ALIX JAMES

ALL BETS ARE OFF

FIRST IMPRESSIONS BOOK ONE

A PRIDE & PREJUDICE VARIATION

Cover Design by GetCovers.com
Cover Image Licensed by Period Images
Background image licensed by Shutterstock

Blog and Website: https://alixjames.com/
Newsletter: https://subscribepage.io/alix-james
Book Bub: https://www.bookbub.com/authors/alix-james
Facebook: https://www.facebook.com/ShortSweetNovellas
Twitter: https://twitter.com/N_Clarkston
Amazon: https://www.amazon.com/stores/Alix-James/author/B07Z1BWFF3
Austen Variations: http://austenvariations.com/

This book almost didn't make it here.

I almost didn't make it here.

Today, I am grateful for my health, for doctors who kept me breathing when I could not breathe on my own, and to God for filling my lungs with the precious breath of life.

Thank you to Joy Dawn King, whose sharp eyes helped me shine this beast when I couldn't trust my own.

And, of course, thank you to my soul mate, the one I dream with, for treating me like his queen and making sure I came back to a loving home to keep doing what I do.

CONTENTS

1. One 1

2. Two 10

3. Three 19

4. Four 28

5. Five 35

6. Six 43

7. Seven 53

8. Eight 64

9. Nine 74

10. Ten 83

11. Eleven 93

12. Twelve 103

13. Thirteen 112

14. Fourteen 122

15. Fifteen 131

16. Sixteen 141

17. Seventeen 149

18. Eighteen 164

19. Nineteen 174

20. Twenty 185

21. Twenty-One 202

22.	Twenty-Two	213
23.	Twenty-Three	222
24.	Twenty-Four	232
Epilogue		240
From Alix		245
Raising the Stakes		247
About Alix James		260
Also By Alix James		261

ONE

"SHE IS TOLERABLE, I suppose, but not handsome enough to tempt me."

Elizabeth nearly choked on her punch.

Tolerable? *Tolerable?*

Her grip tightened around the glass, and for a brief, delicious moment, she imagined spilling the punch all over Mr. Darcy's perfectly tailored coat. She wasn't close enough to pull off the move, but oh, the satisfaction it would bring. He stood across the room, his voice low but clear enough to ring in her ears.

The ballroom seemed to still, the glaring humiliation of his words hanging in the air, stinging as sharply as if he'd directed them right at her. Elizabeth glanced toward Jane, who was entirely absorbed in conversation with Kitty, perfectly unaware of the insult that had just shattered her sister's pride.

Elizabeth's toes curled inside her slippers. She shifted her feet, trying to shake off the burning humiliation crawling up her spine. *Not handsome enough?* Well, if she had any doubts about the man's character, they had just been soundly confirmed.

"Did you hear that?" Charlotte Lucas's voice came from beside her, thick with restrained laughter.

"Every mortifying word," Elizabeth muttered, setting her glass down on the nearest table with a bit more force than necessary. "I suppose I should be grateful he doesn't think me a complete horror."

Charlotte bit her lip, a sparkle of amusement in her eyes. "I never thought a man's bad manners could be so entertaining."

"Entertaining?" Elizabeth shot her a sharp look. "It is outrageous, and I have half a mind to—"

"To what? March up to him and correct his perception of your charms?" Charlotte tilted her head, an eyebrow lifting. "He might take that as a sign of interest, you know."

Interest! Elizabeth would have laughed, but it... well, it wasn't funny. At *all*. She turned back toward Mr. Darcy, who stood brooding like a dark cloud over the festivities. As if anyone could inspire interest in *that* man!

"No. A gentleman so full of himself is hardly worth the trouble," she said, with a haughty lift of her chin. "I'm more likely to *ignore* him."

Charlotte didn't look convinced. "Well, if you're ignoring him, you're doing a poor job of it. You haven't looked away since he insulted you."

Elizabeth blinked. She hadn't realized her eyes were still pinned to Mr. Darcy as though her gaze alone might convey all the contempt she felt. She pulled herself back, smoothing her skirts with a quick brush of her hands. "I don't know why I care. It's not as if I've any reason to impress him."

"Exactly," Charlotte said lightly, "and you've never been one to let some stranger's opinion wound your pride."

"I don't believe it's about my pride," Elizabeth protested, but her words felt weak, even to herself. "It's a matter of decency."

Charlotte let out a quiet laugh, shaking her head. "Well, if you say so."

Elizabeth crossed her arms, but Charlotte's amusement had already worked under her skin. Why *did* she care? A stranger's insult—particularly one from a man as dull and disagreeable as Mr. Darcy—shouldn't have any power over her. Yet here she was, turning three shades of crimson over his words as though they actually held weight.

As if sensing her thoughts, Charlotte stepped a little closer, her voice dropping into a teasing whisper. "In fact, I'd wager that if Mr. Darcy were forced to spend any real time with you, he'd fall quite desperately in love."

Elizabeth let out a bark of laughter. "I think not! The man barely looks capable of emotion, let alone love."

"Oh, I don't know about that. Perhaps if he were shown the proper attention—"

Elizabeth shook her head, cutting her off. "I have no intention of wasting any attention on him. Nor do I care to tempt him, as you so amusingly suggest."

"But that's exactly what makes it interesting!" Charlotte's eyes gleamed now, sensing a game. "I'll bet you, Elizabeth."

"No! No more betting. The last four times I have wagered against you, I have lost—lost more than my pride, too."

"You certainly did." Charlotte stretched forth her arm, rolling her wrist about. "By the by, how do you like my new gloves? And the ribbon on my gown—now, I daresay that green is not usually my color, but I could not let it go to waste, could I?"

Elizabeth grimaced. "I was sure Mama would recognize those and announce it for all the world to hear, but it seems the presence of two wealthy, single gentlemen tonight was quite enough to distract her from the topic of my 'missing' gloves."

"Oh, come, Lizzy, it is not as if anyone is surprised. I *always* win my forfeits."

"Which is why I am not betting against you. *You* flirt with Mr. Darcy as much as you please. I have no intention of suffering further humiliation at his hands... *or* yours."

"What are we talking about?" Jane appeared from behind Charlotte—features flushed and slightly out of breath. "Is Charlotte putting you up to something again, Lizzy?"

"No, because I do not intend to do it. Tell her, Charlotte. Surely, she could use a laugh."

Jane blinked innocently. "Tell me what?"

"Mr. Bingley's friend insulted Lizzy. But honestly, Lizzy, it sounded to me like the sort of thing a man says when he means *precisely* the opposite and is terrified to admit the truth."

"There, do you see, Jane?" Elizabeth gestured toward her friend. "She is at it again. If I am not careful, Charlotte will own my best ball gown, my new bonnet, and half my pin money,"

Jane laughed. "Let me guess, Charlotte. You put Lizzy up to provoking a dance invitation from Mr. Darcy to force him to publicly favor her after being heard insulting her? Lizzy, how could you pass *that* up?"

"Oh, not just a dance," Charlotte corrected. "Lizzy, if you set your mind to it, you could make 'Mr. Darcy of Pemberley with ten thousand a year' fall in love with you. I have every confidence in it."

"Now you're just being preposterous."

Charlotte gave a soft shrug. "Is it preposterous? Or are you afraid it might actually work?"

The challenge sat between them, making the very air crackle. *Impossible!* There was no way a man as proud and insufferable as Mr. Darcy could ever be tempted by her. And why would she want him to be?

"You're serious?" Elizabeth asked, eyes narrowing.

"Absolutely. I stand by my wager."

The absurdly of it was almost too much to consider. "And if I don't succeed?"

"The usual terms," Charlotte said, a glint in her eye. "But I think we both know you're far too clever to fail."

Elizabeth raised an eyebrow. "And if by some miracle I *do* succeed? What then?"

"Then *you* own the forfeit." Charlotte's tone was light, but there was a knowing look in her eyes, the kind that made Elizabeth suspicious.

Elizabeth smiled, her head shaking in disbelief. "I think I would much rather let Mr. Darcy keep his indifference."

But even as she spoke, the idea of forcing Darcy—*Mr. Darcy*—to fall for her, only to have the pleasure of rejecting him, sparked something wicked in her.

"Lizzy, do not let her bait you again," Jane cautioned. "You know she sees you as a soft mark by now."

"Indeed, and yet I let her swindle me time and again, because she is simply too persuasive—and *persistent*—for me to refuse indefinitely."

Charlotte laughed. "What else have I to amuse myself at these Assemblies? I scarcely ever have a dance, but I do usually find other diversions. What say you, Lizzy? Do you feel confident enough to venture it? Or has Mr. Darcy's insult shattered that courage you are so proud of?"

That did it. Somehow, Charlotte always found *just* the right leverage to work upon her. She straightened. "Very well, Charlotte. If you are so confident in this ridiculous wager, I'll play along."

"And your forfeit?" Charlotte asked.

Elizabeth's stomach roiled with denial. She already knew what Charlotte would demand—the thing she had been trying to force for years. The very thought made her bristle. *No.* It couldn't come to that.

Charlotte merely smiled, leaning in closer. "You know what you'll have to do."

Elizabeth tried to swallow the lump forming in her throat, but Charlotte's knowing look only made her heart beat faster.

"No," she decided. "Because I do not intend to lose."

"I have not seen a more spectacular example of buffoonery since Eliza Townsend exposed herself with George Whitmore at Lady Framton's ball," Caroline Bingley declared, sinking into her chair with a sigh of exaggerated suffering.

Darcy kept his focus on the fire, willing himself not to engage. The conversation was predictable: provincial gatherings were beneath her; the company lacked refinement. It was a routine he knew too well.

"Really, Charles, I don't know how you can find any pleasure at all in such company," Caroline continued, swirling her wine. "The conversation was insipid, and as for the dancing—"

"Indeed, the dancing," Bingley interrupted. "I thought it was rather enjoyable. And as for the company, you do them too little credit, Caroline. Why, everyone was lively, their manners pleasing. Perhaps a bit more... vigorous than a London ball, but I have never passed a more delightful evening in my life!"

"Charles, you cannot be serious. Why, there were *children* there—girls not more than fourteen, dancing and flirting shamelessly!"

"Caroline, this is not London. I saw nothing inappropriate—why, every family in the neighborhood was there, and it is rather common in the country for the children to attend such events."

"Well!" Caroline sniffed. "I thought the entire affair rather tawdry."

"Tawdry! You are far too harsh on people you met only this evening. I, for one, have never met so many charming people anywhere. *Even* in London. Darcy, you do not agree with my sister, do you?"

Darcy's mouth twisted in discomfort. He might as well come out with it. "I saw little breeding and no beauty whatsoever."

Caroline Bingley hid a smile behind her glass, but Bingley cried out in dismay. "Surely you exaggerate! You gave yourself little enough trouble to seek enjoyment. Surely you could have joined us on the floor and had a more pleasant evening?"

Darcy turned to meet his friend's gaze, his arms folding across his chest. "I did not see the need."

"No need?" Bingley frowned. "Was it the music, or was the company not to your liking?"

Darcy allowed a pause. The music had been tolerable enough, though the room... not so much. "The company was adequate, but you know how these things go. Too much attention paid to the wrong dance partner, and suddenly, there are expectations."

"Expectations?" Bingley blinked, incredulous. "From a *dance?*"

"Yes, a dance. You have seen it happen. A man dances twice with the wrong woman, and by the next day, half the town believes there is an attachment."

Bingley stared at him as though Darcy had suggested something utterly nonsensical. "Darcy, you're being melodramatic. It was an assembly, not a proposal."

Darcy held his ground. "You underestimate the power of idle chatter. It only takes a little encouragement for desperate ladies to start assuming more than they should."

Caroline let out a delicate laugh. "Oh yes, they must all feel dreadfully forsaken that Mr. Darcy did not condescend to dance. How thoughtful of you to spare the ladies their broken hearts."

He ignored her, his focus still on Bingley. There was no use in trying to clarify himself to someone like Caroline, but Bingley... perhaps Bingley could still be reasoned with.

"You may find it absurd," Darcy continued, "but when you've spent as long as I have fending off fortune hunters and overly ambitious mothers, you begin to tread carefully."

"Fortune hunters? In Meryton?" Bingley was laughing now, his eyes bright with disbelief. "Darcy, I danced with a dozen ladies tonight, and I've no reason to believe any of them expect to marry me tomorrow."

Darcy's expression remained unchanged. "You may be fortunate in that regard, but that has not been my experience."

Bingley leaned back in his chair, crossing his arms. "You truly believe that behaving like a gentleman—a *gentleman*, Darcy, not a cad—necessarily leads straight to matrimony?"

"All too often, when one has wealth and no inclination to marry," Darcy replied curtly. "A few dances here, a bit of polite conversation there, and suddenly a man is trapped in expectations he never intended."

Bingley grinned, clearly unconvinced. "You make it sound like common courtesy is as good as a leg shackle. Surely, a man can be pleasant without every woman assuming he's about to propose."

Darcy shook his head slightly. It wasn't that simple, and Bingley knew it. "You've been spared the worst of it, but not every man can enjoy such freedom."

Bingley sat up straighter, his eyes narrowing with an almost mischievous gleam. "I think you're making excuses."

Darcy raised an eyebrow. "Excuses?"

"Yes. I believe you're avoiding courtesy simply because it's easier to stand aloof and judge the room than actually engage with people."

Darcy fixed him with a sharp look. "That is outrageous."

"Is it?" Bingley's grin widened. "I'll wager that it *is* possible for you to be a perfect gentleman without giving anyone the wrong idea. All I'm saying is that you're overcomplicating things."

Darcy frowned, his patience wearing thin. "I'm not entertaining this."

But Bingley leaned forward, too amused to let the moment pass. "No, listen. Sir William Lucas tells me it is quite the thing here in Meryton to wager—why, even the ladies have their own amusements. Perfectly respectable and expected, and I think it a harmless diversion."

"I do not." Darcy crossed his arms.

"Yes, well, I am now a part of this town, and I shall do as they do. I will wager you, Darcy, and I challenge you on your honor to consider accepting. You claim that behaving as a gentleman leads to unwanted expectations. I am saying it is entirely possible to be polite—dance, talk, the whole lot—without sending anyone rushing to the altar."

Darcy exhaled slowly. Bingley's optimism was charming but misguided. "It is not as simple as that."

"Then prove it," Bingley dared, his smile still in place. "Let us see if your theory holds up. For the rest of our stay in Hertfordshire, you act as a perfect gentleman—dance, converse with every lady in your path, and show the courtesy you claim leads to disaster."

Darcy gave him a long, level look. This was foolishness. A game. "And if I refuse?"

"Then I suppose I'll never know whether you're right," Bingley said, still grinning. "But I'll wager you are overthinking the whole thing."

"I do not need to prove that I am right. I know I am. That is enough."

"Yes, but how are you going to prove it to *me?* You see, I know you, Darcy. You can hardly stand for anyone not to think you are in the right."

He kept his face impassive. "It matters little to me whether you believe me to be right or wrong. I have no intention of putting myself out merely because you desire to engage in some local amusement by trying to provoke me into acting out of character."

"So, you admit that you are unsociable? That you are downright unapproachable and prideful, above your company?"

Darcy narrowed his eyes. "I am no such thing. I simply do not lower myself to indulge in ribaldry."

"Poppycock. That Assembly was everything respectable. *You*, however, were little better than a wall hanging adorning the edge of the room. Can you deny it?"

"I have no wish to deny it."

"Then you may as well admit it, Darcy. You are unpleasant in company because you find it expedient. You will not give yourself the trouble of being merry and engaging because you prefer to be miserable and alone."

Darcy sighed. "I am perfectly willing to return to London if you find my company tiresome."

"No, no, don't you dare!" Bingley laughed. "You cannot show up as my guest, looking like a black cloud, and then leave town the next day. Think of the questions I shall have to answer! I repeat my challenge, Darcy. If you refuse, I shall form my own opinions on your manner."

He pursed his lips. "And if I accept your wager?"

Bingley leaned back, his grin widening. "Then we'll see just how easily you can behave like a gentleman without being 'trapped in expectations.' I daresay you will surprise even yourself."

Darcy considered this for a moment. It was ridiculous. But the idea of proving Bingley wrong—of showing him the truth of how these situations unfolded—was almost tempting. "And if you're right?"

"If I'm right," Bingley said, shrugging lightly, "you owe me nothing. I will have the satisfaction of knowing my dearest friend in the world does not send my neighbors running for the woods in fear of his displeasure."

"And if you are wrong? If I show myself to be everything you deem 'amiable' and half the mothers of Meryton begin buying wedding clothes for their daughters?"

Bingley laughed. "Darcy, if I am wrong, it will not be because of raised expectations among the town, but because you failed to be properly 'amiable.'"

Darcy sucked in a sigh and shifted in his seat. "Try me."

"Very well. If you win... well, then I'll finally take your advice about the business."

Darcy's expression darkened. "The business?"

"You know exactly what I mean," Bingley said, more serious now. "You've been telling me to sell my father's business for years. And I've resisted every time. But if I'm right and you lose the wager, I'll sell it and reinvest as you've been advising."

Darcy studied him in silence. There was no joking in Bingley's tone now. They'd had this conversation before, many times. And though it was in Bingley's best interest to let the business go, the younger man had never been able to sever the sentimental tie. But here was a chance to prove a point—and perhaps to do some real good.

"If you know it is for your own good, why not just sell it now?" Darcy asked testily. "Why try to force me into this charade?"

"Because I have no desire to sell it. You'll have to prove that *you're* willing to listen to *me* when I tell you something that is for *your* own good."

He stared at Bingley, who was still watching him with that maddening grin. Darcy exhaled slowly, the flicker of a smile tugging at the corner of his mouth. "You are incorrigible, Bingley."

"And you're a cynic, but we've always known that."

Darcy shook his head, already regretting the decision, but there was something about the challenge he couldn't resist. "Very well. I accept your wager."

TWO

DARCY UNFOLDED THE LETTER carefully, the firelight illuminating his sister's neat handwriting. Georgiana's letters were always the same—polite, self-effacing, and filled with concerns she wouldn't voice aloud in person. He could see her hesitance in every measured line, the way she danced around her true feelings.

> *My dearest brother,*
> *I hope this letter finds you well. I must apologize for troubling you, but I have received another invitation from Mrs. Pomeroy to join her family at their estate this winter. While I am certain her intentions are well-meaning, I fear she may try to forward a match with her nephew. I cannot help but feel uneasy...*

Darcy set the page down, his fingers tightening against the edges. Mrs. Pomeroy was a perfectly respectable woman. And Darcy had it on good authority that this nephew Georgiana spoke of, a Mr. Eli Fitzsimmons, was already betrothed to a girl from Lincolnshire, of whom it was said he was excessively fond. There could be no reason for Georgiana to fear anything from that quarter. Darcy had made it clear after Ramsgate that such manipulations would not be tolerated, but this was not such a case. However, Georgiana's reluctance to confront even the mildest impropriety made her seem to jump at shadows these days.
She continued:

> *I hope you do not think me ungrateful. Mrs. Pomeroy has been very kind, and I am certain her intentions are respectable. But I feel my presence may only encourage... assumptions. If you believe it is best for me to go, I will, of course, defer to your judgment.*

Assumptions. Georgiana's polite euphemism for the relentless matchmaking she endured whenever Darcy was not present to shield her. At least she was aware of her vunlerability now—a young, unguarded heiress was a prize to be won, to be sure. If any good thing had come from her near brush with disaster this summer, it could be this—that Georgiana was now sensible of her own value to others. But that "value" was not why Mrs. Pomeroy sought Georgiana's company for her daughters. At least... not precisely in the way she feared.

He folded the letter carefully. It was not only Georgiana's dowry and noble connections that made her a target, but also her connection to *him*—a bachelor of seven and twenty, in full possession of a rather large inheritance. And his young sister was old enough now to be in company with some of the same ladies who had set their caps for him.

If he thought Bingley could be made to understand, he would point to this—to Georgiana's "usefulness" to the schemes of anyone interested in cornering a Darcy for themselves. This, *this* was why he was always on his guard! Every encounter, every polite conversation, was another opportunity for someone to misread intentions, to plot, to manipulate. His "ungentlemanly" behavior wasn't just a matter of practicality—it was a shield. Necessary. Effective. He could not afford to let sentiment or civility weaken his resolve.

A tap at the door pulled him from his thoughts. Bingley entered, his face alight with the same easy cheer he'd worn at the assembly. "Darcy, I was looking for you. You slipped away so quickly after dinner."

Darcy placed the letter on the side table. "I did not realize I needed to announce my every movement."

"Well, no, but it might have saved you from Caroline's latest critique of the evening." Bingley grinned, flopping into the chair opposite him. "Apparently, the company was not up to her standards. Again."

Darcy leaned back, his gaze drifting to the fire. "She is not entirely wrong."

"Oh, come on," Bingley said, leaning forward. "It was not so bad. The people were friendly enough. And the dancing—"

"I did not dance," Darcy interrupted flatly.

"Exactly my point," Bingley said. "You stood there like a marble statue while I mingled and enjoyed myself. Tell me, was it really so unbearable to engage with the locals?"

Darcy glanced at the letter again, Georgiana's words flickering in his mind. He exhaled sharply. "Engagement often leads to expectation. I've no desire to give anyone reason to believe I am interested."

Bingley tilted his head, his grin softening. "Not everyone is out to trap you, Darcy. You cannot assume every dance leads to a proposal."

"Perhaps not, but a single dance can lead to speculation. I have seen it often enough."

"Speculation." Bingley shook his head. "You sound as though you are bracing for battle. It is one thing to be cautious, Darcy, but you are taking this to an entirely new level."

Darcy's lips thinned. "You call it caution. I call it experience."

Bingley drummed his fingers on the armrest, studying him with that insufferable air of earnestness. "You know," Bingley began, his voice lighter now, "for a man so quick to judge others, you are not always great at holding up a mirror."

Darcy arched a brow. "I beg your pardon?"

"I mean that you are quick to assume the worst in people, but you do not stop to consider how *you* are perceived."

"I do not concern myself with such frivolities."

Bingley leaned forward, resting his elbows on his knees. "And that, my friend, is exactly the problem. You act as though being cautious is the same as being impenetrable. Do you really think that is what makes you respectable? Walking around like an iceberg, avoiding anyone who might take the slightest interest in you?"

Darcy's fingers tightened on the chair's arm. "Being respected is not about indulgence or frivolous engagement. It is about maintaining one's dignity."

"Dignity, of course. But at what cost? You cannot behave as though everyone is out to scheme against you, Darcy."

Darcy glanced at the letter again, the tight knot in his chest refusing to loosen. "Not everyone, no. But enough to warrant caution."

"Fair enough," Bingley conceded. "But here's a question for you. When was the last time you actually enjoyed a gathering like tonight's? Or allowed yourself to laugh with someone new? To have a conversation without looking for an ulterior motive?"

"I hardly see how that is relevant."

"It is relevant because you have convinced yourself you have to keep the world at arm's length to survive. And maybe, for some people, you do. But not everyone is looking to use you, Darcy. What if there's another way to be?"

Darcy looked back at Bingley, unsettled. There was no guile in his friend's expression, just the relentless optimism Darcy had alternately admired and found maddening since their first acquaintance.

"You think it is as simple as that?" Darcy asked finally.

"I do." Bingley grinned, leaning back. "You think being a gentleman means setting yourself up for heartbreak. I think it means showing people a bit of kindness—without assuming they're all plotting your downfall."

"That is naive."

"Perhaps." Bingley shrugged. "But you are the one who keeps insisting you are right. So prove it."

"Prove it?" Darcy's voice turned wary.

"Yes. You are so certain that engaging with people leads to trouble. I am saying it does not have to. See it through, Darcy. Take the bet."

"I already agreed, did I not?"

"But not wholeheartedly."

Darcy shook his head, leaning back in his chair. "I've no interest in playing your games."

"Then do not think of it as a game," Bingley said, his tone growing more serious. "Think of it as an experiment. Prove to me—and to yourself—that you *can* be a gentleman in every respect—including dancing with ladies you do not know, Darcy—without losing control. That you are not doomed to spend your life dodging every conversation that might lead to... what did you call it? Expectations?"

The fire cracked in the hearth, and Darcy's gaze lingered on the flames. The suggestion irritated him, yet something about it struck a chord. Could it be possible to act with civility without opening himself—or Georgiana—to further vulnerability? Was there a way to strike a balance between engagement and self-preservation?

Not all ladies were harmless, that was the devil of it. Some were, surely. Miss Lucas, whom he had met this evening. Darcy felt he could pass several evenings in her company trading as many or as few civilities as he liked, and he would be quite safe. But there were others, such as Elizabeth Bennet...

Her face flickered unbidden in his mind, sharp eyes and quick wit cutting through the stifling monotony of the evening. She had unsettled him more than he cared to admit. But perhaps—no, surely—her effect on him had been incidental.

Still, the idea of the wager hung in the air, tantalizing in its own way.

"Very well," Darcy said finally. "I shall commit wholeheartedly to this little whim of yours. We shall make a study of it. But do not mistake this for anything more than what it is."

"And what is that?"

"A reminder that there is no winning when you play by society's rules."

Bingley grinned as if he'd won a great victory. "Then we shall see just how much of your dignity survives a few polite conversations and a dance or two."

"It is not my dignity that concerns me the most," Darcy muttered.

CHARLOTTE WAVED THE LETTER over her head. "It is official. We have been invited to dine at Netherfield. My father is already rehearsing his questions for Mr. Bingley. He imagines himself quite the sage advisor."

Elizabeth looked up from her needlework, an amused glint in her eye. "I pity Mr. Bingley. Does your father plan to expound on crop rotations or the precise weight of a prize hog?"

Charlotte folded the letter with a smirk. "Perhaps both."

"I hope he spares Mr. Bingley his thoughts on pig feed. I cannot imagine a less appetizing topic over dinner."

Charlotte sat down beside her, placing the letter in her lap. "If it were not pig feed, it would be the merits of crop rotation or the foolishness of importing sheep. You know how he enjoys an audience."

"Poor Mr. Bingley," Elizabeth said, turning a page. "I imagine his sisters will develop sudden ailments to excuse themselves from the table."

Jane looked up from her embroidery. "I think Mr. Bingley is kind enough to bear such conversations. He has a patience you might do well to emulate, Lizzy."

"Patience is an excellent virtue, Jane, but I see little use for it when the reward is utter tedium."

Charlotte leaned back, her smile turning sly. "What of Mr. Darcy? Do you find him equally tedious?"

Elizabeth arched a brow. "Tedious would be an improvement. At least tedium is *tolerable*."

Jane sighed. "Elizabeth, you ought not to speak so harshly. He may be proud, but there is no harm in giving him the benefit of the doubt."

Elizabeth shut her book with a decisive thud. "After he insulted me in plain hearing? I shall be sure to extend such generosity the next time a gentleman compares me to a cow."

Charlotte laughed. "He did not compare you to a cow, Lizzy."

"No, but 'tolerable and not handsome enough to tempt him' is hardly a compliment."

Charlotte shook her head. "You are fixated on him."

Elizabeth stiffened. "I am not."

"You are," Charlotte said. "You cannot help yourself. He has insulted you, and now you cannot rest until you have bested him. You would not have agreed to the wager otherwise."

"I agreed because you made it impossible for me to do otherwise, and you know it. 'Twas not a fair dare."

"Still," Charlotte said, "you cannot deny he has been on your mind. And the next time you should be in company with him—"

"I shall take great pleasure in avoiding him entirely." Elizabeth picked up her needlework again. "Or perhaps I shall seek him out, just to prove how little I care."

Charlotte raised an eyebrow. "You seem very invested for someone who cares so little."

Elizabeth stabbed her needle into the fabric with more force than necessary. "The wager was your idea, Charlotte. I am only indulging your whim. The moment it ceases to amuse me, it will be forgot."

"Of course," Charlotte said, though her smile suggested otherwise.

Jane sighed. "This may be in poor taste. You ought not to treat another's affections—or your own—as a game."

Elizabeth hesitated. "There are no affections to treat. Mr. Darcy is as impervious as a stone wall, and I... I find the idea of his affections laughable. If he *has* a heart, I am certain it is locked away in some cold and inaccessible chamber, far beyond the reach of ordinary mortals."

"You may laugh now, Elizabeth, but I have every confidence that the gentleman will surprise you. After all, every man has feelings, no matter how shallow they may be."

Jane frowned, her needle paused mid-stitch. "I doubt Mr. Darcy is such a man. I may know little of the gentleman, but his eyes spoke rather too much for me to consider him a man of only shallow sentiments."

"He is no deeper than a mud puddle," Elizabeth said firmly. "Mr. Darcy will return to London entirely unscathed by any weapons I might be able to wield, I am certain of it."

"But he *is* still a man," Charlotte said with a shrug. "And men do experience desire, even if their heart is not lightly touched."

Elizabeth stiffened. "I shall not demean myself to become a strumpet like Lydia just to... to give Mr. Darcy a little 'manly thrill'. I would appeal to... perhaps his intellect, I suppose. I assume he has one."

"Oh, good plan, Lizzy," Charlotte grinned, winking at Jane. "You should have no difficulty winning the wager in that case. You cannot possibly do him any harm, for his 'feelings' will die off as easily as they are inspired."

Elizabeth said nothing, though her needle paused mid-stitch. She had agreed to the wager in jest, her pride stung by Mr. Darcy's insult. Yet now, when she considered the prospect of facing him again, she found herself less certain of her ability to remain unaffected.

"I *shall* win," Elizabeth said at last. "And I shall enjoy the satisfaction of proving him no better than the pompous fool he appears to be."

Charlotte grinned. "Then you must come to tea at my mother's on Thursday. I expect the Netherfield party will be there."

Elizabeth turned, her pulse quickening at the thought. She forced a smile. "Then I shall. I cannot think of anything more delightful than facing Mr. Darcy in full command of my wit."

Jane sighed again, setting down her embroidery. "I hope you know what you are doing, Lizzy."

Elizabeth's smile faltered. "So do I."

CHARLOTTE FUSSED WITH THE tea service with a knowing glance at Elizabeth as the Netherfield party arrive. "You must admire my mother's persistence," she whispered. "Every pot of tea is another step toward securing Mr. Bingley for Maria."

Elizabeth smirked. "I doubt Mrs. Lucas will find him quite so pliable, but I admire her spirit."

The guests entered, and Elizabeth caught sight of Darcy at once. He was the same as the night of the Assembly: tall, severe, and surveying the room as though it were a field of battle. For a moment, his gaze landed on her, and she stiffened, though she could not say why. He nodded briefly, then turned his attention to Sir William.

Elizabeth suppressed a smile. If Darcy thought her unworthy of notice, she would simply have to *make* him notice.

She would not lower herself by playing the flirt. That would only confirm his view of her as an insipid country girl. His mind... she must make his *mind* her plaything. Surely even a man as reserved as Darcy could not fail to appreciate wit and lively conversation.

And if he did, then she would simply enjoy besting him in debate.

When the company was seated, she waited for her moment. Charlotte's father was in the middle of an elaborate speech on the merits of turnips, his words sailing far over the heads of their guests. Elizabeth caught Darcy's expression—carefully blank, though his fingers tapped the edge of his teacup. It was almost... restless.

"You must find this fascinating, Mr. Darcy," Elizabeth said, tilting her head as though genuinely interested.

Darcy blinked, his gaze snapping to hers. "Sorry?"

She smiled innocently. "Sir William's discourse on turnips. Surely such agricultural pursuits are of interest to a gentleman of property."

Darcy's brow creased. "Indeed."

"Tell me, Mr. Darcy, do you believe there is an optimal size for a turnip, or do you think variety is key to cultivation?"

There was a moment of silence. Charlotte coughed into her teacup, while Sir William brightened considerably. "An excellent question, Miss Bennet! A lady with a mind for farming—now that is a rarity!"

Elizabeth kept her gaze on Darcy, who seemed caught between irritation and complete bafflement. "I... I cannot claim to have given turnips much thought," he said finally. "But I suspect... variety might be more desirable, depending on one's soil and climate."

Elizabeth raised an eyebrow. "How diplomatic of you, Mr. Darcy. You are not one for strong opinions, then?"

His gaze sharpened. "I have strong opinions where they are warranted."

"And turnips do not warrant them?"

"Rarely."

Elizabeth bit back a laugh. She had caught him off guard, but he recovered quickly. His tone was measured, his words precise. Still, there was something in the way he looked at her—something that suggested he was not entirely immune to her efforts.

"Perhaps we ought to move to a safer subject," Darcy said. "Do you often enjoy provoking conversations about turnips, Miss Bennet, or was today an exception?"

Elizabeth set her teacup down with deliberate care. "Not turnips specifically, Mr. Darcy. But I do enjoy hearing the thoughts of men who pride themselves on their intellect. It is often quite revealing."

His expression did not change, but his eyes darkened slightly. "And what, precisely, have I revealed?"

"That you are quite practiced at avoiding questions." She smiled sweetly. "I shall have to work harder next time."

His reply was cut off as Mrs. Lucas bustled in with another round of tea. Darcy turned away, giving her little choice but to withdraw. Still, as she sipped her tea, she could not help but feel a flicker of satisfaction.

Darcy might not admit it, but she had seen the spark of something—not interest, surely. But annoyance... yes, annoying him would do. The sort of annoyance that could develop into a grudging respect, with enough little pricks of the pin.

She would consider it a small victory.

Charlotte nudged her. "You engaged Mr. Darcy quite readily."

"Engaged? Hardly," Elizabeth said. "I was simply amusing myself."

Charlotte's lips quirked. "And what do you think Mr. Darcy would say if I asked him?"

Elizabeth tilted her head, pretending to consider. "He would say... nothing at all, I imagine. Silence seems to be his greatest skill."

She laughed lightly, but as Darcy stood to refill his tea, his glance lingered on her for just a moment longer than it should have. Elizabeth's heart gave an unexpected flutter, but she pushed it aside. This was a game, and she had no intention of losing.

THREE

DARCY QUICKENED HIS PACE, his strides purposeful, though he had no destination in mind. He needed movement—something to untangle the knots Elizabeth Bennet had tied in his thoughts. Her voice, her sharp remarks, her maddening smile—they lingered far longer than they should have, disrupting the quiet discipline he relied upon.

How she had managed to turn the conversation at Lucas Lodge to *turnips*—a topic so utterly inane—and yet draw him into it, was beyond his understanding. And that... that *smile* of hers, over *turnips*, of all things! It had unsettled him far more than he cared to admit.

He reached the edge of the field and paused. Why, *why* was he even thinking about her? She was just a country girl—no connections worth noting, probably no fortune, certainly no fashion or... He shook his head with a hiss. She was *not* worth thinking about.

But still, there was something about her that defied reason. She was clever—far cleverer than most of the women he had encountered—but that alone was not reason for him to think of her.

She was unpredictable in her attacks, wielding her wit like a blade. No... not a clumsy, brute force saber. More like a foil—each remark precise, leaving him both challenged and intrigued.

And then there were her eyes. Nothing out of the common way, as far as shape and color went. Indeed, she was not even handsome by his standards, but those eyes had haunted him since his attention first lighted on her at the Assembly. Darcy's jaw tightened as the image came unbidden: her gaze fixed on him, bright and unrelenting, as though she could see through every mask he had ever worn. It had been... disarming.

He drew a deep breath and paced along the field border to the stile. There was no room for such thoughts. Elizabeth Bennet was only a temporary distraction, a puzzle to be solved and set aside. And yet...

"You are going to wear a ditch into the ground if you keep pacing like that," Bingley called out.

Darcy turned to see his friend approaching, his usual good humor written across his face. "I had not realized I was pacing."

"Of course you had not." Bingley fell into step beside him, hands tucked into his coat pockets. "I imagine you were too lost in thought. Or should I say, too lost in Miss Elizabeth Bennet?"

Darcy's jaw clenched. "I do not know what you mean."

Bingley gave him a knowing smile. "Do not pretend, Darcy. I saw the way you were looking at her during tea."

"Like she sprouted a third arm?"

Bingley laughed. "I have not seen you so engaged in conversation since we arrived in Hertfordshire. You actually smiled, or something dangerously close to it."

"If I smiled, it was because her remarks were absurd. She finds great amusement in provoking others."

"And you find great amusement in being provoked."

Darcy stopped. "Do not read too much into it. Miss Elizabeth Bennet is merely... diverting. Nothing more."

"Diverting." Bingley laughed, shaking his head. "I do not believe I have ever heard you describe a lady that way before. Usually, it is all about their connections or their manners. But Miss Elizabeth Bennet seems to have captured your attention in spite of all that."

Darcy looked away, the weight of Bingley's words pressing against the boundaries of his resolve. "She is... different," Darcy admitted reluctantly.

"Different is good."

"Not in this case."

"Why not?"

Darcy hesitated, his gaze fixed on the horizon. "Because different is dangerous. She has no regard for convention, no care for propriety. A man like me cannot afford to indulge in such distractions."

Bingley's smile faded slightly. "Perhaps she is not the one who needs to change, Darcy."

Darcy turned to him sharply. "What are you suggesting?"

"Only that you might try seeing her as she is, rather than as someone who defies your expectations. She is only a lady, after all. No one is expecting you to propose marriage just because she happens to be of the opposite sex."

Darcy opened his mouth to reply but stopped himself. His instinct was to refute Bingley's words, to dismiss them as the ramblings of a man too easily charmed. But the truth was far more complicated.

The sound of hoofbeats interrupted his thoughts, and both men turned to see a rider approaching. It was one of Bingley's servants, who dismounted quickly and handed over a note from the house.

"For you, sir," the man said, bowing slightly before retreating.

"Oh, dear heaven. What now?" Bingley took the note, unfolding it with a sigh as Darcy waited in silence. His friend's brow furrowed as he read, but when he looked up, there was a look of pleased surprise on his face.

"It is from Caroline, naturally." Bingley said. "I've no idea why she could not wait for us to return to the house, but she has a capital idea. She wishes to host a dinner party next week. Apparently, she has already made her order with the butcher. Good show, Caroline! Why, I am perfectly astonished, Darcy. I had not thought she liked the neighborhood so well. This *is* rather a pleasant surprise, is it not?"

Darcy exhaled sharply. Another dinner party. Another evening spent enduring the idle chatter of people who thought far too much of themselves and far too little of everyone else.

Bingley's grin returned as if he had read Darcy's thoughts. "Ah, yes, I see your dread already, my friend. Perhaps Miss Elizabeth will provide some relief from the monotony. She seems to have a talent for drawing you out of your gloom."

Darcy said nothing, his thoughts already spiraling toward the implications of another evening spent in her company.

"Lizzy, do hurry up!" Lydia's voice echoed down the hall, accompanied by the sound of her boots clattering against the tiles. "You will miss all the fun if you take another hour arranging your bonnet."

Elizabeth tied the ribbons under her chin, ignoring her younger sister's impatience. "If you spent less time shouting, Lydia, and more time securing your shoes properly, you might arrive with equal haste."

"I like the sound my boots make," Lydia shot back. "It lets everyone know I am coming."

"Which is undoubtedly something every gentleman in Meryton appreciates," Elizabeth said dryly. "I can think of no finer impression."

She reached for her gloves and followed Lydia down the stairs, where Kitty waited eagerly by the door. Their mother hovered nearby, issuing commands no one would obey.

"Do not dawdle, girls!" Mrs. Bennet clapped her hands at them. "The gentlemen of Netherfield have been seen riding toward the village, and it would be unpardonable if they returned to their estate without acknowledging you."

"Which gentlemen, Mama?" Kitty asked. "All of them? Because I do not give two straws about Mr. Hurst."

"Mr. Bingley, of course! And Mr. Darcy, but if I shouldn't bother about *him*. However, he *is* a friend of Mr. Bingley's, so you may as well greet him, too. If he would but glance at any of you, I daresay his wealth might compensate for his unpleasantness."

Elizabeth rolled her eyes. "How fortunate that wealth excuses all offenses."

"You may laugh, Lizzy, but you shall see how true it is when you are older. Now go along. I would not have my girls miss a chance to greet Mr. Bingley."

Jane and Elizabeth followed their younger sisters as they chattered all the way to Meryton about new bonnets, officers, and every subject of no importance whatsoever. Elizabeth listened with half an ear, her thoughts wandering to and fro—and, more often than not, spinning back to the bothersome Mr. Darcy.

What if she had a chance to make some impression on him in town today? She snorted. Little chance of a favorable one, if her sisters were determined to carry on in their usual way.

"There he is!"

Following her sister's gesture, Elizabeth's eyes landed on... well, Lydia was probably pointing out Mr. Bingley, but Elizabeth's gaze was pulled like a lodestone to the object of her quandary: Mr. Darcy. He stood near the bookseller's shop, speaking with Mr. Bingley and Mr. Philips, a faint frown creasing his brow as he listened to some explanation or other.

Lydia immediately marched forward, dragging Kitty with her, and Elizabeth and Jane had no choice but to follow, though at a more leisurely pace. There was something about Darcy—something in the set of his shoulders and the way his eyes swept over his surroundings—that made her want to test her wit against him again.

Or perhaps to prove to herself that she could.

"Miss Bennet," Mr. Bingley said warmly as they approached, his face lighting up as though genuinely pleased to see them.

"Mr. Bingley." Jane curtsied. "And Mr. Darcy. I trust you are both well?"

Bingley beamed as though her question contained the secret to his entire happiness. "Perfectly well, Miss Bennet! And you, Miss Elizabeth? I trust the morning finds you in good spirits."

"Very good spirits, thank you, sir. I trust you have found much to amuse you in Meryton," Elizabeth answered, glancing at Darcy, who inclined his head stiffly.

Then, he astonished her with an odd statement. He almost sounded... *friendly.* "I hope you found the tea at Lucas Lodge diverting."

"Immensely so," she replied. "Though I suspect you were not so fortunate."

"I do not recall voicing any complaint."

"You did not need to." Elizabeth clasped her hands in front of her, feigning innocence. "Your expression said more than words ever could. You must be grateful Sir William restricted himself to turnips and did not venture into the complexities of cabbages."

There it was—the flicker of something in Darcy's gaze, like amusement carefully tamped down. "You are fond of agricultural topics, it seems."

"Not fond," she corrected. "Simply observant. One learns to find entertainment where one can."

"And do you always succeed?"

"In finding amusement? Nearly always." Elizabeth smiled. "But it is no great accomplishment. Life is a most amusing subject, if one chooses to view it properly."

"That requires skill," Darcy replied.

"Skill and practice. Some of us are fortunate enough to have a natural aptitude for it. Or perhaps it is simply easier in good company. A pity you do not enjoy company yourself, Mr. Darcy."

Darcy straightened slightly, his gaze fixed on hers. "I have never said that. You assume much, Miss Bennet."

"I observe much, Mr. Darcy," she countered. "One must develop the skill when living in a small country town. There is so little to occupy the mind otherwise."

Bingley laughed. "And what conclusions have you drawn, Miss Elizabeth?"

"That Mr. Darcy finds much of the world beneath his notice," she said lightly, her eyes not leaving Darcy's face. "Perhaps even all of it."

Darcy hesitated, just long enough for Elizabeth to feel as though she had hit her mark. "Not all of it."

The remark was so unexpected that Elizabeth found herself momentarily at a loss. He was looking at her, his gaze steady and unreadable, and for the first time, she felt as though the battle between them was not quite so one-sided.

"Then I shall take that as the closest thing to a compliment I am likely to receive from you, Mr. Darcy," she said. "Though it does seem an admission of defeat."

"Defeat?" Darcy echoed. "I had not realized we were at war."

"We are not," she replied. "But if we were, I think I should win."

Bingley's laughter rang out again. "There, Darcy! You are undone!"

Darcy's gaze did not waver from Elizabeth. "We shall see, Miss Elizabeth."

"Well! Jolly good." Mr. Bingley cast a bright gaze round the assembled faces, as if merely by smiling and looking cheerful, he could shift the topic back to somewhat more neutral ground. "I say, Miss Bennet, I sent over an invitation just this morning for dinner next week. I do hope you and your family will be able to join us. My sister Caroline has already begun preparations."

Jane glanced at Elizabeth, blushing so hotly that Elizabeth wondered whether her sister could manage a reply. So, she spoke for her. "We are most obliged, Mr. Bingley. I will be certain my father responds promptly."

"I shall hold you to it," Bingley said. "You must promise me you will attend."

"I do not make promises I cannot keep," Elizabeth replied. "But as my mother is rarely inclined to decline invitations, I believe you can count on at least some of us."

Darcy turned slightly toward her. "And will you be among them, Miss Elizabeth?"

Elizabeth puckered her lips in mock contemplation. "If I must endure your company, Mr. Darcy, then surely you must endure mine."

Bingley laughed, delighted. "There, Darcy! I can think of no finer arrangement."

"I shall endeavor not to test your endurance too much, Mr. Darcy. Though I cannot make any guarantees."

Darcy regarded her for a long moment. "I suspect guarantees would take all the interest out of the evening."

Elizabeth arched an eyebrow. "Ah, then I shall do my utmost to keep it lively."

Bingley clapped his hands together. "It is settled, then. I look forward to seeing you all."

Elizabeth and Jane curtsied lightly. "And we look forward to being seen."

Darcy said nothing more, but as Elizabeth turned to join her sisters, she was keenly aware of his gaze following her.

BINGLEY BURST THROUGH THE library doors with all the subtlety of a hunting dog on the scent. "There you are, Darcy! I thought you had slipped off to the woods or something."

Darcy barely glanced up from the desk where he had been sorting correspondence. "If I had, it would have been in pursuit of silence."

Bingley dropped into the nearest chair, sprawling with an ease that Darcy both envied and found insupportable. "You cannot blame me for wanting to escape my sisters. Louisa has been lamenting the color of the curtains in the breakfast room for an hour now, and Caroline—well, you know how Caroline is."

Darcy set down his quill, arching an eyebrow. "I imagine Miss Bingley was lamenting something equally dire."

"Quite," Bingley said, grinning. "She seems to think my entire fortune is being squandered by tolerating provincial tastes. She has been glaring at the furniture for clashing with her gown."

Darcy leaned back in his chair. "That does sound dire."

"Dire enough to send me seeking better company," Bingley said. "And since you are the only tolerable option in this household—besides my dog—I thought we might discuss the terms of our wager."

Darcy sighed and folded his arms. "I had hoped you would let the matter rest."

"Let it rest?" Bingley leaned forward, his grin widening. "Not when it is becoming so entertaining."

Darcy stood and crossed to the window, the morning light casting long shadows across the grounds of Netherfield. He had retreated to the library after breakfast precisely to avoid this conversation, yet here was Bingley, like a burr stuck to his breeches.

"Entertaining for you, perhaps," Darcy said. "For me, it is merely tedious."

"Oh, I disagree. I think you are finding it far more engaging than you will admit."

Darcy turned to face him, one eyebrow raised. "Engaging?"

"Yes." Bingley's tone grew mockingly solemn. "You are clearly more invested in this than you thought. Or shall we discuss your behavior at Lucas Lodge?"

Darcy stiffened. "I see no reason to revisit that."

"But I do," Bingley said, his grin returning. "You may not have noticed, but I have rarely seen you so attentive during a conversation."

"You made that claim the other day, and I advised you at the time there was nothing in it."

"Oh, I thought it strange at the time, to be sure, but I saw it again yesterday when we saw Miss Elizabeth in town, and you sallied with her like—"

Darcy exhaled sharply. "Miss Elizabeth Bennet has a talent for provocation. That is all."

"Is it? Or is it that she has found the one chink in your armor?."

Darcy's eyes narrowed. "If this is your idea of humor, Bingley, it is poorly executed."

"It is not humor; it is strategy. And I have a proposition for you regarding our little wager."

"Proposition?" Darcy turned to face him.

"Indeed. Darcy, you are going to lose, and you know it. Trying to be receptive and cheerful to an entire town? It is not in your nature."

"You make me out to sound rather an ogre."

"No, merely stating fact. I say you will be wasting your efforts if you are determined to learn to tolerate the eccentricities of *every* person in Meryton. Doomed for failure, I say, for the moment you set your mind to face one, another will bite at your heels."

Darcy crossed his arms. "They would not dare."

"And *that*," Bingley said, pointing at Darcy's chest, "is why you will lose, my friend. This very manner of yours which makes you so forbidding is the very thing that will prohibit you from being amiable. And since I am feeling generous, I propose that we constrict the terms of our wager to one person. One who manages to embody the charm of the town and will challenge you to be at your very best."

Darcy sighed. "Let me guess."

"Oh, I daresay there is no need for you to guess, but I shall state the name, just for the sake of clarity—Miss Elizabeth Bennet."

Darcy tasted bile. "Why are you so fixated on that particular lady?"

"Because she will test you, and if you can remain gentlemanly with her, then I will concede the wager entirely. And no fair dangling your fortune in her face. You must win her *friendship*."

Darcy crossed the room, not looking at Bingley. "And why, precisely, are you so willing to indulge this adjustment, since you seem to feel it is in my favor?"

Bingley shrugged. "Because you have already lost your composure with her once, and I believe you will again. She has found a way to unsettle you, and that makes her the perfect test."

Darcy's jaw tightened. "You mean to stack the deck against me. Before, the terms were generalities. Now, you wish for me to focus all my energies on one person in such a way that I risk raising expectations."

Bingley grinned. "Not at all. I am merely permitting you to be as *un*civil as you please to everyone else, since you seem to have only so many smiles allotted to you each day."

"I know very well what you are doing, Bingley. I cannot possibly win the favor of one lady to your satisfaction while being standoffish with the rest of the neighborhood."

Bingley lifted his shoulders. "As you say, Darcy."

Darcy gritted his teeth. "This entire idea is preposterous. But very well. If Miss Elizabeth Bennet is to be the measure of my civility, then so be it."

Bingley clapped his hands, looking altogether too pleased. "Excellent! I knew you would see reason."

Darcy gave him a pointed look. "Reason has little to do with it. But I will prove you wrong."

"Oh, I have no doubt you will try," Bingley said, standing to leave. "But if there is one lady in Hertfordshire who can break through your defenses, it is Miss Elizabeth Bennet. You had better prepare yourself, Darcy."

Darcy watched him go, his thoughts already tangled with the implications of this new challenge. If Elizabeth Bennet was to be the test, then he would need to steel himself against her wit and charm. There would be no victory without discipline—and no room for error.

FOUR

THE DRAWING ROOM AT Mrs. Phillips's house was far smaller and more crowded than Darcy preferred. Low ceilings and too many bodies made the air stifling, and the cacophony of voices felt as though it was conspiring to drive him out. Darcy stood near a narrow window, half-tempted to pry it open for relief.

He should not have come. The wager was a foolish distraction, and this was no place for a man like him. But Bingley had insisted—loudly and with relentless optimism—that "engaging with the neighborhood" would do them both good. Worse, Darcy had agreed, bound as he was to fulfill his side of the challenge.

And so he found himself enduring Mrs. Phillips's simpering pleasantries, surrounded by people who found his silence inexplicably fascinating.

"Well, Mr. Darcy, I do hope you find Meryton to your liking," Mrs. Phillips was saying, smiling so hard Darcy feared it might cause her injury. "We are not so grand as London, but we have our charms."

"Indeed," he replied, forcing a polite nod.

"Yes," she continued, oblivious to his disinterest, "our assemblies are modest affairs, but they are most agreeable, as you must have seen for yourself. Why, my niece Elizabeth alone could keep a room lively."

At the sound of her name, Darcy turned—just slightly—and saw Elizabeth across the room. She was speaking to her elder sister, her posture relaxed but her hands animated as she gestured through some point. She was smiling.

She was always smiling.

But not in the way of her sister, whose face seemed eternally washed in nauseating serenity. No, Elizabeth Bennet seemed always on the verge of laughter—laughter so infectious that it made him want to lean in and learn what she found so amusing.

Dash it all.

Mrs. Phillips followed his gaze, and the woman was on him like a hawk on a mouse. "Why, Mr. Darcy it seems you must quite agree with me! How silly of me to keep you here with my dull chatter when you could speak with someone far more interesting."

He snapped his focus back. "No, madam, you mistake me. I—"

"No, no, I insist! It would be a shame to miss such excellent company. Do come along, Mr. Darcy. Lizzy?"

Before he could refuse, Darcy found himself propelled toward Elizabeth Bennet like a chess piece moved by an unseen hand.

She turned as they approached, her smile bright and watchful. "Mr. Darcy. What an unexpected delight."

Darcy inclined his head—there was little else he could do, for Mrs. Philips was fairly holding his feet to the fire. "Miss Elizabeth."

"I hope you are finding Meryton tolerable," she said, tilting her head. "Or is *tolerable* too strong a word?"

Darcy hesitated. The wager demanded civility, but Elizabeth Bennet made it devilishly difficult to remain polite without being drawn into her traps. "I believe I am finding it... lively."

Elizabeth laughed softly. "Lively? Now that is unexpected. One might almost think you meant it as a compliment."

"Merely an observation," Darcy replied before he could stop himself.

Elizabeth raised her eyebrows, though the humor in her eyes betrayed her. "I see. A half-compliment, then. I suppose it is better than nothing."

"Do you always persist in finding meaning where none was intended, Miss Bennet?"

"Only when the meaning is amusing," she said, holding his gaze. "And I must confess, you are a most obliging subject."

Darcy's mouth twitched, though he schooled it into stillness. "I am pleased to provide entertainment, though it was not my intention."

"Intentions are overrated," Elizabeth replied airily. "*Results* are far more interesting."

"I cannot think what 'results' you refer to. I should think intentions are what matter."

"Do they? I suppose it depends on what one intends. As for myself, I only intend to keep you speaking. It is such a rare occurrence, Mr. Darcy, that I feel it a duty to encourage it."

He narrowed his eyes. "And what makes you so certain I wish to be encouraged?"

Elizabeth smiled again, though there was a sharpness to it now. "Perhaps I am wrong, and you would prefer to glare at the bookshelves instead. I will not stop you, though I imagine the books have little to say in return."

Darcy exhaled slowly, trying to suppress his irritation. It was not irritation, though—not really. It was the unsettling knowledge that Elizabeth Bennet had managed, yet again, to draw him into conversation without his consent.

He looked at her, truly *looked* at her, and knew in that moment that no amount of "civility" would be enough to satisfy Bingley's terms, and nor could his usual aloofness protect him from her. Her wit was a net, and he was caught.

"I find it difficult," Darcy said finally, "to keep up with you, Miss Bennet."

"Then I shall endeavor to slow down," she replied, though the gleam in her eyes promised no such thing.

Darcy's lips twitched again. He was betrayed by the smallest movement—the kind Elizabeth Bennet always seemed to notice.

"Did you just smile?" she asked, eyes narrowing with exaggerated suspicion. "How extraordinary."

"I did no such thing."

"I could swear you did. Perhaps the books are more amusing than I thought."

Before Darcy could reply—before he could regain the upper hand—a voice edged into his awareness.

"Elizabeth, I believe our aunt wishes to speak with you," Miss Bennet said gently, approaching with her usual bland smile.

Elizabeth turned back to Darcy, giving him a polite curtsy. "Do excuse me, Mr. Darcy. I shall leave you to the books."

As she walked away, Darcy stared at the empty space where she had stood. He had managed to remain polite. He had even managed to carry on a full conversation. And yet, he felt less in control than ever.

"Jane, you are being silly. I have done nothing untoward, and you needn't try to accuse me of any underhanded means. I was perfectly civil yesterday."

The next day dawned gray and brisk, the clouds low and heavy over Meryton. Elizabeth was grateful for the chill as it gave her excuse to walk briskly, arms tucked close to her sides to ward off the damp.

"All I am saying, Lizzy, is that I cannot believe you spoke so tartly to Mr. Darcy," Jane continued, adjusting her shawl. "You will frighten him away."

Elizabeth laughed. "I highly doubt that. Is that why you interrupted us? I had him right where I wanted him."

"Which is where?" Jane asked, hurrying a little to keep up. "Befuddled and frustrated with that rambling sort of exchange you call 'conversation'?"

"Oh, do not pity him so much. Mr. Darcy seems impervious to most things, including good cheer."

"Lizzy!" Jane sighed, though she could not hide a smile. "I only mean to say you might try being kinder."

"Kinder? I am always kind. It is not my fault he takes offense at every sentence."

"Kitty, Lydia, you might slow down," Jane called. "It is still early. I doubt the officers are parading through town at this hour."

Lydia and Kitty—bouncing ahead as usual—seemed oblivious to both the weather and decorum. "They might be!" Lydia shot back over her shoulder. "And what if we miss them?"

Elizabeth shook her head fondly. "Let them tire themselves. I have no desire to chase redcoats through the mud." Just as well, for Kitty and Lydia were long gone, and even if Elizabeth and Jane ran to catch them, they would not manage it at this point.

"Do not speak too soon, Lizzy," Jane said as a peculiar grin overtook her face. "They may not be the only gentlemen you see today."

Elizabeth frowned. "What do you mean?"

Jane gave her a meaningful look just as a familiar figure appeared ahead, rounding the corner near the haberdasher's shop. Mr. Darcy, his tall form unmistakable, walked beside Mr. Bingley, who waved immediately upon spotting them.

"Oh no," Elizabeth said under her breath. "Not the officers, but the generals."

Good heavens, was she constantly to be faced with the man? Mr. Darcy ought to know well enough that his place was at Netherfield, and he ought not to depart from it without her leave. She sighed. This wager was becoming rather vexing, consuming far more of her time and energies than she liked.

"Miss Bennet! Miss Elizabeth! What an excellent surprise!" Mr. Bingley called cheerfully, making his way toward them with little regard for the mud splattering up from his boots.

Mr. Darcy followed, his pace slower, though there was no mistaking his notice of Elizabeth. She felt it like a weight—no, a presence—that lingered even after he looked away.

Elizabeth curtsied as the gentlemen approached. "Good morning, Mr. Bingley. Mr. Darcy."

"Good morning," Bingley replied warmly. "Are you out to take the air?"

"I am not sure there is much air to take this morning," Elizabeth said, glancing up at the leaden sky. "But yes, we are."

"It is brisk," Bingley agreed, apparently untroubled by the chill. "I am convinced a walk does wonders for the spirits, though Darcy insists otherwise."

Elizabeth turned to Darcy, her smile teasing. "Does he? I should think Mr. Darcy prefers the company of his books."

"I am fond of exercise when the occasion requires," Darcy replied. "Though I find this mud less charming than others appear to."

"Ah, but the mud is all part of the adventure," Elizabeth said lightly. "Surely you do not let it deter you?"

Darcy glanced at the hem of her gown, already flecked and soggy where the damp had splashed it. "You seem unbothered."

"One must learn to endure a little inconvenience for the sake of one's spirits," she replied. "Or have you not been lectured on the virtues of fortitude, Mr. Darcy?"

Bingley laughed. "You have him there, Miss Elizabeth."

Darcy's gaze remained on her, though she could not quite determine its meaning. "Fortitude has its place, Miss Bennet, though I doubt it requires ruining one's shoes."

Elizabeth gave a mock sigh, looking down at her half-muddied boots. "A pity, sir, for I was rather counting on clean shoes to make me look respectable. In such a state as this, what am I?"

"A challenge," Darcy said, almost under his breath.

Elizabeth blinked, startled by the quiet remark. For a moment, she wondered if she had misheard him, but no—he was watching her with that same unsettling directness, as though her words and presence had unsettled *him* in turn.

She recovered quickly. "How fortunate that I find challenges invigorating."

"You do seem to," Darcy replied.

Mr. Bingley, fortunately, had been speaking to Jane, and was mercifully oblivious to Darcy's words. He grinned broadly and gestured toward the row of shops lining the street. "Since we are all headed the same way, perhaps we might walk together. Darcy was searching for a book—as you see, we have just come from there—and Caroline has sent me to collect a ribbon—though I fear I shall choose the wrong shade and face her wrath. I say, Miss Bennet, allow me to escort you." Bingley stepped quickly to Jane's side, offering his elbow.

Elizabeth turned her gaze to the quieter of the two gentlemen. "Book shopping! How very industrious of you, sir. But, I see you have no book in your hand, even after departing the finest shop in Meryton. Were the bookshelves too talkative for your liking?"

Darcy raised a brow. "I thought you had declared them too quiet."

"Did I? Then you must forgive me. My opinions are so numerous I sometimes forget them."

Bingley chuckled as he secured Jane's hand in the crook of his elbow. "Darcy does find books better company than most. He likes silence, Miss Elizabeth."

Elizabeth tilted her head. "Not all company need be quiet. Some might argue that liveliness keeps the mind sharper."

"I have never had that particular complaint," Darcy replied.

"No?" She raised an eyebrow. "Then perhaps you simply need a livelier companion, Mr. Darcy."

There it was again—that flicker of something behind his expression, quick as lightning and gone just as fast. He held her gaze for a moment before inclining his head. "I shall defer to your expertise on the matter, Miss Bennet."

The streets of Meryton were busy with morning errands. Shopkeepers swept their stoops, carts rolled past with clattering wheels, and the damp air carried the mingled scents of coal smoke and damp wool.

"You seem very quiet, Mr. Darcy," Elizabeth remarked after a moment. "I trust you are not overwhelmed by the excitement of Meryton."

"Not overwhelmed," Darcy said. "Merely observant."

"And what have you observed?"

Darcy considered his answer. "That you are determined to provoke me."

Elizabeth laughed, her breath clouding in the cold air. "Is that so? I believe I am merely being polite."

"Polite," Darcy repeated. "You have a very peculiar definition of the word."

"I prefer to think of it as... lively."

Darcy almost smiled—almost. "I shall take your word for it."

Elizabeth glanced sideways at him, curious despite herself. There was something oddly compelling about the way he replied—always measured, always controlled, and never without precision. Yet there was something beneath it that looked very much like a cat toying with its prey. He was unlike any man she had ever met, and for all his faults, she could not deny that he intrigued her.

"Here we are!" Bingley's voice carried back to them as he stopped before the ribbon shop. He turned toward Jane with an exaggerated sigh. "Miss Bennet, I beg you will assist me. I shall never choose correctly on my own."

Jane blushed and followed him inside, leaving Elizabeth and Darcy momentarily alone on the street.

Elizabeth turned toward him, folding her hands together. "I believe that is another point in favor of liveliness."

"How so?"

"Mr. Bingley's liveliness has spared us all the horror of Miss Bingley's disappointment," she said. "Surely even you must admit it is useful."

Darcy paused, looking at her intently for a moment longer than seemed polite. "I am beginning to see the appeal."

"Then I have won," Elizabeth replied, smiling.

"Not yet, Miss Bennet," he said quietly. "But you are... persistent."

Her smile faltered—just slightly—because there was something in his voice, something that made her fear that perhaps *she* was the prey the cat was playing with. How unaccountable!

Before she could reflect further on that notion or make any impertinent reply, Jane and Mr. Bingley emerged from the shop, and Darcy stepped back to let them pass.

"Shall we?" Bingley asked, clearly pleased with his purchase. "Miss Bennet, Miss Elizabeth, we must thank you for sharing the morning with us."

Elizabeth and Jane curtsied together. "It was our pleasure."

As they parted ways, Elizabeth glanced back once, just once, to find Darcy still watching her. For all his formality, there was no denying that something had shifted.

And she did not know what to do with that.

FIVE

"YOU ARE STARING OUT that window as though you can melt the snow with the very heat of your glare," Charlotte said as she breezed into Longbourn's drawing room the next day.

Elizabeth turned from the glass, blinking as if caught in a mischief she had not meant to admit. "Nonsense. I was merely admiring the view."

Charlotte arched a brow as she settled into a chair. "Admiring it, or trying to escape it?"

Elizabeth's lips curved somewhat, but the smile felt too thin. "And what precisely would I need to escape, Charlotte?"

"Oh, I don't know." Charlotte leaned forward with a smirk. "Perhaps a certain tall, brooding gentleman who seems to have taken an uncharacteristic interest in you."

Elizabeth scoffed and crossed the room with deliberate ease. "If Mr. Darcy has any interest, it is in finding faults to catalog. I imagine he has compiled an extensive list by now."

"Perhaps he has," Charlotte said. "And yet, he seems determined to look your way all the same."

Elizabeth paused. "You are imagining things."

"Am I?" Charlotte tilted her head. "I watched him at your aunt's tea the other day. He barely spoke to anyone but you."

"Perhaps he finds my faults more entertaining than most," Elizabeth replied, sinking into the chair across from her friend. "I shall endeavor to provide him with more material."

Charlotte laughed softly. "You always deflect, Lizzy. But tell me—how fares the wager?"

Elizabeth waved a hand as though swatting a fly. "As dull and pointless as the day it was made."

"I would not call it pointless. You are winning, after all."

Elizabeth's brow arched. "Winning?"

Charlotte leaned back. "You have him watching you, Lizzy. Speaking to you. Thinking of you, I would imagine."

Elizabeth hesitated, her retort catching on her tongue. Finally, she said, "If he watches, it is only to confirm his low opinion."

"And what if it is not? What if he is beginning to admire you?"

Elizabeth barked a laugh, though it came sharper than intended. "Mr. Darcy? Admire *me?* Pray, Charlotte, do not start writing novels. No one could credit the stories you make up."

"You jest, but I think he finds you more intriguing than you care to admit. I told you you could turn his head!"

Elizabeth snorted. "I am simply fulfilling my part of the bargain by becoming an object of curiosity for a bored man."

"Are you? Or are you starting to enjoy it?"

Elizabeth's breath caught—not enough to be noticeable, but enough for her to feel it. She masked it quickly with a quick wave of her hand. "You give me too much credit. I am merely testing my wits against his pride, nothing more."

"And if it *were* more?" Charlotte asked, her tone gentler now. "Lizzy, you are so determined to win this wager that you may not realize the stakes are changing."

"The stakes," Elizabeth said coolly, "remain the same. I either win or lose."

Charlotte's smile was faint but knowing. "And yet, you will not even consider the horror of what you will owe if you lose."

Elizabeth's face tightened imperceptibly. "It is nothing worth discussing."

"Because you believe you cannot lose? Or because you are afraid you might?"

Elizabeth stood abruptly, brushing imaginary dust from her skirts. "What it would cost me is a bit of pride, nothing more. I have no intention of losing."

Charlotte rose as well. "Be careful, Lizzy. Winning may cost you more than you think."

Elizabeth whirled on her. "What is that supposed to mean?"

Charlotte only laughed. " It is easy to play at a game, but far harder to stop when it begins to play with *you*."

Elizabeth's mouth opened for a retort, but Charlotte had already reached the door. "Good day, Lizzy. I leave you to your view."

The door closed behind Charlotte, and Elizabeth returned to the window, her teacup cradled between her hands. The landscape blurred as her thoughts turned inward. Winning the wager was supposed to have been a matter of pride—a way to restore what Mr. Darcy's insult had taken from her.

And yet...

Elizabeth's brow furrowed as her reflection stared back at her in the glass. It was supposed to be simple. Why did it feel like anything but?

Darcy re-folded the letter with careful precision and reached for a fresh sheet to pen a reply. This was Georgiana's second request now. Her reluctance practically trembled through the page, each word chosen with the same delicate care she used to play her pianoforte. He ran a finger along the edge of the paper, his jaw tightening.

She had sounded hesitant in her last letter, of course. That much was natural. The thought of going anywhere unfamiliar after what had happened in Ramsgate last summer would unsettle anyone, let alone a girl as sensitive and trusting as Georgiana. When she had written to him then, he had replied, urging her to set aside her fears—to think not of the shadows of the past but of the opportunities the visit could offer.

He had meant every word. He had believed it was for the best. But now...

Darcy re-opened her letter before him as though it were a ledger of debts he could not balance. Georgiana's reply had come today, more unhappy than before, more direct in her quiet plea. Her words were circumspect, of course—she never spoke plainly when she feared disappointing him—but the message was clear. She did not want to go with Mrs. Pomeroy's family.

He dipped his quill into the ink, but the paper remained blank. What was there to say? He had already reassured her once. He had reminded her that Mrs. Pomeroy's family was well-respected, that she would be among girls her own age. That she would, he had said carefully, be 'looked after.' There would be no... incidents.

And yet Georgiana had written again.

Darcy set the quill down and rubbed a hand over his face. He could not fault her for her fears. They were, after all, too fresh. He remembered all too well the tears in her eyes when she had confessed what nearly happened. How she had trusted the wrong man. How she had nearly...

He drew a sharp breath and sat straighter. Georgiana was strong in ways she did not yet understand, but how was she to grow if he allowed her to avoid every challenge? This visit was a chance for her to see a different world, to spend time with companions of her own age, to leave the memories of Ramsgate behind her. Would it not be wrong—selfish, even—to shelter her so completely?

The door opened behind him, and he glanced up to see Bingley stepping in. "Ah, there you are! I had begun to wonder if you had locked yourself away for good."

"Not for good," Darcy replied, setting his quill aside. A reply would have to wait.

"Then only for now." Bingley laughed, moving to lean against the mantel. "What has you so grim this morning? Your valet did not cut you shaving, I trust? Nothing the matter with your breakfast?"

Darcy shot him a look but said nothing, folding Georgiana's letter and slipping it into his pocket.

Bingley's gaze flickered to the papers on the desk. "Ah. Correspondence. That explains it. You always look as though the fate of the empire rests on your pen."

"I do not tend to waste time on trivial matters."

"And is this matter trivial?"

"No," Darcy said after a beat. "But it is private."

Bingley raised his hands in mock surrender. "Say no more. I shall leave you to it. Though I do hope you plan to take some air at least. Brooding is bad for the constitution. I am going for a ride, if you care to join me."

With a final grin, Bingley departed, closing the door behind him. Darcy exhaled slowly and returned his attention to the blank page.

He dipped the quill again and began to write.

My dearest Georgiana,

I have read your letter with the greatest care, as I always do, and I can see how earnestly you feel about this visit. Let me say first that I would never press you to do anything I believed to be truly against your well-being. You are my highest priority, always.

You know, however, how deeply I believe in your strength and goodness, even when you do not see it yourself. The family of Mrs. Pomeroy are well thought of in every respect, and I assure you, you will be as safe with them as you would be at Pemberley itself. The daughters of the house are known for their cheer and good nature, and I feel it would be a great opportunity for you to grow comfortable in the company of your peers.

It is only natural, after all, to feel uncertainty about unfamiliar surroundings, but those uncertainties often prove baseless when we face them. I hope you will think on this, my dearest sister, and know that I trust entirely in your ability to meet any challenge with grace and courage.

If, however, after giving it all due consideration, you still feel strongly against the visit, I will not press you further. Your peace is more important than any plan, and I trust your instincts implicitly.

Yours always,
Fitzwilliam

Darcy blotted the ink and folded the letter, slipping it into an envelope and sealing it with a firm press of his signet. As he held the envelope for a moment longer, his mind turned, inexplicably, to Elizabeth Bennet. She would be here at Netherfield tomorrow with her family for dinner, so he must face her again, and soon. An odd thought pierced him, that his anxious dread of that scenario was a sort of mirror for how his sister must be feeling about going with the Pomeroys.

But that was... well, it was preposterous. The two situations were nothing alike! One was the growth of an impressionable young lady, and the other was the dignity of an eligible gentleman. In one instance, a little boldness in the face of trial was perfectly wise, but as for the other...

He shook the thought away and placed the letter with the others to be sent. This was no time for distraction.

THE CLINK OF SILVERWARE and the hum of conversation filled the air at Netherfield's dining room, the candlelight flickering over fine china and polished crystal. Elizabeth could feel the heat of it flaring against her skin—the weight of too many stares, too many opinions.

At least two of those stares belonged to Mr. Darcy and Miss Bingley, though their purposes could not have been more opposite.

Miss Bingley was on the offensive tonight, her tone sharp and her remarks carefully aimed. And it became rapidly apparent what the point of this dinner party was meant to be—Miss Bingley was claiming her turf, exerting her superiority, and every other female in Meryton was meant to feel it. From the moment Elizabeth had stepped into the room, Caroline Bingley's smile had been too sweet, her comments too pointed. The subtle mockery in her voice was an art form, and Elizabeth could not deny its skill, though she had no intention of losing to it.

She lifted her glass of wine with practiced ease, tilting her head just so as Miss Bingley leaned forward with a conspiratorial air.

"Do you not find it charming, Miss Eliza," Caroline said, her voice dripping honey, "how country gatherings such as these bring out such... candid personalities?"

Elizabeth's lips thinned, the beginnings of a smile forming. "I suppose it is rather charming. One does learn so much about one's company when people speak freely."

Caroline's smile tightened, but she pressed on. "Indeed. Of course, there are times when one wishes for a touch more... refinement."

"Refinement is an admirable goal," Elizabeth said lightly, "though I confess I find it less entertaining than honesty."

Across the table, Mr. Darcy's fork paused briefly above his plate. His eyes flicked toward Elizabeth, not so much with surprise as with interest—as though her words were pieces of a puzzle he had not yet solved.

Miss Bingley laughed. "Oh, Miss Eliza, you are too generous. Surely you would agree that a certain level of refinement is necessary for—well, for harmony."

"Harmony is a fine thing, but I fear too much of it leads to dull company. Do you not agree, Mr. Darcy?"

His gaze held hers for a moment longer than was proper, his fork now forgotten. "I believe harmony and honesty are not mutually exclusive, Miss Bennet."

"Indeed? Then perhaps we must agree to disagree. I find too much harmony quite stifling."

Darcy's cheek twitched, the faintest trace of amusement crossing his otherwise serious face. "Then I suspect you are never stifled, Miss Bennet."

Elizabeth felt a small jolt at his reply—not just at the words themselves, but at the way he delivered them. She detected no mockery in his tone, no disdain. If anything, it was... admiring.

Miss Bingley's laugh, however, was quite the opposite. "Oh, Mr. Darcy, you are far too indulgent. Miss Eliza has quite the way with words, does she not?"

"She does," Darcy said simply, his gaze never leaving Elizabeth.

Elizabeth blinked, caught off guard by the frankness of his statement. There was no irony in his voice, no polite veneer. He meant it. She felt the warmth of it spread through her chest... and she hated that she felt it at all.

But then Mrs. Bennet's voice broke through like a thunderclap. "Of course, Mrs. Hurst, everyone dearly loves my Lydia. She does have such a lively nature. Just this morning, she was quite determined to go to Meryton, and you know I could not possibly stand in her way. All the officers would have been so disappointed to miss her, you know!"

Across the table, Sir William Lucas gave a hearty laugh. "Lively spirits are the heart of any gathering, are they not, Mrs. Bennet? And I daresay all the young men must surely agree. Why, I remember many such youthful excursions in my day!"

Elizabeth's stomach churned as her mother prattled on, unaware—or worse, uncaring—of the glances her words invited. Mrs. Goulding, seated further down, whispered something to her husband, who nodded gravely while reaching for his wine. Lydia, perched near the end of the table, was too busy giggling with Kitty to notice the mortified expression on Elizabeth's face.

Elizabeth caught Jane's eye, and her sister offered a small, helpless smile. From the far side of the table, Mrs. Purvis—one of the neighborhood's more reserved ladies—shifted uncomfortably in her seat, as though contemplating escape.

"I do hope your family has a similar appreciation for liveliness, Miss Bingley," Mrs. Bennet continued, her tone almost triumphant.

Caroline smiled thinly, her eyes flicking toward Darcy as though to gauge his reaction. "I find a lively spirit charming in moderation," she said smoothly. "Though I confess, I prefer quieter pursuits."

"Quiet pursuits," Elizabeth said lightly, "can often disguise the loudest ambitions."

Caroline turned toward her, her smile tight as a bowstring. "I suppose you would know, Miss Eliza. You do have such a way of making yourself heard."

Elizabeth's smile brightened. "Thank you, Miss Bingley. I find it impossible to stay silent when there is so much of interest to remark upon."

Across the table, Mrs. Purvis's delicate sigh broke through the tension, her fan fluttering lightly against her cheek. "Such spirited conversation this evening. It is always a pleasure to see. My congratulations, Miss Bingley, on a thrilling evening."

Darcy coughed softly, though Elizabeth thought it might have been a laugh. Caroline's eyes narrowed, her composure cracking just slightly, and Elizabeth felt an undeniable rush of satisfaction.

SIX

DARCY SET DOWN HIS wineglass, his fingers brushing the stem with meditative slowness. Across the table, Miss Elizabeth Bennet's smile sharpened like the point of a quill, her wit slicing through Caroline Bingley's carefully laid remarks with the kind of effortless precision that left even him taken aback.

He coughed lightly, though the sound seemed to draw her attention. She glanced at him, her eyes bright with amusement, and for a moment—just a moment—he felt the flicker of a smile threatening to escape.

No. Not here.

He reached for his knife instead, slicing a neat line through the roast on his plate, though he barely tasted it. Across the table, Caroline shifted in her seat, her expression schooled into something meant to resemble poise. Darcy knew better. He could see the tightness in her jaw, the slight rigidity of her shoulders. Miss Bennet had scored a hit, and Caroline was preparing her counter.

"Miss Elizabeth," Caroline began, her voice sweet enough to curdle. "I must say, your loyalty to your neighbors is rather inspiring. It is such a delight to see someone so... spirited."

Elizabeth inclined her head, her expression neutral but her eyes alive with challenge. "How kind of you to say, Miss Bingley. I do hope I have not bored you with my observations."

"Not at all," Caroline said, her smile tight. "Indeed, I was only just thinking of how important and rare true, spirited conversation is—particularly among ladies. My dear friend Georgiana, for example, always appreciates a good wit."

Darcy's hand froze briefly above his plate. The mention of Georgiana was calculated, of course. Caroline wielded her supposed intimacy with his sister like a weapon, and it was a tactic he found increasingly tiresome.

"Your sister is such a treasure, Mr. Darcy," Caroline continued, turning toward him now with an indulgent smile. "She often writes to me, you know, sharing her thoughts on music, art... so many subjects. Such refinement for one so young."

Elizabeth's gaze flicked toward him briefly, curiosity flashing in her eyes. Darcy set down his knife with deliberate care. "Georgiana is indeed talented," he said evenly. "Though I was not aware she corresponded with you so regularly."

Caroline's smile wavered, just for an instant. "Oh, well, perhaps not regularly," she admitted, her tone airy. "But we have exchanged letters. She is always so eager to hear my thoughts on matters of taste."

Elizabeth's mouth curved faintly, like a wolf catching the scent of blood, though she said nothing. Darcy resisted the urge to shift in his seat.

"Your guidance must be invaluable to her, Miss Bingley," Elizabeth said at last, her voice carrying just enough sweetness to match Caroline's. "How fortunate that she has you to look up to."

Caroline straightened, clearly interpreting Elizabeth's words as genuine. "Indeed. Georgiana is such a darling girl, and I do feel quite protective of her. It is only natural, of course, given my closeness to Mr. Darcy and his family."

Darcy's grip tightened briefly on the edge of the table, but he remained silent, his expression impassive. Elizabeth, however, was not so restrained.

"How noble of you, Miss Bingley," she said, tilting her head slightly. "To take such an interest in a young woman's development. I am sure Mr. Darcy values your mentorship of his sister greatly."

Caroline hesitated, clearly unsure whether Elizabeth's words were sincere or mocking. "Of course," she said after a moment, her tone clipped. "Could I do less for such a sweet young friend?"

"No, indeed," Elizabeth replied, her eyes glittering. "Though I must confess, it surprises me that someone of your sophistication and many obligations would have so much time for correspondence."

Darcy fought valiantly, but in the end, he managed to suppress the urge to smile. Caroline, on the other hand, faltered visibly, her reply catching on her tongue before she could deliver it.

"It is no trouble," Caroline said finally, her voice brittle. "One must always make time for those in need of guidance."

"Especially those so young," Elizabeth added lightly. "I daresay she must look upon you as a second elder sister."

This time, Darcy did not bother to hide the slight upward curl of his mouth. He reached for his wineglass, taking a measured sip as Caroline's composure cracked further, her smile slipping just enough to reveal her frustration.

Across the table, Sir William Lucas was regaling Mr. Philips with an account of some long-past hunting adventure, his voice carrying with the cheerful obliviousness of a man accustomed to being indulged. "...and there I was, face to face with the beast! It was a stag of the largest size, I assure you—though I would not expect anyone to believe me without seeing the rack for themselves!"

"Indeed," Mr. Bennet mused as he lowered his drink. "So large it would not fit through the door of your study, hence the reason you did not take it."

"Well! I had only just fired and had not yet the opportunity to reload, of course," Sir William chuckled. "But I assure you, it was the largest ever seen in Hertfordshire."

"Oh, naturally, naturally."

Mrs. Purvis, seated nearby, made a polite noise of interest, though she barely looked up from her plate. Darcy caught Elizabeth's glance flicking briefly in their direction, her lips curving slightly as if in private amusement.

"Mr. Darcy," Caroline said, turning to him with a forced laugh. "You are far too quiet tonight. Do say something to defend me."

He set the glass down carefully, his gaze resting on Caroline for a moment before shifting to Elizabeth. "I was not aware that you required any defense, Miss Bingley."

"Require it? Of course not, but I feel my words have been little understood this evening. You, however, are much more intimately acquainted with my tastes and manner, and surely I need not explain myself to *you*."

"Miss Bennet seems to be managing the conversation quite well without my interference."

Elizabeth's brows lifted slightly, and for a moment, their gazes held. There was something in her eyes—amusement, yes, but also something sharper, something that made the hair on the back of his neck prickle.

Meanwhile, Mrs. Philips leaned closer to Mrs. Bennet at the far end of the table, her voice dropping to a conspiratorial whisper. "Do you see how Mr. Bingley looks at Jane? I daresay something will come of it soon. Mark my words."

Mrs. Bennet, practically glowing with anticipation, nodded enthusiastically. "Oh, I have every confidence. Every confidence!"

Caroline's laugh rang hollow in the silence that followed her exchange with Darcy. "Well, I see I am outnumbered."

"You speak as if opinions are arrayed against you, Miss Bingley," Elizabeth said. "How could anything be further from the truth? You have such a talent for commanding attention."

Darcy cleared his throat, setting his glass down with more force than necessary. "Miss Bingley, I believe the next course is being served."

Caroline blinked, her irritation poorly masked as she turned toward the servants now entering the room. "Of course. How delightful."

Elizabeth's gaze lingered on him for a moment longer, and then she turned back to her plate. And it was as if he never existed.

Darcy focused on his own meal, though he could feel the lingering tension in the room like a taut string waiting to snap. It was not Elizabeth's words that stayed with him, though they had been sharp and clever as always.

It was the way she had looked at him—curious, questioning, as though trying to see something beneath the surface. He wished she would stop.

And he wished, in equal measure, that she would not.

ELIZABETH CLASPED HER HANDS tightly in her lap, her eyes darting between her mother and Lydia as they fluttered around the drawing room like magpies in a glittering treasure chest. The Bingley sisters sat poised on the elegant settees, their expressions composed as bone china to the casual observer but painfully transparent to Elizabeth. Every raised brow, every faintly curled lip, was a silent declaration: How unfortunate to share a room with such company.

Across the room, Lady Lucas busied herself with a cup of tea, her polite murmurs to Mrs. Philips barely masking her own appraisal of the furnishings. Sir William stood by the fireplace, his stance as jovial as ever as he engaged Mr. Purvis in a loud recounting of the evening's finer points.

"Oh, look at these curtains!" Mrs. Bennet exclaimed, running her fingers along the edge of the brocade. "Such fine workmanship. Do you not agree, Lydia? They must have cost a fortune!"

"Certainly not what we have at Longbourn," Lydia agreed. She leaned in closer to the mantle, her fingers trailing dangerously near the delicate porcelain figures displayed there. "I wonder if they're real gold."

Elizabeth's breath caught. "Lydia," she said, her voice sharper than intended, "perhaps it would be better to admire the room from a little farther back."

Lydia waved her off with a careless laugh. "Do not be such a bore, Lizzy. You can admire things much better up close."

"Admiration does not require touching," Elizabeth snapped. She glanced at Caroline Bingley, whose prettily pursed lips spoke volumes. A faint hum of laughter passed between her and Louisa, and Elizabeth's stomach tightened. Nearby, Lady Lucas exchanged a pointed glance with Mrs. Goulding, her fan fluttering lightly against her cheek.

Mrs. Bennet clasped her hands together and beamed. "What an exquisite room! Such refinement. Oh, I must tell Mr. Bennet how splendidly Mr. Bingley has furnished his home. May I suppose it was you who oversaw all these arrangements, Miss Bingley?"

Caroline Bingley's smile was smooth, but there was a faint edge to her voice as she replied, "Most of the credit belongs to my brother, Mrs. Bennet. He does have a certain... exuberance when it comes to pleasing his guests."

"Exuberance!" Mrs. Bennet laughed, her fan fluttering. "Well, it is a credit to his taste, then. Though I daresay he must have sought your advice for such details. Gentlemen rarely have an eye for these things."

Elizabeth clenched her hands tighter, praying the earth might open and swallow her whole. Charlotte, devil take her, had been distant and quiet all evening, talking with Jane at the edge of the room. From the corner of her eye, she noticed Lady Lucas's polite smile tighten, though she said nothing, her gaze lingering on Lydia, who had now moved to the far corner, examining a collection of small silver boxes with far too much interest. Caroline's gaze followed her, a faint sneer tugging at the corners of her mouth.

"Lizzy," Jane whispered from the seat beside her, "perhaps you should—"

But Elizabeth was already rising. "Lydia," she called, her voice firmer now, "I am certain you will find the view from here just as impressive."

Lydia turned, a pout forming on her lips. "You are no fun, Lizzy. No one minds."

Elizabeth's gaze flicked to Caroline, who was now watching the exchange with the air of a cat observing cornered mice. Sir William's booming laugh punctuated the tension from across the room, though Elizabeth barely noticed. "I mind," she said firmly, stepping closer. "Come sit with me for a moment."

Lydia groaned but obeyed, plopping onto the settee with all the grace of a child denied sweets. Elizabeth sat beside her, smoothing her skirts and forcing her expression into one of calm. It was not difficult to see the disdain in Caroline's posture, the slight angle of her chin as she turned to whisper something to her sister. Louisa laughed quietly, the sound just loud enough to carry. Lady Barrow's fan fluttered again, though this time it seemed more to conceal a smile than cool her face.

Elizabeth's jaw clenched. She could not deny the truth of it—her mother's gushing, Lydia's impulsiveness, the loud and ungraceful way they filled the room—it was all painfully out of place in a setting like this. But she hated, hated, the way Caroline wielded her disdain as though it were a weapon. As though the Bennets' flaws were a source of her personal amusement.

"Miss Eliza, you must tell me—do you find the countryside offers much in the way of... refined society?"

Her mother—dash it all—overheard the remark Caroline had directed at Elizabeth and responded herself. "But of course! We dine with four and twenty families! Some of whom you see here, so I should say 'refined,' indeed!"

Elizabeth closed her eyes faintly and held her breath at Miss Bingley's poorly concealed amusement. She gritted her teeth and added, "I suppose that depends on your definition of 'refinement.' I find the variety of the countryside keeps one quite sharp. It is difficult to fall into dullness when there is always something—or someone—to keep you on your toes."

Caroline's lips pressed together, but she said nothing. Instead, she turned to her sister, murmuring something Elizabeth did not catch, though the faint smirk that followed spoke volumes.

The sound of the gentlemen's approach was a welcome reprieve. Lydia sprang to her feet at the sight of Mr. Bingley entering the room, and Mrs. Bennet was quick to follow, engaging him in animated conversation as though he were the answer to all her prayers. And Jane's blush warmed her cheeks as Mr. Bingley came to stand rather casually beside her chair.

Darcy entered last, his dark eyes scanning the room briefly before settling, as they so often did, on her. Elizabeth felt her spine stiffen under his gaze, but she refused to look away. If Caroline wished to play at superiority, Elizabeth would not indulge her further by ceding ground.

DARCY ENTERED THE DRAWING room, letting his gaze sweep over its occupants with the practiced ease of someone who could both observe and remain unseen. Mrs. Bennet was holding court near the fireplace, speaking to Mrs. Hurst while her youngest daughter hovered nearby, her laughter loud enough to bounce off the walls. Miss Jane Bennet stood slightly apart, serene as ever, though Darcy thought he detected the faintest hint of tension in her posture.

And then there was Elizabeth Bennet.

She was seated near the far settee, her expression calm but her eyes alert, as though bracing herself for a storm. Darcy's gaze lingered on her for half a beat longer than it should have, drawn by the quiet resolve in her posture. She was, he realized with some unease, the only member of her family who seemed entirely aware of how they were being perceived.

"Do come and sit, Mr. Darcy," Caroline said, her voice lilting as she gestured to the chair nearest her own. "The evening has been most entertaining--, though I daresay we could use a bit of your... ahem... decorum to settle our spirits after the meal."

Darcy inclined his head and took the seat, and then he took up a book that was resting on the table beside him. He had no intention of indulging Caroline tonight—not when she had spent the better part of the evening making Elizabeth Bennet her target. Her attempts had been as transparent as they were tiresome.

"Mr. Darcy," Caroline began, her tone honeyed but brittle at the edges, "I was just about to observe to Miss Eliza how charming it must be to grow up in the countryside. Such an inspiring setting for simpler pursuits, I imagine—needlework, flower arranging... perhaps a bit of poetry?"

Elizabeth's lips curved into a faint smile, though Darcy, from his place near the fire, caught the glint of challenge in her eyes. "Indeed, Miss Bingley. The countryside is a wonderful muse for those with the creativity to appreciate it. Though I confess, I find poetry to be a pursuit fraught with danger."

"Danger?" Caroline laughed. "What could be dangerous about poetry, of all things? It is the purest expression of love."

"Oh, I think nothing is more certain to extinguish affection than bad poetry. A single, overwrought verse can do what no rival ever could."

Darcy's gaze flicked up from his book, though he kept his expression neutral. He filed away her words with silent amusement.

"Surely you exaggerate," Caroline said. "Poetry is timeless, an art that moves even the most unfeeling hearts."

Elizabeth's brows lifted, her smile sharpening. "Is that why it is so often the refuge of the rejected? A poor sonnet scribbled in haste, with rhyme as its only merit, is a surefire way to drive love out the door."

Caroline opened her mouth, but Elizabeth was not finished. "Do you not agree, Mr. Darcy?" she asked, turning her gaze to him with mock innocence. "Surely, as a man of letters, you must have encountered your share of poetic catastrophes."

Darcy, caught off guard, lowered his book. "I suppose I have seen examples where the effort outweighed the effect."

"How graciously put," Elizabeth said, inclining her head toward him. "Though I suspect you are merely too kind to share your honest opinion."

"Mr. Darcy is always kind," Caroline interjected quickly. "Particularly when others mistake their efforts for accomplishments."

Elizabeth's eyes danced with amusement. "How fortunate for us all. There can be no danger in attempting to impress, so long as Mr. Darcy is there to offer his measured approval."

"Or disapproval, as the case may be," Darcy said mildly, his gaze meeting hers.

The air between them crackled before Caroline cleared her throat, drawing the attention back to herself. "I am sure Miss Eliza's preferences are merely a reflection of her… rustic tastes. Simplicity has its own charm, I suppose."

"Indeed," Elizabeth replied, her tone careless. "Simplicity is often underrated. It requires no artifice to make an impression."

Darcy's gaze lingered on her for a moment longer before returning to his book. He did not need to look up again to know she had bested Caroline entirely.

Caroline's eyes narrowed just slightly, then she crossed her hands over her lap and fixed her gaze petulantly across the room.

"Lydia, come away from that!" Mrs. Bennet called, flapping her fan as Lydia approached a delicate vase perched on a nearby table. "You'll knock it over, and I daresay it must have cost a fortune."

"It is quite stable, Mama," Lydia Bennet replied, though her hands hovered near the vase as if testing its balance. "I am only looking."

"You have a way of looking that involves too much touching," Elizabeth said sharply, rising to intercept her sister. "Come, Lydia. Sit with me."

Miss Lydia huffed but complied, flouncing onto the settee with an exaggerated pout. Mrs. Bennet, however, seemed unperturbed, turning back to Bingley. "Oh, Mr. Bingley, your house is so exquisitely appointed. I do hope you will call on us soon at Longbourn! I have often thought our drawing room felt so much more cheerful when a gentleman was present." At this, she shot a withering glance at her husband, who gave every appearance of ignoring her.

Elizabeth stiffened. Darcy saw the faintest flicker of color rise to her cheeks, though she quickly recovered, sitting straighter as though she could physically lift herself above the moment.

"Oh, Mrs. Bennet,"Miss Bingley said, "I am sure your drawing room is perfectly charming. I imagine it reflects your family's... unique character."

Darcy felt his ears actually burning, a wave of secondhand embarrassment prickling at his skin. He watched Elizabeth closely, his pulse quickening despite himself. Would she rise to Caroline's bait, or would she let the remark stand?

Elizabeth turned her head slightly. "Indeed, Miss Bingley. Our drawing room *is* quite unique—though I imagine it would benefit greatly from your advice. You seem to have a particular gift for... curating *appearances*."

Caroline's smile faltered, her eyes narrowing. There was just enough ambiguity in Elizabeth's tone to force her to consider whether the remark was truly a compliment or something far more barbed.

From across the room, Charlotte Lucas coughed delicately, her gloved hand lifting to her mouth, though the faint quiver of her shoulders betrayed her mirth. Darcy's gaze shifted between the two women, his pulse quickening as he watched Caroline Bingley's composure waver.

"Thank you, Miss Eliza," Caroline said at last, her voice clipped. "It is always a pleasure to hear your observations."

Elizabeth's smile widened, a picture of innocent triumph. "The pleasure, Miss Bingley, is entirely mine."

Darcy felt a strange surge of satisfaction, though he quickly forced his expression into its usual stoicism. She had not merely answered Caroline's condescension—she had dismantled it, piece by elegant piece.

She was clever—too clever. And beautiful, though she made no effort to be. Most unsettling of all, she was utterly unafraid to challenge anyone, even him.

This fascination was dangerous. It pulled at the edges of his carefully constructed control, threatening to unravel everything he had spent years mastering. Elizabeth Bennet was a puzzle, yes—but she was also a distraction. And distractions were the one thing he could not afford.

"Mr. Darcy?" Caroline's voice cut through his thoughts, her tone sharp with impatience.

Darcy blinked, his expression smoothing as he turned toward her. "Yes, Miss Bingley?"

Caroline's smile returned, though it was tight. "I was simply asking if you would care to add your observations. You have been so quiet this evening."

Darcy glanced toward Elizabeth once more before replying. And dash it all if the lady was not looking at him with something akin to hope. "I believe Miss Bennet has already said all that needs to be said."

That was the worst thing he could have said, for Miss Elizabeth actually favored him with a smile.

SEVEN

THE STUDY AT NETHERFIELD was quiet save for the occasional crackle of the fire and the rhythmic tapping of Darcy's boot against the floor. He sat stiffly in his chair, arms folded tightly across his chest, while Bingley leaned back on the sofa, all careless ease and infuriating cheer.

"You laugh," Darcy said flatly. "But this is no laughing matter."

"I fail to see why not," Bingley replied, grinning as he waved Darcy off. "Come now, Darcy. You make it sound as though you've been caught in some grand scandal. All you need do is continue as you have been—polite, civil. That's all."

"It is far from all," Darcy shot back, rising abruptly to pace the room. "Do you not see what she is doing?"

"Who?" Bingley blinked, his grin widening. "Miss Bennet?"

"Miss *Elizabeth* Bennet," Darcy corrected. "She has made me her target. Every glance, every word—it is as though she has resolved to unravel me entirely."

Bingley snorted. "Darcy, you do love to dramatize."

Darcy spun to face him, his brows drawn tight. "This is precisely the sort of behavior I warned you about. A young lady setting her sights on a gentleman who shows her too much regard—drawing him into a trap until there is no honorable way out. Ruined reputations, entanglements, expectations—have you forgotten the sort of danger such situations invite?"

Bingley raised his hands in mock surrender. "Forgive me, but I hardly see Miss Elizabeth as the scheming sort. She seems more inclined to mock than to entrap."

Darcy's jaw tightened. "Mockery is but a step away from manipulation."

"You give her far too much credit," Bingley said lightly. "And yourself far too little."

Darcy exhaled sharply, turning back toward the window. The faint light of dawn crept over the horizon, painting the fields in pale golds and blues. He clasped his hands behind his back. "This wager... it was foolish. I will not continue it."

"That's unfortunate," Bingley said. "Because I intend to."

Darcy turned sharply. "What do you mean?"

Bingley grinned and reached into his pocket, pulling out a folded sheet of paper. "I received this letter yesterday. It's from my man at the mill. He's been discussing some fascinating opportunities for expansion."

Darcy's stomach sank. "The mill?"

"Yes," Bingley said, unfolding the letter and scanning it with obvious satisfaction. "The numbers look promising. With a bit of investment, we might double the output within the year. And the war is sure to end sooner or later, making the cotton from the Continent that much easier to obtain."

"Bingley, no." Darcy strode across the room, snatching the letter from his friend's hand. "You cannot be serious. The mill is a drain on your resources, not a boon. I told you months ago—two years ago! It ought to be sold."

Bingley chuckled. "And I told you, Darcy, I'm rather fond of the thing. It was my father's pride and joy."

"And now it is your liability," Darcy countered, glaring at the letter. "You are throwing good money after bad. You have no head for business, and no need to depend on it. Sell it. Invest the proceeds wisely."

Bingley leaned back, his grin undiminished. "You know, I might take that advice... if I thought you were holding up your end of our little wager."

Darcy froze, the letter crumpling slightly in his grip. "You cannot be serious."

"Oh, but I am," Bingley said cheerfully. "I agreed to consider selling the mill, provided you saw this bet through. You've been doing splendidly thus far, Darcy. Miss Elizabeth hasn't fled in terror, and you haven't stormed off in one of your infamous silences. It's practically a triumph."

Darcy's glare could have melted glass. "This is extortion."

"No," Bingley corrected, wagging a finger. "This is motivation. You hold up your end, Darcy, and I'll consider holding up mine."

"You would risk your fortune over a wager?" Darcy demanded.

"You would abandon your efforts to 'improve my prospects' because you fear a witty young lady?" Bingley countered, his grin turning sly.

Darcy's jaw tightened, his hand crushing the letter further before he thrust it back at Bingley. "You are insufferable."

"And you are predictable," Bingley said, rising to his feet and clapping Darcy on the shoulder. "Now, stop pacing and think of it this way—if you can survive the clever remarks of Miss Elizabeth Bennet, surely you can survive anything. Oh! You recall that we are to dine with Colonel Forster this evening, I hope. I believe I shall retire to dress."

Darcy said nothing, his gaze fixed on the glowing horizon beyond the window. He did not reply when Bingley left the room, whistling a jaunty tune as though he had just won a great victory.

The truth settled heavily on Darcy's chest, suffocating in its simplicity: he was trapped. And worse, the trap was one he had walked into willingly.

"Five shillings says Mrs. Long will be late for the next Assembly," Mrs. Philips announced, her fan snapping shut with finality.

Lydia, perched on the arm of a settee, jingled her coin purse. "I'll take that bet, Aunt! I know for a fact that her niece has a scheme because she wants to see the officers first."

"Mrs. Long is always late," Mrs. Philips insisted. "You mark my words, she will not arrive before the third dance. Never has, never will."

Mrs. Bennet fanned herself with exaggerated vigor. "But she might surprise us! Last week, she was nearly punctual for morning service."

"That was not punctual," Elizabeth said from her seat by the window. "The sermon was already halfway through."

"Well, it was punctual for her," Mrs. Bennet declared. "I say she arrives before the first dance is over. Five shillings says I am right."

"Done," Mrs. Philips said with a delighted clap of her hands. "I shall enjoy spending your money, sister."

Elizabeth sighed, glancing over at Jane, who sat quietly with her embroidery. "How can you sit there smiling while they wager over such nonsense?"

Jane lifted a shoulder. "It passes the time."

"Passes the time! It encourages their folly."

"It buys *us* a moment's peace, does it not?" Jane murmured, her voice so low that Elizabeth barely heard her over Lydia's triumphant laugh.

"Ha! See this?" Lydia cried, shaking her purse. "I won this morning when the butcher's pig weighed exactly as I said it would—twelve stone and not an ounce more!"

Kitty, seated on the floor near the hearth, looked up with a pout. "I said twelve stone, too."

"But you did not put up your coin, Kitty," Lydia retorted, dangling her purse mockingly. "And now I shall spend it on ribbons and sweets, while you sit there looking cross."

Elizabeth pinched the bridge of her nose. "Why do you waste your winnings so quickly?"

"What else should I do with them?" Lydia asked, blinking as though the question were incomprehensible.

"Save them," Elizabeth replied. "Or, if that is too ambitious, spend them on something of consequence."

"Ribbons and sweets *are* of consequence. A life without adornments or treats is no life at all."

Before Elizabeth could respond, a servant entered with a letter, handing it to Jane. Mrs. Bennet stopped fanning herself at once, her entire focus narrowing in on her eldest daughter.

"Who is it from?" she demanded eagerly, leaning forward.

Jane unfolded the letter carefully. "It is from Miss Bingley. She invites me to dine with her and her sister at Netherfield tomorrow."

Mrs. Bennet clasped her hands together, practically glowing with satisfaction. "Oh, this is excellent news! Jane, you must go at once."

"Of course I will go," Jane said calmly, though Elizabeth caught the flicker of hesitation in her expression.

"And you must ride on horseback," Mrs. Bennet continued, her tone turning decisive.

Jane's needlework dropped into her lap. "Ride? But the weather—"

"Exactly! The weather will make you look all the more modest and unassuming," Mrs. Bennet said with a knowing nod. "Mr. Bingley will like that, he is such an amiable young man. Arriving by carriage would be far too ostentatious. Mark my words, he has never seen the like of you, my Jane."

Elizabeth gaped. "You mean to send her out in the rain, looking half-drowned, to impress Mr. Bingley?"

"Precisely," Mrs. Bennet replied, as though Elizabeth had just delivered a compliment.

"It is only a little rain," Lydia interjected. "She will not melt."

Kitty giggled. "Perhaps Jane will be like that old nursery story and grow roots wherever she falls."

Elizabeth turned to Jane, her voice firm. "You do not have to ride in this weather. Take the carriage. There is no sense in falling ill for the sake of appearances."

Jane hesitated, glancing between her mother and Elizabeth. "I do not wish to offend anyone..."

"Offend!" Mrs. Bennet cried. "Jane, you must think of your future."

"I shall hardly be presentable when I arrive, Mama."

Their mother pointed with her fan. "So much the better! They will see to your comforts and you will be the gracious recipient of their efforts."

Elizabeth groaned. "If Jane's future depends on the state of her hemline, we are all doomed."

Mrs. Philips chuckled, folding her embroidery. "I'll wager she will arrive perfectly presentable and composed either way. Jane is too sensible to let a little weather get the better of her."

"I'll wager two shillings she arrives with her bonnet entirely ruined," Lydia pronounced. "And if it is, I'll buy her a new one—with pink ribbons."

Jane gave Elizabeth a small, helpless smile, but Elizabeth's jaw tightened. "This is absurd."

"Then wager against us, Lizzy," Lydia teased. "Or are you too afraid of losing again?"

Elizabeth opened her mouth to retort but stopped herself with a sharp exhale. There was no point. The tide had already turned in Mrs. Bennet's favor, and Jane would not push back. With a resigned sigh, Elizabeth turned toward the window, watching as the rain began to fall in earnest.

ELIZABETH STRODE BRISKLY THROUGH Meryton's market square, her bonnet tied tight against the wind and her skirts held just high enough to avoid the muddy streets. The rain had relented to a light drizzle, but the damage was done—word had already spread that Jane Bennet, invited to dine at Netherfield the previous evening, had arrived soaked to the bone and was now bedridden. And the town had wasted no time turning her misfortune into entertainment.

"She'll be better in three days, mark my words," declared Mr. Goulding, standing outside the greengrocer with a knot of villagers. "Mrs. Bennet will see to that."

Mrs. Long clucked her tongue. "Three days? I say it will be five, at least. Her mother may want her well, but not before she has secured a *certain* gentleman's affections."

"Four," Mrs. Philips interjected, her coin purse jingling in her hand. "Fanny Bennet is too clever to let her daughter look like a real invalid. What point in ensnaring a gentleman's affections if she appears too ill to marry him?"

Elizabeth stopped short, her stomach twisting as the conversation reached her ears. "You cannot be serious."

The group turned, startled to see her standing there, her expression a mixture of disbelief and indignation. Mrs. Goulding chuckled nervously. "Ah, Miss Elizabeth! Just a bit of fun, you know. Nothing harmful."

"Fun? Wagering over my sister's health is your idea of fun?"

Mrs. Philips pursed her lips, glancing at the others. "It's only harmless speculation, Lizzy. We all know Jane will recover soon enough."

Elizabeth stepped closer, her gaze icy. "Do you? Do you know how unwell she is? Or how she fared riding through that storm? Or how she is being cared for at Netherfield?"

No one answered. Elizabeth's hands tightened into fists at her sides. "Of course not. Because instead of offering concern, you are placing bets as though she is a horse in a race."

Mrs. Long bristled, muttering something about "taking things too seriously," but Elizabeth had already turned on her heel, marching toward the road to Netherfield.

BY THE TIME ELIZABETH reached Netherfield, her boots were caked in mud, and her shawl was damp from a persistent drizzle that had arrived halfway through her walk. The grandeur of the house loomed ahead, its perfectly symmetrical windows glowing softly with the light of fires within. She squared her shoulders and knocked firmly on the door.

The butler's eyes widened slightly as he opened it, taking in her bedraggled state. "Miss Bennet?"

"I am here to see my sister. Please inform Mr. Bingley or Miss Bingley that I will wait out of the way until I have spoken with her."

The butler hesitated, but Elizabeth's firm tone left little room for argument. He stepped aside, and she was ushered into the drawing room to wait.

She had scarcely removed her shawl when the door opened, and Mr. Darcy entered, his dark eyes narrowing slightly at the sight of her. By the look on his face, she could only surmise that he had happened upon her accidentally—perhaps, indeed, he had fled to this particular drawing room to escape his eager hostess for half an hour.

"Miss Elizabeth," he said, his voice betraying his surprise. "To what do we owe this... unexpected visit?"

Elizabeth straightened, clasping her hands before her. "I am here to see my sister."

"I believe is resting," Darcy replied. "Miss Bingley and the housekeeper have ensured she is receiving the best care."

"I am certain they have. But I would like to speak with her myself."

Darcy studied her for a long moment, his brow furrowing. "Surely you did not walk here in this weather."

"I did, from Meryton," Elizabeth said, her chin lifting slightly. "And I will gladly walk back to Longbourn, once I am satisfied that my sister is in good comforts."

Before Darcy could respond, the door opened again, and Bingley entered, his usual cheerfulness lighting up the room. "Miss Elizabeth! How very good of you to come. I had sent an offer of a carriage, in case you or your mother wished to call on your sister, not half an hour ago"

Elizabeth turned to him with a warmer smile. "That was very kind of you sir, but as you see, I managed on my own. May I ask, how is my sister this morning?"

"Oh, quite comfortable, I assure you. Caroline only just informed me that Miss Bennet is sleeping rather soundly and ought not to be disturbed. I can have the maid inform her of your arrival."

"I would rather look in on her myself," Elizabeth replied. "I need not rouse her if she is sleeping."

Darcy's expression tightened, but Bingley only looked as easy and pliable as ever. "Of course, of course. Allow me to escort you."

Elizabeth entered Jane's room to find her sister propped up in bed, her cheeks flushed with fever but her smile warm. And not sleeping, as had been reported.

"Lizzy," Jane said softly. "You should not have come in this weather."

Elizabeth sat beside her, taking her hand. "And leave you to be the subject of the town's wagers without learning how you truly are? Never."

Jane frowned. "Wagers?"

Elizabeth squeezed her hand gently. "It does not matter. I am here now, and I will not leave until I am certain you are well."

"You will stay?" Jane asked. And then she coughed.

"For now, at least," Elizabeth said firmly. "Let them try to send me away."

THE CRACK OF A billiard ball echoed through the dimly lit room as Darcy lined up his next shot. He adjusted his grip on the cue stick, his movements deliberate and controlled. Focus, precision, restraint—these were the virtues that steadied him, that kept the storm inside at bay.

But this afternoon, even billiards could not distract him.

He drew back the cue and sent the ball spinning across the table, pocketing a red with a sharp clink. It should have been satisfying, but it was not. Not when the very house felt as though it were conspiring against his peace. He had spent the better part of the day avoiding the drawing room, the halls, even the dining room, lest he accidentally cross paths with *her*.

Miss Elizabeth Bennet.

Every time he was near her, he could feel his resolve unraveling. The sharp wit, the glint of challenge in her eyes—she was far too clever, far too perceptive. If he were not careful, she might notice the way his gaze lingered too long, or the way his carefully measured words seemed to fail him when she spoke. And if she noticed, others would, too. Then what?

He tightened his grip on the cue. This would all pass soon enough. Elizabeth Bennet would return to Longbourn once she had been satisfied that her sister was well looked after, and he could return to his life of orderly solitude.

"Darcy! There you are," came Bingley's cheerful voice as the door swung open. Darcy froze mid-motion, his carefully maintained calm splintering at the intrusion.

"I assumed you'd taken to hiding," Bingley said, strolling in with the air of a man who had not a care in the world. He crossed to the table and began racking the balls for a new game. "It seems you've made a habit of disappearing these days."

Darcy straightened, forcing his expression into neutrality. "I prefer quiet. You know that."

"Too much 'quiet' can be the death of a man," Bingley said with a grin, setting the cue ball into position. "And I daresay Miss Elizabeth would agree with me."

Darcy's fingers twitched against the cue stick. "I do not know why I should care what Miss Elizabeth thinks on the matter." He watched as Bingley took his first shot, scattering the balls with a practiced ease that set his teeth on edge.

"Ah, and speaking of Miss Elizabeth," Bingley continued, his tone almost too casual, "I have ordered that her belongings be sent for."

Darcy blinked, the words striking him like a physical blow. "Sent for?"

Bingley nodded, leaning on the cue stick. "Indeed. She will be remaining here until her sister is fully recovered."

Darcy's stomach sank. His carefully constructed plans for avoidance crumbled in an instant. "She... she is staying?"

Bingley straightened, tilting his head as he regarded Darcy with faint amusement. "Why do you sound as though you fear a ghost? Surely you are not afraid of Miss Elizabeth?"

"Of course not," Darcy snapped, though the sharpness in his voice betrayed him. He turned away, pretending to adjust the position of a ball on the table.

"Good," Bingley said, laughing softly. "Because I cannot fathom why you would be. She is a lady, Darcy, not some wild beast. And you are no churl. You will do very well."

Darcy's hand tightened on the cue stick as he stared down at the green felt. "It is not a matter of being a churl," he said stiffly. "It is a matter of propriety."

"Propriety!" Bingley repeated with a laugh, taking his next shot. The ball rolled neatly into the corner pocket. "You worry too much. Miss Elizabeth is not so very terrifying as that. Besides, you are nothing if not proper."

Darcy opened his mouth to protest, but no words came. He could hardly explain the truth to Bingley—that the mere presence of Elizabeth Bennet was enough to throw him entirely off balance. That he felt as though his carefully ordered self-control was slipping with every sharp glance and witticism she directed his way.

"She may well be a fortune hunter," Darcy protested. "I daresay her mother would have her so, and who is to say her sister has not already enacted the first stage of their strategy?"

"Strategy!" Bingley barked. "How very like you, Darcy, to assume a fever and a cough were intentional elements of some battle plan waged against single gentlemen."

"Not against us, but against our bank accounts," Darcy huffed. "It would not be the first such attempt I have seen."

"Well, I have every confidence in your discretion, Darcy," Bingley added, moving to line up another shot. "You'll manage this just as you manage everything else—with hauteur and that practiced curl of your lip. And I fancy I shall write Simmons and authorize those improvements at the mill…"

Blast the man! Bingley *would* jest about that foolish wager now, of all times! Darcy's cravat suddenly felt far too tight around his neck. He resisted the urge to tug at it, instead placing the cue stick on the table with deliberate care.

"I am not certain you understand the situation," Darcy said, his voice strained. "Prolonged proximity to Miss Elizabeth… it is not without its complications."

"Complications?" Bingley's grin widened. "Darcy, you do insist on making it sound like a battle worthy of Wellington himself."

Darcy said nothing, his pulse hammering in his chest. It *was* a battle—against himself, against the feelings he could neither name nor allow to take root.

Bingley glanced at him as he lined up his next shot. "You'll see, Darcy. All will be well. Quite well, indeed."

Darcy stood motionless as Bingley resumed his cheerful game, the soft clatter of billiard balls echoing in the room. His cravat still felt like it might strangle him, but this time, he welcomed the discomfort—it sharpened his focus.

So, Elizabeth Bennet would be staying. For days, perhaps even a week. The thought was both exhilarating and horrifying, a tangle of contradictions that had no place in his carefully ordered world.

If she *must* remain at Netherfield, then he would act. He could not afford to let her charm, her wit, her eyes—egad, her *eyes*…

He shoved the thought aside with brutal efficiency. He would not countenance permitting her to unsettle him any further. Nor could he allow her to misread his attentions, to think he was a man who could be trifled with.

If civility demanded he speak to her, then so be it. He would engage. He would listen. He would smile. He would be the most polite gentleman to be found from London to Northampton.

But Elizabeth Bennet would come to understand, in no uncertain terms, that he was a man of boundaries.

She was clever—cleverer than most. Surely she would perceive the deeper meaning beneath his words, the warning that lay behind every polite remark. She would know he was no fool to be toyed with, no gentleman to be drawn into games of flirtation and folly. He would show her what it meant to face Fitzwilliam Darcy: unflappable, resolute, and utterly unyielding.

"Darcy? You've gone quiet again. Thinking up strategies for the billiards table?"

Darcy turned to his friend, his expression unreadable. "No," he said. "Strategies for far more important matters."

Bingley chuckled. "Well, do not tax yourself too much. I know you usually best me, but I mean to give you an honest challenge this afternoon."

An honest challenge... Darcy's lips pressed into a thin line. Bingley could have no possible idea... "I think I can manage two things at once."

Bingley laughed and walked around the table to consider his next shot, leaving Darcy standing alone in the corner. His gaze drifted to the doorway, and for a fleeting moment, he could almost imagine her standing there, her sharp eyes challenging him with that faint smile playing on her lips.

He inhaled deeply, steadying himself. Very well. If the wager demanded proximity, he would use it to his advantage. He would remain the picture of propriety, and yet he would draw a line so clear that even the most determined woman in the world could not miss it.

EIGHT

ELIZABETH STEPPED INTO THE breakfast room with her usual brisk confidence, though the moment her eyes landed on Mr. Darcy seated by the window, her stride faltered for the briefest of heartbeats. He was there alone, the sunlight streaming through the tall panes behind him, casting a faint glow around his silhouette. He appeared uncommonly relaxed, a book in one hand, his other resting idly on the table beside a half-empty teacup.

And he looked rather... *ahem*.

Well, she could not very well say *what* he looked like, but there was a faint sheen of sweat on her upper lip when she ran her hand over it. How very silly!

For an absurd moment, she considered retreating—but no, that would not do. She had wagered her pride and her wit on this game, and she would not cede the field so easily.

"Good morning, Mr. Darcy," she said brightly, stepping further into the room. Her tone was warm, her smile practiced but disarming. If he thought he could avoid her with polite indifference, he was sorely mistaken. She would *make* him notice.

Darcy's head lifted, his dark eyes locking onto hers with a brief flicker of what might have been surprise before his expression smoothed into something more obscure. He rose from his chair with impeccable courtesy. "Miss Bennet."

Elizabeth made her way to the sideboard, filling her plate with leisurely disinterest. She could feel his gaze lingering, though whether it was out of politeness or wariness, she could not yet tell. "You are an early riser," she remarked, her voice light and conversational. "I find the house is far quieter at this hour."

"Indeed," Darcy replied,. "It affords one the chance to collect one's thoughts without distraction."

Elizabeth turned, plate in hand, and raised an eyebrow as she took a seat across from him. "And have you much to think about, Mr. Darcy? Or do you merely enjoy solitude for its own sake?"

Darcy hesitated for a fraction of a second, then set his book down with deliberate care. "Both, I suppose. Reflection is a necessary exercise."

"I imagine it must be difficult to achieve, then, in a house so filled with activity."

His gaze met hers, steady but guarded. "It requires discipline."

"Discipline," she repeated. "What a noble virtue. Though I confess, it seems rather a dry way to spend one's morning."

Darcy's lips tightened—was that almost a smile?—before his expression returned to its usual reserve. "Not everyone shares your appetite for early morning activity, Miss Bennet."

"True," Elizabeth said, her fork pausing midway to her mouth. "But I have found that even the gravest of dispositions can benefit from a little animation to stimulate the blood early in the day. Do you not agree?"

"I find animation is best when balanced by purpose."

Elizabeth's smile widened, though her confidence wavered just slightly. He was more adept at this game than she had given him credit for. She would have to be sharper. "I daresay you do excel at purpose, Mr. Darcy. Though one must hope it does not prevent you from ever enjoying yourself."

Darcy studied her for a moment, his gaze thoughtful in a way that made her pulse quicken. Then, with the barest flicker of amusement in his eyes, he said, "I enjoy many things, Miss Bennet. Solitude among them."

It was not quite the rebuttal she expected, and it left her momentarily at a loss. She took another bite of her breakfast to buy herself time, her mind racing for the next volley. But before she could speak, Darcy stood.

"Please excuse me," he said. "I have letters to attend to."

Elizabeth inclined her head, masking her frustration behind a practiced smile. "Of course, Mr. Darcy. I would not dream of keeping you from your reflections."

Darcy's gaze lingered on her for the briefest of moments, something unreadable flickering there, and then he bowed and departed the room.

Elizabeth sat back in her chair, her fork resting against her plate as she stared after him. The quiet confidence she had felt when she first stepped into the room had been replaced by something altogether more unsettling. Darcy was polite, certainly. Reserved, absolutely. But there was something in his manner that hinted at layers she had not anticipated.

For the first time since accepting Charlotte's wager, Elizabeth found herself wondering if she had underestimated her opponent.

DARCY TUGGED ON HIS gloves, his expression carefully neutral as he waited for the others to assemble near the front entrance of Netherfield. The morning had cleared to a brisk, sunny day, and it was decided—much to Darcy's dismay—that a walk through the grounds would be an ideal activity after breakfast.

He had considered claiming a prior engagement, but Bingley's infectious cheer had worn him down. Now, as the door opened to admit Elizabeth Bennet, bright-eyed and fresh as the dew in her walking dress, he cursed his momentary lapse in judgment.

"You are joining us, Mr. Darcy?" Elizabeth asked lightly as she pulled on her gloves. Her tone was pleasant, but there was a glint in her eye he did not trust. The vixen.

"I am," he replied evenly. "The morning is... agreeable."

"It is indeed. I imagine even you cannot find fault with it."

Caroline Bingley, appearing at his elbow, interjected before he could respond. "Mr. Darcy finds fault with nothing, Miss Eliza," she said with an air of superiority. "For that would be ungentlemanly. He, of course, is the very model of civility."

Elizabeth glanced at him, her brows lifting in mock surprise. "How fortunate for us all. I confess, I had begun to wonder if Mr. Darcy ever allowed himself the luxury of a flawed opinion."

Darcy's jaw tightened, though he kept his expression neutral. "I find opinions are most useful when grounded in reason."

"And yet," Elizabeth countered, "reason alone can make the world rather dull."

Caroline's smile faltered as Elizabeth's words hung in the air, but Darcy merely inclined his head. "Reason is often misunderstood, Miss Bennet. It is not an enemy to joy and enthusiasm, but a companion to it."

Elizabeth blinked, momentarily caught off guard by his response. Before she could reply, Bingley strode into the room, his voice booming with enthusiasm.

"Everyone ready?" he called, clapping his hands together. "Oh, dash it all, I see Hurst will not be joining us. But I say we shan't let that spoil our morning. I thought we might take the path by the pond—Caroline, Louisa, you must see the swans."

As the group began their walk, Darcy deliberately slowed his pace, keeping a calculated distance from Elizabeth. But fate—or perhaps Bingley's endless enthusiasm—had other plans.

"Darcy, you must walk with Miss Elizabeth," Bingley said, gesturing with a grin. "She will at least provide interesting conversation. I fear Caroline and Louisa might bore you with talk of London fashions."

Miss Bingley rounded on her brother with a sharp protest, but Bingley, the bounder, cut her off by taking her arm and marching her down the path. "I say, Caroline, I was thinking of hosting a ball," he said, loudly enough for everyone to hear them. "I will, of course, depend on your wisdom and talents there. Did not Lady Aston write a fortnight ago about a new musician she had brought on for her last ball? I was hoping you might..."

Bingley's voice trailed off as they gained distance, and Darcy found himself reluctantly strolling beside Miss Elizabeth. Her brows arched as she looked his way. "Do not worry, Mr. Darcy. I shall do my best to prevent your morning from becoming dull."

The words were polite, but Darcy felt the faintest tug of challenge in her tone, as though Elizabeth Bennet were daring him to falter. She was testing him again, probing for some crack in his demeanor. Darcy inclined his head. "Your company is rarely dull, Miss Elizabeth."

They walked on in relative silence for a few moments. Darcy welcomed the quiet, using the time to steady his thoughts. Yet, he could sense Elizabeth's restlessness beside him, as if her very presence demanded conversation.

"You seem unusually subdued this morning, Mr. Darcy," she said at last. "Surely the beauty of the autumn countryside inspires some thought or reflection. One must be an ogre, indeed, to fail to appreciate those colors."

Darcy followed the direction of her gaze. "It is, indeed, beautiful. But I find it more conducive to quiet observation than conversation."

"Ah," she replied, her voice light, though he detected the faintest hint of mischief. "So, it is silence you seek. I marvel, then, at your enjoyment of Mr. Bingley's company."

Darcy stopped, turning to face her fully, weighing his response. "Mr. Bingley is an exceptional friend. His good nature is an asset I do not take lightly."

"A loyal defense, Mr. Darcy. Though I must wonder if you were not tempted to strangle him when he paired us together for this walk."

Darcy hesitated, his calm facade wavering just enough for a flicker of irritation to pass through him. She was too perceptive for his liking—and far too comfortable pressing him. "I assure you, Miss Bennet, I am quite capable of exercising patience."

She laughed—a clear, melodic sound that startled him with its warmth. He looked away quickly, his thoughts spiraling toward the vexing realization that he had noticed, too keenly, how her presence unsettled him.

"Patience, Mr. Darcy? I am impressed," she teased. "I had thought you too unflappable altogether to require the exercise of such a virtue."

Darcy's jaw tightened. It would not do to let her provoke him further. "Speaking of patience, Miss Bennet, I trust your sister continues to improve under your care. No doubt your attentiveness brings her comfort."

Her expression shifted slightly, though her smile remained. "Jane is much better this morning, thank you. Though I confess, it was not my attentiveness that helped her rest—I believe it was my restlessness that kept her from it. Thus, my temporary removal from the room has probably purchased her more comfort this morning than my presence could have done."

Darcy blinked, caught off guard by the ease of her retort. "I see," he said, unable to suppress the faint lift of his brow. "In that case, I hope this walk proves sufficient to ease your restlessness, for her sake."

"Indeed, Mr. Darcy," she replied with a slight curtsey, her smile deepening. "For her sake."

Before he could find a suitable reply, Caroline's voice carried over the path. "Mr. Darcy, you must come and see the swans! They are magnificent this year."

Seizing the opportunity for reprieve, Darcy inclined his head. "Excuse me, Miss Bennet," he said, his tone polite but firm, before striding ahead toward the Bingleys.

As he approached the others, he resisted the urge to glance back. He could still feel the lingering effect of her laughter and the sharpness of her wit, like the faintest tug at the edges of his resolve. Her presence was entirely too vivid, too insistent, and he despised how easily she unraveled his carefully guarded composure.

ELIZABETH SAT RIGIDLY IN the library, her embroidery hoop lying forgotten in her lap. She had taken it up in a half-hearted attempt to appear industrious, and this room had some of the best lighting in the house for the task, but her needle had hovered motionless for several minutes. Across the room, Mr. Darcy occupied a solitary chair near the window, seemingly engrossed in a book. If he noticed the tension threading through the air, he gave no indication.

The man was impossible.

She had spent the better part of the morning attempting to draw some measure of civility—no, warmth—from him, only to be met with politeness so cold and measured it could have rivaled a frosty January morning. It was galling. For all his elegance and wealth, Mr. Darcy had the social charm of a well-carved statue, and Elizabeth could feel her patience fraying.

She had to struggle to remind herself why she cared at all. Jane's sly smile and Charlotte's brash confidence as they dared her into this wretched bet resurfaced in her mind. To win his *approval*—not his actual love, heaven forbid, but the faintest mark of regard—was to prove that her wit could breach even the stoniest of barriers. Yet, the longer she studied his detached demeanor, the more she questioned the wisdom of her endeavor.

Still, Elizabeth Bennet did not shy away from challenges.

She glanced at him, noting the precise manner in which he turned the pages of his book, each movement deliberate and unhurried. Her frustration mounted. Surely, no one could be so absorbed in a single volume. She cleared her throat lightly, enough to catch his attention. He looked up, his dark eyes meeting hers with a questioning tilt of his brow.

"Mr. Darcy, what are you reading with such profound concentration? I wonder what holds such sway over your attention."

For a moment, he said nothing, and Elizabeth wondered if he might ignore her entirely. Then, closing the book with an infuriating slowness, he answered, "It is a volume of poetry, Miss Bennet."

"Poetry! Surely not the melancholy sort? I would have imagined you a reader of history or philosophy."

"I find poetry... instructive," he replied. "It conveys truths about human nature that are often obscured in other forms of writing."

Elizabeth leaned forward slightly, her smile sharpening. "Then you must share a passage that you find particularly revealing. I confess, I am eager to hear which truths you hold in such high esteem."

His lips pressed into a thin line, as if weighing whether to humor her or retreat into his solitude. Finally, he opened the book again, his voice almost impossibly deep and harmonic as he recited a short stanza. It was a reflection on constancy and the quiet strength of enduring devotion—an apt choice, though Elizabeth suspected his selection was carefully deliberate.

She pretended to ponder his words. "It is beautifully written, I grant you, but does it not run the risk of being overly earnest? There is such danger in laying bare the heart—especially in verse."

His brow lifted slightly, a faint flicker of amusement crossing his face. "A true sentiment is not less true for being plainly spoken."

"Perhaps. But a plain truth rendered in rhyme often becomes an unintentional comedy. I confess, bad poetry is one of my great terrors. I find it the surest way to extinguish any affection."

There it was again—the faintest flicker of something almost cunning in his expression, gone so quickly she thought she might have imagined it. His tone remained perfectly composed as he said, "Then I shall be sure to choose my stanzas carefully in your company, Miss Bennet."

Elizabeth raised a brow, her lips curving into a teasing smile. "Do you mean to say you write poetry, Mr. Darcy?"

"I mean only that one must always consider one's audience."

Her pulse quickened at the subtle edge in his words. For a moment, she thought she had caught a glimpse of something beneath his polished exterior—a hint of passion, of conviction—but it vanished as quickly as it appeared.

"You speak as one who holds his principles dear," she said lightly, masking her thoughts behind her usual wit. "I fear you may find me lacking in that regard, Mr. Darcy. I am far too easily swayed by whim."

"And yet," he said quietly, "I do not find you lacking."

Elizabeth blinked, caught off guard, but before she could reply, Darcy returned his attention to the book, his expression unreadable. The conversation was over—or so he seemed determined to make it.

She searched his face for any trace of mockery but found none. How maddening that he could unsettle her with so few words when she had spent the morning attempting the same with no success.

"Well, sir," she said, regaining her composure, "I thank you for your good opinion, though I shall not let it go to my head."

"Indeed," he said, his mouth curving slightly, though whether it was a true smile or merely the shadow of one, she could not say. "You seem far too grounded for such vanity."

Before she could muster a response, Caroline Bingley swept into the room, somewhat out of breath. "Mr. Darcy! Oh... and Miss Bennet. There you are. Mr. Hurst is organizing a game of cards in the dining room. Shall we join them?"

Darcy was holding his breath, she was sure of it. He had clenched his hand above the page of his book, and the muscles of his jaw appeared to be twitching in the light from the window. But an instant later, he forced a polite expression and set his book aside. "By all means, Miss Bingley."

"There, just as I hoped! I told my brother I was certain you would wish to join us. I am afraid, though," she added, frisking Elizabeth with another glance, "that we've only *one* empty chair at the table."

Elizabeth rose. "No matter, Miss Bingley. I shall entertain myself by the fire." She followed Miss Bingley into the drawing room, her thoughts darting between her lingering frustration and the mounting determination to adjust her strategy. He was not a man to be lightly touched—that much was obvious. A passing good nod from him would never suffice if she meant to make his mind her plaything. So, how could she... *break* him, for lack of a better word?

As they entered the drawing room, she glanced behind her to see Mr. Darcy hesitating just briefly before he complied with Miss Bingley's urging to join them. His expression remained neutral, but the slight tightening of his jaw betrayed his reluctance.

Taking her seat, Elizabeth kept one eye on him as he moved to his place at the card table. His every motion was deliberate, his demeanor composed, but there was no mistaking the faint flicker of irritation that crossed his face when Miss Bingley leaned toward him, smiling in that overly practiced way she seemed to reserve for his attention alone.

Elizabeth studied the exchange with interest. Miss Bingley's comment, whatever it had been, drew only a brief, monosyllabic reply from Mr. Darcy. He did not turn toward her fully, nor did his expression soften in the least. He treated her with the barest veneer of politeness, offering no more than was necessary to maintain decorum. His disengagement was so apparent that Elizabeth marveled at Miss Bingley's obliviousness to it.

It struck her then that Miss Bingley's attempts to charm Mr. Darcy lacked any subtlety. She flattered him excessively, fawned over his every word, and deferred to him on every point, no matter how trivial. And yet, for all her efforts, Mr. Darcy barely spared her a glance unless compelled by circumstance. He seemed, Elizabeth thought, quietly weary of her attentions.

The realization deepened as Elizabeth considered the broader picture. A man of Darcy's wealth and status would undoubtedly be accustomed to such behavior—not only from Miss Bingley, but from countless other women who saw him as a prize to be won. To him, such fawning must be tiresome, if not outright irritating. Miss Bingley, for all her elegant manners and fine gowns, was likely just one more in a long line of ambitious women vying for his favor.

Her gaze flicked back to Darcy, now engaged in conversation with Mr. Bingley. His tone, though restrained, carried a touch more warmth. And then there was the way he had spoken to *her* earlier. It was different—not warm, precisely, but sharper, more engaged. He debated with her, answered her challenges, and even, on occasion, offered something resembling a compliment. It was hardly the behavior of a man who dismissed her outright. But then again, it was hardly encouragement, either.

Elizabeth's fingers tightened on her embroidery hoop as she mulled over the distinction. She could not, *would not,* become another Miss Bingley, hovering like a moth around a flame, desperate for even the faintest flicker of approval. She did not even like the man! She certainly had no intention of demeaning herself to turn his head, even if such measures had any chance of success.

No, if she was to gain his regard, it would have to be on her own terms. She would need to provoke his interest—not with empty flattery, but with something more substantial.

But how?

Jealousy? Oh, hardly! How could *she* make such a man jealous? She would have to dangle something before him that he wanted above all other things, and she had nothing of the kind within her power to offer.

But he *did* like to be right. And he liked it best when he had a chance to *prove* he was right, rather than every word of his being accepted with all the eclat of a proverb.

Her thoughts churned as she watched Darcy rise briefly to retrieve the cards, his movements precise, his expression intentionally composed. His manner bespoke a man who kept others at arm's length, who had little patience for superficiality or pretense.

If that was the case, then perhaps the answer was simpler than she thought. She would not seek to please him, nor would she attempt to curry his favor. Instead, she would do what she did best: be herself. But more herself, even, than she had been. Bold, observant, and unapologetically forthright.

The corner of her mouth lifted slightly as her resolve hardened. She would win this wager yet—not by simpering or flattering, but by reminding Mr. Darcy that she was unlike any other woman he had encountered. If that meant ruffling his feathers a little more, so much the better.

After all, she had never been one to shy away from a challenge.

NINE

"You play with such conviction, Miss Elizabeth. One might think you mean to make a point rather than entertain."

Elizabeth's hands did not falter on the keys, though her smile widened slightly, a glint of mischief flashing in her eyes. "Why, Miss Bingley, I was not aware music required one to sacrifice purpose for entertainment. I rather thought the two might coexist."

Her response was as swift and pointed as the notes she struck, and Darcy found himself both irritated and intrigued. He leaned back in his chair, his gaze fixed on her as she played with a confidence that seemed designed to command attention—not to charm, as others might, but to provoke thought.

She was succeeding.

The room's focus was entirely on her, but Elizabeth seemed oblivious to it. Her performance was not a bid for admiration or applause; it was a conversation—one she controlled with every sharp trill and measured pause. The piece she selected was one he recognized immediately—Haydn, spirited and complex, with a rhythm that seemed intent on defying confinement.

Though her skill was not a match for Georgiana, or even Miss Bingley, her hands moved swiftly, confidently, across the keys, producing a sound so rich and unrestrained that it seemed at odds with the very idea of predictability. It was deliberate, he realized. Perhaps even a challenge to his defense of poetry as a means of expression. She had taken his words and turned them into music, as though daring him to critique what was undeniably skillful.

His gaze settled on her again, this time with renewed focus. Her expression was not one of polite concentration, as was often seen in performers eager to please. No, Elizabeth Bennet played as though she were addressing each note to someone specific—someone whose reaction mattered. Her eyes did not seek out Mr. Bingley, or Miss Bingley, who sat stiffly nearby, but they flicked toward him, if only for a fleeting moment, before returning to her task.

It was maddening.

When the final notes faded, a polite smattering of applause broke out, led by Mr. Bingley, who leaned forward in genuine admiration. "Brilliant! That was absolutely brilliant, Miss Bennet. You must play another."

Elizabeth shook her head with a polite smile. "You are too kind, Mr. Bingley, but I would not wish to weary my audience."

"Nonsense," Bingley protested. "No one here could tire of such talent."

"Oh, I am certain they could, sir. But I am not so impervious to praise that I cannot be worked upon."

There it was again—that sharpness, so finely tuned that it might have been missed by anyone who did not know to listen for it. Darcy was certain she meant to unsettle him, and worse, she was succeeding. He had dealt with countless women who sought his approval, but Elizabeth Bennet was unlike any of them. She did not flatter. She did not simper. She challenged, and he found it... irksome.

"Then, you will play again," Bingley asked, almost petulantly.

She laughed. "Thank you, Mr. Bingley, but I should not wish to monopolize the evening. Perhaps another guest might favor us with a performance?"

Miss Bingley immediately rose, her mouth drawn into a tight smile. "What a charming sentiment, Miss Bennet. Indeed, we cannot expect our audience to be satisfied with only one piece. Mr. Darcy, do you not agree? We must have more to admire."

Her sudden appeal drew his attention, though he barely resisted the urge to sigh. "Miss Bennet's performance was admirable enough," he said simply.

Elizabeth's eyes sparkled as she rose from the pianoforte, her expression too serene to be sincere. "High praise indeed, Mr. Darcy. I shall treasure it."

The words were delivered with perfect composure, yet Darcy detected the subtle edge beneath them, a glimmer of satisfaction at having unsettled him. He could feel the faintest heat rising at the back of his neck.

As she moved to retake her seat, she glanced at him again, her smile faint but unmistakable. Darcy returned the look with studied indifference, though his thoughts churned. There was something new in her manner—something irreverent and perfectly unrepentant—that set his nerves on fire tonight.

Miss Bingley's hands were now poised over the keys, but Darcy found he could not summon the energy to feign interest in her playing. Instead, his mind lingered on Elizabeth, on the way she had so effortlessly turned the performance into an exchange, a contest, a challenge.

And, much as he loathed to admit it, she had won.

ELIZABETH STEPPED ONTO THE upper balcony, wrapping her shawl tightly around her shoulders. Laughter and chatter from earlier in the evening had long since faded into whispers, and the household had gone quiet as it settled for the night. Though reassured by Jane's steady breathing when she had looked in on her moments before, she fancied the idea of a bit of fresh air for herself.

Stars scattered across the clear sky as her gaze drifted to the shadowed gardens below. The solitude was a welcome balm after the strain of polite conversation, yet it did little to ease the vice twisting her mind. The wager she had made now seemed frivolous, a childish game entangled in a man far too complex to decipher.

Three days she had been in this house. Though she had not come with the intention of working upon Mr. Darcy, the opportunity was not one she could readily pass up. But three days now of twisting her mind to wring out some answer, some easy victory, had exhausted her energies. Darcy was not easily won over—nor easily understood—and with every passing moment, her own motives felt increasingly muddled.

Behind her, the quiet click of a door opening broke her reverie. She turned sharply, freezing as Mr. Darcy stepped onto the terrace. His attention was fixed on the horizon, his expression unguarded in a way she had never seen before. He appeared distracted, even haunted, his hand resting against the railing as though to steady himself, entirely unaware of her presence.

Elizabeth hesitated, torn between retreating unnoticed and announcing her presence. Before she could decide, Darcy's eyes wandering the sky caused him to glance her way. He started slightly, his composure returning so quickly that she might have imagined the flicker of surprise. "Miss Bennet," he said, his voice quieter than usual, almost tentative. "Forgive me—I did not realize you were here."

"There is nothing to forgive," Elizabeth replied. "I did not mean to disturb you."

"You disturb nothing," he said quickly, his eyes meeting hers briefly before skimming back to the horizon. For a moment, silence settled between them, laden with unspoken thoughts. Then, more softly, he added, "I was... seeking air."

"As was I." She studied him as he looked away. There was something uncharacteristically unsettled in his posture—the way his shoulders tensed, the faint line between his brows. "You seem preoccupied, Mr. Darcy. Is everything quite well?"

He hesitated, his jaw tightening briefly before he exhaled. "It is nothing of consequence."

"Then it must be a very loud 'nothing.' You look as though the weight of the world rests upon your shoulders."

His lips curved faintly, though his eyes remained distant. "A heavy imagination, perhaps."

"Or a heavy letter," Elizabeth said gently, glancing at the folded paper in his hand. "Though I would not presume to pry."

Darcy glanced at the letter absently, as though only now remembering he held it. "It is nothing that should concern you."

"Concern? No, not likely. And yet, I find myself curious. A rare thing, Mr. Darcy, for I do not often find myself curious about those who avoid conversation."

His brow lifted slightly, and this time, he met her gaze with more intent. "You find me deficient in conversation?"

"Deficient? No. Selective, perhaps."

He studied her for a moment, his expression unreadable. Finally, as though against his better inclination, he said, "Do you ever find yourself mistaken in your judgment, Miss Bennet?"

Elizabeth blinked. Mr. *Darcy*? Questioning his own judgment? How very curious. "Frequently. Though I confess I am often reluctant to admit it."

Darcy's lips pressed, almost forming a smile. "A reluctant admission is better than none at all," he murmured. He straightened, his hand tightening slightly on the railing. "I received a letter this evening—two, rather—that troubled me."

"Oh?"

"It pertains to my sister," he continued after a pause. "Georgiana."

"I have heard of her, yes."

He nodded briefly, as if satisfied that she recognized the name. "She is but fifteen. I do not suppose you were aware of that fact."

Her brows rose. "Indeed, I was not. Why, Miss Bingley spoke of her as young, but I supposed almost any unmarried lady might fall under that category for her."

Darcy coughed—or perhaps he was choking on a laugh. She could not be sure. "Indeed. My sister is... very young. Impressionable," he said carefully. "Too trusting, perhaps."

Elizabeth caught the hesitation in his voice. She stepped closer, folding her hands. "And this letter has made you worry for her?"

His jaw tightened again. "I have always worried for her."

The admission hung in the air, quiet but profound. Elizabeth felt her breath hitch slightly, the rawness in his tone unexpected. "She is fortunate to have such a devoted brother," she said softly.

Darcy turned to her then, his gaze sharp, as though searching for any trace of mockery. Finding none, he relaxed—minutely. "Devotion is one thing," he said. "Wisdom is another. I fear I have sometimes failed her in the latter."

Elizabeth opened her mouth to reply, but before she could speak, he straightened fully, the mask of composure sliding back into place. "Forgive me. I have spoken too freely."

She smiled faintly. "You have said nothing that requires forgiveness, Mr. Darcy. Only that which invites understanding."

She saw the faint workings of his throat and the clenching of his jaw in the moonlight. A long, indrawn breath, and then a slow exhale. "Indeed. Then... perhaps you will humor me some while longer, Miss Bennet."

"If it pleases you, sir. I have nowhere else to be."

The edge of his mouth turned up. "I sent her to stay with a family in Bath for the winter—people I trust and respect. It seemed the best decision for her. But tonight, I received two letters that have made me doubt myself."

"What did the letters say, if I may ask?"

"The first was from my cousin, Colonel Fitzwilliam," he said. "And my sister's other guardian, I might add. He wrote to urge me to consider Georgiana's own wishes, which he implied I have... neglected to account for. The second was from Georgiana herself. She..." He paused, his voice catching briefly. "She sounded... rather unhappy."

Elizabeth's heart softened at the quiet anguish in his tone. "And you regret your decision?"

"I do." His admission was blunt, his gaze fixed on the darkened garden below. "Georgiana depends on me entirely. Her letters, her confidences—they often reveal more than she intends. I believed I was acting in her best interests—still, I believe that. I think it would be profitable for her to gain some experience in the world. She *must* learn to be comfortable in company, and such a thing takes practice."

Practice? And this, coming from the man who never gave himself such trouble? Elizabeth could hardly restrain the burst of laughter that threatened. But she sobered just in time. "Does it?" she asked instead, hoping desperately that he did not hear the thick irony in her voice.

"Naturally. And this would have been a prime opportunity for her, but now... now I am not so sure." He turned to face her. "She is unhappy. No, it is more than that. She sounds positively desolate. How is she to... to..." He stopped, his hand clenching in the air. "Forgive me. You have no context. I suppose this makes little sense to you."

Elizabeth stepped closer, though unsure why she did so. "Mr. Darcy," she said gently, "it is clear to me that you care deeply for your sister. Whatever doubts you may have, your concern alone speaks volumes."

Darcy lifted his head slightly, his eyes meeting hers. "Concern is not enough if it leads to mistakes. She trusted me to know what was best for her. If I have failed her yet again..."

"You have not failed her," Elizabeth interrupted. "You acted with the information you had at the time, and it is clear you are willing to listen and adjust. That is no failure, Mr. Darcy. That is care."

He regarded her for a long moment. "You speak with a certainty I do not feel," he said at last.

Elizabeth smiled faintly. "Certainty is a luxury I rarely afford myself. But I do believe, Mr. Darcy, that your sister is fortunate to have someone who takes his responsibilities so seriously."

A shadow of gratitude passed across his face, and he inclined his head slightly. "Thank you, Miss Bennet," he said. "I do not often confide in others, but tonight... I find your perspective unexpectedly welcome."

Her breath caught briefly, surprised by the candor of his words. For a moment, the usual battle lines between them blurred. The silence between them stretched, heavy and charged, wrapping around her like the night itself. The stars above were unrelenting in their brilliance, sharp pinpricks of light that felt too distant, too indifferent to the storm inside her.

The wager—how utterly absurd it seemed now!—mocked her, a shallow, meaningless endeavor that could not survive the raw humanity she had just glimpsed. This was not the Fitzwilliam Darcy she had crafted in her mind—the cold, haughty figure she had so eagerly battled against, all for the pleasure of thwarting him once the victory was hers. What she saw tonight was a real man, one with feelings that were on the verge of breaking, his control brittle and barely holding.

Whatever he was most of the time, tonight at least, he was not arrogant; he was human, carrying a weight so personal, so crushing, that it pulled him into himself. And she had been toying with him—mocking him—while he stood there unraveling. Shame coiled hot and tight in her chest, but beneath it, something deeper stirred: the aching realization that she had misjudged him completely.

When Darcy finally spoke again, his voice was low and rough. "I should let you retire, Miss Bennet. The hour grows late."

Elizabeth nodded, sensing the conversation had reached its natural end. "Good night, Mr. Darcy," she said softly. "And... I hope you will not be too harsh on yourself. Even the best of brothers must learn as they go."

His gaze lingered on her for a moment longer before he inclined his head. "Good night, Miss Bennet."

As he stepped back inside, Elizabeth turned toward the garden once more, the cool air soothing her flushed cheeks. Her resolve to unsettle him had vanished entirely, replaced by something far more complicated—and far more troubling.

THE FIRE HAD BURNED low in the grate, casting flickering shadows across the walls of Darcy's room. He stood by the window, arms folded tightly across his chest, his gaze fixed on the moonlit grounds below.

Elizabeth Bennet.

He exhaled sharply, dragging a hand through his hair as if the motion could dispel the image of her standing on the balcony. Her words had been gentle, her voice warm with genuine concern, and it had disarmed him completely. How had she managed it? How had she reached into a part of him he thought fortified beyond intrusion? He had been so careful—so determined to keep her at arm's length—and yet, tonight, she had breached every defense without effort.

And it had been... comforting.

He turned from the window, pacing the length of the room, his boots muffled by the thick carpet. The events of the day turned over in his mind, each moment more vexing than the last. She had been irreverent, impertinent, maddeningly witty at the pianoforte. She had toyed with him, caught him off guard, and delighted in his discomfort. And yet, when she had spoken to him tonight—when she had offered him solace with that piercing sincerity—it had felt as though she truly saw him. Not the man society revered or envied, but the flawed, burdened soul beneath. The one whose existence he worked so hard to deny.

He despised how much he had let her affect him.

Darcy paused, leaning heavily against the mantel. He should not have confided in her. That much was certain. His concerns for Georgiana were his alone to bear, and sharing them with Elizabeth Bennet—no matter how innocently done—had been a mistake. She was nearly a stranger, barely more than an acquaintance, and yet, in that moment, she had felt like the only person who might understand. The thought made a rush of heat scald his face. Egad, he had told her so much!

He had been reckless. Foolish. To allow a woman like Elizabeth Bennet—sharp-tongued, unpredictable, wholly unsuitable—to occupy so much of his thoughts was unforgivable. He was a man of reason, of discipline, and yet he had spent the day entirely undone by her presence. Worse still, he knew this had been building for weeks. Ever since that first encounter in Meryton, she had lingered at the edges of his mind, challenging every expectation, every judgment.

His jaw clenched as he turned back toward the window. She was nothing like the women he had known, and that was precisely the problem. He had always valued order, predictability. Elizabeth was chaos—beautiful, compelling chaos—and she had no place in his carefully constructed life. To even entertain the thought of her was absurd. She had neither fortune nor connections, and her family—he grimaced at the memory of Mrs. Bennet's cloying chatter—was an embarrassment.

And yet...

Darcy's hands tightened into fists at his sides. He could not ignore the truth, no matter how much he wished to suppress it. Her wit, her courage, her refusal to defer to him—they both frustrated and fascinated him. But fascination was a dangerous thing. It clouded judgment, bred mistakes. He could not afford mistakes.

The moon hung high in the sky, its pale light spilling over the garden paths and illuminating the shadows of the trees. Darcy's gaze lingered there, his thoughts as tumultuous as the clouds drifting across the horizon. He had resolved long ago that his life would be dictated by duty, by responsibility—not by passion. He would not deviate from that path, no matter the temptation.

And Elizabeth Bennet was temptation itself.

Straightening, Darcy drew a deep breath, forcing himself to still the chaos within. Tomorrow, he would be better. Tomorrow, he would redouble his efforts to maintain his distance. She would not unsettle him again. She could not.

And yet, as he extinguished the lamp and climbed into bed, the memory of her voice—soft and steady, cutting through his doubt like a lifeline—lingered in his mind, refusing to be banished.

TEN

ELIZABETH PERCHED ON THE edge of Jane's bed, her arms crossed and her expression equal parts affectionate and exasperated. "Jane, you are the most stubborn patient I have ever met."

Jane smiled faintly, her cheeks still pale but no longer fevered. "That is a fine thing to say, Lizzy, considering I am trying to follow your orders."

"By insisting you are well enough to march to the drawing room tonight?" Elizabeth arched a brow. "I would hardly call that obedience."

"I feel much improved. And it would be ungrateful to leave without expressing my appreciation for all their kindness."

Elizabeth groaned, throwing herself back on the bed. "You are too good, Jane. No one will think ill of you for escaping back to Longbourn the moment you are able to stand upright. I would think it a triumph."

Jane laughed softly. "You would. But I must show them I am better before we leave. It would feel ungracious otherwise."

Elizabeth propped herself up on one elbow, eyeing her sister critically. "You could nearly have it in your power to determine the fortunes of every house in Meryton, you know."

Jane blinked, confused. "What do you mean?"

"I mean," Elizabeth said with a grin, "that half the town has wagered on how long it will take for you to recover."

Jane's eyes widened in alarm. "Surely not."

"Surely yes." Elizabeth sat up, counting on her fingers with mock solemnity. "The Lucases, the Philipses, even Mr. Long himself has joined in. Mama pretends to be scandalized, but not so scandalized as to prevent her from placing her own wager. Papa said as much in the note he sent with my trunk when it was brought."

Jane pressed a hand to her cheek, her laugh faint but horrified. "Lizzy, that is dreadful!"

"It is," Elizabeth agreed cheerfully. "And entirely within character for our neighbors. And so, if you mean to go home tomorrow, would you like to know who is favored to win? I suppose it would help if we named a time..."

"Certainly not! I would rather not think of myself as the subject of such... frivolity."

Elizabeth cast a hand over her heart. "They wager because they care."

Jane snorted, then crumbled into a reluctant laugh as she cupped a hand around her mouth. "And am I supposed to believe you have no stake in this yourself?"

"Me? No, no, I lost two days ago."

Jane doubled over, holding her stomach. "Oh, Lizzy, do not make me laugh! I will start coughing again."

Elizabeth sighed. "And yet, you insist on going downstairs tonight. I shall repeat myself—you are always too gracious for your own good. Truly, you are not required to sit with them tonight if you are not ready. No one will think you unkind."

"I feel ready to try. If I can sit with them for an hour, then we will leave in the morning. That is my plan."

Elizabeth sighed, knowing better than to argue further. "You are determined, then?"

"I am."

Elizabeth sighed. "Very well. But do not think I will let you martyr yourself. If you so much as blink too sluggishly, I will throw you over my shoulder and drag you back to bed myself."

Jane laughed again, leaning back against her pillows. "I believe you would."

"Believe it entirely," Elizabeth said with a mock glare. She hesitated, then asked, more softly, "Are you certain you do not wish to know the wagers? It might be diverting."

"Lizzy!" Jane swatted at her lightly. "I do not. But do not forget there is *another* wager Charlotte will want to hear of."

Elizabeth's smile faltered entirely, and a hot rush flooded her cheeks. She looked down.

Jane leaned in a little more closely. "And how are you faring, Lizzy? Charlotte will indeed ask."

Elizabeth drew back slightly, her face carefully neutral. "How am I faring? Why, splendidly. I have not offended Mr. Darcy so much that he has fled Netherfield."

"*Yet*," Jane teased gently. "But truly—how is it to be under the same roof as him? You must have gained some ground."

Elizabeth looked away, fiddling with the edge of Jane's blanket. "I hardly know. He is as inscrutable as ever. At times, he seems... less unpleasant than I first thought. But then he says or does something that makes me want to throttle him. It is rather exhausting, if I am honest."

Jane tilted her head. "Does he still stare at you so?"

Elizabeth huffed a laugh, standing to retrieve Jane's shawl from the nearby chair. "I imagine he stares at everything that displeases him, which must include half the world. Now, enough of that—Charlotte will have to wait for her answers. Let us focus on getting you through tonight without causing another flurry of bets."

Jane smiled, letting the subject drop, but her thoughtful expression lingered as Elizabeth draped the shawl around her shoulders.

THE MURMURS OF CONVERSATION reached him before he rounded the corner, voices low but unmistakably familiar. Darcy paused, drawing back into the shadows of the hallway just beyond the drawing room.

"I am relieved, I must confess," Caroline's voice carried into the corridor. "Miss Bennet is a... a charming girl—fair company when there is so little else to be had, but her lingering presence has quite disrupted the house."

"But surely, they shall be going tomorrow," Mrs. Hurst opined. "It cannot be so very much longer now. I hear her fever broke this morning."

"Yes, and now, surely we shall have to entertain them both in the drawing room this evening before they go tomorrow. Would that he had simply offered the carriage this afternoon! We both know Mrs. Bennet has no interest in hastening her daughter's return, but I cannot imagine why Charles feels the need to let the thing drag on."

Louisa hummed in agreement. "It is all very tiresome. And Miss Eliza? The way she parades herself about as though she belongs here—it is insufferable."

Darcy's hand tightened around the edge of the doorframe. Elizabeth Bennet? Parading herself? He almost laughed aloud at the absurdity. If anything, her stubborn independence stood in sharp contrast to the obsequious airs of the company Caroline preferred.

"She will be leaving soon," Caroline continued, her tone airy. "And none too soon, I daresay. I can only imagine the relief Mr. Darcy will feel to be free of her sharp tongue."

Darcy's throat tightened. Relief? Yes, of course—relief. That was exactly what he should feel. He stepped back, taking another path through the house to avoid further hearing what he could not unhear. The sisters' petty disdain needled him more than it should.

By the time Darcy reached the quiet of his room, his thoughts had unraveled into a tangled mess. The image of Elizabeth on the balcony the night before lingered in his mind, her wit tempered with surprising softness, her sharp eyes turned curious, even kind.

He pressed a hand to his temple. This would *not* do. He had resolved to remain guarded, and yet, in her presence, he found his defenses slipping—worse, crumbling. If this carried on, and with Bingley's injunction against any sort of incivility hampering his usual defenses, Darcy could well find his honor engaged before he could make his escape to London.

His breath in his throat, Darcy sat at the writing desk and took up a sheet of paper. If civility and distance had failed to curb Elizabeth's disconcerting effect on him, then perhaps another approach was needed. He had one evening left, after all, in which to make his stance known for good.

He stared at the blank page, Elizabeth's mocking words echoing in his mind: *"Bad poetry is one of my great terrors. I find it the surest way to extinguish any affection."*

A small, sly smile tugged at the corner of his mouth. *Bad poetry.* If Elizabeth found it repellant, then perhaps it could serve a higher purpose.

Reaching for his pen, he dipped it into the ink and began to write.

DARCY TRAILED INTO THE drawing room after dinner, his palms damp despite the coolness of the hall. He clasped his hands behind his back, willing the perspiration to subside. It was absurd. *He* was absurd. *How* had it come to this?

Elizabeth Bennet. That was how.

She had been seated opposite him at dinner, and it had taken every ounce of discipline not to stare. Every sharp turn of her wit, every arch of her brow as she replied to Miss Bingley's thinly veiled remarks, had unraveled his composure bit by bit. By the time she excused herself to escort her sister back down to the drawing room, his toes were curled inside his shoes, the roots of his hair felt like they were on fire, and he was halfway through his second glass of wine.

Now, she reentered the room with Miss Bennet on her arm, the latter still pale but looking hale enough to at least maintain her feet. Darcy's heart hammered as Elizabeth's smile softened while she guided her sister to a seat near the fire. It was a smile full of care and sweetness, utterly disarming in its sincerity. And for a fleeting instant, last evening came rushing back to him—her genuine concern and patience in the face of his doubts. Lucky would be the man Elizabeth Bennet chose to lavish her affections on...

That was when he started coughing.

Elizabeth glanced his way, one eyebrow edging upward. Darcy cleared his throat and claimed a seat, fixing his gaze on the fire. The rug. The steaming coffee service that had just been brought in. Anything but Elizabeth Bennet.

"My sister is feeling much better," Elizabeth said brightly, answering a question nobody had yet asked. "The warmth of the fire will do her good."

Bingley all but leaped from his seat to arrange a cushion for Jane Bennet. "You must tell me at once if you feel chilled, Miss Bennet. Or fatigued. Or—well, anything at all."

Miss Bennet murmured her thanks, but Darcy's attention was elsewhere. Elizabeth sat beside her sister, her hands folded in her lap, her gaze flicking briefly toward him before focusing on the conversation between her sister and Bingley.

Miss Bingley, seated nearby with her embroidery untouched, gave a hollow laugh. "It is such a relief to see you feeling better, Miss Bennet. We were all so dreadfully worried. Were we not, Louisa?"

Mrs. Hurst, who was perched beside her sister with a glass of sherry, nodded. "Oh, quite. We have been simply beside ourselves."

Elizabeth's expression remained polite, but there was a faint, familiar edge to her smile. "You have both been such kind hostesses. I am certain the strain of your worry must have cost you many hours of sleep."

Darcy bit back the urge to smirk. She was so good at that—cutting just deep enough without ever drawing blood. Miss Bingley seemed not to notice.

In the corner, Hurst grumbled something incoherent about cards—no doubt, he was petulant that no one else wished to join him—and poured himself another drink. Darcy ignored him, his focus narrowing again to Elizabeth. She sat straighter now, leaning slightly toward her sister as though shielding her from the insincerity radiating from the Bingley sisters.

The paper in Darcy's pocket crinkled faintly as he shifted. The poem. The utterly idiotic poem.

Earlier, the idea had felt inspired. He had convinced himself that it was a clever way to put her off, to gain the upper hand and make her feel all the same unease that had begun to torment him.

But now... now it felt like a reckless gamble. Surely, she would see through it. Surely, she would know he was baiting her. And yet, the alternative was to let her continue infiltrating his thoughts unchecked.

"Mr. Darcy," Elizabeth said suddenly. "You are very quiet this evening. Is something on your mind?"

Darcy stiffened, his gaze snapping to hers. She sat poised, her head tilted ever so slightly, the flicker of a challenge gleaming in her eyes. Her tone was polite, everything ladylike and respectable—but the teasing undercurrent was unmistakable. It was like a gauntlet thrown at his feet.

"Quiet, Miss Bennet? Perhaps I am simply observing."

"Observing what, I wonder?" Elizabeth said, leaning slightly forward, the firelight catching the sparkle in her eyes. "Surely not the weather—it has hardly changed all day."

Darcy arched a brow. "Must one always speak to be occupied?"

"Not always. But silence often speaks louder than words. I cannot help but wonder what yours might be saying."

He hesitated, feeling the faint stir of heat creeping up his collar. "Perhaps it says nothing of interest."

"Oh, I doubt that," she replied with a smile—sharper now, like the edge of a blade concealed behind silk. "I have always suspected you of being a man of hidden depths, Mr. Darcy. But perhaps I am mistaken and you truly are as dull as any other man."

He swallowed. Was that a trickle of sweat itching beneath his cravat? *Impossible!* "Dull? That would not be for me to judge, Miss Elizabeth, but I would not have taken you for one to make such mistakes lightly."

Elizabeth laughed softly, the sound as infuriating as it was captivating. "Even I cannot claim infallibility. But I do pride myself on my intuition. And just now, my intuition suggests that your thoughts are far from dull."

"Your intuition flatters me," Darcy said, forcing the words past the tightness in his throat. "But I am afraid you overestimate the complexity of my thoughts."

Elizabeth's brow lifted, a knowing glint flashing in her eyes. "Then perhaps you might share them, so I might judge for myself."

"Share them?" He hesitated, the papers in his pocket crinkling against his fingers. The idea had seemed daring, even clever, earlier in the safety of solitude. Now, under her keen gaze, it felt reckless—yet maddeningly tempting.

"Yes," Elizabeth said, her voice softening slightly but losing none of its edge. "I confess, I am curious. Surely even a man as composed as yourself cannot be entirely immune to intrigue or interest?"

His jaw tightened. "You think me composed, Miss Bennet?"

"Oh, excessively so," she said with mock seriousness. "I cannot imagine you ever giving way to whimsy—or indulgence. Do you even allow yourself the luxury of frivolous thought?"

Darcy stiffened, his hand twitching against his side. A sharp reply hovered on his tongue—something cutting, deflecting, anything to push her back. But then Bingley turned, looking at him expectantly, his brows slightly raised as if bracing for Darcy's usual brusque retort.

Politeness Bingley had demanded... he could not dare respond in his accustomed way. He had to go above and beyond in civility—civility so pungent, so cloying and loathsome that she would nearly trip over herself to back away from him. And yet, Bingley would have nothing of which to accuse him on the matter.

Darcy's jaw tightened. He could feel the edges of the papers in his pocket like a taunt. *The poem.* He had written it for precisely this reason: to steer her away, to show her how ridiculous this game was. All he needed was the nerve to follow through.

He took a breath, steeling himself. "Perhaps I will concede, Miss Elizabeth. There may be *some* value in frivolity. I was thinking—" he said slowly...

Did he dare do it? He had to decide before the next words left his— "that this evening might benefit from a touch of... diversion."

There. He had said it.

Bingley straightened. "A diversion?"

Darcy nodded, sliding his hand into his pocket. The paper felt heavier than it should have. "I have been experimenting with... with verse."

Bingley's mouth dropped open. "You? Writing poetry?"

"Yes," Darcy said firmly, though his throat felt dry and his stomach felt like a twisting brood of vipers. "I thought I might recite something."

Miss Bingley sat up taller, her eyes lighting with transparent delight. "Oh, Mr. Darcy! How marvelous! I had no idea you possessed such a talent."

Elizabeth, meanwhile, tilted her head, her expression suddenly dark with curiosity. "A poem, Mr. Darcy? That is... quite the revelation."

Her tone was neutral, but the glimmer in her eye betrayed her skepticism. He swallowed hard. His hand trembled faintly as he withdrew the paper, but he forced himself to ignore it. "I hope you will be kind enough to forgive its imperfections."

Bingley blinked rapidly, as though trying to reconcile this Darcy with the one he had known for years. Miss Bingley practically glowed, clearly assuming the effort was for her benefit.

And Elizabeth... she leaned back slightly, her arms crossing loosely over her lap, her expression full of a thousand questions and her gaze unwavering. "Oh, I am certain there could be no imperfections at all, if you are the author, Mr. Darcy."

Darcy straightened his shoulders, determined not to falter now. "If you will indulge me," he said, the words catching in his throat but refusing to be retracted.

ELIZABETH SHIFTED SLIGHTLY IN her chair, watching Mr. Darcy retrieve a crumpled paper from his pocket with an air of grave determination. She was not sure what she had expected when he had proposed to share his thoughts, but this... this did not feel promising.

"Did you..." Miss Bingley's voice faltered slightly as she leaned forward, her face lighting with hopeful curiosity. "Write this recently, Mr. Darcy?"

"I did," Darcy replied, his tone stiff. He unfolded the paper carefully, his eyes scanning the words with what could only be described as grim resolve. "I composed it today."

Elizabeth blinked, her brows lifting as Mr. Darcy cleared his throat. He was truly going to read this? *Mr. Darcy?* The idea was absurd, incongruous—utterly baffling. And yet, there he stood, as though ready to recite something epic and eternal.

He cleared his throat, his voice deepening as he began:

> *"O fairest star that graces night,*
> *Thy glow doth set my heart alight.*

Thy laughter rings, a silver chime,
A melody that halts all time."

Elizabeth's stomach turned. She cast a furtive glance at Jane, who had turned an alarming shade of pink and was now staring fixedly at her lap. Mr. Bingley had shifted forward, one hand pressed firmly to his mouth, his shoulders faintly trembling.

Darcy's eyes flicked up, then back to the page as his voice grew stronger, almost fervent:

"Thy gentle eyes, like pools of dew,
Reflect a world both kind and true.
Thy spirit fierce, yet soft as spring,
Doth make my silent soul to sing."

Elizabeth gripped the arm of her chair, her jaw tightening against the onslaught of saccharine rhymes. Was it possible to die of secondhand embarrassment? She risked a glance at Miss Bingley, who was leaning forward with a strained but delighted smile, as though determined to absorb the poem as a personal ode.

Darcy's shoulders were bunching under his coat, but he droned on, apparently oblivious to the collective agony of his audience as his voice rose with an almost theatrical intensity:

"O angel bright, in mortal guise,
Thou art the sun to my sunrise.
Thy every word, a honeyed grace,
Doth lift my heart to heaven's embrace."

The silence in the room grew oppressive, broken only by the faint, muffled sound of Mr. Hurst snoring in the corner. Elizabeth's pulse thundered in her ears. She dared not look at anyone now, certain her composure would shatter.

Darcy drew a deep breath for the final stanza, his voice nearly trembling with conviction:

> *"And though I'm bound by duty's chain,*
> *My love for thee shall not be vain.*
> *For fate itself cannot efface,*
> *Thy name, my heart's eternal place."*

As the last syllable fell into the heavy air, Darcy lowered the paper. His face was ashen and his brow prickled with beats of sweat, as though the exercise had cost him every shred of his fortitude. And his gaze swept the room, as though daring anyone to challenge the earnestness of his expression.

No one moved. No one spoke.

The silence stretched, thick and stifling. Elizabeth stared at her hands, willing herself not to burst into laughter or tears—she was not sure which would win. Jane had turned impossibly red, her lips clenched together between her teeth in what seemed like an attempt to suppress either a giggle or a sob. Mr. Bingley's hand remained firmly over his mouth, though his wide eyes betrayed his disbelief.

Miss Bingley was the first to break the stillness, her voice high and brittle. "Oh, Mr. Darcy! How... how beautiful! Such... passion!"

Darcy inclined his head slightly, his face impassive. "Thank you."

"I trust," Miss Bingley preened, her lashes fluttering, "that these sentiments have their inspiration in present company?"

Darcy cleared his throat. "Merely strings of words that I fancied sounded well together, Miss Bingley."

Elizabeth finally looked up, her eyes locking with his. He seemed utterly unaffected by the devastation his poem had wrought, as though he had read a military dispatch rather than the most cloying verses ever composed.

Forcing a smile, Elizabeth cleared her throat delicately. "Mr. Darcy," she said, her voice betraying only the faintest tremor, "you have outdone yourself."

He blinked, tilting his head slightly, as if unsure whether to take her words as a compliment or not. "I appreciate your kind attention, Miss Bennet."

Eleven

"All secure, Mr. Hill?" Elizabeth asked, glancing at the neatly tied baggage atop the coach. The morning air was crisp and damp, the mist clinging to the hedgerows, but her spirits soared with the promise of escape. At last—freedom. A week at Netherfield had felt an eternity, with every polite exchange and stolen glance a fresh trial. Now, with Jane recovered and the open road before them, she could breathe again.

Jane emerged from the house behind her, swathed in a warm shawl. Though her cheeks had regained some of their color, her movements were still tentative due to her lingering headache. A pity their mother would never heed Elizabeth's admonishments! Give her another wealthy, single man, and Mrs. Bennet would send her eldest daughter off again in a storm without a second thought.

"Are you certain you are well enough to travel, Jane?" Elizabeth asked, scanning her sister's face for any sign of fever or faintness.

Jane smiled faintly, her hands clasped tightly in her lap. "I am quite well, Lizzy. Truly. It will be a comfort to be home again."

Elizabeth nodded, though she felt far from reassured. Jane's modesty often led her to downplay her own needs, and Elizabeth worried that three miles out in the cold might be more taxing than her sister admitted. Still, there was no denying the relief of leaving Netherfield behind.

A rustle of movement drew Elizabeth's attention back to the house, where Mr. Bingley and Mr. Darcy had emerged to see them off. Mr. Bingley's cheerful demeanor was as steady as ever, and Elizabeth could not help but note how his gaze lingered on Jane, his concern evident in the way he hovered near the carriage door.

"Miss Bennet," Bingley said warmly, offering Jane his hand through the door of the carriage. "I trust the journey will not tire you too much. Please do not hesitate to send word if there is anything you require."

"You are very kind, Mr. Bingley," Jane replied. "I cannot thank you enough for your hospitality and care during my illness."

"Think nothing of it," he said, his expression brightening. "It has been a pleasure to have you both here."

Elizabeth inclined her head to their host, but could not help the way her eyes drifted to the man standing behind him. Ah, yes... The Poet.

Darcy, standing a few steps behind Bingley, said nothing, his expression as inscrutable as ever. His dark eyes flicked toward Elizabeth briefly, a momentary glance that conveyed neither warmth nor irritation. If he harbored any relief at their departure, he hid it well, though Elizabeth imagined he must be as eager as she to put their curious and contentious interactions behind them.

"Mr. Darcy," she said, nodding to him before the footman closed the door. "I trust you will find Netherfield more peaceful without us."

His brow furrowed slightly, as though weighing her words for hidden meaning. "I would not presume to call your presence disruptive, Miss Bennet. Your sister's health was a matter of genuine concern."

Elizabeth inclined her head, unwilling to engage further. She leaned back and permitted the footman to close the door, pulling the blanket more snugly around her sister's lap.

Bingley stepped away, his cheerful farewells ringing in the air as the driver prepared the horses. Darcy remained silent, his hands clasped behind his back, his gaze fixed somewhere beyond the mist-shrouded hedges. Elizabeth found herself watching him for a moment longer than she intended. And then she blinked, snapping herself back to sanity. Whatever had possessed her to regard the man with anything more than strategic curiosity?

The carriage lurched forward, breaking her train of thought. As Netherfield's shadow receded into the distance, Elizabeth exhaled. Finally, she could have a few moments of peace.

Jane's voice drew her attention back. "Lizzy, do you think... do you think Mr. Bingley regards me too highly?"

Elizabeth blinked, surprised by the question. "Why should that trouble you?"

Jane hesitated, her hands twisting the edge of her shawl. "He is so amiable, so generous. I cannot help but wonder if he perceives more in me than there truly is to admire."

"Jane," Elizabeth said firmly, taking her sister's hand, "if Mr. Bingley admires you—and I believe he does—it is because he sees what I see. Your kindness, your grace. Do not diminish yourself in his eyes or your own."

Jane's cheeks flushed, but she said nothing more. Elizabeth sat back, her thoughts turning inward as the familiar landscape of Hertfordshire rolled past.

ELIZABETH HAD BARELY STEPPED out of the carriage before the sound of Mrs. Bennet's exclamations filled the air. "Oh, my dearest Jane! My poor, sweet girl—how pale you still look! But we shall have you feeling better in no time. Lizzy, where is her shawl? Does she not need another shawl? And Mr. Bingley, I suppose, sent you off with nothing but kind words and no further assurances?"

Elizabeth sighed inwardly as she helped Jane down. Before they could even cross the threshold, Mr. Bennet appeared at the door, his expression wry as he greeted them.

"Welcome home, girls," he said. "I trust you survived Netherfield unscathed. We have missed you sorely, but you will be delighted to hear that we have been well compensated for your absence with an extended visit from Mr. Collins."

Elizabeth blinked. "Mr. Collins? Your cousin, Mr. Collins? I did not even know we were to expect him!"

"Oh yes, did I not tell you? I suppose I did not. Yes, indeed, he arrived at two o'clock, the day before yesterday. And he has made quite the impression. Why do you think your mother was kept away from visiting her dearest Jane at Netherfield during her illness?"

Elizabeth's heart sank. "Probably because she was busy trying to 'secure the future' of another of my sisters."

"Aye, I would imagine some coins have changed hands over the matter already. Oh, do not scowl so, Lizzy. I daresay you will find him diverting."

The word "diverting" held enough irony to make Elizabeth wary. Her suspicions were confirmed the moment they entered the drawing room. A man of rather expansive height and girth rose from a chair, his face lit with an eager smile that showed more teeth than necessary. He was dressed impeccably, though with a stiffness that suggested he cared more for appearances than comfort.

"Ah, my fair cousins!" he exclaimed, bowing deeply. "How delightful to at last make your acquaintance. I am your most humble servant, William Collins, rector of Hunsford Parish and honored clergyman under the patronage of the esteemed Lady Catherine de Bourgh."

Elizabeth exchanged a glance with Jane, whose faint smile betrayed her amusement.

"We are pleased to meet you, Mr. Collins," Jane said.

"And I, dear cousin, am overjoyed to find you safely returned," Mr. Collins continued, his gaze shifting to Elizabeth with an expression that made her distinctly uncomfortable. "And you must be Miss Elizabeth Bennet. Your reputation for wit and beauty precedes you."

Elizabeth raised an eyebrow, unsure whether to thank him or recoil. "You are very kind, sir."

He beamed, clearly taking her mild response as encouragement. "I hope to spend much time in your company, Cousin Elizabeth. I consider it my duty to foster familial ties during my stay, and you, I am certain, will be an engaging conversational partner."

Elizabeth offered a tight smile, already devising ways to avoid such conversations. "Yes, well, if you will forgive me, Mr. Collins, my sister is still feeling rather poorly, and I would like to help her upstairs to rest."

"Oh! Of course, of course. Indeed, I did think Miss Bennet seemed rather pale, but I had supposed that was only in contrast to your more... vivid coloring." He spoke the last with almost a gasp in his breath, and when Elizabeth rounded sharply on him, he was dabbing his mouth as if he had just finished eating.

Lydia leaned closer to Elizabeth, her whisper loud enough to be heard by all. "You watch, Lizzy. I bet I can make him say 'Lady Catherine' three times in one breath before dinner."

"Lydia," Elizabeth warned, her tone sharp enough to cut her sister's laughter short. The last thing she needed was for Mr. Collins to overhear and mistake Lydia's teasing for genuine interest.

"Lizzy's right," Kitty whispered. "You should be ashamed of yourself, Lydia."

"But why? I could do it," was Lydia's petulant response.

"Because that is too easy. It should be four times. No! Make it five."

Elizabeth shot them both a glare, but Mr. Collins seemed, mercifully, to suffer from that peculiar sort of hearing impairment that is selective in nature. He was speaking again to their mother, and indeed, the name Lady Catherine had left his lips at least twice in one sentence—the lady's virtues, her generosity, her wisdom, and her superior taste in furnishings.

Mr. Bennet, seated comfortably in his chair, looked on with amused detachment. "And there you have it, Lizzy," he said when Mr. Collins finally paused for breath. "Our cousin is a man of many fine words and, it would seem, even greater admiration for his patroness."

Elizabeth suppressed a smile, though she longed to escape the room. "It is always enlightening to hear of such devotion."

"Indeed, Miss Elizabeth!" Mr. Collins exclaimed. "I believe it is my duty to speak well of those who have so kindly supported my station. Lady Catherine's wisdom—"

Elizabeth quickly interrupted. "We are most fortunate, Mr. Collins, to hear of her many merits. I am sure my father will be eager to discuss them further during dinner. Come along, Jane. Let us make you comfortable."

As Elizabeth turned Jane to fairly drag her out of the room, Lydia and Kitty crowded after them. "You'll take the bet, won't you Lizzy? Come, now, it is not like you to be shy."

Elizabeth shook her head. "Perhaps later, Lydia."

"Oh, but it's no good later. If I wait too long, you'll see that I'm right and you won't take the bet at all."

Elizabeth rolled her eyes as they mounted the stairs. "Very well, I shall consider myself warned. I will not take your bet at all. Satisfied?"

Lydia stopped at the bottom of the stairs, her arms crossed as she pouted up at them. "You're no fun, Lizzy."

DARCY SAT AT THE far end of the drawing room, his fingers tightening around the book he had not turned a page of in at least ten minutes. The muted hum of conversation grated on his nerves, particularly Miss Bingley's laughter—discordant, like the notes of a poorly tuned instrument. Across the room, Hurst dozed with the effortless indifference of a man for whom boredom was a lifestyle.

Darcy's focus strayed to the others. Miss Bingley was leaning toward her sister, her tone hushed but animated, her glances in his direction far too frequent for comfort. He forced his attention back to the pages in his lap, but the words blurred, and his thoughts churned with unwelcome insistence.

That blasted poetry. Why, *why* had he done it? Now Miss Bingley probably thought he had written it for *her*.

Elizabeth's face when he had read aloud returned to him unbidden: the faint flickering of her jaw, the way she bit her lip as though physically restraining herself from comment. He could almost hear the laughter she had refused to voice. Oh, he had made his point, indeed. She had told him the very best way to drive her away, and he had pulled it off with élan. Sort of.

But rather than to put her back on her heels, as he had hoped, now she was just laughing at him.

Well... did that, after all, achieve his ends? Hang his pride for a moment. Why should he care what a country miss thought of his dignity? Was she prepared to cease her assault on his senses? *That* was the material question.

And why was she so determined to pluck him apart in the first place? It did not appear to be the usual flirtation—she hardly seemed interested in complimenting him or making herself agreeable in the common way, so he could only surmise that she had chosen him as some sort of social rival in a game to which he had never been told the rules. Was his self-inflicted humiliation enough to send her elsewhere for her amusement?

Enough! He snapped the book shut, the sharp sound startling Hurst, who grunted in his sleep. He had spent far more than enough time this evening fretting about a woman who was not even in the house.

"Oh, Mr. Darcy, will you not join us?" Miss Bingley called. She rose and crossed the room, settling herself on the settee nearest him with an air of possessive ease. "Surely you are not still brooding over the Bennets' departure? I daresay we shall have our fair share of entertainment soon enough."

"I am brooding over nothing, Miss Bingley."

"Of course not," she said with a coy smile. "You would never, naturally. But I think, perhaps, the absence of *one* lady in particular has cast a rather unexpected pall over the house."

Darcy lifted his head abruptly. "What? I—"

"I was only observing, Mr. Darcy, that my brother is somewhat... diminished this evening."

Darcy released his breath slowly and darted a glance at Bingley. "I see nothing amiss in his manner."

"Do you not? Well, perhaps it is less apparent to another man. But a lady cannot help but notice the, ah, *energy* Jane Bennet has inspired."

Darcy narrowed his eyes. "To what does your observation tend, Miss Bingley?"

"Why, half the town must already believe she and my brother are engaged. Do you not think it amusing?"

Darcy's expression darkened. "Gossip is rarely amusing, particularly when it concerns a lady's reputation."

Miss Bingley faltered, but only briefly. "Oh, I mean no harm, of course. But speaking of amusing..." Her eyes sparkled with a mischievous edge as she added, "I must say, Mr. Darcy, your recital last night was quite unexpected. Such... fervor."

Darcy's jaw tightened. "I am glad it provided you with amusement."

"Not merely amusement!" she exclaimed, clasping her hands dramatically. "I found it quite moving. You must have another verse to share."

"I do not," Darcy said flatly, his grip on the arm of the chair firm enough to leave marks.

"Surely you cannot mean that. A man of your talents?" Her gaze lingered on him, her smile widening. "Now that I think of it, I must wonder what inspired such sentiment. Could it be that your muse has departed this morning?"

He stiffened, heat rising to his face. Miss Bingley leaned closer, her tone lowering conspiratorially. "I have noticed, Mr. Darcy, that you have been... how shall I say... more willing to indulge whimsy of late. I cannot help but wonder if this has anything to do with that silly wager you made with my brother."

Darcy froze, his breath catching. "The wager has nothing to do with poetry."

"Oh, I am sure it does not," she said lightly, though her eyes gleamed with something sly. "But I do think Charles has forgot all about it. He has been rather preoccupied with Miss Bennet, as you must have noticed. It would be such a shame if all your efforts toward forced and unnecessary 'civility' went unnoticed."

Her words crawled under his skin, needling at him in ways she could not possibly understand. He rose abruptly, cutting her off mid-sentence. "If you will excuse me," he said coldly, "I find I am in need of some air."

Miss Bingley blinked, momentarily thrown, but quickly recovered with a simpering smile. "Of course, Mr. Darcy. Do enjoy the evening air. Perhaps it will soothe your spirits."

He ignored her, striding from the room and into the cool night. The gardens of Netherfield stretched before him, silvered by moonlight. He walked briskly, the sharp air doing little to calm the storm in his mind.

Elizabeth Bennet.

Her presence lingered like a shadow he could not shake. Her laughter—her *almost* laughter—during his recital still echoed faintly in his ears. She had refused to mock him outright, but her eyes had betrayed her amusement, and he could not decide if he was sympathetic at her mirth over the spectacle he had made of himself, or infuriated.

But then the memory of her sitting beside Miss Bennet near the fire rose unbidden, her care for her sister so clear, her quick defense of that sister before Miss Bingley so perfectly aimed. She was unlike anyone he had ever known—so full of contradictions. Bold yet tender. Clever yet infuriating.

And entirely too captivating.

Darcy stopped abruptly, his hands clenching at his sides. He hated it. He hated that he could not forget her. And most of all, he hated that she had got under his skin in ways he could neither explain nor endure.

THE PATH TO MERYTON was alive with the usual bustle of villagers going about their errands, but Elizabeth's thoughts were elsewhere as she walked alongside Charlotte Lucas. Jane had been too pale and tired to join them, and for a mercy, all three of her younger sisters had found something else to do.

"So, Lizzy," Charlotte began with a sly smile, "you had a week at Netherfield. How is your wager progressing? Have you managed to thaw the infamous Mr. Darcy into swooning admiration for you, or are you preparing to admit defeat?"

Elizabeth sighed. "Must we discuss it, Charlotte? The man is insufferable. I doubt he even notices whether one exists to thaw or not."

"Ah, but you forget—winning his approval is not about him noticing you. It is about you *making* him notice you."

Elizabeth glanced at her friend with narrowed eyes. "I see. So I am to resort to fluttering my lashes and simpering, am I?"

Charlotte laughed. "Hardly. You could not simper convincingly if your life depended on it. But you do have charm, Lizzy. Wit, intelligence—all those things men claim to admire until they realize they cannot best you. Surely even Mr. Darcy can be made to appreciate that."

"He appreciates nothing but his own pride," Elizabeth said sharply, then caught herself. Charlotte's teasing had drawn her out more than she intended, and her irritation surprised even her. "Besides," she added more lightly, "I am growing weary of the game."

"Oh no, you don't. You are *not* giving up now. We agreed on the terms, and I am holding you to them."

Elizabeth frowned. "I am reconsidering the wisdom of those terms."

"That is precisely why they are so effective," Charlotte said with mock solemnity. "Think of it, Lizzy—oh, I have already great plans for your forfeit. And you know I will appreciate winning far less than you will feel the sting of losing."

The jab hit its mark, and Elizabeth's frown deepened. "You are a cruel woman."

"I am merely practical," Charlotte replied, her grin widening. "And I suspect you would be just as merciless if the wager went the other way."

Elizabeth opened her mouth to retort, but the hum of voices ahead distracted her. A cluster of women stood near the apothecary, their heads bent close in avid conversation. As Elizabeth and Charlotte approached, she caught snippets of their words—enough to know that Mr. Collins had become the topic of town gossip.

"It must be one of the Bennet girls," one woman said. "Why else would he visit now, unless to secure a wife?"

"Well, it certainly won't be Mary," another laughed—rather too confidently for Elizabeth's taste. "Or Jane, for everyone knows Mrs. Bennet thinks she can secure Mr. Bingley. And no clergyman alive would try managing those younger two girls. Five shillings says it will be Miss Elizabeth. She's the second prettiest of the lot, and quick-witted, too. He would do well to choose her."

Elizabeth halted abruptly, her indignation rising. Charlotte stopped beside her and raised an eyebrow. "It seems your cousin is already the subject of some matchmaking."

"And *I* am to be the sacrifice, am I?" Elizabeth shot back. "Of all the presumptuous assumptions—"

"Oh, come now, Lizzy! They are only having a bit of fun. You know there is never a thing in it."

"Until a 'harmless' wager becomes prevailing sentiment and so many assumptions are made that I cannot withdraw gracefully!"

Charlotte lifted a shoulder. "You should be flattered. The heir to Longbourn, no less! Imagine the poetic justice of it all. Mrs. Goulding absolutely relishes the notion that the famous Bennet sisters, who always attract such notice, really are—"

"Yes, yes, I *know*." Elizabeth turned a withering glare on her friend, though the effect was lost on Charlotte, who seemed more amused than sympathetic.

"Well, why not set her on her ear by marrying the heir? It is not a terrible idea, Lizzy."

"If you think I would ever entertain such a notion—"

"Relax, Lizzy. You forget that I met him two days ago when Maria and I called on Mary. The man may be pompous, but he is hardly an ogre or a beast. You will manage."

"I have no intention of *managing* anything," Elizabeth retorted. "If Mr. Collins has set his sights on me, he will find them very poorly aimed."

"I *meant* that you would manage to put him off easily enough," Charlotte chuckled. "In all seriousness, though," she said, "about Mr. Darcy. You are not really considering forfeiting the wager, are you?"

Elizabeth sighed, her shoulders sagging slightly. "I do not know, Charlotte. The thought of continuing is exhausting. Mr. Darcy is..." She trailed off, searching for the words to describe the knot of frustration and curiosity he inspired. "He is not a man to trifle with. And I am not entirely sure what I hope to gain by this."

Charlotte nodded thoughtfully. "It's not just about the wager anymore, is it?"

Elizabeth hesitated, then shook her head. "No, I suppose it is not."

"Well," Charlotte said briskly, "whatever it is, I expect you to see it through. After all, if you lose, I expect you will never speak to me again, and that would be a pity."

Elizabeth's blood spiked in her veins. Charlotte was teasing... she *had* to be, but it still curdled her stomach to think of the stakes. As the familiar outline of Longbourn came into view, she resolved to push aside her doubts—for now. There was still time to win, and losing was simply not an option.

Twelve

"Miss Elizabeth, might I have the honor of your company for a walk this afternoon?"

Elizabeth looked up from her plate, caught mid-bite by Mr. Collins's sudden address. His voice carried a tone of solemn expectation, as though he were bestowing a favor too great to be refused.

"Thank you, sir, but I am sure one of my sisters would be better suited to the honor," she replied, setting her fork down with deliberate care. "Perhaps Mary. I believe she would welcome a chance to discuss the finer points of virtue."

Mr. Collins blinked, clearly unprepared for such a suggestion. "Ah, but it is you, Miss Elizabeth, whom I wish to accompany. I feel certain we would benefit greatly from a shared conversation. Lady Catherine often speaks of the value of pairing good intellects on such occasions. Indeed, I think she must be right."

Her mother rose from her seat. "Lizzy, you shall go, of course! A walk will do you good, and Mr. Collins has so kindly extended his invitation."

Elizabeth bit back a retort and glanced at Jane, who offered her a small, sympathetic smile. "If it pleases Mr. Collins, I shall be ready shortly." .

"Splendid!" Mr. Collins exclaimed, rising to his feet as though the matter had been triumphantly resolved. "We shall set out as soon as you are prepared. Lady Catherine recommends morning walks most highly and often remarks that the brisk air sharpens one's faculties. I have made it a point to heed her advice in all things."

He bowed deeply and left the room, leaving Elizabeth to watch him go with a mix of resignation and disbelief.

"Lizzy," Lydia said under her breath, "do you think he can talk and walk at the same time? Or will he stop every few steps to bow to the hedgerows?"

Kitty stifled a laugh, and Elizabeth shook her head, refusing to indulge them. Jane caught her eye and smiled faintly, offering silent encouragement. "I wish I felt well enough to accompany you. I might have been able to offer some sort of help."

"Oh, I am certain Mr. Collins will prove an engaging companion all on his own," Elizabeth said dryly, rising from her seat. "I mean to satisfy my curiosity on that point, if only to see how far his admiration for Lady Catherine can stretch."

"Will you try to count how many times he mentions Lady Catherine before you reach the first turn in the lane?" Lydia asked.

"Do not encourage her, Lydia," Mary interjected. "Such behavior is unkind."

"Unkind?" Lydia said, her eyes wide with mock innocence. "I am merely asking for information, Mary. It is entirely scientific."

Elizabeth shook her head. "If I counted every reference to Lady Catherine, we would never reach the lane at all. I suspect I shall have to endure her praise in uninterrupted measure."

Lydia laughed, but Mrs. Bennet was already bustling around the table. "Do not be difficult, Lizzy," she said. "You must see how advantageous Mr. Collins's attentions are. A man of his standing! And the heir to Longbourn! It is more than you deserve, I might add, with your sharp tongue and willful ways."

Elizabeth rose from her seat and moved toward the hall for her gloves and bonnet, unwilling to prolong the conversation. "I shall endeavor to represent the family with all the grace I can muster," she said, slipping past her mother before another admonition could follow.

In the hall, she lingered for a moment to secure her bonnet, letting the familiar motions calm her irritation. Mr. Collins's attentions were unwelcome enough, but her mother's insistence that she accept them with gratitude only worsened the ordeal. As she tied the ribbons beneath her chin, she resolved to endure the walk with as much patience as she could manage. Surely even Mr. Collins would run out of words before long.

Darcy closed his book and set it on the table beside him, its pages unread. The drawing room at Netherfield felt unusually stifling that afternoon, the kind of quiet that invited unwelcome thoughts. He stood and crossed to the window, his hands clasped behind his back as he gazed out at the misty horizon.

No matter how resolutely he tried to banish Elizabeth Bennet from his mind, her unpredictable words and enigmatic smiles returned to taunt him. It had been days since she had left for Longbourn, yet her presence lingered—an aggravatingly persistent specter. She had unsettled him in ways he could neither explain nor dismiss, and the memory of her laughter—most particularly, the stifled chuckles when he had embarrassed himself, gnawed at his composure.

The creak of the door broke his reverie, and he turned to see Bingley entering the room.

"Darcy," Bingley said as he walked toward the hearth. "I have taken a notion into my head."

"Dare I ask?"

"Miss Bennet is said to be recovering well," Bingley said, leaning casually against the mantle. "Her mother has informed Mrs. Philips, who was kind enough to spread the word in Meryton."

"That is good to hear," Darcy said evenly, though his grip on the book's spine eased.

"I thought so as well." Bingley moved to the hearth, turning to face Darcy with a spark of mischief. "It has set me thinking, actually. With Miss Bennet on the mend, I believe it would now be in decent taste to consider a proper gathering. A ball, perhaps."

"Oh." Darcy sighed. Of course, a ball. It was probably the proper thing to do—Netherfield was the largest house in the area, and the idea had been launched about town more than once since their arrival. "I see."

"Not with much pleasure, I take it. Come, Darcy, the neighborhood is overdue for a bit of cheer, and what better occasion than the season's first frost? Of course," Bingley added with a grin, "Caroline is already threatening to take to her bed at the very idea. I believe she dreads the militia being included."

Darcy scoffed. "Why? You could hardly fail to invite them without causing talk."

"Oh, she is utterly persuaded that including the militia would ruin the evening entirely. But I cannot imagine excluding Colonel Forster and his men, especially when they have been such a fixture in the neighborhood."

"Your sister's feelings aside, it does seem you are determined."

"I am. After all, what is the point of taking a house like Netherfield if one does not host at least one grand gathering?"

Darcy turned back toward the window, his thoughts flickering to Elizabeth again. A ball would mean her presence. The thought stirred an unwelcome mixture of anticipation and dread. He had been determined to maintain his distance, to let reason prevail over sentiment. Yet every encounter with her seemed to chip away at that resolve.

Bingley's voice broke into his musings. "Oh, and speaking of Longbourn, they have a guest."

"A guest?"

"Yes, a Mr. Collins. Their cousin, I was told. Apparently, he is the heir to Longbourn. Mrs. Philips mentioned him this morning when I was in town. Apparently, he has arrived with some rather... specific intentions."

Darcy frowned. "What sort of intentions?"

"Matrimonial ones," Bingley said, laughing. "It seems Mrs. Bennet is in raptures over the idea. From what I gather, he is making no secret of his desire to secure a match."

Darcy stiffened, his brow furrowing. "And has he singled out a particular daughter?"

"Well, that's the entertaining part. The whole town is abuzz with speculation. There are even wagers in Meryton about how quickly he will propose and to whom."

"Wagers?" Darcy's tone hardened.

"Indeed. Mrs. Long has placed her bet on Miss Catherine, though I hear others are favoring Miss Mary. I understand, however, that Miss Elizabeth is by far the favorite in the odds."

Darcy's fingers tightened. "Indeed?"

Bingley shrugged. "Apparently, Mr. Collins has already made a number of flattering remarks about her."

"Flattering remarks?" Darcy echoed, his tone colder now.

"Something about her 'not being unsuitable'," Bingley said, chuckling. "Though I daresay his standards of flattery leave much to be desired."

Darcy turned sharply, striding back toward his chair and gripping its back with unnecessary force. "And what does Miss Elizabeth make of him?"

Bingley tilted his head thoughtfully. "I cannot say, but knowing her, I suspect she finds it all amusing. I have not met the man myself, though, so how could I tell her impressions of him?"

"He sounds hardly clever enough to value a lady of worth," Darcy snapped. Then he cleared his throat. "I—I mean that as... a generality, of course. I am not saying that—"

"Oh, I think I know exactly what you are saying. Collins' backhanded sort of compliment sounds rather like declaring a lady 'tolerable,' does it not?"

Darcy narrowed his eyes. "I was not trying to court the lady when I said that. Persistent men, no matter their other qualities or lack thereof, have a way of wearing down even the strongest objections," he said, his voice clipped. "And family pressure can be... compelling."

"Darcy," Bingley said, raising a brow, "you sound almost concerned."

Darcy hesitated, his jaw tightening. Why would he care? The matter did *not* concern him. But still... "I merely find it unfortunate that such a woman should have to endure the attentions of an unworthy suitor."

"What makes you think he is unworthy? I know nothing of the man."

Darcy forced his jaw to relax as he turned. "Quite right. It was only an assumption. But if he were a desirable match, it seems there would be more names put forward, and other families might be vying for the attention of such a man. Heir to Longbourn, that must be no small thing in this neighborhood."

Bingley studied him for a moment, his expression curious but amused. "And interesting extrapolation. You may be right, Darcy, but Miss Elizabeth seems more than capable of handling herself."

Darcy said nothing, though his thoughts churned. The idea of Elizabeth tethered to a man she could not like—and Darcy could not imagine any possibility that this Collins fellow was someone she *would* like—was intolerable.

And yet, what right had he to interfere? She was nobody to him. Just the subject of a stupid wager he never should have agreed to.

He clasped his hands behind his back again, trying to force himself to remain still, but it was an exercise in futility.

Bingley clapped him on the shoulder. "Do not overthink it, Darcy. Let the cards fall where they may."

Darcy's teeth ground. The cards were falling, indeed—into chaos. And he had a sinking suspicion he was already losing control of the game.

"Miss Elizabeth, I am most gratified by your willingness to indulge my humble request," Collins began, gesturing for her to take the lead down the path. "A morning walk is, I find, a most edifying activity, particularly when one is blessed with such unseasonably fine weather and excellent company."

Elizabeth inclined her head but said nothing, letting her silence fill the space where he clearly expected flattery in return. She stepped onto the gravel path and began walking at an even pace, wishing to neither rush nor prolong the ordeal.

"Lady Catherine de Bourgh," he continued as soon as they had passed the first hedgerow, "often remarks upon the value of exercise, especially for young ladies. She believes it cultivates a graceful carriage and a sound constitution. Admirable foresight, naturally, for young ladies of good health must, surely, make more desirable partners in life. Such wisdom is, of course, one of her many extraordinary qualities."

Elizabeth cast him a sidelong glance. "It seems Lady Catherine's wisdom touches on every facet of life."

"Oh, indeed! Her guidance is as boundless as her benevolence. Why, I recall one particular instance when she took the trouble to personally instruct Mrs. Jenkinson—her daughter's companion, you understand—on the correct method of arranging her shawl to capture a properly modest manner while still adorning the lady's figure in the most flattering fashion. Such attention to detail is the hallmark of true superiority."

Elizabeth stifled a sigh, her resolve to remain civil wearing thin. "An impressive example, no doubt. Though I wonder, Mr. Collins, do you find your own judgment lacking in such matters that you require Lady Catherine's constant guidance?"

He blinked, momentarily thrown off balance. "Lacking? Oh no, Miss Elizabeth, I would not say lacking. Rather, I endeavor to align my opinions with hers, as I find her judgment to be—how shall I put it?—unassailable. It is my duty, as her clergyman, to reflect her views faithfully."

"And do you find that duty a rewarding one?"

"Exceedingly so! It is a privilege to serve such a lady, just as it is an honor to inherit such an estate as Longbourn, which, I trust, you and your family will be glad to know I intend to maintain with the utmost care."

Elizabeth's jaw tightened. "I am sure we are all most relieved to know the estate will be in such capable hands."

Mr. Collins beamed, utterly oblivious to her tone. "I do believe, Miss Elizabeth, that my decision to visit Longbourn was both timely and wise. Lady Catherine herself encouraged me to take this step, for she feels that a clergyman with property ought to set an example of familial duty. It was she who first suggested that I turn my thoughts toward matrimony, a subject I must confess has occupied my mind a great deal of late."

Elizabeth's steps faltered, but she recovered, her pulse quickening. "Indeed?"

"Lady Catherine impressed upon me the importance of choosing a wife who would be a credit to my position. Naturally, my thoughts turned to the daughters of my esteemed cousin, Mr. Bennet. And though I do not wish to presume, Miss Elizabeth, I find myself most drawn to—"

Elizabeth halted abruptly, turning to face him with as much composure as she could muster. "Mr. Collins," she said, cutting him off before he could finish, "it is a fine morning, and I would hate to spoil it by rushing into matters better left for another time."

Mr. Collins blinked, startled by her interruption, but quickly recovered. "Of course, Miss Elizabeth. Your sensibility is admirable. There is no need to hasten what is surely a matter of great importance."

"Precisely," Elizabeth said, resuming her walk. "Shall we continue?"

"By all means! I was merely remarking to myself what a charming landscape this is. Lady Catherine would approve most heartily of the arrangement of those shrubs. They remind me of the ornamental hedges at Rosings Park..."

As he monologued on with yet another paean to Lady Catherine's taste, Elizabeth allowed her gaze to wander over the fields in the distance. She focused on the crispness of the air and the rustle of leaves in the breeze, willing herself to endure what remained of the walk with her composure intact. She could feel her irritation simmering, but a small, grim satisfaction surfaced as well. She had diverted him for now, though she suspected his intentions would resurface sooner than she liked.

"CHARLES, MUST WE REALLY go through with this ball?" Caroline Bingley lamented from the settee as Darcy entered the drawing room. She sat primly, her hands folded over an open book she had no intention of reading, her expression one of carefully curated irritation.

Bingley, who had been leafing through a pile of correspondence, looked up with mild surprise. "'Must?' Caroline, it was my idea. Of course, we must."

"Then perhaps I should ask whether we *should*," she said with a delicate sigh. "It seems... excessive. Surely a smaller gathering would suffice. Have we not already hosted a fine dinner party? I thought that would have satisfied the neighborhood."

"Ah, so *that* was your intent. I fear you are to be disappointed, Caroline, for I mean to keep my promise."

"An unnecessary promise!" Miss Bingley declared. "No one expected it, until you had to run on about it in town."

Darcy settled into the armchair near the hearth, his face impassive as he watched the exchange. He had seen Caroline maneuver her brother before, and this had all the hallmarks of another of her campaigns.

Bingley shook his head, smiling faintly. "Indeed, they did, and my answer remains the same. I have already spoken with Mrs. Nichols, and the preparations are underway. We have but to name a date and send the invitations. It is a ball, Caroline, not an invasion."

"Perhaps," she said lightly, smoothing her skirt, "but must we include the militia? It lowers the tone considerably."

Darcy glanced at her, his brow arching slightly. "Colonel Forster and his officers are hardly the rabble."

Caroline turned her gaze to him, her eyes narrowing almost imperceptibly as she gauged his tone. "Perhaps not," she conceded, "but there is something to be said for exclusivity. One would not want the room to feel... crowded."

Bingley laughed. "Caroline, you'd have the room feel empty at this rate. The militia has been good company to half the neighborhood."

"Half the neighborhood lacks any sort of discernment," she said sharply, then softened her tone when she turned back to Darcy. "Of course, I defer to my brother's enthusiasm. But I do wonder, Mr. Darcy, whether you will find the evening as diverting as my brother hopes. A man of your tastes, surrounded by such a lively company..."

"I am sure I will endure the company as well as any other," he interrupted.

Caroline's smile was thin, but her eyes glittered with calculation. "I do hope so. After all, one cannot escape the reality of who will attend. The Bennets will be there, naturally."

Bingley, oblivious to the trap she was setting, beamed. "Naturally! We could not do without them. Such a relief that Miss Bennet is well again because I could hardly plan such a thing with one of the daughters of the neighborhood still ill after a visit to my home."

"Indeed," Caroline said. "Miss Bennet's recovery is very fortunate. But I wonder... does this mean *all* the Bennet sisters will attend? Even the younger ones?"

Darcy's hand stilled against the arm of his chair. He glanced at her briefly. "I imagine they will."

"Well! My own mother never would have permitted me out at such an age, but there, at least they shall have Miss Eliza to rein them in. There's a mercy."

Darcy narrowed his eyes and said nothing."

"Yes, it is a fine thing for Miss Eliza, for I daresay her parents do little enough to keep decorum in that house." Caroline said, watching him closely now. "But the lady herself, now, she does have a certain... presence. I must admit, her wit is rather sharp. Though I wonder if that sharpness does not sometimes cut the wrong way."

Darcy's gaze remained on the fire. "Miss Elizabeth's wit is her own, and she wields it expertly."

Caroline tilted her head, the faintest frown tugging at her lips. "How kind of you to say so, Mr. Darcy. I am sure she will be delighted by your... approval."

Bingley chuckled, glancing up from his correspondence. "Elizabeth Bennet is a delight to everyone but Caroline, it seems."

"Not at all," Caroline said, smoothing her expression into one of false contrition. "I merely think it prudent to temper one's enthusiasm for certain qualities."

"Such as?" Darcy asked, his voice sharper than intended.

"Oh, I could not say," Caroline said airily. "It is simply that Miss Elizabeth is so... unaffected. One hopes she does not mistake confidence for charm."

The silence that followed was sharp enough to cut glass. Darcy leaned forward, resting his forearms on his knees as he studied her. "Miss Elizabeth has no need to mistake anything, Miss Bingley. She knows her worth."

Caroline's smile tightened again, and she turned back to Bingley, her tone as sweet as honey. "Well, I hope the ball lives up to your expectations, Charles. I'm sure it will be an evening to remember."

Bingley laughed, oblivious to the undercurrents. "Of course it will! Everyone is looking forward to it."

Caroline glanced toward Darcy once more, her gaze lingering. "Everyone, indeed."

Thirteen

"Mr. Collins," Elizabeth said with a touch of exasperation, "I do not believe there is anything of theological importance to be found in a ribbon shop."

"Nonsense, Cousin Elizabeth," Mr. Collins replied, puffing out his chest. "Every endeavor, however humble, may serve to glorify the higher principles to which we aspire. Even ribbons."

Lydia snorted loudly, earning a sharp look from Jane. "Well, I think they glorify bonnets," Lydia said with a grin, tugging Kitty's arm. "Come, let us look at that one with the blue trim."

The two younger Bennets skipped ahead, leaving Elizabeth to follow at a more sedate pace. Mr. Collins hurried alongside her, gesturing broadly toward the shop displays. "Lady Catherine herself is most particular about ribbons. She insists that her household be adorned with the most tasteful embellishments—nothing garish, of course, but always elegant. And, of course, Miss de Bourgh's gowns are the very model of taste and femininity."

"I am sure," Elizabeth sighed. She exchanged a glance with Jane, whose faintly amused expression betrayed her own struggle to remain composed.

A week had passed now since their return from Netherfield, and Jane was now quite recovered. And again, as they had nearly every day this week, the party from Longbourn had found themselves venturing toward Meryton—all for disparate reasons, and all encouraged and abetted by Mr. and Mrs. Bennet… again, for disparate reasons.

As the group lingered outside the milliner's shop, Lydia's attention wavered from one display to another. She was in the middle of declaring that she must have a bonnet trimmed with blue when two officers approached, their red coats bright against the dull gray of the day.

"Ah, Miss Bennet!" called one of them, a familiar face from the previous week's assembly. Lieutenant Denny, all cheer and confidence, tipped his hat with a broad smile. "I trust you are enjoying your morning?"

Jane smiled politely. "Very much so, Lieutenant. And you?"

"Well enough, thank you," he replied before gesturing to the man beside him. "May I have the pleasure of introducing my friend, Mr. George Wickham? He has just joined us here in Meryton. Wickham, may I present Miss Jane Bennet, Miss Elizabeth Bennet, Miss Mary Bennet, Miss Catherine Bennet, and Miss Lydia Bennet, as well as their cousin, Mr. Collins."

The man at Denny's side stepped forward with an easy bow. "It is an honor to make your acquaintance, ladies." His gaze swept over the group, his expression warm and unhurried. "And Mr. Collins, of course."

Elizabeth noted the slight hesitation in his voice when he addressed Mr. Collins, but it was quickly smoothed over with a courteous smile. She glanced at her cousin, who, puffed up with self-importance, was already preparing to make himself known.

"Mr. Wickham," Collins began grandly, "it is a pleasure, indeed. I am Mr. Collins, clergyman of the parish of Hunsford, serving under the esteemed patronage of Lady Catherine de Bourgh."

Wickham bowed again. "The very name of Lady Catherine commands respect, Mr. Collins. I am well acquainted with her—by reputation, of course—and I am honored to meet one of her trusted clergy."

"You are *acquainted* with her? Why, sir then you must know the honor you do me, for I have been sadly alone in my comprehension of the great lady's goodness. Miss Elizabeth, *this,* indeed, is a gentleman well worth knowing better!"

Elizabeth managed to tune out most of her cousin's effusions, her attention drifting to Mr. Wickham as he exchanged a wry glance with Lieutenant Denny. His composure never faltered, though the faintest flicker of amusement crossed his face.

"You are newly arrived, then, Mr. Wickham?" Jane asked.

"Indeed, Miss Bennet," Wickham replied, turning to her. "And I must say, I am already most impressed with the welcome I have received. The warmth of this town is unparalleled."

"Oh, how charming!" Lydia exclaimed, stepping forward. "And will you be attending the next Assembly, Mr. Wickham? Surely you must come—it would be a crime for a new officer not to attend!"

"I would not dream of missing it," Wickham said, his smile broadening. "Especially if all the young ladies of Meryton are as delightful as you, Miss Lydia."

Lydia giggled, and Elizabeth bit back a smile of her own. There was something undeniably magnetic about Mr. Wickham, though she could not yet decide if it was genuine or merely polished. His manner was effortless, as though he had been born to charm, but there was nothing yet to suggest anything untoward. In fact, he seemed entirely agreeable.

"And what brings you to Meryton, Mr. Wickham?" she asked, curious to hear more.

"A change of scenery, Miss Elizabeth," he replied. "The regiment offers an opportunity to serve and to explore new parts of the country. I find that variety is one of life's greatest pleasures."

"An admirable sentiment. I hope you find Meryton's charms sufficiently varied."

"I have no doubt," he said with a slight bow, the twinkle in his eye suggesting he had already formed a favorable opinion of the town—and perhaps its inhabitants.

Lieutenant Denny clapped Wickham on the shoulder. "I told you, didn't I? Meryton has the friendliest neighbors a man could hope for."

"Indeed, you spoke the truth," Wickham said, glancing between them, "But I am afraid, ladies, that we are keeping you from your morning errands. Lieutenant Denny and I have duties to attend to, but I hope to see you all again soon."

"The pleasure was all ours, sir," Elizabeth said.

Lieutenant Wickham tipped his hat, preparing to take his leave, when the sound of approaching footsteps shifted the mood entirely. Elizabeth turned her head just as Mr. Darcy stepped out of the stationer's shop. His gaze swept over the group, halting briefly on Wickham.

Elizabeth expected the usual polite nod, but instead, Darcy's expression froze, his eyes narrowing almost imperceptibly.

"Ah... Mr. Darcy," Wickham said with a tight smile, his earlier ease visibly fraying. He hesitated, then offered a stiff bow. "A happy coincidence, I'm sure."

Darcy did not return the gesture. "Mr. Wickham."

Elizabeth's gaze flicked between the two men. Darcy's stance had stiffened slightly, his usual air of control edging into something more brittle, while Wickham stood as though rooted to the spot. For the first time since their introduction, Wickham appeared unsure of himself.

"You are acquainted, then?" Elizabeth asked.

Wickham hesitated again. "We are... familiar. A long time ago, Miss Elizabeth."

Darcy's eyes locked on Wickham with the precision of a blade. "Not long enough."

The silence that followed was thick with unspoken history. Wickham shifted his weight but made no attempt to meet Darcy's gaze again. Instead, he turned to Elizabeth, his expression carefully composed.

"Meryton is fortunate to have such a lively community," Wickham said, his voice lighter now, as if determined to reclaim the ease of their earlier conversation. "I am certain I shall enjoy my time here."

Elizabeth nodded, her attention still divided. Darcy, for his part, seemed entirely uninterested in Wickham's efforts to steer the conversation.

"Miss Bennet," Darcy said abruptly, turning to her with a sharpness that felt deliberate. "I trust your family is well?"

Elizabeth blinked at the sudden change of focus. "Quite well, thank you, Mr. Darcy."

"I am glad to hear it." His gaze lingered on her for a moment, then shifted to Collins beside her, who, for once, seemed flabbergasted into silence. "I believe I have an engagement to keep," he said at last. "Good day."

Without sparing Wickham another glance, Darcy turned on his heel and walked away, his retreat as abrupt as his arrival.

Elizabeth turned back to Wickham, who was now watching Darcy's receding figure with an expression she couldn't quite place—something between frustration and resignation.

"Well," Wickham said lightly, watching him go. "It seems Mr. Darcy has not changed."

Elizabeth's curiosity burned brighter, but she merely tilted her head. "And what, Mr. Wickham, would you say Mr. Darcy was before?"

Wickham hesitated just long enough to be noticeable before smiling again. "A subject for another time, perhaps. I would not want to darken such a pleasant day."

Elizabeth frowned but let the matter drop, her thoughts churning as the group resumed their walk.

DARCY STOOD JUST OUTSIDE the bookseller's shop, gazing down the busy Meryton street. His earlier encounter with Wickham had stirred his irritation, but it was the second encounter—Elizabeth Bennet's radiant smile turned toward that scoundrel—that had truly set his mind in motion.

He had been too reactive, too defensive. He had made his disdain too odiously clear, and in pubic, even!

That would not do. Egad, someone as perceptive as Elizabeth Bennet would already be imagining scenarios, trying to discern the cause of his dispute with Wickham and imagine a woman to be at the heart of it.

And a woman—especially one with an active mind such as hers would immediately leap to that prospect, and she would not be too far wrong. She probably even thought he was *jealous* of her attentions to Wickham!

If Elizabeth Bennet thought to trifle with him, to tease him into losing his composure, she would find herself sorely mistaken. His bet with Bingley required gentlemanly civility, yes—but civility had many forms. He could be every inch the gentleman and still outmaneuver her.

What about her cousin, that Collins fellow? He had stood stupidly watching the entire exchange, with scarcely a coherent thought sparking in his murky dull eyes. Darcy's lips quirked in a faint, humorless smile. The man was a buffoon, yes, but even buffoons could serve a purpose.

His thoughts were interrupted by the very figure who had consumed them. Elizabeth Bennet appeared down the street, her arm linked with her sister's as they strolled past a milliner's window. Mr. Collins trailed behind them, his chest puffed out and his head tilted upward, as though the rooftops were studying his profile.

Darcy did not hesitate. He stepped into their path, bowing slightly as the group approached. "Miss Bennet," he said, touching his hat courteously. "Miss Elizabeth. How fortunate to meet you again."

Elizabeth's smile faltered for the briefest of moments before she composed herself. "Mr. Darcy," she said, inclining her head. "You are quite the fixture in Meryton this afternoon. I had thought you were already on your way back to Netherfield."

"It seems the town offers more interest than I anticipated."

"Oh, we do our best to entertain," Elizabeth said lightly. "Though I would not have thought Meryton suited to your tastes."

"On the contrary," Darcy said. "It has a certain charm. And of course, the company is unparalleled."

Elizabeth's brow arched slightly. "I do not believe I had the pleasure of introducing you to my cousin when we met earlier. Mr. Collins, this is Mr. Darcy." She clasped her hands before her and smiled sweetly. "Mr. Darcy is a rather fine poet, Cousin."

Darcy coughed. Oh, the crafty snipe! She *would* throw that back at him...

Mr. Collins stepped forward, his hat doffed. "Mr. Darcy! Why, sir, you are not *the* Fitzwilliam Darcy of Pemberley, are you? I wished to enquire earlier, but I was in such awe... pray, sir, are you the very same?"

Darcy's eyes flickered to Elizabeth's for an instant. He could not say why he sought reassurance there, but the look she returned—a sly quirk of her lips and an inviting tilt of her head—made his stomach curdle. That look was not a welcome, but a dare.

"Indeed, I am."

"Why, sir!" Collins threw a hand over his heart. "I have the very great honor of being named Rector to Hunsford Church, by the great Lady Catherine de Bourgh, who, I understand, is—"

"My aunt," Darcy finished with a half smile. Oh, this just got even easier. If Lady Catherine had chosen Collins, Darcy could nearly print out a list of the man's merits and faults merely by type. And toying with the man for his own purposes would be child's play.

"What an honor to meet you here, sir." Darcy shook the man's hand, though his grip was firmer than necessary. "I trust you are enjoying your visit to Longbourn."

"Oh, quite so, quite so! It is a most delightful household, and Miss Elizabeth has been... *most* accommodating."

Darcy's gaze flicked to Elizabeth, who was pressing her lips together in what he could only interpret as thinly veiled irritation. "Indeed," he said, his tone taking on a faintly conspiratorial edge. "Miss Elizabeth is known for her *engaging* company. I do not wonder that you find her a delightful presence."

The look she shot him—half astonishment, half betrayal—that was all the indication Darcy needed to know he was on the right track.

Collins beamed, clearly missing any subtext. "Oh, most engaging! I daresay I am quite fortunate to have such opportunities to... to deepen my acquaintance with her."

Darcy nodded thoughtfully. "And you are wise to seize them, Mr. Collins. Such opportunities are not to be taken lightly."

Elizabeth's jaw clenched. "I am certain Mr. Collins's visit will be a memorable one."

"Oh, undoubtedly," Darcy agreed, turning back to Collins. "You must find Miss Elizabeth's wit and intelligence quite stimulating."

"Oh, yes," Collins said eagerly. "Though, of course, one must temper wit with modesty, and Miss Elizabeth excels at both. Lady Catherine herself would undoubtedly approve."

"Ah, Lady Catherine, indeed," Darcy said, his tone turning faintly reverential. "Her discernment is unmatched. No doubt she would commend your excellent judgment in choosing to spend your time so... wisely."

Elizabeth's eyes flashed. "Mr. Darcy, your high opinion of Mr. Collins does him great credit."

There was danger there, but the fire was not yet kindled so brightly that he did not dare to dance close to the flame.

"Only what is deserved. Mr. Collins clearly has an eye for quality."

Collins puffed up further, and Darcy had to resist the urge to laugh outright. Elizabeth's irritation was as excruciatingly obvious as her attempts to mask it, and he found himself enjoying the sight of her composure beginning to fray. Finally, he had found a way under her skin!

"Well, we must not keep you from your errands," Elizabeth said finally, her tone clipped but polite. "Come, Jane, Mr. Collins."

"Oh, but Miss Elizabeth," Collins said, hovering awkwardly near Darcy, "perhaps Mr. Darcy would favor us with further conversation. I am sure he has much wisdom to impart."

"Another time, perhaps," Darcy said, bowing slightly. "I would not intrude further on the ladies' afternoon."

Elizabeth inclined her head, her smile forced. "How considerate of you, Mr. Darcy."

"Always, Miss Elizabeth," he replied, his voice quiet but deliberate. "Always."

As they walked away, Darcy allowed himself a small, private smile. He had seen the way her hand tightened around Jane's arm, the tension in her posture. Whatever game Elizabeth Bennet thought she was playing, she was not the only one who could wield strategy. And with Mr. Collins so eager to hover at her side, Darcy had a ready-made ally—one who, despite himself, might just help Darcy keep his distance.

For now.

THE TEA AT LUCAS Lodge was already in full swing when Elizabeth arrived with her mother and younger sisters, the room alive with chatter and the faint clink of teacups. Papa had claimed he would come, right up to the moment they all mounted the carriage and he found that his "gout" was troubling him. Elizabeth had given him a rather stern look, but the only response she got was a faint chuckle as he closed the door.

Still, the Bennet ladies expected to be well entertained. Charlotte—bless her—had strategically placed her family to intercept their more tiresome guests, leaving Elizabeth free to mingle—or at least attempt to find some amusement among the company.

It was not long before Mr. Wickham appeared, his charming smile bright enough to cut through the din of conversation. He greeted her warmly, sliding seamlessly into her company as though he had been invited specifically for her entertainment.

"Miss Bennet," he said, inclining his head. "You appear to be the brightest star in the room this evening."

Elizabeth laughed. "And you, Mr. Wickham, appear to be an excellent flatterer."

"A man must develop certain skills to survive in such dazzling company. Though I must confess, your wit leaves me at a distinct disadvantage."

Elizabeth arched a brow. "Perhaps you are more skilled than you let on."

"Ah, but my skills pale in comparison to present company," Wickham said with a laugh. "I daresay I am always at the mercy of a pretty face, no matter how clever I fancy myself."

"Perhaps we should test that theory," Elizabeth replied. "What say you to a wager?"

Wickham's grin widened. "A wager? My kind of game. What shall we wager on?"

Elizabeth glanced across the room where Sir William Lucas had cornered a hapless young officer and was animatedly extolling the virtues of his family's recent improvements to their garden. "How long do you think Sir William will speak on that subject before the poor man escapes?"

Wickham followed her gaze, his expression turning sly. "An excellent wager. I give him... six minutes."

Elizabeth smirked. "I give him ten."

Wickham extended his hand. "Done. And what shall we wager?"

Elizabeth considered for a moment. "A shilling, perhaps? Nothing too extravagant."

"Agreed," Wickham said with a flourish. "Though I warn you, I am rarely on the losing end of a wager."

The two turned their attention to Sir William, who was now gesturing expansively toward an imaginary flower bed. Wickham leaned in closer, his voice low. "He does seem particularly inspired today. I may have underestimated him."

Elizabeth laughed, and they continued to watch the scene unfold. Sure enough, the officer finally managed to escape precisely nine minutes later. Elizabeth clapped her hands together triumphantly. "Nine minutes! Ten is closer to nine than six. I win."

Wickham placed a hand over his chest in mock dismay. "Ah, you have bested me, Miss Bennet. I am undone."

"Then you owe me a shilling," Elizabeth said with a grin, extending her hand expectantly.

Wickham hesitated, patting his waistcoat pocket with exaggerated movements. "Ah, well, you see... I seem to have left my coins in my other coat."

Elizabeth's smile faltered slightly, but she said nothing. Mercy's sake, it was only a shilling. Wickham turned to the nearby officer, Lieutenant Denny, lowering his voice. "Denny, be a good fellow—lend me a shilling, will you? I'll repay you tomorrow."

Denny blinked, then barked a laugh that drew the attention of several nearby guests. "Lend you a shilling? You owe me more than a week's pay from gaming last night!"

Wickham stiffened, his charming facade cracking just enough for Elizabeth to notice. He recovered quickly, turning back to her with a self-deprecating smile. "Ah, well. It seems I must concede defeat entirely. I cannot bear to disappoint a lady, but my poor pockets betray me."

Elizabeth tilted her head, her eyes narrowing slightly as she studied him. "It seems, Mr. Wickham, that your skills as a gambler may not extend to your finances."

He laughed again, though it sounded hollow this time. "You wound me, Miss Bennet. But rest assured, I will make good on my debt."

"Never mind," she said with a wave of her hand. "It was not a fair bet. You had no possible way of knowing the depth of Sir William's lungs."

"A lady as gracious as she is beautiful," Wickham replied, with a hand over his chest. "I do not receive such mercies lightly, I assure you. You have made a devoted servant of me, Miss Elizabeth."

Elizabeth said nothing further, but the moment lingered in her mind long after Wickham had moved on to charm another guest. His polished manners and ready smile suddenly seemed thinner, less substantial, as though they could collapse under the weight of a stronger wind.

What in Heaven's name had happened between this fellow and Mr. Darcy? She was prepared now to think there might be some genuine complaint. Whatever history existed between them, it was unlikely to be a matter of simple jealousy.

Elizabeth's lips curved into a faint smile. If Wickham was as slippery as he appeared, he might just be the perfect tool for her wager. Darcy was already unsettled by his presence; what might happen if she encouraged it further?

This could be very useful, indeed.

Fourteen

"Lizzy, do fix that ribbon properly," Mrs. Bennet called. "You will be walking home from church with Mr. Wickham, no doubt, and we cannot have the tail of that ribbon flipping up into your face when you try to speak. Such a charming man! And so attentive to you last time."

Elizabeth glanced at her mother in the hallway mirror, adjusting the errant ribbon with a sigh. How quickly her mother had shifted her interest from Mr. Collins! "Mama, you mustn't interpret every pleasantry as an intention to propose."

"Intent to propose, how silly! On only your third meeting—or is it the fourth now? But you will see, Lizzy. I know a man with intentions when I see one."

"Mama, I am quite certain Mr. Wickham's attentiveness was no more than politeness."

"Nonsense, child!" Mrs. Bennet declared, pausing to assess her youngest daughters' bonnets. "A man does not smile that way unless he means to. You must learn to notice these things."

Her father stopped in the hall as he waited for Hill to fetch his coat. "It is a wonder Mr. Wickham has time for such charm, given all the effort required to keep his boots polished. I daresay, such a dandy has never graced the regiment."

Elizabeth bit back a laugh, while her mother huffed. "Oh, Mr. Bennet, you never take these matters seriously!"

"I take them quite seriously, madam. So seriously that I have decided to hasten us along before the sermon at church turns into a sermon at home."

Jane stepped into the hallway, still adjusting her muff, and caught Elizabeth's gaze. "Come, Lizzy. Shall we walk ahead with Mary? The morning air is lovely today and I, for one, am eager to stretch my legs."

Elizabeth nodded, glad for the reprieve. As they gathered their things, she glanced toward the window. The prospect of seeing Mr. Darcy at church was almost thrilling. After all, she had yet to try her shiny new weapon on him in her assault on his manly sentiments. Envy was a fine blade, when wielded with skill. But it could turn about and cut the one holding the sword just as easily.

The Bennets arrived at the chapel to find the yard already bustling. Ladies exchanged greetings in hushed tones while gentlemen lingered in groups, discussing crops or the latest news from Meryton. Elizabeth spotted Mr. Wickham standing near the entrance, his polished charm on full display as he spoke with a small crowd of admirers. But the moment she entered his periphery, he seemed to straighten, and she caught the instant his head began to turn her way.

Excellent. He would do nicely.

She avoided his gaze, turning instead toward Jane. "Shall we join Charlotte in her pew today?" she asked, gesturing to where her friend stood with her family. "If so, we ought to catch them up now, before they go inside."

"Ah, Miss Elizabeth," Collins interrupted. "Is it not better for you to sit in your family's pew?"

Elizabeth paused, sliding an eye toward Collins. "We often exchange pews with the Lucases. Maria frequently sits beside Lydia and Kitty in our place."

"But is that... entirely proper? Her ladyship always emphasizes the importance of proper devotion on the Sabbath. She is most particular about the conduct of true worship."

Elizabeth rolled her eyes and closed her mouth. It was not worth wasting her air. The regiment's officers stood near the churchyard gate, their scarlet coats bright in the morning sun. And Lieutenant Wickham at last grew tired of her ignoring him to break away from the group. He approached the Bennet family, his stride confident and his smile a study in suave mastery.

"Miss Elizabeth Bennet," he said, tipping his hat. "You brighten an already fine morning."

"Mr. Wickham," Elizabeth replied. "How good of you to join us."

"Indeed, I could hardly miss services," Wickham said. "Though I confess, the company afterward is nearly as inspiring as the sermon itself."

Mr. Collins, who had overheard, bristled. "Sir, that is hardly the proper spirit for the Sabbath. Lady Catherine would never approve of such frivolity taking precedence over sacred reflection."

Wickham's smile flickered with amusement. "Ah, but surely even Lady Catherine values the fellowship of good neighbors after service. Does she not?"

Elizabeth glanced at Wickham, her mouth almost rioting with suppressed laughter. "I am sure she would not *dis*approve of the good people of the town showing their patriotism by a bit of friendliness toward the members of the militia. Particularly on a holy morning."

Collins blinked and gave his lapels a jerk. "Well. Well... just so."

That was precisely the moment that the Netherfield party arrived. Elizabeth turned to watch the carriage park—for Netherfield was, apparently, too far for a Sabbath day's walk for Miss Bingley.

Mr. Bingley approached with a warm smile, offering a bow to their mother.

"Good morning, Mrs. Bennet," he said. "What a fine day for the service. The journey from Netherfield was quite pleasant in such weather."

Mrs. Bennet beamed. "Indeed, Mr. Bingley! Such a blessing to have fine weather this late in the season."

Bingley's gaze lingered on the group before he added, "I trust your family is well?"

"Quite well, thank you," Mrs. Bennet replied. "As you can see for yourself. Do not my girls look well today?"

Mr. Bingley's gaze now had permission to trip freely over Jane before he was obliged once again to fix his eyes on Mrs. Bennet. "They do, indeed."

Mr. Darcy stood slightly apart, acknowledging the group with a brief nod. His eyes caught Elizabeth's for a moment, but before she could decipher his expression, he turned to address... of all people... her *cousin*. What the devil?

"Mr. Collins," Darcy began, "I understand you recently delivered a sermon on the virtues of charity. Was it well received?"

Collins's face lit up as though Darcy had just elevated him to the status of a bishop. "Oh, most assuredly, sir! Oh, my goodness, Lady Catherine must have been mightily impressed to have written to *you* about it!"

Darcy's cheek twitched, and if Elizabeth had learned anything about his expressions, it almost looked... smug. As if his venture had been a mere lucky guess. "Indeed, sir."

"Oh, my. Truly, sir, it was one of my finest orations. The congregation was deeply attentive, and I was fortunate to draw upon the wisdom of Lady Catherine, who has always stressed the vital importance of almsgiving. Her guidance, of course, shaped my every word."

Darcy gave a slight nod. "I see. Lady Catherine's influence is, no doubt, considerable. As is her wisdom. I have often turned to her for advice in matters at Pemberley."

Elizabeth stared in disbelief. Was... was *Mr. Darcy* truly entertaining this nonsense? Worse, Collins had puffed himself up like a preening bird, casting furtive glances around the churchyard to ensure all present witnessed this distinguished exchange.

"Oh, indeed, sir! You could not have sought wiser counsel. I, too, have often turned to that noble lady for advice, and, I flatter myself, I am proving a *most* adept student to her ways."

Darcy offered an approving response, something polite but noncommittal, and Elizabeth bit the inside of her cheek to keep from laughing—or groaning. For all his faults, she had never expected Mr. Darcy to willingly align himself with a man like Collins.

She turned sharply to Jane, muttering, "It seems Mr. Darcy finds Mr. Collins's company every bit as stimulating as I do."

Jane suppressed a smile and gave a slight shake of her head. "Lizzy, do behave."

DARCY SETTLED INTO HIS pew, casting a discreet glance toward the section where Elizabeth sat beside Miss Lucas. From this angle, he could see her profile as she leaned slightly toward her friend, exchanging a quiet word before the service began. There was a grace to her movements, a natural energy that commanded his attention even in stillness.

In the Bennets' pew, just ahead of Darcy and somewhat to the left, Mr. Collins sat upright, his gaze fixed on Elizabeth with an intensity that bordered on absurd. Darcy felt a flicker of satisfaction; the man was clearly smitten—not with the lady, no. He was not clever enough to truly love someone like Elizabeth Bennet.

But he was certainly in awe of his good fortune to claim a connection to her. Infatuated with the idea of a pretty wife, and silly enough to imagine his affections being returned. It would require little effort to encourage him further in his attentions, ensuring Elizabeth's focus remained far from more dangerous quarters—namely, himself.

Perhaps he ought to feel guilty over toying with the man so. Had his first reaction upon hearing of Collins' interest in her not been indignation? Darcy was no fool, had seen it often enough—a brilliant young lady forced to surrender her light to the nearest man with a comfortable home. It was the way of things, and Elizabeth Bennet would likely fare no better than most ladies of similar circumstances. It was not his fault, and it was not his problem.

But still... it did not mean he liked seeing it, and even less did he like suggesting any merit in such a match.

Oh, but no matter. If a woman existed in Hertfordshire who was just stubborn enough to disgrace herself by refusing an eligible match, it was this lady. She was... probably in no danger from Collins. No, *Darcy* was the one in danger, from *her*, so he would use Collins as he saw fit for now.

When the final hymn concluded, Darcy rose along with the congregation, taking his time to make his way outside. The churchyard, now alive with chatter, offered the perfect opportunity to press his strategy further. He approached Collins, who stood near Elizabeth, practically vibrating with the opportunity to linger in her company.

"Mr. Collins," Darcy said, drawing the man's attention, "a fine sermon this morning, would you not agree?"

"Oh, indeed, Mr. Darcy!" Collins exclaimed, bowing deeply. "The lessons on diligence and virtue were most edifying."

Darcy's gaze shifted briefly to Elizabeth, whose eyes met his for the barest moment before she dipped a curtsey and turned away to speak with Miss Lucas. "And yet," Darcy continued, "it seems that some virtues, such as liveliness and wit, were somewhat overlooked. I say, what true merit is there when other virtues are only displayed half-heartedly? Wouldn't you agree, Mr. Collins?"

Collins's face lit up. "Ah, yes, Miss Elizabeth is a shining example of such qualities. Her liveliness is a credit to her upbringing. Why, just the other day, she spoke with such energy on the subject of—"

Darcy held up a hand, cutting him off with a measured smile. "Miss Elizabeth's qualities are indeed remarkable. I imagine Lady Catherine herself would commend your discernment in recognizing them."

Collins beamed, his chest puffing out with pride. "You truly think so, sir?"

"I do. It takes a man of ambition to appreciate the value of a partner who could elevate all aspects of his life."

Collins's eyes widened as though the idea had only just occurred to him. "A partner of such caliber—yes, indeed! Lady Catherine would surely see the wisdom in such a match."

"I have no doubt," Darcy replied. "And as you are already well-placed to make your intentions known, I trust you will seize the opportunity."

Collins bowed again, his movements jerky with excitement. "Mr. Darcy, your advice is always most insightful. I shall not delay!"

Darcy inclined his head, stepping back as Collins turned toward Elizabeth with re-newed determination. Watching the interaction from a distance, Darcy allowed himself a small, satisfied smile. Collins, for all his absurdities, was a convenient distraction—one that might keep Elizabeth occupied and away from Wickham's charms.

For now, it was a strategy. And judging by Collins's eager demeanor, it was one already taking effect.

ELIZABETH STROLLED UP THE lane from the chapel with Charlotte, the murmur of parishioners fading behind them. Behind her, Lydia and Kitty's laughter carried as they lingered near the regiment's officers. It was no surprise when Mr. Wickham detached himself from the group and strolled toward Elizabeth.

"Miss Elizabeth, you appear to have appreciated today's sermon on virtues."

"Do I? Why, Mr. Wickham, you must have been watching me rather closely."

He chuckled. "I confess, I found myself glancing toward you for inspiration."

Elizabeth raised an eyebrow, her lips curving faintly. "Flattery so early in the day, Mr. Wickham? I had not expected you to be so bold."

"For such company, Miss Bennet, I can only be bold."

From the corner of her eye, Elizabeth saw that Darcy had paused mid-conversation with her cousin, his attention shifting sharply to Wickham. He did not approach, but his posture stiffened, his gaze darkening as it rested on the pair.

Perfect.

Elizabeth caught the glance and turned back to Wickham with deliberate cheer. "And yet, boldness is a quality that requires careful cultivation. Don't you agree, Mr. Wick-ham?"

Wickham grinned. "Careful cultivation, yes, but also a touch of daring. A balance I believe some find... invigorating."

"Action without foresight often leads to regret," came Darcy's voice, cool and clipped. He had stepped closer, his presence now impossible to ignore.

Elizabeth's head tilted slightly, her tone light but pointed. "An interesting observation, Mr. Darcy. Though I wonder if foresight sometimes lends itself to hesitation."

"Or wisdom," Darcy replied evenly, his gaze locked on hers.

Wickham's smile did not falter. "Wisdom is admirable, of course. But life demands moments of spontaneity, would you not say, Miss Elizabeth?"

"Indeed," Elizabeth said brightly. "Spontaneity can be most entertaining." She turned her smile toward Darcy, letting it linger. "Though I imagine Mr. Darcy prefers his life governed by careful deliberation."

"I do," Darcy said. "Spontaneity is not always synonymous with sound judgment."

"Ah, Mr. Darcy, ever the voice of prudence!" Collins interrupted, suddenly at Elizabeth's side. "Your wisdom reminds me of Lady Catherine's unparalleled advice on making decisions. She often says that careful reflection is the mark of true distinction."

Elizabeth's jaw tightened slightly. Oh, dash it all, why was *he* interrupting? This was going so nicely before he blundered in!

Collins placed a hand over his heart as he continued. "And Miss Elizabeth, too, has shown remarkable discernment in her company today. It is a testament to her excellent upbringing."

"Indeed," Darcy said, cocking an odd glance at Wickham, who grimaced faintly. "Miss Elizabeth has a way of drawing out... unique perspectives."

Elizabeth met his gaze, her eyes narrowing. "I find variety most enlightening, Mr. Darcy. Each encounter provides its own lessons."

Wickham chuckled. "A most gracious sentiment, Miss Bennet. Though I hope my lessons prove more agreeable than most."

"Some lessons are more valuable than others," Elizabeth replied curtly.

Collins beamed, clearly interpreting her words as praise for himself. "Miss Elizabeth, ever so perceptive! I am sure our discussions will continue to be enlightening for us both."

Darcy's lips twitched faintly, and Elizabeth could not decide if it was frustration or reluctant amusement. Either way, the flicker of emotion was enough to bolster her confidence.

As the church doors closed for the day, Elizabeth let the crowd drift forward, lingering for a moment by the low stone wall. She watched as Darcy sent a poisonous glance at Wickham one last time on his way to the Netherfield carriage. Their exchange was little more than a glance, but the way Darcy's lip fought against curling in disdain and the conscious flicker in Wickham's stride were enough.

Elizabeth smiled to herself. Whatever was between them, she cared not. Oh, indeed, she was curious, and she would learn the truth of it eventually, but for now, Wickham was proving an effective countermeasure, and she had every intention of wielding him wisely.

For now, the game was firmly in her hands.

DARCY STOOD BY THE window in Netherfield's drawing room, watching as faint streaks of gold broke through the overcast afternoon sky. Sunday services were behind them, and the house was uncharacteristically quiet—too quiet, in his opinion. The stillness seemed designed to amplify his restless thoughts, all of which seemed to circle back to Elizabeth Bennet.

He clenched his hands behind his back and made a deliberate effort to focus on the scene outside. The sight of rolling fields, wet with the day's drizzle, was a balm, if only a fleeting one. Her face—her wit, her pointed remarks—had lodged itself firmly in his mind, and no amount of rational effort could dislodge it.

The door opened, and Bingley strode in. "Darcy, I've been looking for you! How long have you been hiding here?"

"I was unaware that standing in a drawing room constituted hiding."

"It does when you're avoiding all company," Bingley replied cheerfully, settling into a chair near the fireplace. "Come now, man, it's Sunday. A perfect day for lively conversation and entertainment."

"I thought Sundays were for reflection."

Bingley grinned. "Reflection, conversation—they can be one and the same. Though I doubt Miss Bennet would agree, considering how often her younger sisters interrupt her."

Darcy tensed, though his expression betrayed nothing. "And what, pray, does Miss Bennet have to do with this conversation?"

"Nothing at all," Bingley said innocently. "Only that I spoke with her outside the church, and she said something to that effect when Miss Lydia kept trying to change the subject. Rather amusing, I thought."

"Amusing."

"That sounds rather like sarcasm, Darcy."

"Your point, Bingley?"

"My point?" Bingley feigned surprise. "Oh, I've no point at all. Just an observation. In fact, I saw you conversing most animatedly with Mr. Collins and Miss Elizabeth. Was that... a smile I saw on your face? Egad, Darcy, I had not known you were capable of it."

Darcy folded his arms. "I sense a jest."

Bingley laughed, leaning back in his chair. "Not at all! No, no, I daresay you were quite charming enough to satisfy the terms of our wager."

A spark of hope kindled in his chest. Perhaps Bingley was prepared to concede! "You are satisfied, then?"

Bingley swept an arm as he bent in a courtly bow. "Darcy, you are the very model of civility, even in the face of a very tempting woman and a somewhat vexing man."

"Did you expect otherwise?"

Bingley chuckled. "Indeed, I did. You proved me wrong, my friend. Though, it *was* only one encounter. If I may test your composure further—"

"I would prefer you did not."

"Too late," Bingley interrupted. "I've been giving thought to the mill."

Darcy's brow furrowed. "But the matter is settled. You are to sell it."

"We have 'settled' no such thing. I've decided to make the investment—expansion, repairs, perhaps even some new machinery. What do you think?"

"I think you are wasting your resources," Darcy said flatly. "You would be better off selling it."

Bingley chuckled. "Ah, there it is—the Darcy certainty. Tell me, is it not possible that I might succeed where others have not?"

"It is possible. But it is also unlikely."

"Unlikely, perhaps," Bingley said, his grin unshaken. "But I do enjoy a challenge. Much like you enjoy remaining polite in difficult company."

"I have no difficulties—"

"Excellent!" Bingley clapped his hands together. "Then I daresay another fortnight at most ought to satisfy the terms. Oh! Perhaps we shall conclude after the ball. Long enough for due reflection, I think, but not so long that either of us would find the waiting odious. What say you, Darcy?"

Darcy's teeth were nearly ground to powder, but he forced a trembling sort of grimace in place of a smile. "Very well, but not one day longer."

Fifteen

"Five shillings says the Netherfield Ball is held within the week," Lydia declared. She jingled her small purse triumphantly as Kitty nodded in fervent agreement.

"You are too optimistic," Mary replied without looking up from her book. "Such matters take time and planning if they are to be done with decorum. We've not even seen the invitations. Two weeks, at the very least."

Mrs. Bennet, who had been inspecting a length of ribbon for her bonnet, snapped her head up. "Nonsense, Mary! Why, Mr. Bingley has been hinting at it for a fortnight or more. Did you not hear him speak of bringing the neighborhood together when he visited last?"

Elizabeth exchanged a glance with Jane, who was carefully folding a piece of embroidery in her lap. "I seem to recall he said no such thing," Elizabeth said lightly. "Though I would not discourage Mama from placing her own wager. I am sure it would liven up the odds."

Mrs. Bennet turned a sharp look on her second eldest. "Do not tease, Lizzy. I have every confidence that the ball will be announced soon—and when it is, you must be ready to dance. And do be sure to save a set for Mr. Collins."

Elizabeth arched a brow. "I was not aware we were taking reservations."

"Oh, Lizzy!" Lydia interrupted with a loud laugh. "You will not need to save a dance for Mr. Collins. He is so slow, I am sure you could finish two sets before he even finds the floor."

"That is enough, Lydia," Jane said gently, though her lips twitched with amusement.

Lydia jangled her coin purse again. "I only said what you all were thinking. Will you place a wager, Lizzy? Surely you have an opinion on the timing of this grand affair. Perhaps you would like to bet on the number of dances Mr. Collins will attempt with you."

Elizabeth sighed. "If I were to bet, Lydia, I would wager that Mr. Collins will find a way to be intolerably verbose, regardless of the number of dances or the date of the ball."

Mr. Bennet, seated in the corner with a copy of *Don Quixote*, chuckled. "A safe wager, indeed. Perhaps he will find himself a Dulcinea at the ball, as well."

"Stuff and nonsense! He will dance with Lizzy," Mrs. Bennet sniffed. "Or Mary would do very well, I suppose. I'll not countenance any foreign tarts coming in and stealing his notice."

Foreign...? Elizabeth's mouth dropped open and her gaze drifted to her father, who only chuckled and turned his page without explaining who Dulcinea was. Not that it mattered—her mother had already shifted topics again.

"Of course, it will all depend on Mr. Bingley's timing," she said. "An honor to Jane, to be sure, for did he not wait until she was recovered to even speak of it? Mark my words, my dear, this ball will be your moment. He cannot wait forever to declare himself."

Jane's cheeks flushed a delicate pink. "Mama, please. It is not certain there will even be a ball."

"Not certain?" Mrs. Bennet exclaimed. "Oh, you are too modest, Jane! Why, everyone knows Mr. Bingley has been thinking of it. And once he proposes, think how grand it will be to be the mistress of Netherfield! So close to your family, too. I declare, Jane, there will be nothing like it. I always said you could not be so beautiful for nothing!"

Elizabeth bristled at her mother's words. Their mother made too much of Jane's beauty. None of the praise was undue, of course, but it always made Jane uncomfortable, to say nothing of how it made the rest of their sisters feel. And for once, she found she could not hold her tongue as she ought. "And what of my prospects, Mama?" she blurted. "Surely you have some grand prediction for me as well."

"Of course, I do," Mrs. Bennet said, waving a hand. "Mr. Collins is perfectly respectable, and he has already shown such marked attention to you."

"Respectable and marked attention," Elizabeth said wryly. "What more could a woman ask for?"

"Exactly! You must encourage him, Lizzy. It would be a fine match, indeed. And then—oh, just think! Once Jane is married to Mr. Bingley, and you are settled with Mr. Collins, we shall be the envy of all Meryton."

Elizabeth caught her father's eye. He had lowered his book just enough to peer over it with an arched brown and pursed lips. His eyes narrowed, but then he raised his book again and lost himself. Apparently, there was no help to be found there.

"Well, if you will excuse me," she said, rising, "I believe I shall take a walk. I feel the need for fresh air after all this planning."

"Oh, do not stay out too long, Lizzy," Mrs. Bennet called after her. "You will want to look your best when Miss Bingley calls with the invitations for the ball!"

Elizabeth marched to the door, her pace brisk as she escaped the din of the sitting room. Outside, the late afternoon air was crisp, carrying the faint scent of damp earth and falling leaves. She breathed deeply, letting the quiet of the garden soothe her frayed nerves.

A ball at Netherfield. It was a certainty, she supposed, but the thought of enduring Mr. Collins's attentions under the watchful eyes of the neighborhood made her stomach churn. And then there was Mr. Darcy—his inscrutable expressions, his maddening composure. If a ball did come to pass, she resolved to face it as she did all challenges: with wit and determination.

The rest, she thought with a faint smile, would be left to chance.

"I still say it is foolhardy," Caroline said, pacing in front of the fireplace. "The last gathering we hosted brought nothing but chaos."

"It brought good company," Bingley replied, glancing up from the desk where he was carefully drafting the guest list.

"Good company?" Caroline turned sharply. "If you mean the Bennets, then I despair of your judgment entirely."

Bingley set his pen down and leaned back. "Do not despair, Caroline. The ball will happen, whether or not you approve. The neighborhood expects it."

"They wager on it, you mean," Caroline snapped. "I have heard the rumors. The butcher's wife insists it will be next Tuesday, while the dressmaker has pinned her hopes on Thursday. And we are to reward such absurdity?"

Bingley laughed. "Why not? It's harmless fun."

"Harmless!" Caroline threw up her hands. "You are inviting crassness and presumption into this house, Charles. Mark my words, it will end in disaster."

Darcy shifted in his chair. "She is not entirely wrong."

Bingley turned to him. "Oh, not you too. I had hoped for support."

Darcy closed the book he had been skimming. "I do not object to the ball itself, but you must be prepared for what follows. It will spark speculation."

"It already has," Bingley said. "Everyone in the village talks of nothing else. If anything, announcing it will put an end to their guessing."

Caroline folded her arms. "And what of the guests? You cannot seriously expect me to endure another evening of these simple country misses fairly seducing drunken officers in my drawing room."

"You endured it before," Bingley said, his tone growing sharper. "And I recall no complaints then."

Caroline's lips thinned. "A dinner party is nothing to a ball for drunken revelry. I shall not countenance it, Charles! I had hoped the novelty would wear off for you by now."

Bingley sighed. "Caroline, I will not hear another word on the subject. The ball is my decision. I will see to the arrangements myself if I must."

She stopped pacing, her posture stiff with indignation. "Do as you please. But do not expect me to salvage the evening when it inevitably falls to pieces."

Bingley waved her off with a grin. "I would not dream of burdening you."

Caroline swept from the room, her skirts rustling loudly in her wake. When the door clicked shut behind her, Bingley turned to Darcy.

"You do not agree with her, do you?"

Darcy hesitated. "Her concerns are not without merit."

"Concerns," Bingley said, shaking his head. "All this fuss over a harmless evening. The neighborhood will enjoy it, and I will enjoy seeing them do so. Must everything be weighed so heavily?"

Darcy rose, walking to the desk. "You do not see the weight because you are not its bearer. Speculation can lead to expectations."

Bingley arched a brow. "You speak of Miss Bennet."

Darcy's silence was answer enough.

Bingley leaned forward, resting his elbows on the desk. "I do not wish to hurt her, Darcy. Surely you see that."

"I do," Darcy said. "And that is why you must tread carefully."

"Carefully," Bingley repeated with a small laugh. "Carefully is not the word the neighborhood would use to describe me, I think. They wager on everything I do."

"They wager on everything everyone does."

Bingley smiled faintly. "Even you, I imagine."

Darcy said nothing, his gaze fixed on the guest list. One name in particular stood out—Elizabeth Bennet. Of course, she would attend. And this ball was to be his final test of civility—endure an evening of her smiles, her enchantments, or die trying.

"One week," Bingley said, picking up his pen again. "The invitations will go out tomorrow. Prepare yourself, Darcy. It will be a splendid evening."

ELIZABETH ADJUSTED HER BONNET and shifted the weight of her basket, filled to the brim with her mother's endless list of "essentials." She caught sight of Charlotte Lucas near the apothecary and waved. "Charlotte!"

Charlotte waited for a carriage to pass before crossing the street. "Good afternoon, Lizzy. On an errand from your mother, I see?"

Elizabeth hefted the basket a little. "Yes, well, Lydia was 'supposed' to be helping me, but she has gone off Heaven knows where. I am sure she is questioning everyone she finds about the rumors of a ball at Netherfield."

"Ah, well, to that I say the answer depends entirely on who you believe. Mrs. Long insists invitations will be issued tomorrow, but Mr. Goulding swears it will not be for another fortnight."

Elizabeth laughed. "I think it is all rather absurd."

Charlotte glanced toward the street, shielding her eyes from the sun as a figure approached from the direction of the inn. "Is that... Mr. Wickham?"

Elizabeth's gaze followed hers. The man's easy gait and familiar features confirmed it before he came within earshot. She folded her arms loosely, a faint smile tugging at her lips. "Indeed, it is. My favorite toy."

Charlotte's eyes widened. "Oh? Do tell, Lizzy."

But Elizabeth crossed one arm over her chest and offered only a smug grin. "I shall not give up my secrets that easily, you know. I still have a wager to win."

Charlotte pursed her lips. "I think you may be cheating, Lizzy."

"Perhaps."

By the time Wickham reached them, he was already smiling. "Miss Elizabeth, Miss Lucas. I could not have hoped for a more agreeable encounter this afternoon. I was looking for a bit of amusement, and I am sure I can count on both of you to see me right. Tell me, what has you both smiling today?"

Charlotte chuckled. "Any number of things, Mr. Wickham, but I imagine wagers over a prospective ball would be the most promising sort of entertainment."

"Ah, yes! At Netherfield, correct? Even among the officers, speculation abounds. I daresay half of Meryton has already made it a sport."

Elizabeth's brow arched. "And what is your stake in it, Mr. Wickham?"

"I've refrained thus far," he replied, flashing a grin. "Though if wagering were the custom of every gentleman, I suppose I might be tempted."

"Better to refrain," Elizabeth said. "You may find yourself out of pocket by the end of the month, if this town's enthusiasm is anything to judge by."

Wickham laughed. "A fair warning, Miss Bennet. But perhaps I will place a wager after all—on something more certain than the date of a ball."

Charlotte's eyes flicked between the two of them before she took a step back. "I must beg your pardon, but I have an errand to finish. Do excuse me."

Elizabeth shot her a quick look, but Charlotte was already retreating into the nearest shop, leaving her alone on the street with Wickham. He turned his full attention on her, his expression one of amused interest. "Well! Your friend is rather abrupt today."

"You might call it abrupt. I would use the word 'purposeful'."

Wickham grinned. "A lady after my own heart. Well, then, I shall waste no time in placing my wager."

Elizabeth shifted her basket. "By all means, let there be no suspense. Are you betting on the number of dances, or the length of the guest list? Perhaps the main course, or the size or the number of musicians?"

He leaned closer. "I had rather thought of something much more amusing. I wager, Miss Elizabeth, that I will be able to solicit your hand for more than one dance."

"Oh, now, that is hardly sporting! Why, you have only to ask me, and as I have the power of refusal or acceptance, the wager stands on the pleasure of an interested party. Now, say, should we make the stakes rather interesting… say, perhaps, five shillings? Why, then, you see, I would be in the enviable position of being able to simply refuse your hand for a second set, thus winning the bet."

"Yes," he replied, his brow furrowing. "That is a bother. Well, may I propose a counter wager?"

Her smile deepened. "And what might that be?"

"Well, I can hardly expect you to grant me two dances if your evening is full, can I?"

"Oh! So, you would place bets on a lady's unpopularity? Rather ungallant, would you not say?"

"Far be it from me to imply anything of the kind. Perhaps I will wager that... ah, I have it! I wager that Darcy will beg a set of you."

Elizabeth's brows shot up. "Mr. Darcy? The man who scarcely notices my existence but to disapprove of it?"

Wickham laughed. "The very one. And if he does ask, Miss Elizabeth, you shall have the pleasure of refusing him and saying that you had promised that set to me."

She puckered her lips in thought. "Interesting, Mr. Wickham. And what happens if you are already engaged with another lady by the time Mr. Darcy asks... assuming he does? Is the wager forfeit?"

"Well," he chuckled, "I suppose I leave such terms to you to sort, Miss Elizabeth. Ah! And speak of the very devil himself."

Elizabeth turned to see Mr. Darcy approaching from around the corner, his gaze flicking briefly to her before settling on Wickham. His features remained impassive, giving little indication of his thoughts.

"Mr. Darcy," Wickham greeted, his earlier ease noticeably absent. "I did not expect to encounter you today."

Darcy gave a brief nod in response but did not speak. The pause that followed felt deliberate, drawing attention to everything unspoken between them.

Elizabeth tilted her head slightly, her tone unnaturally light as she broke the pause. "Mr. Wickham and I were just discussing the likelihood of a ball at Netherfield. You might know better than anyone. Are we to expect the pleasure of such an event soon?"

"I am afraid it is not my place to speak on the matter, Miss Elizabeth," was his clipped reply.

"Then perhaps you may at least be able to tell me if the town is wasting their time in speculation. It is all the talk, you see."

Darcy's eyes met hers, guarded. "I expect your curiosity will be satisfied soon enough."

"There, that is as good as an announcement," Elizabeth decided. "Everyone will be terribly pleased, sir."

Wickham's smile sharpened. "I trust you will attend, Mr. Darcy. Surely, no event would be complete without you."

Darcy's lips thinned. "I was unaware my presence held such significance."

"Oh, but it does. You always draw interest, whether you seek it or not."

Darcy's gaze flicked briefly back to Elizabeth. "As it happens, I do not. Good day, Miss Bennet. Mr. Wickham." With a curt nod, he turned and walked away, his strides brisk and deliberate.

Wickham watched him go, his grin returning. "It seems I struck a nerve."

Elizabeth gave him a sideways glance. "You seem adept at that."

He laughed, but Elizabeth's gaze remained on Darcy's retreating figure. His sudden departure did not unsettle her—it intrigued her. Whatever tension existed between the two men clearly worked in her favor, and she intended to make the most of it.

"An invitation from Netherfield!" Mrs. Bennet's voice echoed through the house, louder than the bells at St. Mary's on a Sunday morning.

Elizabeth glanced up from her book as Lydia darted into the drawing room, waving a cream-colored envelope triumphantly. "It's here, it's here!" Lydia sang, spinning on her heel. Kitty trailed behind her, nearly tripping over her own excitement.

Jane looked up from her embroidery, her cheeks pinking slightly. "Is it truly—?"

"Indeed!" Mrs. Bennet swept into the room with all the grandeur of a queen bearing news of a royal decree. "A ball! At Netherfield! Oh, Jane, my dear, this is your moment! Mr. Bingley shall have no choice but to propose after such a splendid evening."

Elizabeth set her book aside, unable to suppress a smile. "And what role, precisely, does a ball play in securing a proposal?"

Mrs. Bennet waved her hand dismissively. "Oh, Lizzy, you are far too cynical. A ball is the very height of romance. Why, your father and I first danced together at a ball. And look at us now."

Elizabeth's brows lifted. "Indeed, Mama. What a glowing endorsement."

"Do not tease your mother," Mr. Bennet said from behind his newspaper. "It is unkind to mock those who cling to their dreams."

Mrs. Bennet ignored him entirely. "Jane, my dear, we must ensure you have a gown that leaves no doubt as to your charms. Perhaps something with ribbons. Or lace. And pink—it *must* be pink!"

"Something sensible will suffice, Mama," Jane said gently, though her blush deepened.

"Sensible! Jane, you cannot be sensible at a ball. It is entirely the wrong idea."

Lydia plopped down beside Elizabeth, still clutching the envelope. "I wonder how many dances I shall have. Ten, at least. Maybe twelve."

"Surely you will leave some for the other guests," Elizabeth said.

Kitty huffed. "Only if they ask quickly enough. Lydia always steals the best partners."

"And I'll bet Mr. Wickham asks me first," Lydia said, tilting her chin up triumphantly. "He said he loves dancing."

Elizabeth raised a brow. "How fortunate for you."

"Lizzy," Mrs. Bennet called, her tone suddenly sharp. "Do not think you can sit in the corner making clever remarks all evening. You must dance as well."

"Do I usually abstain?"

"No, but I would not put it beyond you to vex me on *this* night, of all nights! And I am sure Mr. Collins will be most attentive to you. He will no doubt insist upon at least two sets."

Elizabeth's faint smile hardened. "How reassuring."

"Now, Jane," Mrs. Bennet said, returning her focus to her eldest daughter, "we must make the best use of this time. There are gowns to be chosen, accessories to be polished, and—oh, the hair! We must call Mrs. Hill at once. Yes, she must see if she can get an extra maid from the village to help you all dress."

"Perhaps we might let Jane breathe first," Elizabeth suggested.

Mrs. Bennet glared at her, but Jane intervened with a soothing smile. "Lizzy is right, Mama. There is still plenty of time before the ball."

"Time enough to make every possible preparation!" Mrs. Bennet declared. "Oh, Jane, my dear, you will be the fairest star of the evening. And after Mr. Bingley proposes, we shall have such celebrations!"

Elizabeth exchanged a glance with Jane, who looked both flattered and overwhelmed. Rising from her chair, Elizabeth moved to her sister's side, resting a reassuring hand on her arm. "Do not let Mama's enthusiasm frighten you. A ball is just a gathering, nothing more."

"A gathering where every eye will be on us," Jane murmured. "And every ear will be listening."

Elizabeth squeezed her arm. "Let them. You will dazzle them all."

"Will you not dazzle them too, Lizzy?" Lydia teased, spinning across the room.

"Only if they appreciate sharp tongues and scathing remarks," Elizabeth replied.

"I daresay Mr. Darcy might," Kitty muttered.

Elizabeth's head whipped toward her sister. "What nonsense is that?"

Kitty shrugged. "Only that he looks at you often enough to suggest he finds something interesting."

"Perhaps he is wondering whether I have horns hidden under my hair," Elizabeth said.

"Or perhaps," Jane said, leaning close to Elizabeth's ear, "you are nearer to winning that wager with Charlotte than you think."

Sixteen

Elizabeth slowed her pace as the path curved toward Oakham Mount, the breeze tugging lightly at her bonnet strings. It was the kind of afternoon that invited contemplation, the horizon stretching wide and pale beneath a sky heavy with winter light. She had come here seeking quiet, a reprieve from the crowded chaos of Longbourn. The air was crisp, the ground firm beneath her feet, and for a time, she allowed herself the luxury of wandering without aim.

As she paused near a weathered outcrop to take in the view, the distant sound of hooves reached her ears. She turned, half-expecting to see a farmer tending his fields below, but instead, a rider crested the rise. The dark figure on horseback moved with an easy grace, and recognition came swiftly.

Mr. Darcy.

He dismounted a short distance away, tying his horse to a low branch with practiced efficiency. He seemed unaware of her presence at first, his attention fixed on the path ahead. Elizabeth considered retreating quietly down the hill before he noticed her—an option that grew increasingly appealing as he straightened and turned in her direction.

Too late.

"Miss Bennet." He inclined his head, his tone neither surprised nor overly familiar.

"Mr. Darcy," she replied, keeping her expression as neutral as his. There was no easy excuse to slip away now, not without appearing deliberately rude, and so she remained where she was, watching as he approached.

Darcy halted a few paces from her, his gaze sweeping briefly over the landscape before returning to her with measured politeness. "I was told the view from Oakham Mount was worth the ride. It seems the recommendation was not misplaced."

Elizabeth tilted her head, studying him. "It is quite the popular spot. I had not expected to meet anyone here, however."

"Nor I," he admitted. "But it is a pleasant surprise."

Pleasant, was it? Elizabeth permitted herself the ghost of a smile. Perhaps she was on her way to winning this wager, after all. For a moment, they stood in silence, the wind threading through the grass around them. There was a tension in his bearing—calm on the surface, but tightly controlled beneath. He did not seem entirely at ease, as though something weighed upon him that he was unwilling to share.

She stole a glance at him. His brow was faintly furrowed, his focus turned inward. Whatever occupied his mind, it was not something he meant to divulge easily. Elizabeth knew enough of Mr. Darcy to expect reticence, yet she could not help but wonder what had brought him here, alone.

"You are enjoying the morning air, I see," she said at last.

Darcy's gaze flicked briefly toward her before returning to the path ahead. "Yes. The countryside is particularly pleasant in the early hours."

Elizabeth smiled faintly. "I find it refreshing, though I suppose it lacks the grandeur of Pemberley. Or so I have heard from Miss Bingley and Mr. Collins."

A muscle in his jaw twitched slightly, but his tone remained even. "Grandeur is not always what one requires."

"Oh? And what does one require, in your estimation?"

He hesitated, as though weighing whether to answer. "Tranquility."

Elizabeth tilted her head, studying him curiously. "You do not strike me as a man easily disturbed, Mr. Darcy."

"Appearances can be deceptive."

The admission, though simple, caught her off guard. She had not expected him to engage so directly, and it stirred a flicker of curiosity she couldn't quite ignore.

"Is it the company here in Hertfordshire that disturbs you, or something else?"

Darcy's lips pressed into a thin line. "I did not say I was disturbed."

"No," she agreed, her eyes gleaming with mischief, "but you implied it rather strongly."

He glanced at her then, something flickering in his expression—wry amusement, perhaps, or grudging respect. "You are quite determined to draw conclusions, Miss Bennet."

"Only when you leave me such tempting gaps to fill."

Another pause followed, but this time it felt less strained. Darcy's posture relaxed slightly, though his guarded demeanor remained intact.

"It is my sister," he said at last, the admission emerging slowly, as though each word required deliberate effort. "She is... still very unhappy."

Elizabeth flicked her gaze back to his face. "I am sorry to hear it. Has something changed since we last spoke of her?"

"She remains in Lincolnshire with acquaintances. They are well-meaning, good people. But I have come to believe they are ill-suited to her temperament." His voice was steady, almost careless, but Elizabeth detected a hint of something beneath it—concern, perhaps, or frustration.

She tilted her head thoughtfully. "Then why not bring her here? To Netherfield, I mean. Surely she would find the company more agreeable."

Darcy's reaction was swift, his eyes narrowing ever so slightly before he quickly masked whatever had unsettled him. "That would not be possible."

Elizabeth arched a brow, intrigued by his sudden defensiveness. "Not possible, or not preferable?"

He hesitated, clearly weighing how much to reveal. "It is simply not an option."

"Then perhaps you might return to London yourself and bring her to stay with you there. Or if that is also impractical, could you not take her back to Pemberley?"

Darcy regarded her with an odd expression, as though her suggestion were both unexpected and strangely disconcerting. "You would encourage me to leave Hertfordshire?"

She shrugged, a teasing glint in her eyes. "Why not? It is not as though anyone here expected you to stay. Besides, the people of Meryton are hardly inclined to miss a poet."

A flicker of conscious embarrassment crossed his face at the mention of poetry, and Elizabeth's lips curved into a mischievous smile. "What, Mr. Darcy? Have you so soon forgot your newfound literary talents?"

Darcy's mouth tightened, though whether from amusement or irritation, she could not tell. "I see you continue to enjoy your sport at my expense."

"And you continue to provide ample material. Perhaps it is you who should be blamed for your predicament."

They stood there for a moment, the view stretching out before them, but Elizabeth's focus remained on Darcy. He appeared pensive, as though weighing her words with greater care than she had intended.

At last, he straightened, his composure firmly in place. "Thank you for your suggestions, Miss Bennet. They have... given me something to consider."

She inclined her head. "I do hope you find a solution that brings her some measure of happiness."

Darcy nodded, his expression unreadable once more. "Good day, Miss Bennet."

"Good day, Mr. Darcy."

As he turned to leave, Elizabeth watched him for a moment, her thoughts swirling with the oddness of the encounter. He was still as frustratingly reserved as ever, yet beneath that impenetrable exterior, there was something more—something she could not yet name but found herself wanting to understand.

Elizabeth Bennet had... surprised him.

He had gone to Oakham Mount that morning seeking solitude, only to find her already there. It should have been an inconvenience, another moment of forced politeness in a town where civility was more exhausting than the expectations of London society. And yet, somehow, it had not felt like that at all.

Her suggestion had caught him off guard. She had not pleaded for his company, had not hinted at wanting him to remain longer in Hertfordshire—far from it. She had coolly suggested he might leave, even teased him about being missed by no one. He frowned slightly, remembering her parting words: "Poets may not be appreciated here, Mr. Darcy, but perhaps your sister would fare better with you elsewhere."

It was unexpected. He had assumed, like so many others, that she might be angling to keep him near, driven by the same mercenary motives he had grown so accustomed to guarding against. And yet she had practically encouraged him to go, as though his presence were inconsequential to her.

Darcy leaned back in his chair, fingers steepled beneath his chin. He found himself reconsidering everything he had assumed about her. It was disconcerting—irritating, even—that she continued to evade every expectation he set.

Elizabeth Bennet was a woman of contradictions. Her cleverness was undeniable, her conversation lively and engaging enough that she *could* lay any snare she liked, and yet there was no apparent calculation in her manner. If she sought to trap him in the web of marriage—like so many before her—she was going about it in the strangest way possible. In fact, she seemed intent on doing the opposite, treating him with a degree of irreverence that was both infuriating and oddly... refreshing.

His lips tightened as he picked up the pen again. Georgiana's unhappiness gnawed at him, but for the first time, he allowed himself to consider Elizabeth's suggestion. It had been flippant, no doubt meant in jest, but perhaps there was wisdom in it. Georgiana had always fared better in familiar company—among those who truly cared for her, rather than those who viewed her merely as an heiress to be entertained.

He stared down at the unfinished letter. Break off his stay in Hertfordshire and return to Pemberley? It was a tempting thought, though complicated by timing. He could hardly leave Hertfordshire now without raising questions. Besides, Bingley would never let him hear the end of it if he disappeared just before the ball.

And yet the idea lingered.

Darcy frowned again. This was precisely why he had been avoiding her. Elizabeth Bennet was a distraction—a maddening, unpredictable distraction—and if he was not careful, she would upend more than just his carefully laid plans.

With a resolute sigh, he dipped the pen into ink and began to write, determined to focus on Georgiana rather than the woman who, despite his better judgment, had taken up far too much space in his mind.

My Dearest Georgiana,

I hope this letter finds you well. I have given further thought to your concerns...

But even as the ink flowed, his thoughts betrayed him, circling back to Elizabeth Bennet—irrepressible, intriguing, impossible to ignore.

ELIZABETH STOOD AT THE window, her fingers tapping idly on the wooden sill as she stared out over the fields. She was not certain why the conversation with Mr. Darcy continued to occupy her mind, but it did. She turned away, crossing the room once more, her restless energy finding no outlet. His manner had shifted—subtly, yes—but it had been enough to catch her attention. Concern for his sister had softened some of his reserve, though he had hardly invited her sympathy.

She paused mid-step, her brow furrowing. Why did it matter? Whatever turmoil troubled him, it was none of her concern. Yet here she was, pacing the length of the parlor as if searching for a resolution to a puzzle she had not intended to solve. With an exasperated sigh, she seated herself in the nearest chair, the distant murmur of voices from another room offering little distraction.

Elizabeth was not accustomed to feeling unsettled, and Mr. Darcy's guarded glimpse of vulnerability had done precisely that.

The creak of the door pulled her from her thoughts. Charlotte Lucas stepped inside, a basket in hand. "Elizabeth! I hoped I might find you here. Your mother mentioned you had returned from your walk."

"Charlotte!" Elizabeth hurried forward to greet her. "I was in desperate need of sensible company. Please, sit."

Charlotte smiled and set the basket down, taking the offered seat. "I cannot stay long. My mother is expecting me shortly, but I wanted to deliver this before I forgot." She opened the basket to reveal a small bundle wrapped in linen. "Mama insisted we send along some of her preserves. She claims you were admiring them last week."

Elizabeth chuckled, grateful for the distraction. "Your mother's preserves are the envy of the neighborhood. Thank her for me."

Charlotte studied her friend for a moment, her expression thoughtful. "You seem... preoccupied. I hope the morning's walk was pleasant?"

Elizabeth hesitated, unsure how much to share. "It was... enlightening, in an unexpected way."

"Enlightening?" Charlotte's brow lifted in curiosity. "Dare I hope it involved something—or some*one*—of interest?"

"Perhaps," Elizabeth said with a mischievous smile. "I encountered Mr. Darcy on the path."

Charlotte blinked. "Mr. Darcy? And did he speak, or merely glare at you in his usual fashion?"

"Oh, he spoke," Elizabeth said lightly, though her tone did not quite match the unease lingering in her mind. "In fact, he surprised me. He spoke of his sister."

"His sister?" Charlotte leaned forward, intrigued. "That is a rare topic indeed. I do not believe I have ever heard him mention her before."

"Nor had I," Elizabeth admitted. "He seemed... conflicted. Apparently, she is unhappy in her current situation, though he did not elaborate much beyond that. I told him he ought to collect her from Lincolnshire, where he has sent her, and take her back to London himself. It was as if it was the first time the notion had ever occurred to him!"

Charlotte considered this, her hands clasping neatly in her lap. "How very strange! I had always thought Mr. Darcy indifferent to the troubles of others, but perhaps I was mistaken."

Elizabeth frowned slightly. "I would not go so far as to say he is indifferent. Reserved, certainly. Guarded. But there was something genuine in his concern for his sister. It was... disarming."

"Disarming?" Charlotte echoed, a knowing gleam in her eye. "Elizabeth Bennet, I do believe you are beginning to see Mr. Darcy in a different light."

Elizabeth scoffed, though it lacked real conviction. "Do not read too much into it, Charlotte. He is still insufferable most of the time."

"Most of the time," Charlotte repeated, smiling faintly. "But not *all* of the time, it seems."

Elizabeth waved a hand dismissively, though the gesture lacked its usual vigor. "Enough of Mr. Darcy. I shall not waste my breath defending a man who barely speaks enough to defend himself."

But Charlotte was not so easily deterred. "Enough of Mr. Darcy, indeed." She paused, then added, "Except you have just given him advice that, should he follow it, will take him far from Hertfordshire—far from you."

Elizabeth blinked, taken aback by Charlotte's pointed observation. "I did no such thing," she protested. "I merely suggested that he do what is best for his sister."

"And what if what is best for his sister means he leaves immediately?" Charlotte leaned forward slightly, her voice calm but firm. "If Mr. Darcy departs, you may as well concede the wager now. After all, you cannot win over a man who is no longer in the vicinity."

Elizabeth opened her mouth to respond, then closed it again, realization dawning slowly. Her own words came back to haunt her—encouraging him to go, shrugging off his presence as though it mattered not whether he stayed. Had she truly been so foolish?

"I did not think of that," Elizabeth admitted at last, her tone quieter, more thoughtful.

"I can see that." Charlotte tilted her head, studying her friend with a mixture of amusement and concern. "It seems to me that you are playing a rather dangerous game without even realizing it. First, you spend days, weeks, even, sparring with him, and now you all but invite him to leave. Are you trying to win this wager, or have you grown tired of the contest?"

Elizabeth frowned. "I have not grown tired of anything. I simply…" She trailed off, uncertain how to finish the sentence. The truth was, she had not considered the implications of her advice to Darcy—only that it had felt right in the moment.

Charlotte raised an eyebrow. "Well, I suppose if you wish to see him go, that is your choice. Though I must say, it would be a rather dull outcome. You were just beginning to enjoy the challenge, were you not?"

Elizabeth shot her a sharp look. "Enjoy is not the word I would use."

"No? Then what word would you use?"

Elizabeth hesitated, torn between brushing off the question with humor or admitting to something more. "Very well," she said at last. "It has been… engaging."

"Engaging," Charlotte echoed, her smile deepening. "I see. And would it be so terrible to admit that perhaps you do not wish for him to leave after all?"

Elizabeth straightened in her seat, her chin lifting slightly. "Whether he stays or goes is entirely his decision. I only suggested what might be best for his sister."

"But not necessarily what might be best for you," Charlotte pointed out gently.

Elizabeth fell silent, considering her friend's words. It was a strange thought—that she had, perhaps unwittingly, influenced Mr. Darcy in a way that could affect her own standing in the wager. Worse still was the realization that she wasn't entirely sure she wanted him to leave.

"I did not expect him to take me seriously," Elizabeth said finally, as though voicing the thought aloud might make it less absurd.

Charlotte chuckled softly. "Elizabeth, if there is one thing I have learned about Mr. Darcy in the past few weeks, it is that he takes *everything* seriously—including, it seems, you."

Elizabeth's lips tightened, but she could not deny the truth in Charlotte's observation. Darcy had, for all his flaws, listened to her—really listened. And in doing so, he might cost her something she held rather dear.

"Well," Elizabeth said briskly, rising from her seat with an air of determination, "if he does leave, I shall simply find another way to win the wager."

Charlotte smiled knowingly. "Of course. Though perhaps next time, you might think twice before offering advice that could send your object running."

SEVENTEEN

DARCY SWUNG DOWN FROM his horse outside Meryton's post office, handing the reins to a waiting boy with a brief nod. The bustle of the small village carried on around him—hawkers calling out their wares, carts rumbling over uneven stones—but Darcy paid them little mind. He reached into his coat for the letter he had penned that morning, intent on posting it himself. A trivial errand, perhaps, but it provided an excuse to clear his head.

He had barely stepped onto the path when an all-too-familiar voice greeted him with effusive cheer.

"Ah, Mr. Darcy! What an honor it is to cross paths with you on such a fortuitous morning!"

Darcy paused, turning just in time to see Mr. Collins bustling toward him, a grin plastered across his face and his hat clutched in both hands as if in reverence.

"Mr. Collins," Darcy acknowledged. "A surprise."

"A most delightful one, sir!" Collins beamed. "And might I say, your presence graces our humble village. I see you have a letter. May I presume, sir, that you are engaged in correspondence with some fair maiden?"

Darcy's expression remained impassive, though he immediately understood Collins's insinuation. Collins, ever eager to curry favor, would assume the maiden in question was none other than Miss de Bourgh, in line with Lady Catherine's long-standing hopes. But he was not entirely wrong, and... perhaps it would serve Darcy's interests to let the man have his assumptions.

"I was writing to a lady, yes," Darcy said. "It is a matter of some importance."

Collins practically quivered with approval. "Ah! A lady of great distinction, no doubt! Lady Catherine, of course, will be most gratified by this news. I dare say, sir, that your thoughtfulness toward the fairer sex is an example to us all."

Darcy resisted the urge to roll his eyes. "I am sure the lady will be pleased to hear from me."

Collins leaned in conspiratorially, his voice dropping to a stage whisper. "And may I ask, Mr. Darcy, whether you included some of your celebrated poetry? A lady of such refined sensibilities would surely be moved by a well-crafted verse."

Darcy's jaw tightened imperceptibly. So Elizabeth had told her cousin about the incident at Netherfield. He could imagine her recounting it with that mischievous glint in her eye, turning his humiliation into an amusing anecdote. The thought irritated him more than it should have.

"I did not," he said curtly. "The letter's purpose was of a more practical nature."

Collins nodded eagerly, undeterred by Darcy's cool tone. "Of course, of course! Practicality is, after all, the cornerstone of any sensible engagement. But a dash of sentiment never goes amiss, eh?"

Darcy fixed Collins with a steady gaze, his patience wearing thin. "I am sure the lady will appreciate my efforts. Perhaps she will even elaborate her approval when I see her in person."

"Indeed, sir!" Collins said, beaming. "And might I add, what a fine idea it would be for you to visit in some haste! A gentleman's presence always carries more weight than mere words on paper."

Darcy gave a slight nod. "I am considering it."

Collins nearly bounced on his heels in excitement. "Splendid! I must say, Lady Catherine would no doubt applaud your decisiveness. She has often remarked upon your excellent judgment in such matters."

"Quite," Darcy said briskly. "Now, if you will excuse me, I have other business to attend to."

"Of course, of course!" Collins said, stepping aside with an exaggerated bow. "A pleasure, sir, as always. Do give my regards to Lady Catherine when next you see her. If I am not mistaken, you may precede me. It may be that our individual hopes might even be answered within the same week!"

Darcy merely inclined his head and walked into the office. As he rode back toward Netherfield some minutes later, he allowed himself a moment of reflection. Collins's absurd insinuations about Anne de Bourgh were of little consequence, but Elizabeth's role in spreading word of his ill-fated poem lingered uncomfortably in his mind.

If she thought to unsettle him, she was succeeding all too well. But two could play at that game.

ELIZABETH SIDESTEPPED A PUDDLE as she and Jane made their way through the bustling streets of Meryton. Lydia flitted ahead, stopping at intervals to peer into shop windows or flirt with passing officers. The air was filled with the hum of chatter, louder and more excitable than usual.

"It seems all of Meryton has turned out today," Jane remarked, glancing at the growing clusters of townsfolk gathered in animated conversation.

"Indeed," Elizabeth said dryly, "and I suspect it has less to do with fine weather and more to do with fine gossip."

As they passed the baker's shop, the unmistakable voice of Mrs. Long reached Elizabeth's ears. "Oh yes, yes! Mr. Darcy will be leaving before the ball, mark my words. Mr. Collins said it was on the best authority."

Elizabeth stopped mid-step. "Mr. Collins? On the best authority? That hardly bodes well."

Jane hesitated, her expression uncertain. "Do you think it could be true?"

"I think," Elizabeth said with a grimace, "that if Mr. Collins were the sole authority on the rain holding off, one would do well to carry a parasol even in a drought."

Before Jane could respond, Mrs. Philips emerged from a nearby haberdashery, clutching a parcel of fabric in one hand and a feathered hat in the other. She leaned toward Mrs. Long, her eyes gleaming with the thrill of fresh gossip. "An engagement, you say? To Lady Catherine's daughter?"

"Oh yes," Mrs. Long whispered. "Mr. Collins claims it is practically settled."

Lydia, who had been inspecting bonnets with Kitty, spun around and dashed toward the knot of gossipers. "An engagement for Mr. Darcy? How positively dull! I thought he was far too proud to marry anyone at all."

"Lydia!" Jane whispered, scandalized.

"Oh, do not be such a bore, Jane," Lydia said with a wave of her hand. "This is far more interesting than lace trimmings. Besides, if he does leave, that means we can place bets on when he goes. I daresay he stays through the ball—I should wager two shillings on it!"

Elizabeth groaned quietly. Before she could drag her sister away, a familiar voice sounded from behind.

"Do you see what I mean?" Charlotte Lucas fell into step beside Elizabeth, her eyes alight with amusement. "The entire town is in an uproar."

"And all over something ridiculous," Elizabeth muttered. "Does anyone truly believe that Mr. Darcy intends to marry Miss de Bourgh?"

Charlotte tilted her head. "You know as well as I do that belief in Meryton requires far less evidence than it ought."

Elizabeth sighed. "You sound like you find this amusing."

"I do," Charlotte said, her voice calm but pointed. "But you should not. If Mr. Darcy leaves before the ball, I believe you forfeit your wager."

Elizabeth stopped walking. "Surely you cannot mean that. This is idle speculation at best."

Charlotte gave her a knowing look. "Idle speculation or not, if he is gone before the ball, it matters little. He will have left, and you will have lost."

Elizabeth opened her mouth to argue, but found no suitable retort. Charlotte pressed on, her tone softening. "Lizzy, I know you never truly cared for gaining his affections—no matter how little you like the idea of losing the wager—but do not pretend his departure would mean nothing to you. You dislike the idea more than you are willing to admit."

Elizabeth crossed her arms, feeling a prick of irritation—not with Charlotte, but with herself. She had practically handed Mr. Darcy the suggestion to leave when they last spoke. And now, absurd though it was, the notion that he might actually take her advice left an unexpected tightness in her chest.

"You think too much of it," she said, resuming her pace with renewed briskness. "The entire thing is preposterous."

"Perhaps," Charlotte agreed, though the gleam in her eye suggested she thought otherwise.

They had barely gone another ten paces when Lydia bounded back, her cheeks flushed with excitement. "Elizabeth! Charlotte! You will never guess—Mrs. Philips says Mrs. Goulding has already put down a shilling that he will be gone by Thursday!"

"I should wager on it myself," Elizabeth muttered under her breath.

Charlotte heard and raised a brow. "Truly? That would be quite the vote of confidence in your own success."

Elizabeth gave her a sharp look. "Who said I was not going to wager the opposite?"

"Pity," Charlotte said lightly. "You might have won *something*, at least."

THE BELL ABOVE THE door chimed as Elizabeth stepped into the bookshop, the cozy quiet welcoming her more than anything else had that day. She moved to the back, scanning the shelves without any real intent, more interested in the calm than in finding something to read.

"Miss Bennet."

She turned at the sound of Darcy's voice, eyebrows lifting in mock surprise. Good heavens, was the man following her? "Mr. Darcy. Of course. Where else would one find you but lurking near the poetry?"

Darcy gave a slight bow, a faint smirk touching his mouth. "And where else would I find you but bent on teasing me?"

"I suppose it is only fair. You do seem drawn to opportunities for torment."

"I was under the impression you found my poetry entertaining," he said dryly, gesturing toward the nearby shelf.

"Oh, immensely so," she replied. "It was unforgettable. Truly."

He returned the book in his hand to the shelf with deliberate care. "If you are here to continue that line of critique, I must warn you that I've yet to recover from your last appraisal."

Elizabeth chuckled softly, moving to a nearby shelf. "Consider this my act of mercy, then. I've no intention of critiquing anything today."

"Mercy from you, Miss Bennet?" Darcy arched a brow. "Now that is unexpected."

"Occasionally, I am magnanimous," she said lightly, glancing at a row of novels. "Besides, I would hate to disturb your 'quiet.'"

"It is difficult to find, particularly in Meryton."

"Ah, yes. One imagines it must be quite a trial for you," Elizabeth said, turning to face him. "Everyone is terribly curious about any single gentlemen, of course. Our quaint little town and its noisy, excitable residents must be dreadfully taxing on your composure."

Darcy didn't answer immediately, though a trace of amusement lingered in his expression. "Perhaps it is not the town itself, but certain residents, who make it... lively."

Elizabeth tilted her head, feigning a thoughtful expression. "Surely you are not including Mr. Collins among those?"

Darcy narrowed his eyes. "Why do you choose that name in particular?"

"Oh—" Elizabeth let her fingers stray down the spine of a nearby book. "It seems you are rather friendly with my cousin. Some might even say he is in your confidence." She turned an arched brow at him.

"I had someone else in mind entirely."

Their eyes met, and for a moment, the silence grew noticeably heavier. Elizabeth, not one to leave awkward pauses unattended, picked up the nearest book and opened it without looking at the title.

"Tell me, do you recommend this one?" she asked, holding the book up.

Darcy leaned slightly to see it. "That depends. Do you enjoy political treatises?"

Elizabeth shut the book with a snap. "Perhaps I will save it for a particularly sleepless night."

"A wise choice." He looked away, then, almost as if he were dismissing her.

Elizabeth flipped idly through the book she had grabbed, casting a sidelong glance at Darcy. There must be *something* she could say to provoke him. Something to coax a confession of sorts from him, so she could learn how much of the day's gossip was true. She landed on a weak prospect and gave it rein.

"I do not suppose I have told you, Mr. Darcy, but my aunt hails from Derbyshire."

"You have not said that, no." He never even looked up.

"She often speaks of the beauty of the area. I imagine she would be familiar with your home if I asked her. After all, according to Miss Bingley, Pemberley is the finest jewel in the county."

He blinked, and she saw a flicker where his jaw muscles clenched, then relaxed, but his only sound was a noncommittal hum.

Something she said was stirring him, though she could not know whether for good or ill. But she had no better ideas, so she stepped a little closer. "It must be quite something to manage a great estate like Pemberley. Constantly coming and going, letters to write, people to manage..." She trailed off casually, letting the words hang just long enough to seem natural.

Darcy, who had been pretending to examine the titles on the shelf beside him, turned slightly toward her, a hint of curiosity in his gaze. "It is a responsibility, yes. But a necessary one."

"I suppose it leaves little time for more... leisurely pursuits. Travel, for example?"

Darcy's brow lifted slightly, a reaction so subtle that had she not been watching closely, she might have missed it. "I travel only when it is required."

"Or when your presence is requested by a friend? That is, after all, why you are at Netherfield, I suppose."

"Just so."

Elizabeth nodded slowly, turning a page without reading it. "And yet, all the tittle-tattle says you may soon be required to leave Hertfordshire."

There it was—the bait.

Darcy did not react as she expected. No startled denial, no accidental confirmation. Instead, his lips curved ever so slightly in what could only be described as a knowing smile.

Darcy gave a slight bow. "Curiosity, after all, is what makes life interesting. And can there be a more perfect expression of curiosity than the local gossip?"

Elizabeth arched a brow. "In a town like Meryton, gossip is practically currency. And at present, you seem to be quite the valuable commodity."

He gave her a sidelong glance. "I am not sure whether to be flattered or alarmed."

"Perhaps both," she replied lightly, then, with a seemingly casual air, added, "I suppose it is inevitable when someone of your standing—so full of... mystery—lingers in the neighborhood."

Darcy's lips curved slightly, though whether it was amusement or irritation, Elizabeth could not tell. "Mystery, Miss Bennet, is often simply another word for discretion."

"And discretion often invites speculation," she countered. "You cannot be surprised that people are curious. Especially when there are whispers of you leaving, possibly to visit... significant acquaintances."

She saw it—a flicker of something in his expression before he masked it. "Significant?"

"Oh, come now, Mr. Darcy," Elizabeth said, tilting her head. "I know not how many people have heard of your sister, but that is not the nature of the general speculation. It is hardly a secret that Lady Catherine de Bourgh wishes to see you... settled."

Darcy's gaze sharpened, though his tone remained maddeningly calm. "I had not realized your interest extended to my personal arrangements."

Elizabeth suppressed a smile. "Merely idle curiosity. After all, if you do plan to leave, it would only be fair to warn the town. There are bets riding on how long you shall remain."

"Bets?" he repeated, incredulous.

"Of course," she said sweetly. "It is Meryton, after all. Though," she added, with mock gravity, "if you were to leave before the ball, I imagine you would disappoint a great many people."

"And would you count yourself among them, Miss Bennet?"

The question was delivered with such quiet force that it gave her pause. Elizabeth blinked, momentarily caught off guard, before regaining her composure. "I would count myself among those curious to see how you manage an evening among such tedious company. I, for one, am entirely certain you will do all in your power to avoid it."

His jaw flexed. "You may rest assured, Miss Bennet, that should I attend, I will strive not to disappoint."

"Well, then," Elizabeth said brightly, placing her book back on the shelf. "I suppose we shall have to wait and see if the wagers are won—or lost."

Darcy inclined his head, his expression inscrutable once more. "Indeed. Though, as with most wagers, the outcome is never certain."

The side of Elizabeth's mouth turned up. "Which means, of course, that anything can still happen."

DARCY PLACED THE SMALL volume of poetry on the counter and withdrew the necessary coins, nodding curtly to the shopkeeper. He had intended to leave the shop moments earlier, but Elizabeth had exited ahead of him, and he found himself lingering, watching as she paused just outside the door to speak with a cluster of red-coated officers. One of them, unmistakably Wickham, was standing far too close.

Darcy's fingers tightened around the coins as he watched Wickham's easy manner, the way he leaned in just slightly, speaking with that polished charm Darcy knew too well. Something cold and sharp twisted in his chest. Wickham was too skilled at ingratiating himself, too adept at hiding his true nature behind a mask of affability. And Elizabeth—clever as she was—had no idea who she was dealing with.

He should not care. It was none of his business whom she spoke to, and yet, the thought of her laughing with Wickham, letting him charm her... it set his teeth on edge. No, he could not allow it.

Darcy placed the coins on the counter with a decisive clink and turned toward the door. It had barely closed behind him when Wickham's voice reached his ears.

"Miss Bennet, might I have the honor of escorting you back to Longbourn?"

Darcy's pulse quickened, and before he could think better of it, he closed the remaining distance between them with measured strides. "I believe that privilege has already been spoken for."

Elizabeth turned to him, her brow lifting slightly. Wickham's smile slipped for just a moment before he masked it with an exaggerated bow. "Of course. I would not wish to intrude."

Darcy ignored Wickham's too-polite tone and glanced at Elizabeth, hoping she would play along. She studied him for a beat, then offered a gracious smile. "Indeed, Mr. Darcy did ask earlier. I had quite forgot."

Wickham's smirk widened as he inclined his head. "Ah, Mr. Darcy, ever the gentleman. How fortunate Miss Bennet is to have such attentive company."

Darcy's gaze flicked to Wickham, cool and unwavering. "Indeed, fortunate timing."

Wickham's eyes gleamed with something sharp beneath the surface, but he merely offered another bow. "A pleasure, Miss Bennet. Perhaps another time." He lingered for a moment before turning back toward the other officers.

Elizabeth suppressed a chuckle as they walked away. "Attentive company, Mr. Darcy? How gallant of you."

"I merely acted in the interest of propriety. It would be unwise to walk alone with... certain company."

"Certain company," she repeated, amused. "How mysterious. And yet, I find myself less curious about your meaning than about what Mr. Wickham did to earn such disdain."

Darcy's lips pressed into a thin line, his gaze fixed ahead. "He is not a man to be trusted."

Elizabeth tilted her head, waiting for more, but none came. "Is that all? Surely you can offer something more specific."

Darcy hesitated, then said carefully, "His reputation among those who know him well speaks for itself."

Elizabeth frowned slightly. "I see," she said lightly. "You prefer to let whispers and rumors do the talking."

"I prefer not to speak of him at all," Darcy replied curtly. "Save to say this—you would do well to be on your guard about him."

Elizabeth studied him, then burst out in to a laugh so merry and sarcastic that he stopped, flushed, and stared at her. "Why, Mr. Darcy, do you honestly imagine I did not take my measure of the man within the first evening of my acquaintance with him? You think I require such warnings like a silly schoolgirl?"

His jaw hardened. "You would not be the first."

"Spare me. When a man makes a one shilling wager with a lady and cannot pay his forfeit—and has not even make a gallant gesture in apology in the fortnight since his loss—he has little standing in this neighborhood."

Darcy's cheek twitched, and she could see him visibly forcing air into his lungs. "Perhaps... Meryton's odd penchant for frivolous betting has proved a... a magnifying glass of sorts."

"Perhaps it has, Mr. Darcy. Unless you have something particular to say about the lieutenant, I shall keep my own counsel. Now, shall we continue in silence, or would you prefer some poetry to lighten the mood?"

Darcy shot her a sharp look, though there was a flicker of amusement in his eyes. "Spare me."

"Not in the mood for conversation, I see," she said, arching a brow. "Well, since you were so eager to join me, you may have to suffer through my company."

Darcy resisted the urge to sigh. Her teasing always had a way of unraveling his carefully maintained composure. He caught her gaze flickering toward the small book he still carried, wrapped in paper.

"And what is this treasure you've acquired?" she asked, her tone innocently curious, though the mischief in her eyes gave her away.

Darcy held the book slightly closer to his side. "Merely a volume of... of poetry."

"Poetry! Surely not more of the sentimental kind, Mr. Darcy."

Darcy gave her a sidelong glance. "It is hardly sentimental. It is Cowper."

Elizabeth's eyes gleamed with interest and something else—challenge. "I should like to see this unsentimental poetry of yours." Without waiting for permission, she deftly plucked the book from his hand.

"Miss Bennet—"

"Oh, come now, Mr. Darcy," she said, flipping open the pages with an exaggerated air of importance. "What do we have here? Shall I read it aloud?"

Darcy tensed, caught between amusement and alarm. "If you insist on making a spectacle of it, at least choose something suitable."

Elizabeth flipped through the pages with a gleam of mischief and, settling on a poem, cleared her throat as though preparing to deliver a proclamation to a packed hall. She raised the book high, tilting her head with mock solemnity before launching into an overly dramatic reading:

> *"Obscurest night involv'd the sky,*
> *Th' Atlantic billows roar'd,*
> *When such a destin'd wretch as I,*
> *Wash'd headlong from on board,*
> *Of friends, of hope, of all bereft,*
> *His floating home for ever left."*

Her voice rose on '*roar'd*' and lingered on '*board,*' her hand sweeping out as if presenting a grand celestial scene to an invisible audience. Darcy, watching from beside her, raised a brow, his arms folding over his chest.

> *"No braver chief could Albion boast*
> *Than he with whom he went,*
> *Nor ever ship left Albion's coast,*
> *With warmer wishes sent.*
> *He lov'd them both, but both in vain,*
> *Nor him beheld, nor her again."*

Elizabeth cast a pointed glance at Darcy, widening her eyes theatrically and fluttering her lashes with exaggerated delicacy. She paused meaningfully, lowering her voice to an absurd hush for effect:

> *"Not long beneath the whelming brine,*
> *Expert to swim, he lay;*
> *Nor soon he felt his strength decline,*
> *Or courage die away;*
> *But wag'd with death a lasting strife,*
> *Supported by despair of life."*

Her tone dropped into an overdone whisper on *'die away,'* her fingers clasping over her heart. Darcy's lips pressed tightly, the corners twitching despite his best efforts.

> *"'He shouted: nor his friends had fail'd*
> *To check the vessel's course,*
> *But so the furious blast prevail'd,*
> *That, pitiless perforce,*
> *They left their outcast mate behind,*
> *And scudded still before the wind.'"*

Her intonation soared ridiculously on *'fail'd'* and *'wind,'* as though each word carried the weight of the cosmos. She placed a hand over her brow, mimicking a swoon.

> *"'Some succour yet they could afford;*
> *And, such as storms allow,*
> *The cask, the coop, the floated cord,*
> *Delay'd not to bestow.*
> *But he (they knew) nor ship, nor shore,*
> *Whate'er they gave, should visit more.'"*

On *'bestow,'* Elizabeth made a grand sweeping gesture, her hand trailing through the air like the flight of an imaginary raven. Darcy exhaled audibly, the closest he would allow himself to come to a laugh.

She finished with a final flourish, lowering her voice to a whisper as though concluding a great soliloquy:

> *"'He long survives, who lives an hour*
> *In ocean, self-upheld;*
> *And so long he, with unspent pow'r,*
> *His destiny repell'd;*
> *And ever, as the minutes flew,*
> *Entreated help, or cried—Adieu!'"*

She snapped the book shut and turned to Darcy with an impish grin. "There, how was that for poetry? Did I capture its essence?"

Darcy, at last, gave a soft exhale that might have been a laugh had it escaped with more force. "You are mangling the meaning entirely."

Elizabeth feigned shock, clasping her hand to her chest. "Mangling it? Why, Mr. Darcy, I read the words exactly as they were printed, changing not a single syllable."

"Yes, but your emphasis is all wrong. You contort the intent and have entirely undone the rhythm."

"I thought I was giving it life! Surely you appreciate a little... creative interpretation."

"Interpretation?" he repeated, stepping closer and plucking the book from her hand. "What you were giving it was melodrama. Poetry is meant to be felt, not paraded about like a stage performance."

Elizabeth's eyes gleamed with challenge. "Then, by all means, show me how it is done properly."

Darcy hesitated. He knew her game, but something about her challenge—and the undeniable curiosity in her gaze—made it impossible to refuse. With a resigned breath, he took the book from her hands and opened it to the same poem, his fingers resting lightly on the worn edges of the pages. Without theatrics or flourish, he began:

> "*At length, his transient respite past,*
> *His comrades, who before*
> *Had heard his voice in ev'ry blast,*
> *Could catch the sound no more.*
> *For then, by toil subdued, he drank*
> *The stifling wave, and then he sank.*'"

His voice, while calm, drew subtle attention to "*catch the sound no more,*" the faintest emphasis lending a quiet reverence to the words. He paused just slightly before continuing, his gaze focused on the text as though it held some profound truth:

> "*No poet wept him: but the page*
> *Of narrative sincere;*
> *That tells his name, his worth, his age,*
> *Is wet with Anson's tear.*

And tears by bards or heroes shed
Alike immortalize the dead.'"

There was no excess in his delivery, no exaggerated emphasis—only a thoughtful cadence, as though he were savoring the words for their own sake. His voice dipped slightly
on *'tears,'* giving it a weight that lingered in the air. Elizabeth's smile, which had begun as
all amusement, was now fading into something more contemplative.

"'I therefore purpose not, or dream,
Descanting on his fate,
To give the melancholy theme
A more enduring date:
But misery still delights to trace
Its semblance in another's case.'"

Here, his voice softened almost imperceptibly, the rhythm becoming more fluid, as
though mimicking the gentle movement of the heavens themselves. His pauses were
deliberate, his inflections subtle, creating a quiet intensity that made the poem seem less
recited and more felt.

Elizabeth's teasing expression was long gone. She watched him closely, her steps slow-
ing. When he reached the final lines, his voice grew quieter still, carrying a strange,
unexpected warmth:

"'No voice divine the storm allay'd,
No light propitious shone;
When, snatch'd from all effectual aid,
We perish'd, each alone:
But I beneath a rougher sea,
And whelm'd in deeper gulfs than he.'"

When he finished, Darcy closed the book, his eyes meeting hers for a beat longer than
was proper. "Satisfied, Miss Bennet?"

Elizabeth blinked, seeming to shake off some sort of sheen over her eyes. "Well," she said, "That was... tolerable."

Darcy raised a brow, the barest hint of a smile tugging at his lips. "Tolerable?"

"Yes, tolerable," she insisted, though the teasing edge in her voice was less sharp than usual. "Perhaps even acceptable. But I suppose even a good reading cannot save overly sentimental poetry."

Darcy inclined his head slightly, the smirk fully forming now. "Perhaps you have higher standards than I imagined."

Elizabeth tilted her head, her teasing smile returning in full force. "Oh, I do. But perhaps you might meet them one day."

They continued walking, the playful tension lingering between them like the echo of the poem's final lines, neither entirely willing to break it.

Eighteen

Elizabeth breezed into Longbourn with a lightness in her step, her bonnet dangling from her fingers and a smug little smile tugging at the corners of her mouth. For once, fortune seemed to be tilting in her favor. Darcy had not only intervened with Wickham at the bookshop but had also walked her home afterward—an act that, while cloaked in cool civility, carried more than a hint of possessiveness. If she could maneuver him into a dance or two at the upcoming Netherfield ball, she would surely win Charlotte's wager.

"Lizzy, is that you?" Jane's voice called from the sitting room.

Elizabeth made her way in, still smiling. "Indeed it is, and I bring excellent news."

Jane looked up from her embroidery, her serene expression marred only by a faint crease of worry at her brow. "Oh? Has something happened?"

"Nothing dreadful, I assure you. In fact, it is quite the opposite. Mr. Darcy has finally shown himself capable of gallantry—or something that closely resembles it." Elizabeth tossed her bonnet onto a nearby chair and sat down beside Jane. "I believe I can coax a dance or two out of him at the ball. Enough to win the wager with Charlotte. I shall lose my wager with Mr. Wickham, but he is already a shilling in my debt anyway, and I care nothing for that."

Jane's eyes widened slightly. "Wait... you have competing wagers? And... what is this about Mr. Wickham?"

"Merely hedging my bets. But I daresay it is nearly a foregone conclusion at this point. I shall have the better of Charlotte at last—it was in all Mr. Darcy's looks this afternoon."

"You seem rather confident for someone who swore that gentleman was incapable of feeling. Has he suddenly developed some, after all?"

Elizabeth waved a hand dismissively. "Enough, I imagine. Where is Mama?"

Jane began gesturing toward the stairs, her mouth ready with a reply, when the sitting room door opened.

"Ah, my dear cousin!" Collins exclaimed. "I heard you had just returned from town. And was that Mr. Darcy who saw you to the door? An excellent man, very good of him. I was just about to seek you out, for, you see, there was a matter of greatest import I wished to speak of with you."

Elizabeth's mood plummeted like a stone. "Mr. Collins," she said evenly, forcing a smile that felt more like a grimace.

He bowed deeply, his hand pressed to his chest. "I hope, dear cousin, that you will not find my request presumptuous, but as your nearest relation, I feel it my duty to reserve your hand for the opening dance at the Netherfield ball."

Elizabeth barely stifled a groan. She had half a mind to refuse outright, but Jane's gently reproving gaze stopped her. Besides, a single dance was no great sacrifice, especially if it meant sparing herself and her family from one of his long-winded speeches about propriety and gratitude.

"Of course, Mr. Collins," she replied with as much grace as she could muster. "I would be honored."

Mr. Collins beamed, clearly delighted by what he saw as her enthusiasm. "Wonderful! I knew you would agree, for I have always believed you to be a most sensible young lady. And rest assured, I plan to remain close by your side throughout the evening. A gentleman must always ensure his partner is well attended, after all."

Elizabeth's smile froze. "Throughout the evening?"

"Indeed, yes! It is only fitting that we should spend the majority of the evening in each other's company. Why, the other guests might even begin to speculate on the nature of our... attachment."

Elizabeth's pulse quickened, though not from any pleasant emotion. "Mr. Collins, I think you misunderstand—"

"Oh, say no more!" he interrupted, holding up a hand. "I understand perfectly, cousin. I, too, feel that there is no need to rush things. These matters must be handled delicately, but I am confident that by the end of the evening, we shall find ourselves much... closer."

Elizabeth's stomach turned. Collins was under some ridiculous delusion about securing her favor, and the thought of enduring his particular attentions for an entire evening made her want to flee to her room and barricade the door.

"Mr. Collins," Jane interrupted, "surely Elizabeth will wish to dance with other partners as well. It would be unfair to monopolize her time."

Mr. Collins chuckled indulgently. "Oh, of course, of course. I would not dream of de-priving her of other dances entirely. But naturally, as her cousin and—dare I say—closest male relation present, I must take precedence."

Elizabeth gritted her teeth. "How thoughtful of you."

He beamed again, clearly mistaking her sarcasm for approval. "Until then, dear cousin, I shall count the hours!" With another deep bow, he excused himself, leaving Elizabeth and Jane in stunned silence.

Elizabeth turned to her sister, eyes wide with disbelief. "Did he just...?"

Jane nodded, her expression sympathetic. "He did."

Elizabeth slumped back against the sofa, pressing a hand to her forehead. "I cannot believe it. The one night I needed to be free of him, and he's determined to play the gallant suitor."

Jane reached over and took Elizabeth's hand in hers. "You'll think of something, Lizzy. You always do."

Elizabeth sighed, her earlier optimism now a distant memory. "I certainly hope so, Jane. Otherwise, this wager might be lost before the ball even begins."

ELIZABETH WAS STILL SEETHING over Mr. Collins's audacious presumption when the front door creaked open and closed with a faint thud. Mary stepped into the room, carrying a basket.

"Mary, you've been out?" Elizabeth asked, more out of politeness than curiosity.

"Yes, I was visiting Maria Lucas," Mary replied as she removed her gloves. "She wished to consult me on the suitability of certain verses for a letter she means to write. I found her selections rather lacking."

Elizabeth gave a half-smile, more amused by the familiar primness of Mary's tone than the subject itself. "How dutiful of you to offer your assistance."

Mary ignored the teasing tone and sat straighter, a serious expression forming on her face. "I also happened to speak with someone in town, who offered me a word of caution."

Elizabeth raised an eyebrow. "A word of caution? Concerning what, or whom?"

Mary hesitated, clearly weighing her words. "Concerning you."

"Me?" Elizabeth blinked, caught off guard. "And what am I to be cautious of?"

"I was told," Mary said slowly, "that your attention toward a certain gentleman is ill-advised. That it will lead only to disappointment and embarrassment."

Elizabeth stilled, her mind racing. She had little doubt as to which gentleman Mary referred—there was only one whose attention she actively sought at present. But who had said such a thing to Mary? Elizabeth narrowed her eyes, thinking of potential culprits. Wickham? Perhaps. He would have reason enough to sow discord, given her recent snub.

But then again, Charlotte had always been a clever schemer when it suited her. And when would Mr. Wickham have encountered Mary? He probably barely knew she existed, but Mary had come from Lucas Lodge...

Elizabeth cleared her throat. "And who, pray, delivered this dire prophecy of doom?"

Mary hesitated, casting a wary glance toward the doorway. "I do not think it proper to name names. Suffice it to say, Lizzy, I believe your admiration for Mr. Darcy is misplaced."

Elizabeth rolled her eyes. "Come now, what nonsense is this?"

"I am merely repeating what I was told," Mary said, her voice steady but solemn. "You are free to ignore it, of course, but I felt it my duty as your sister to warn you. You should not pin your hopes on a man like him."

Aha. Yes, that sounded very like what Charlotte might have said, merely to stir the pot, and Mary was nothing if not a dutiful messenger. "How thoughtful of you, Mary. I trust the one who warned you of this has some vested interest in my well-being and reputation?"

Mary frowned, clearly missing Elizabeth's sarcasm. "No, none that I am aware of. But it does not matter who my source is. What matters is that I believe this to be true, and I will go to Papa if I must."

Elizabeth's amusement evaporated. "Go to Papa? Mary, you cannot be serious."

"I am. He may not care about Kitty or Lydia's flirtations, but I believe he will take a firmer stance if he knows you mean to encourage a man like Mr. Darcy."

"A man like Mr. Darcy! Tell me, what is so odious about his reputation more than any other gentleman?"

"It is not that," Mary said hesitantly, toying with nervous fingers over her stomach. "It is only that he is known to be practically engaged. That he gives every appearance of flirting and dallying where he should not, and—"

"Flirting! Mr. Darcy could not even define the word if you put it to him."

Mary's jaw went rigid. "He is not acting the part of the gentleman, Lizzy. I know his attentions are insincere."

Elizabeth stood, pacing the length of the room, trying to rein in her irritation. She knew Mary well enough to recognize that once her sister latched onto something she deemed 'virtuous,' she would cling to it with infuriating persistence. Worse, if she truly intended to involve their father, it could complicate Elizabeth's plans for the ball in ways she could ill afford.

"Very well," Elizabeth said at last, forcing herself to sound calm. "You've delivered your warning. There's no need to trouble Papa over something as trivial as a few dances at a ball."

Mary's expression did not soften. "I hope you will heed it, Lizzy. I would hate to see you humiliated. Your reputation affects us all, as you well know."

Elizabeth turned back toward her sister, her jaw tightening. "Thank you for your concern, Mary, but I assure you, I am quite capable of managing my own affairs."

Mary said nothing further, but the look she gave Elizabeth before turning and leaving the room spoke volumes. Elizabeth let out a sigh of frustration as soon as the door closed behind her.

And she began to wonder if she might be in over her head after all.

DARCY PLACED HIS WINEGLASS carefully on the table, watching as the ruby liquid stilled. Across the table, Caroline Bingley prattled on about some friends in London and how she still suffered some delusions of returning to Town before the end of the month. But his attention was elsewhere—fixed on his own thoughts, where Elizabeth Bennet's voice and laughter had begun to linger with an unsettling permanence.

"...and truly, the lace at Madame Fauchet's is unmatched. Do you not agree, Mr. Darcy?" Caroline's voice broke through his reverie, drawing his gaze.

"I beg your pardon?"

Caroline's eyes gleamed with satisfaction, as though she had caught him in some great lapse of manners. "I was merely observing that Madame Fauchet's lacework is superior. But I see you have weightier matters on your mind."

Darcy inclined his head slightly, unwilling to engage further. He had long since mastered the art of appearing impassive in the face of Caroline's attempts to command his attention. Tonight, however, the effort seemed greater.

Beside her, Louisa Hurst reached for her glass, her movements languid. "One can hardly expect Mr. Darcy to occupy his thoughts with mere lace. He is a man of substance, after all."

"I suppose," Caroline added with a feigned air of nonchalance, "that he has been rather preoccupied since his little stroll in Meryton this afternoon."

Darcy's hand tightened slightly around his fork, but he made no outward sign of displeasure.

"A stroll?" Mr. Hurst asked, glancing up from his plate, his expression one of mild interest.

"Oh, yes," Caroline continued, her tone light and teasing. "It seems our Mr. Darcy was observed escorting a certain Miss Elizabeth Bennet home from town. Quite gallant, would you not say, Louisa?"

Louisa gave a small smile. "Gallant, indeed."

Bingley, seated beside Darcy, looked up with a bemused expression. "Is that true, Darcy? You escorted Miss Elizabeth home?"

Darcy maintained his composure, though his mind was already calculating the implications of Caroline's remark. The last thing he needed was for this to become a subject of speculation—or worse, gossip. "It was hardly worth noting," he replied evenly. "We merely happened to leave the bookshop at the same time, and there was unsavory company about. I did as any gentleman ought."

"Indeed," Caroline said, her smile sharpening. "And yet, for a man who prides himself on avoiding unnecessary entanglements, it does seem a curious deviation from your usual practice."

Darcy's jaw tightened, but he forced his voice to remain calm. "I see no cause for such exaggeration, Miss Bingley."

"Oh, but there is no exaggeration," she said sweetly. "I merely found it amusing. After all, one does not often see you in the company of young ladies—except under strict social obligation, of course."

"Come now, Caroline," Bingley said, his tone mildly reproving. "You are making far too much of a simple courtesy."

Caroline gave a delicate shrug, unbothered by her brother's intervention. "Perhaps, but one cannot help but wonder... A man who claims to be guarding himself so carefully, escorting a young lady home? What are the poor townspeople to think?"

Darcy set his fork down with deliberate precision, the metallic clink against the plate louder than he intended. He could feel the tension rising in his chest, a mixture of annoyance and something far more dangerous—guilt. Caroline's words struck closer to the mark than he cared to admit. He had been careless, not in action, but in thought. Allowing himself to enjoy Elizabeth's company, even fleetingly, was a perilous indulgence.

"The townspeople may think as they please," Darcy said, his voice cool and measured. "It is of no consequence to me."

"Oh, naturally," Caroline replied with a sly smile. "But I do hope you are not finding Meryton more diverting than you expected. One would hate for you to become entangled in a place like *this*."

Darcy shot her a sharp glance, but before he could respond, Bingley interjected with a good-natured laugh. "Enough, Caroline. You are determined to tease Darcy tonight."

Caroline's eyes glittered with triumph, but she relented, turning her attention back to her plate. Darcy, however, found no relief. The conversation had only deepened the conflict within him—a conflict he could not afford to entertain, yet could not seem to ignore.

LATER, AFTER THE UNCOMFORTABLE dinner had mercifully ended, Darcy found himself standing beside the fire in Bingley's study, a glass of brandy in hand. Bingley joined him, sinking into a chair with his usual affable ease, though his expression remained thoughtful.

"I must say, Darcy, Caroline's remarks at dinner were rather pointed," Bingley said, swirling the amber liquid in his glass. "She seemed most intent on provoking you. What have you done to rile her?"

Darcy exhaled slowly. "She is determined to remind me of the wager. I think she is hoping I will lose."

Bingley leaned forward slightly, his brow furrowing. "Forgive me, but why let it trouble you? You've done nothing improper. Surely no one would think less of you for escorting Miss Bennet home. It was the gentlemanly thing to do."

"It is not the action itself, Bingley," Darcy replied, setting his glass down on the mantel. "It is the attention it invites. Your sister was not wrong about Meryton's love for gossip.

Such talk could lead to expectations—expectations I cannot afford to encourage. I told you this would all end poorly."

Bingley considered this for a moment, then said, "I think you worry too much. Elizabeth Bennet is hardly the sort to presume anything from a simple act of kindness. In fact, I think her rather an admirable lady."

Darcy stiffened. "Admiration is one thing. Entanglement is another."

"And you have reason to fear entanglement here?"

"I fear complication," Darcy said sharply. "My life, Bingley, is not one that allows for impulsive decisions. My family's name, my estate, my responsibilities—they demand prudence, not distraction."

Bingley's smile faded, replaced by quiet understanding. "And you believe Miss Elizabeth could become such a distraction?"

Darcy ran a hand through his hair, frustration creeping into his voice. "She already is. I find myself thinking of her when I should not. I look for her in every room, and when she is present, I—" He stopped himself, realizing he was revealing far more than he intended.

Bingley studied his friend for a long moment before speaking. "Darcy, I've known you a long time. You are not a man given to whims or fancies. If Elizabeth Bennet occupies your thoughts, it is because she has earned her place there."

Darcy turned away from the fire, pacing the length of the room. "It does not matter. I cannot afford to lose my composure or my objectivity. Caroline's remarks tonight were a reminder of what is at stake."

Bingley stood, setting his glass aside. "If you ask me, Caroline is merely trying to get under your skin. You should not let her."

Darcy stopped pacing, his expression grim. "Perhaps. But it serves as a warning all the same. I cannot afford to give anyone reason to believe there is more between myself and Miss Bennet than civility."

Bingley leaned back in his chair, tilting his glass lazily. "Civility, is it? Well, if that is your aim, I wish you luck, my friend. From where I stand, it looks as though it might be a more difficult wager than you anticipated."

Darcy's jaw tightened as he turned back toward the fire, the golden light flickering across his face. He had no desire to admit how accurate Bingley's observation was, but the truth gnawed at him, undeniable.

"I entered this wager," Darcy said at last, his tone clipped, "believing it to be a matter of simple decorum. Show politeness, avoid entanglements, and leave with my reputation intact."

Bingley sat up straighter, setting his glass aside. "I only meant to suggest that you could demonstrate common civility without risking—"

"Common civility does not exist in our world," Darcy interrupted. "For men like me, like you, there is only propriety, or scandal. One dance too many, one smile held too long, and suddenly the world imagines attachments where there are none."

"You are overthinking this," Bingley said after a pause. "No one is expecting you to propose marriage after escorting Miss Bennet home. You have always held yourself above such nonsense. Why let it trouble you now?"

Darcy turned away, the muscles in his shoulders taut. "Because this time, it is different." He drew a slow breath, steadying himself. "Elizabeth Bennet is not like the others. She is—"

He stopped himself abruptly, unwilling to finish the thought aloud. It was too dangerous, even in Bingley's presence, to give voice to what had begun to take root in his mind. Elizabeth Bennet was not merely a passing amusement, nor a trivial test of his will. She was clever, quick-witted, and undeniably captivating. But more than that, she had a way of making him forget, if only for a moment, the weight of expectation he carried. And even more thrillingly, to imagine something... *beyond*.

"Different how?"

Darcy shook his head. "It does not matter. What matters is that I maintain control. If I do not, I risk far more than losing a wager. I risk dragging both of us into a situation neither of us can escape without damage."

Bingley's brow creased in concern. "I still think you are reading too much into other people's opinions."

"Because I *must*. You do not understand, Bingley. Your good nature, your wealth—they shield you. But for me, everything is scrutinized. If I were to marry below my station, society would tolerate it, but only just. But to show interest without intention? To raise a young lady's hopes, even unintentionally, only to leave her to face the fallout alone? That is not something I can countenance."

Bingley said nothing for a moment, his expression thoughtful. He swirled the remnants of his brandy, then took a slow sip before setting the glass aside. "I did not mean to make light of your concerns, Darcy. But if I may—perhaps you should worry less about what society expects and more about what you want. You are always thinking of duty, of propriety, of reputation. When was the last time you allowed yourself to want something for yourself?"

Darcy's grip tightened around the stem of his glass, but he did not respond. He could not. Admitting the answer, even to himself, would mean acknowledging that his desire for Elizabeth Bennet had grown beyond mere attraction. It would mean admitting that she was no longer simply an opponent in a game of wits, but a temptation he longed to indulge.

And that, he could not allow.

Instead, he said quietly, "What I want is irrelevant. It always has been."

NINETEEN

"Now remember, Jane, you must not refuse Mr. Bingley if he asks for a second dance," Mrs. Bennet declared. "None of your modesty for *this* night! A gentleman so besotted is sure to propose before the evening is out."

Elizabeth rolled her eyes and adjusted her gloves, casting a sideways glance at Jane, who offered a calm, noncommittal smile in response. The carriage rocked gently beneath them as the grand house loomed closer, its windows glowing with the promise of warmth and festivity. Elizabeth tried to ignore the restless flutter of nerves in her chest. This evening was not about Jane's impending engagement, nor her mother's endless matchmaking schemes—it was about winning her wager and, perhaps more pressingly, finding a way to survive Mr. Collins's attentions unscathed.

The carriage rolled to a stop, and the Bennets alighted, their arrival met with the glow of lamplight spilling from the great house and the soft murmur of voices and music beyond the open doors.

"Come, girls," Mrs. Bennet said, bustling them along. "Do not dawdle."

Inside, Netherfield's grand hall was already filling with guests, the air humming with the anticipation of an evening's revelry. Elizabeth scanned the room quickly, her eyes seeking out familiar faces. Mr. Bingley stood near the entrance to the drawing room, already surrounded by well-wishers, his cheerful disposition drawing people in like a flame. Elizabeth gave her sister a gentle nudge.

"Go on, Jane. I believe your evening has just begun."

Jane hesitated for a moment, then allowed herself to be guided forward. Elizabeth watched as Bingley's face lit up at Jane's approach, and for a moment, she felt a flicker of satisfaction. At least Jane would have a promising night.

Her own satisfaction, however, was short-lived.

"Such a grand house, is it not, Cousin Elizabeth?" Mr. Collins declared as he stepped beside her, effectively cutting off her view of the entrance hall. His gait was brisk, his voice overly loud, and he offered her an arm with an air of importance that made Elizabeth grit her teeth. "Mr. Bingley is to be commended for his fine taste, though, of course, it cannot rival the splendor of Rosings Park."

Elizabeth kept her expression carefully neutral, though inwardly she sighed. "Yes, it is quite elegant."

Collins beamed, clearly taking her lukewarm response as wholehearted agreement. "Indeed, indeed! I am sure the guests shall be just as impressed by our entrance. And may I say, Cousin Elizabeth, that you look most radiant tonight. I daresay your appearance shall be the talk of the ball." He adjusted his cravat as if preparing for an audience.

Elizabeth plastered on a smile. "You are too kind."

"Not at all, not at all," he insisted, straightening and offering his arm. "Come, we must find a place near the dance floor. As you know, it is my privilege to open the ball with you, and I would not wish to miss the opportunity."

Elizabeth took his arm reluctantly, casting a quick glance around the room. Her gaze landed on Darcy, standing a short distance away, his eyes already fixed on her. He did not move toward her, nor did he offer any sign of greeting. Instead, he turned slightly, as though deliberately distancing himself from her line of sight.

Elizabeth's irritation flared. If he was so intent on avoiding her, then why had he been watching her in the first place?

"Shall we take in the room, Cousin?" Collins prompted, his grip tightening slightly on her arm as he began leading her forward. Elizabeth bit back a sigh and allowed herself to be escorted, though her mind was already working furiously. She had planned to approach Darcy early in the evening, hoping to coax a dance from him before anyone else could lay claim to his attention. A smile on the dance floor, perhaps even a second dance to seal the deal beyond any doubt, and that would be sufficient.

Now, however, she found herself shackled to Mr. Collins and at the mercy of his overzealous attentions.

"What a splendid assembly this is! And how grand of Mr. Bingley to host such an event. It is a testament to his fine character, would you not agree, Cousin Elizabeth?"

Elizabeth nodded absently, her eyes once again drifting toward Darcy again. He stood with Bingley now, their heads bent in quiet conversation. Bingley's face bore its usual open cheerfulness, but Darcy's was more guarded, his gaze flicking briefly in her direction before returning to his friend.

She could not tell what passed between them, but the sight of Darcy speaking with Bingley only served to heighten her frustration. If only she could find a way to rid herself of Mr. Collins...

"Cousin Elizabeth, are you quite well?" Collins asked, his tone solicitous. "You seem... distracted."

"I assure you, Mr. Collins, I am perfectly well," she replied, forcing a smile. "Merely taking in the atmosphere."

"Ah, yes," he said, nodding sagely. "Such grandeur can be overwhelming to a young lady. But fear not, dear cousin. I shall remain at your side throughout the evening, ensuring you are never without proper company."

Elizabeth's smile stiffened. "How very thoughtful of you."

As they reached the edge of the dance floor, the music swelled, signaling the start of the first set. Collins turned to face her fully, his chest puffed out with pride. "Shall we?"

Elizabeth had no choice but to nod and allow herself to be led into position. All the while, she could feel Darcy's eyes on her, watching from the periphery of the room. He remained where he was, a silent observer, yet his presence was as tangible as if he stood beside her.

And so the dance began, with Mr. Collins stepping on her toes at least twice before the first turn was complete.

FROM WHERE DARCY STOOD, he could see Elizabeth Bennet entering the room, her eyes flicking about as though taking in every detail at once. He noted, with some satisfaction, the faint crease of concentration on her brow—until Mr. Collins, ever-oblivious and ever-intrusive, shifted his large frame beside her, leaning in too close and speaking too loudly.

Darcy's jaw clenched as he watched the man hover by Elizabeth's side, puffed up with importance, no doubt imagining himself her gallant protector for the evening. As much as Darcy somehow loathed the idea of Elizabeth being subjected to Collins's tiresome company, he could not help but see the man's usefulness. For all his faults—and they were plentiful—Collins was a convenient barrier. As long as the clergyman remained glued to Elizabeth's side, Darcy would have little cause to be drawn into closer proximity to her.

"Darcy, there you are." Bingley's voice broke through his thoughts. "I am simply beside myself with how grand the room looks tonight. Do you not agree?"

Darcy blinked, refocusing his attention on his friend. He gave a curt nod. "Yes. Your housekeeper has done well."

"Still as enthusiastic as ever about these gatherings, I see," Bingley teased lightly, but Darcy offered no reply. His eyes had drifted back to Elizabeth, who now stood at the edge of the dance floor, Collins gesturing animatedly beside her. Her expression was carefully composed, but Darcy could sense the frustration simmering beneath it.

Bingley followed his gaze, a knowing smile forming on his lips. "Ah, Miss Elizabeth. She does look well tonight, does she not?"

"She always looks well," Darcy said quietly before he could stop himself.

Bingley's smile grew. "High praise, coming from you."

Darcy forced himself to look away. He could feel Bingley's scrutiny, but he had no intention of indulging it. His goal tonight was clear: remain distant, remain excessively polite, and most importantly, remain unnoticed in regard to Elizabeth Bennet. Any appearance of particular attention would only serve to stoke the unwholesome flames of gossip that Caroline Bingley had so gleefully kindled.

But as the first strains of music filled the air, and the dancers took their places, Darcy found his resolve tested. Elizabeth had taken to the floor with Collins, and though Darcy had no desire to be in the clergyman's place, he could not look away. Collins stumbled through the opening steps, his movements clumsy and exaggerated. Elizabeth, by contrast, moved with grace, her expression a mask of polite endurance.

Oh, dash it all, what was the use? Everyone else was looking at her. Elizabeth Bennet did capture attention—*his* attention, most dangerously of all. And that was precisely why he had to ensure that no one else noticed.

It was a delicate balance. He had no intention of indulging his own feelings, but he could not deny that he felt protective of her, especially with Wickham probably lurking somewhere in the crowd. The man had a knack for inserting himself where he was least wanted, and Darcy had no doubt he would attempt to engage Elizabeth before the night was through.

"Darcy, you have not forgot the supper set, have you?" Bingley asked. "Our deal?"

Darcy's grip on the stem of his glass tightened slightly, though his outward composure remained intact. "I had not forgot."

"Good," Bingley replied, smiling faintly. "One dance, Darcy. Then you may safely ignore her for the rest of the evening. That is all it will take to silence Caroline's teasing and prove your point. And I..." he sighed reluctantly. "I suppose I will be obliged to write to my solicitor and sell the mill."

Darcy made no immediate reply. The very idea of dancing with her left him uneasy.

"I shall ask her," he said at last, his voice low. "At the appropriate time."

"Excellent," Bingley said with satisfaction. "You might even enjoy it, Darcy."

Darcy said nothing in response, though inwardly he braced himself. One dance might satisfy Bingley's challenge, but half an hour on the dance floor, followed by an hour or more sitting beside her at supper...

His gaze drifted back to Elizabeth, who was still enduring Mr. Collins's attentions with remarkable patience. He allowed himself one brief moment of indulgence, imagining how different the evening might be if he could approach her without consequence, without the burden of reputation weighing upon every action.

But such thoughts were dangerous, and Darcy had no intention of entertaining them further. He would ask Elizabeth for the supper set, fulfill the terms of the wager, and ensure that no one—not even himself—could mistake it for anything more.

ELIZABETH HAD SCARCELY FINISHED the third dance with Paul Goulding when she noticed Darcy approaching. *At last!* His expression was as composed as ever, yet there was something in his bearing—something deliberate—that caught her attention.

"Miss Bennet," he said as he reached her, bowing slightly. "Might I have the honor of the supper set?"

For a moment, Elizabeth could only blink at him. This was... entirely too easy. She had imagined a game of cat and mouse throughout the evening, with herself as the cunning predator, coaxing Darcy into revealing more than he intended. Yet here he was, asking her directly, as though it were the most natural thing in the world.

She smiled, masking her surprise. "Certainly, Mr. Darcy. I would be delighted."

Mr. Collins, who was still lingering too close for comfort, looked fit to swoon. "Ah, Cousin Elizabeth! You are much sought after this evening, but I trust you will not forget your humble relation. Perhaps you might join me for another—"

"I believe, Mr. Collins, that Sir William was hoping to speak with you," Darcy interrupted. "I trust you were aware? Sir William is quite keen to hear more about your recent efforts at Hunsford. On my honor, I heard him speaking to Mr. Bennet about it not five minutes ago."

Collins's face lit up. "Indeed? Well, if that is the case, I must not delay."

With an elaborate bow, he excused himself, leaving Elizabeth momentarily stunned by the ease with which Darcy had dispatched him. She scarcely contained her amusement as she turned back to Darcy. "That was well done."

"I have found that certain conversations are best left to those who appreciate them."

Elizabeth laughed softly. "Poor Sir William. He may never forgive you."

"I am willing to risk it," Darcy replied, a faint smile playing at the corner of his mouth. After a brief pause, he added, "Would you care for some punch, Miss Bennet? Or are you otherwise engaged?"

Elizabeth hesitated for a moment, caught slightly off guard by the unexpected civility of the offer. "Yes, thank you. That would be most welcome."

Darcy inclined his head and turned toward the refreshment table, leaving Elizabeth to watch his retreating form with a mix of curiosity and newfound amusement. She had expected Darcy to keep his distance tonight, but instead, he seemed intent on behaving like... like a *gentleman*. Without even being provoked to it. How very unexpected—and how very intriguing.

They approached the refreshment table together, and Darcy selected a glass of punch and handed it to her.

Elizabeth accepted the glass, offering a small smile. "I must admit, I did not expect to enjoy myself tonight."

"I can hardly credit that statement. You always seem to enjoy yourself in company."

"And you do not."

He swallowed and raised a brow. "You intend to change my mind, Miss Elizabeth? Or are you merely being contrary for the sake of provoking a debate, as you seem fond of doing?"

She permitted her smile to widen. "I leave you to discern that on your own. Meanwhile, I shall perhaps observe that balls are generally predictable affairs."

"Predictable in what sense?" Darcy asked.

"Oh, the usual," Elizabeth said lightly. "Too many people in too small a space, far too many opinions on matters of little importance, and always the same assortment of characters—gossips, dancers, and those who merely endure it."

Darcy inclined his head slightly, considering her words. "And which are you?"

Elizabeth smiled wryly. "I suppose I fall somewhere between the last two."

"That would explain why you often find yourself at the center of attention, yet never entirely content with it."

Elizabeth blinked. "Why, Mr. Darcy, you would teach me to doubt my own feelings!"

"I am correct, am I not? Tell me that you do not immediately seek to deflect the focus of others from yourself and toward one of your sisters when you feel the sun shines a little too warmly on you?"

She laughed. "I think what you call deflection is the natural result of having one sister, at least, who can outshine the sun."

He raised his glass toward her. "There, you are doing it again."

Elizabeth sipped her wine and shook her head. "And you, Mr. Darcy? Where do you place yourself in my little cast of characters?" She made a mock pout. "For surely, I did not take you for a gossip, but you seem perfectly content to blather nonsense at the moment."

Darcy's mouth curved, and he twirled the stem of the glass in his hand. "I endure it," he said simply, though there was a flicker of something wry in his eyes. "Balls are necessary obligations, nothing more."

"And yet here you are, obliging yourself to fetch punch for me," Elizabeth teased, tilting her head slightly. "Surely that is not merely obligation?"

Darcy met her gaze evenly, his expression calm but unreadable. "It is civility."

"Ah," Elizabeth said, feigning disappointment. "Civility. How very dull."

To her surprise, he smiled—a real, unguarded smile that transformed his normally severe features. "Perhaps civility need not always be dull."

"I suppose it depends on the company," she said softly, meeting his eyes briefly before glancing away.

Darcy inclined his head slightly, acknowledging her words without further comment. For a moment, the conversation lapsed into silence, but it was a comfortable silence, one that needed no urgent filling.

"I should join my friends," Elizabeth said at last, though she found herself reluctant to leave. "Thank you, Mr. Darcy. For the punch."

"You are welcome, Miss Elizabeth."

"The Boulanger," Elizabeth remarked as they stepped into line, her hand resting lightly in Darcy's. "An interesting choice for a supper set, is it not? Lively enough to keep everyone awake, yet formal enough to remind us all of propriety."

Darcy inclined his head slightly, his grip steady but precise as they moved into place. "It serves its purpose. A balance between energy and decorum."

Elizabeth smiled, as though she had anticipated such an answer. She glanced away, scanning the crowded ballroom as if assessing her surroundings, but Darcy noticed the faint curve of amusement lingering at the corners of her mouth. It was a look he had grown familiar with—Elizabeth Bennet, perpetually entertained by the world around her, and often at his expense.

Around them, couples moved into place, preparing for the opening steps. The buzz of conversation filled the air, punctuated by the occasional rustle of skirts and clink of glassware from the supper room beyond. Darcy noted the eyes of several guests drifting their way, some curious, some speculative.

He forced himself to focus on the rhythm of the music, the precision of the steps. And yet, even as the first notes sounded, and the people around them began to move into his sphere, his attention remained anchored to Elizabeth. She moved with a willowy sort of seduction, each step light and sure, and though he maintained the proper distance between them, he could not help but be acutely aware of her—of the warmth of her fingers in his, of the delicate rustle of her gown as it swirled around her feet.

"You have fallen quiet again, Mr. Darcy," Elizabeth remarked as they stepped together. "One might think you are concentrating."

Darcy met her gaze briefly, then looked past her toward the other dancers. "Is that not expected during a dance?"

"It is expected," she agreed, tilting her head slightly, "but I find it rather disappointing. Surely a man of your talents could manage both concentration and conversation."

"And what would you have me say, Miss Bennet?" he asked, his tone as measured as his steps. "Am I to offer witticisms, or merely endure your observations in silence?"

Elizabeth's eyes sparkled with mischief as they parted for the next figure. "Oh, I would not dream of imposing too greatly upon your wit. Perhaps you could recite poetry instead."

Darcy raised a brow as they turned through the group, his voice carrying over the music. "You mean to mock me, Miss Elizabeth?"

"Oh, no!" she cried innocently. "But you find the exercise a pleasure, and so if I wish to make myself agreeable for the half hour, I can do you the courtesy of listening."

Darcy arched a brow as they reached the end of their line. "I fear that would be a far greater imposition than silence."

When they came back together, Elizabeth smiled up at him. "Then I must insist upon it. Surely a man as accomplished as yourself has no shortage of verses to recite."

"I do not recall boasting of any such accomplishment," Darcy replied. "But if you insist, I could attempt a line or two."

"Please do," Elizabeth said, her smile widening as they turned again.

Darcy took a steadying breath, his mind racing. He had not intended to humor her, but something about the sparkle in her eyes and the way she leaned ever so slightly closer as they moved was impossible to resist.

When they met again in the steps, he said, his tone as serious as if he were quoting Byron himself:

> *"The moon is high, the night is fair,*
> *Yet I find myself trapped in this despair."*

Elizabeth blinked, then laughed—a bright, genuine sound that drew glances from the nearby dancers. "Trapped in despair, Mr. Darcy? Over a mere dance? How melodramatic of you."

"Perhaps my muse is too stern," he said, the corner of his mouth twitching. "I shall try again."

"Please do," she replied, her tone encouraging, though her laughter still lingered.

As the dance brought them apart again, Darcy's thoughts turned toward the absurd. He could scarcely believe he was indulging her like this, yet the challenge in her eyes spurred him onward.

When they rejoined, he added, with mock solemnity:

> *"A ballroom bright, a crowd unkind,*
> *And yet, your sharp wit fills my mind."*

Elizabeth feigned shock, pressing a hand to her chest. "Why, Mr. Darcy, I believe that is almost a compliment."

"It was not my intention to flatter," he replied, his voice perfectly dry.

"Ah, but that is what makes it so rare," she countered, her eyes gleaming.

Darcy held her gaze a moment longer, feeling a warmth that had nothing to do with the heat of the room. She was unlike anyone he had ever encountered—clever, quick-witted, and entirely unafraid to meet him on equal footing.

"Shall I try again?" he asked as they moved through the next sequence.

"Oh, please do," Elizabeth said, her tone bordering on delighted.

As they met once more, Darcy leaned in just enough to lower his voice, a glimmer of mischief entering his own expression.

> *"Though words may falter, steps may fail,*
> *I find no wit in your travail."*

Elizabeth gasped theatrically. "Now that is quite unkind, sir! My steps have been nothing short of perfection."

Darcy allowed himself a faint smile. "I concede the point. My muse must be defective."

Elizabeth laughed again, shaking her head. "Then perhaps we should leave the poetry to others. I should hate to see you ruin your reputation with such efforts."

Darcy inclined his head, his tone gentler now. "And what of yours, Miss Bennet? Surely such provocations risk damaging your own standing."

"Oh, my reputation is quite ruined already," she said airily, her grin as bright as the chandeliers overhead. "But I find I enjoy myself far more this way."

As they turned for the final figure of the dance, Darcy realized that he, too, was enjoying himself more than he had in years. The weight of the ballroom, the expectations, the constant eyes upon him—all of it seemed to fade in the presence of Elizabeth Bennet's quick tongue and sharper mind.

As the music swelled to its conclusion, they came to a graceful stop. Darcy released her hand, though the warmth of her touch lingered longer than it should have.

"Thank you, Mr. Darcy," Elizabeth said, her voice light but sincere. "That was almost enjoyable."

"Almost?" he echoed, raising a brow.

"Well," she said with a playful tilt of her head, "you did insist upon trying poetry."

"At your insistence, madam."

"And you were naive enough to take my words at their face value!" She clucked her tongue. "I thought you might have known better by now, Mr. Darcy."

Darcy allowed himself a chuckle as he bowed. "Then I shall endeavor to avoid such mistakes in future."

Elizabeth curtsied in return, her eyes still dancing with humor. "A wise decision."

As the other couples began to disperse, Darcy extended his arm. "Shall we take our place for supper?"

Elizabeth hesitated for only a moment before accepting his offer. "I suppose I must, if I hope to observe more of your endurance."

Darcy gave no outward sign of amusement, but inwardly, he braced himself. The supper set, he reminded himself, was merely another obligation to be met. And yet, as he led Elizabeth toward the refreshment room, he could not shake the feeling that this particular obligation might prove far more difficult—and far more dangerous—than he had anticipated.

Twenty

THAT WAS IT. THE wager was won.

Elizabeth shot Charlotte Lucas a triumphant look as she took Darcy's arm, allowing him to lead her toward the supper room. Charlotte raised her brows meaningfully, then rolled her eyes in exaggerated exasperation. The gesture said everything: *Well done, now finish it.*

Wait... she was... serious?

Elizabeth shook her head faintly, pantomiming that she did not understand, so Charlotte spelled it out for her by mouthing the words. *"Turn him down."*

She blinked. Charlotte was really holding her to *that* part of the wager? The petty, spiteful part, the part Elizabeth had agreed to only out of wounded pride? She pursed her lips and sucked in a breath. Could she do it? Did she even need to?

Oh, surely she had satisfied the terms. Charlotte could not be so cruel... could she? But as Elizabeth slid her gaze toward Darcy, then back to her friend, Charlotte made one final gesture. A little brushing of her thumb against her fingertips, a little signal that said plain as day, "Prepare to pay up."

Elizabeth felt a pang of something unfamiliar—guilt, perhaps, or reluctance—as she turned away from her friend.

Her attention snapped back to the gentleman at her side as his fingers closed around hers. It was a perfectly ordinary gesture, yet the weight of the eyes following them made it feel oddly significant. Elizabeth glanced up at him, finding his expression composed as ever, though there was a faint tension in his jaw, as if he were bearing the scrutiny with stoic resignation. The realization struck her: He knew they were watching too.

The room seemed to hum with the energy of so many unspoken thoughts, so much speculation. Elizabeth could almost feel the pressure of the whispers—who would have imagined Mr. Darcy, the aloof and inscrutable master of Pemberley, sharing the supper set with one of the Bennets? She had no doubt Caroline Bingley's fury could have set the chandeliers alight, and Mary Bennet's thinly veiled disapproval had not escaped her notice either.

But as they reached their table, Elizabeth forced herself to focus. She had secured the supper set—whatever remained was no longer Darcy's choice, but fully within her own power. Her wager with Charlotte was as good as finished. The thought should have brought triumph, a sense of satisfaction at having proven her friend wrong. Yet as she settled into her chair and Darcy poured her a glass of punch, the feeling that stirred within her was something far more complicated.

"Is the punch to your liking, Miss Bennet?" Darcy asked, breaking the silence.

Elizabeth glanced down at her glass, then back at him. His tone was polite, even cordial, yet she detected the faintest hint of something more—hesitation, perhaps, or curiosity. "Perfectly, thank you," she said lightly. "Though I confess I find the conversation thus far to be lacking."

His lips quirked slightly, the ghost of a smile. "Then allow me to remedy that."

"How very considerate of you," Elizabeth replied, her smile widening.

She had not expected to feel this way—to enjoy herself so thoroughly, to see Darcy not as a wager to be won but as a man she genuinely admired. The thought of rejecting him, of fulfilling the final term of her agreement with Charlotte, now felt... wrong. It was no longer a jest, no longer a harmless game. It was real.

Elizabeth stole another glance at Charlotte, who was seated on the far side of the room, deep in conversation with Maria Lucas. Charlotte turned slightly, catching Elizabeth's eye, and gave her a subtle but pointed look. Elizabeth quickly looked away, her pulse quickening.

Darcy's voice drew her attention back. "You seem distracted, Miss Bennet."

She blinked, startled. "Oh, not at all. I was merely... reflecting."

"On what, if I may ask?"

Elizabeth hesitated, searching for an answer that would not betray her thoughts. "On how unexpected this evening has been."

Darcy's brow furrowed slightly. "Unexpected in what way?"

"In many ways," she said, her tone deliberately vague. "But mostly in how much I have... enjoyed it."

His expression softened, and for a moment, the intensity of his gaze left her breathless. "I am glad to hear that," he said quietly. "It is not often that I enjoy such evenings myself."

Elizabeth felt her cheeks warm, and she looked away, reaching for her glass to cover her flustered state. "Would you go so far as to declare yourself happy at the moment?"

"Happiness is a matter of perspective."

"And what, pray, is your perspective?"

"That happiness is best pursued quietly," Darcy replied, meeting her gaze.

"How utterly tragic," Elizabeth declared, leaning forward slightly. "I suppose that means you avoid public displays of joy? No raucous laughter, no spirited exclamations?"

"I leave those to others," he said evenly.

"Ah, so you merely endure happiness."

Darcy paused, his glass halfway to his lips. "I do not endure happiness, Miss Bennet. I prefer it to be... private."

"Private happiness," Elizabeth repeated thoughtfully. "That sounds like the sort of thing one reads about in that rather... *bad* poetry of yours."

Darcy's hand froze, his expression briefly faltering. "I beg your pardon?"

"Oh, you cannot be under the impression that you are a talent!" she said, her eyes sparkling with mischief. "Your lines are filled with solemn pronouncements on the virtue of quiet suffering and the agony of secret longing."

"I know you are no lover of verse, but I was not aware you had such a low opinion of my efforts. I believe I am insulted."

She leaned forward. "Mr. Darcy, though it pains me to grieve you, you are the *worst* poet I have ever heard."

"I find that difficult to credit, coming from one who dislikes the form in general. What gives you the authority to judge?"

"Is it not subjective? I have my own preferences, and that is sufficient. Perhaps it would surprise you to know that I do not hate *all* poetry."

Darcy set his glass down, his composure returning. "And what sort would you prefer?"

Elizabeth hesitated, caught off guard by the question. "The sort that... amuses, I suppose. Or surprises. Perhaps even delights."

"That is a tall order," Darcy said, his tone thoughtful. "Perhaps you should demonstrate."

"Demonstrate?" she repeated, narrowing her eyes suspiciously.

"If you have such strong opinions on the matter, surely you can provide an example."

Elizabeth opened her mouth, prepared to refuse, but the glint of challenge in Darcy's eyes gave her pause. She could not very well back down now, not after teasing him so thoroughly.

"Very well," she said, straightening in her chair. "But I warn you, Mr. Darcy, I am no poet."

"I am prepared to be amazed."

Elizabeth pursed her lips, considering. Then, with a theatrical sigh, she recited:

> *"A gentleman grave, his manner austere,*
> *But what lies beneath? A heart full of cheer?"*

Darcy's lips twitched. "Is that meant to describe me?"

"It might," Elizabeth said airily. "Though I suppose the cheer is debatable."

Darcy leaned back slightly, as though accepting her challenge. "Allow me to retort."

> *"A lady so clever, her wit sharp and fine,*
> *Yet often she leaves disaster behind."*

Elizabeth gasped, though her smile betrayed her amusement. "Disaster? That is most unjust."

"Is it?" Darcy countered, his tone dry. "I heard something about a certain occasion involving Mr. Collins and a tray of tea, shortly after he came to Longbourn."

Elizabeth's mouth dropped open. "You have spies, I see!"

He sipped his wine, rather smugly, and set his glass aside. "No. I have Bingley, who has spent an inordinate amount of time in conversation with your sister. He said something about an odd wrinkle in the rug that had not been there moments before. Apparently, it cost Mr. Collins his favorite cravat."

"That was not my fault!" Elizabeth protested, laughing despite herself. "If anyone was to blame, it was the rug."

"The rug was innocent. *You*, however, I am in doubt of."

Elizabeth shook her head, her laughter drawing the attention of a few nearby guests. "You are entirely incorrigible, Mr. Darcy."

"I prefer incorrigible to austere," he said, raising his glass slightly.

Elizabeth studied him for a moment, her amusement softening into something warmer. She had not expected this—this playfulness, this ease. It was a side of him she had glimpsed before but never so fully, and it was... disarming.

"Well," she said at last, lifting her glass in return. "To incorrigible gentlemen and clever ladies."

"To private happiness," Darcy added quietly.

Their glasses clinked softly, the sound nearly lost amid the buzz of the room. Yet for Elizabeth, it felt like a declaration—of what, she could not quite say. All she knew was that for the first time in their acquaintance, she felt entirely at ease in Darcy's presence. And that, she realized with a pang, was more dangerous than any wager.

Darcy watched Elizabeth laugh, her eyes sparkling as she recovered from their poetic sparring. He had not expected the conversation to take this turn, and yet he found himself oddly grateful for it. She had a way of disarming him, of coaxing out parts of himself he thought long buried. The weight of the room—the glances, the whispers, the expectations—had faded into background noise, eclipsed entirely by her presence.

But just as he began to settle into the ease of their conversation, Elizabeth's expression shifted. Her laughter quieted, and her gaze flickered briefly across the room. Darcy followed it instinctively, noting that her friend Miss Lucas seemed to be watching them with a pointed look. When Elizabeth's eyes returned to his, they held a new coolness, her warmth momentarily dimmed. It was so subtle, so fleeting, that he might have imagined it—if not for the faintly guarded tone that crept into her voice when she spoke again.

"You are rather reflective all of a sudden, Mr. Darcy. Dare I ask what occupies your thoughts?"

Darcy hesitated, unsure how to answer. The truth—that his thoughts were entirely consumed by her—seemed far too dangerous to admit. He forced himself to look away, focusing instead on the flicker of the candlelight on the table.

"Many things," he said at last, keeping his tone even. "But mostly, I find myself wondering how you manage to defy expectation at every turn."

Elizabeth's laughter returned, soft and musical, yet Darcy noted that it did not linger as long this time. "That, Mr. Darcy, is simply a matter of principle. I make it a point never to be predictable."

"You succeed admirably," he said, his lips curving into a faint smile.

For a moment, her smile softened into something less playful, more contemplative. But then her gaze flicked away again—this time toward her sisters. Lydia's shrill laughter rang out from the far side of the room, and Elizabeth's expression tensed almost imperceptibly. Darcy followed her gaze once more, wondering what thoughts swirled behind her eyes, what weight she carried that she would not share. When her attention returned to him, her smile was firmly in place, though it no longer reached her eyes.

Their conversation lulled as the servers cleared away their plates. Darcy caught himself studying Elizabeth as she turned her attention to the room again, her gaze sweeping over the other guests with quiet observation. There was a thoughtfulness to her, an intelligence that shone through in every glance, every word. She was not merely clever; she was perceptive, and he had no doubt that she saw more of the world—and of him—than most people ever did.

But tonight, there was something else in her expression, something Darcy could not quite name. A flicker of hesitation, of conflict, as though she were at war with herself. Each time she let her warmth show, it seemed quickly followed by a moment of retreat, as though she were reminding herself of some invisible boundary she dared not cross.

The inconsistency left him restless. What was holding her back? Why did her openness feel so fleeting, her joy so tempered? She had never been thus before. Was something troubling her this evening? It... it could not be Wickham, could it? An almost possessive ire shot through him at that idea. Darcy shot a glare across the dining room, but Wickham was not even within ready line of sight, and furthermore, Darcy had not seen him approach Elizabeth all evening.

He longed to ask, to understand, but he knew better than to press. Instead, he kept his silence, hoping that if he waited, she might offer him a glimpse of whatever thoughts weighed on her so heavily.

Darcy's attention drifted to Elizabeth's face as her gaze wandered across the room, settling on her sisters. Miss Lydia and Miss Catherine were giggling loudly with their partners, their behavior drawing amused—and disapproving—glances from the surrounding guests. Miss Mary, seated near Mr. Collins, was speaking with displeased urgency about something or other, her voice carrying across the room with unrestrained earnestness.

Elizabeth's expression tightened slightly, though she did not sigh or frown. Instead, there was a faint set to her jaw, a frustration she was clearly attempting to conceal. Darcy noted the flicker of something deeper in her eyes—sadness, perhaps, or resignation. She did not meet his gaze at first, but when she finally turned and caught him watching her, her lips curved into a faint, self-deprecating smile.

"One cannot account for younger sisters," she said quietly, her tone wry but tinged with something softer. "One is concerned for them, of course, but... well, they cannot entirely be managed."

Darcy hesitated, considering her words. "You speak from experience."

She gave a small shrug, her gaze drifting briefly back to the table where Lydia had now spilled something onto the floor. "Lydia is lively, and Kitty follows where she leads. They mean no harm, but sometimes... sometimes I wonder if they understand how their actions reflect on the rest of us."

Darcy inclined his head slightly, his voice low as he replied, "You are not alone in such concerns."

Elizabeth glanced at him, her expression shifting subtly. There was curiosity in her eyes now, mixed with a hesitation he had not seen before. She seemed to weigh her next words carefully before speaking.

"And your own sister," she began, her tone softer now, "has her situation improved? I recall you mentioned she was visiting a family she had not wished to travel with. I hope her spirits have... recovered."

Darcy blinked, momentarily caught off guard by the question. He had not expected her to remember such a detail, let alone ask about it with such genuine concern. For a moment, he said nothing, unsure how much to reveal.

"I have promised her that I will collect her next week and return to London with her, to spend the rest of the winter with our Matlock relations."

"Ah." She nodded, and there was in her expression some sort of mixture of approval and regret. "I imagine that pleased her."

"I hope so. For now, she is managing. Though I fear her reluctance to go with that family was not entirely unfounded. Georgiana is... sensitive. Shy. She finds it difficult to adapt to unfamiliar company."

Elizabeth nodded thoughtfully, her gaze steady on his. "That is understandable. I imagine it is difficult to feel at ease in such situations, especially for someone so young."

Darcy hesitated again, the words catching in his throat. There was something about Elizabeth's manner—her empathy, her quiet curiosity—that made him want to share more. He leaned slightly forward, lowering his voice as he continued. "She has had... experiences that make her wary of others. I wish I could shield her from such things, but I know it is not entirely within my power."

Elizabeth's brow furrowed slightly, her tone growing even softer. "Tell me, Mr. Darcy... what is she like?"

The question hung between them, and Darcy felt an odd tightness in his chest. He rarely spoke of Georgiana in such detail, even to Bingley. But the sincerity in Elizabeth's expression—the absence of judgment, the quiet understanding—compelled him to answer.

"She is..." He paused, searching for the right words. "She is kind. Gentle. Perhaps too gentle for her own good. She has a talent for music and a love for reading, though she can be painfully shy in company."

Elizabeth smiled faintly, her eyes softening. "She sounds lovely."

"She is," Darcy said quietly. "But her kindness makes her vulnerable. She sees the good in everyone, even when it is not deserved. And I fear there are those who would take advantage of that."

Elizabeth's expression grew serious, her gaze steady. "She is fortunate, then, to have a brother who sees the world more clearly."

Darcy met her eyes, struck by the quiet conviction in her voice. "I do what I can," he said after a moment. "But there are times when I wonder if it is enough."

Elizabeth leaned forward slightly, her fingers brushing the edge of her glass. "I think, Mr. Darcy, that it is enough to care. To try. That is more than many would do."

Darcy felt the weight of her words settle over him, their sincerity cutting through the noise of the room. She spoke with such ease, such clarity, and he found himself wondering—not for the first time—how it was that she seemed to understand so much of what he could never say.

"Thank you," he said at last, his voice low. "For speaking so plainly."

Elizabeth smiled then, a small, warm smile that sent an inexplicable warmth through him. "Well," she said lightly, "I should warn you, Mr. Darcy, that plain speaking is something of a habit with me."

"It is a habit I find myself appreciating," he replied.

Elizabeth blinked, surprised by the sincerity of his tone. Then, with a soft smile, she said, "Well, I shall consider that a compliment."

"It is meant as one," he replied.

Their eyes met, and for a moment, the noise of the room seemed to fade entirely. Darcy could feel the pull of her presence, the undeniable gravity that seemed to draw him closer to her. It was a feeling he had fought against for weeks, a battle he had told himself he could win. But sitting here, looking at her, he realized with startling clarity that he had already lost.

"Miss Bennet," he began, his voice low, each word carefully chosen. "I find myself—"

"Mr. Darcy," Elizabeth interrupted, her tone sharp but not unkind. Her eyes widened slightly, and she glanced away, her fingers tightening around the stem of her glass. "Please... do not."

Darcy froze, the unspoken words caught in his throat. For a moment, he simply stared at her, the flicker of something—hesitation? fear?—in her expression catching him entirely off guard. She wasn't angry. If anything, she looked almost regretful, as though stopping him had cost her something, too.

"I beg your pardon," he said finally, his tone carefully neutral. "I did not mean to make you uncomfortable."

Elizabeth's gaze darted back to him, and though her expression was carefully composed, there was a tremor of uncertainty in her voice when she replied. "You did not. It is only that... some things are better left unsaid."

Darcy's chest tightened, confusion and frustration warring within him. He had thought—no, he had felt—something between them tonight. A connection that transcended the games and wagers and social conventions that had brought them together. But now, as she sat before him, her eyes shadowed with some unspoken thought, he was no longer certain of anything.

"Of course," he said after a moment, inclining his head slightly. "I would never presume to speak where my words are unwelcome."

Elizabeth winced, a small but unmistakable reaction, and Darcy cursed himself for the unintended sharpness of his tone. She opened her mouth as if to respond, then seemed to think better of it, her lips pressing into a thin line.

They sat in silence for a moment, the charged energy between them replaced by an awkward stillness. Around them, the hum of the room returned, the clinking of glasses and low murmur of voices grounding them once more in the reality of the evening.

Elizabeth shifted slightly in her seat, her fingers brushing against the tablecloth. "I think I should... return to my friends," she said, her voice softer now, almost tentative. "Thank you, Mr. Darcy, for your company."

Darcy rose immediately as she stood, his movements instinctive and precise. "The pleasure was mine, Miss Bennet."

Her gaze lingered on his for a heartbeat longer than necessary, as though she wanted to say more. But whatever words she might have spoken remained unvoiced. Instead, she offered him a small, almost apologetic smile before turning and weaving her way back toward the crowded ballroom.

Darcy watched her go, his thoughts a whirlwind of contradictions. She had stopped him before he could say the thing he had scarcely allowed himself to admit, even in the privacy of his own mind. And yet, she had not rejected him outright. There had been no disdain in her manner, no triumph or amusement, only discomfort—and something else he could not quite name.

THE HUM OF THE ballroom enveloped Elizabeth as she moved back toward the dance floor, the remnants of her supper conversation with Darcy lingering in her mind. It had been unexpectedly enjoyable—no, more than enjoyable. It had been disarming, leaving her mind spinning into an abyss of... was *that* was desire was? It was certainly something.

The Darcy she had encountered tonight was not the aloof, judgmental man she had once dismissed with scorn. He was thoughtful, even kind, and for the first time, she began to see him as something more than the sum of his faults. He was human, imperfect, and—she dared admit—remarkably similar to herself. A fellow cynic, forced to weather the world with wary eyes, he had revealed a side of himself that felt unexpectedly familiar.

And tonight, he had done it... rather pleasantly. Darcy had been charming, surprisingly warm, and even vulnerable in his quiet way. The memory of his expression when he spoke of his sister sent a pang through her chest—an ache that felt dangerously close to admiration. She shook her head slightly, as if to dislodge the thought, but it clung stubbornly, a persistent echo of their conversation.

Elizabeth pressed her lips together, her hands tightening briefly at her sides. She had not rejected him outright. That was the most damning part of all. She had stopped him, yes, but only because she could not bear to hear what he might have said. The thought of his sincerity, of the possibility that he might feel as deeply as she now suspected, left her trembling.

And worse still, she had not finished the terms of the wager.

Her gaze flicked across the room to Charlotte, who stood near the far wall, her expression one of quiet expectation. Elizabeth's stomach twisted. She could not go on with it—not now, not after tonight. Whatever Charlotte might think of her, whatever teasing remarks or smug glances she might endure, Elizabeth could not bring herself to treat Darcy so callously.

No, it was time to surrender. To admit defeat. She would cross the room, find Charlotte, and tell her plainly: "You were right. I cannot do it."

She had taken only a single step in Charlotte's direction when a young militia officer approached, his red coat bright against the muted colors of the crowd. He bowed deeply, his expression earnest and eager. "Miss Bennet, may I have the honor of this dance?"

Elizabeth hesitated, glancing toward Charlotte, whose eyes met hers briefly before darting away. A quiet sigh escaped her lips. She had been ready to end this charade—to lay down her arms and declare herself vanquished. But now, here was a polite interruption, one that demanded her attention and delayed the inevitable.

With a small, practiced smile, she inclined her head. "Of course, sir. I would be delighted."

As he led her to the dance floor, Elizabeth tried to muster the lightness that usually came so easily. But her mind was elsewhere—on Darcy's weighted gaze, on the warmth that had crept into his voice, and on the weight of everything she had nearly allowed him to say.

The music began, and they moved into the steps of The Duke of Kent's Waltz. The officer was a competent dancer, if a bit stiff, and his conversation stayed firmly in the realm of polite trivialities. Elizabeth found herself responding automatically, her attention drifting elsewhere.

Across the room, she caught sight of Darcy, standing near one of the columns, his dark eyes fixed on her. She faltered for the briefest moment in her step, recovering quickly enough that her partner did not notice, though her heart gave a curious little flutter. Darcy's gaze was steady, unreadable, and yet it seemed to hold an intensity that made her pulse quicken.

What was he thinking? The thought distracted her throughout the remainder of the dance, her replies to her partner growing increasingly absentminded. By the time the set ended, she was grateful for the opportunity to retreat to the side of the room for a moment of refreshment.

Elizabeth made her way to a small table near the far wall, where glasses of punch and plates of biscuits had been laid out. She took a glass and sipped, letting the cool, sweet liquid soothe her dry throat. She glanced around the room, scanning the lively crowd, and her gaze inevitably landed on Darcy once more. He had moved closer, though still at a respectable distance, and was now speaking with Mr. Bingley. Even as he nodded in response to whatever Bingley was saying, his attention flickered back to her.

Elizabeth felt a curious mix of irritation and warmth. Why was he watching her so intently? Did he not have more pressing matters to occupy his time?

"Miss Eliza!" came a familiar, saccharine voice. Elizabeth turned to find Caroline Bingley standing beside her, resplendent in a pale orange gown that shimmered in the light. Her smile was as sharp as the cut of her sleeves. "You seem quite occupied this evening. Might I intrude upon your thoughts for a moment?"

Elizabeth set her glass down and returned Caroline's smile with one of her own, her tone cool but polite. "Of course, Miss Bingley. I am always delighted by your company."

"How gracious of you," Caroline said, her voice lilting with practiced charm. She moved closer, her eyes sweeping the room with calculated disinterest before settling back on Elizabeth. "I must say, you have had quite the evening. Mr. Darcy has been... attentive, has he not?"

Elizabeth tilted her head, feigning ignorance. "Attentive? Nothing out of the common way, I imagine."

"Oh, come now, Miss Eliza," Caroline said with a small, tinkling laugh. "Everyone has noticed. He danced with you, sat with you at supper—why, I daresay he has scarcely looked away from you all evening."

Elizabeth's cheeks warmed, though she kept her expression neutral. "I suppose Mr. Darcy is fulfilling his duty as a gentleman. Nothing more."

"Is that what you think?" Caroline said, her voice dropping slightly. "How charmingly naive of you."

Elizabeth stiffened slightly but kept her expression even. "I cannot imagine what you mean by that, Miss Bingley."

Caroline's gaze flicked briefly across the room, and Elizabeth followed it, her stomach sinking as she spotted Lydia and Kitty near the refreshment table. Lydia was laughing loudly at some joke made by a young officer, her voice carrying above the hum of conversation. Kitty, not to be outdone, swayed slightly as she giggled into her punch cup, clearly enjoying the attention of another officer who was leaning far too close.

Caroline sighed delicately. "Your sisters do seem to be enjoying themselves tonight. Though I wonder if perhaps their enthusiasm might be a touch... immoderate."

Elizabeth's jaw tightened, but she kept her tone light. "They are young, Miss Bingley. Youth is often exuberant."

"Indeed," Caroline said, her tone laden with false sympathy. "It is such a pity, though, when exuberance leads to... unfortunate misunderstandings. I only say so because I care, of course."

Elizabeth turned to face her fully, her smile frozen in place. "How very thoughtful of you."

Caroline tilted her head, her expression one of feigned concern. "I only wish to be helpful, Miss Eliza. After all, I would hate for anyone to misconstrue Mr. Darcy's behavior tonight. He is a man of duty, as you said, and his honor is above reproach. Surely you understand."

Elizabeth's heart began to race, though she kept her voice steady. "I cannot imagine anyone would think otherwise."

"Oh, I should hope not," Caroline said with a sigh of relief. "It would be such a shame for you to misinterpret his attentions. You see..." She leaned in slightly, lowering her voice as though sharing a secret. "His behavior this evening is no doubt tied to the wager he made with my brother."

Elizabeth's stomach dropped. "A... a wager?"

"Oh, yes, though I'm sure it was all in good fun. Darcy, Heaven bless him, has been trying for years to persuade my brother to sell that dreadful warehouse in London, but Charles has been *so* stubbornly attached to it. Darcy knew, of course, that he would not let it go without a little extra incentive. Of course, as part of the arrangement, Mr. Darcy promised to show... a certain *civility* to my brother's guests and neighbors."

Elizabeth narrowed her eyes and turned them fully on Miss Bingley. "Civility?"

"Oh! You know Darcy. He can hardly swat the ladies away fast enough when he is in company, so naturally, he has taken the defense of disliking everyone at first brush. Charles is terribly naive about the thing, though, and he took it into his head that Darcy *must* make himself amenable to... everyone. Although, I understand that later, the terms of the wager were restricted to merely indulging *your* family."

Elizabeth gripped the edge of the table to steady herself. "How kind of him."

"Oh, indeed," Caroline said brightly. "Mr. Darcy is nothing if not honorable. But I thought you ought to know. It would be dreadful if you were to imagine his attentions were... personal."

Elizabeth forced a tight smile, her heart pounding in her chest. "Your concern is noted, Miss Bingley. Thank you for your thoughtfulness."

Caroline's expression turned positively saccharine. "Of course. It is always a pleasure to be of service."

With that, she swept away, leaving Elizabeth standing alone, her thoughts churning. A wager. That was why Darcy had been so attentive, so polite. It was not because he wished to be, but because he was bound by some ridiculous agreement with Bingley.

Her cheeks burned as she glanced across the room, her eyes landing on Darcy once more. He was speaking to Mr. Hurst now, but his gaze flicked toward her as though he could sense her attention. His expression was calm, unreadable, but to Elizabeth, it now seemed calculated. Every gesture, every word from him tonight—it had all been a performance.

Straightening her shoulders, she set her glass aside and lifted her chin. Whatever games Mr. Darcy and his friends wished to play, she would not be their unwitting pawn. Not tonight. Not ever.

DARCY STOOD AT THE edge of the ballroom, his gaze drawn involuntarily to Elizabeth Bennet as she danced with a young militia officer. The officer was grinning like a schoolboy, clearly enamored with his partner, while Elizabeth moved with her usual energy, nearly sparkling in the candlelight. Darcy's chest tightened unexpectedly, a flicker of jealousy sparking in a way he could neither understand nor control.

He forced himself to look away, his eyes scanning the room. It was then that he noticed Wickham, standing near the far wall and watching the same dance with a peculiar intensity. Darcy's jaw clenched. Wickham had spent the evening carefully avoiding him, slinking into the shadows whenever their gazes met. And yet, he had lingered near Elizabeth more than once, his interest in her as unwelcome as it was unseemly.

Darcy's fingers curled into his palm as he resisted the urge to intervene.

His attention flickered back to the dance floor, where Elizabeth was laughing lightly at something her partner had said. There was no artifice in her manner, no coyness—only her usual vivacity, which seemed to draw people toward her effortlessly. Darcy's throat constricted with something he refused to name, and he turned sharply to survey the room once more, needing to distract himself.

That was when he saw it.

Wickham had moved across the room and was now speaking with Miss Mary Bennet. Darcy's brow furrowed, unease prickling at the back of his neck. Mary Bennet was the last person Darcy would have expected Wickham to approach. Her solemn, pious demeanor was a far cry from the lively, flirtatious women Wickham typically sought out. And yet, there he was, leaning in slightly as he spoke, his expression uncharacteristically serious.

Mary stood stiffly, her hands clasped tightly in front of her as she listened with rapt attention. The oddity of the interaction struck Darcy immediately. Wickham was many things—charming, duplicitous, manipulative—but he rarely wasted time on endeavors without purpose. What could he possibly want with Mary Bennet? And why did she seem so... enthralled?

Darcy's gaze darted back to the dance floor, where Elizabeth was now executing a turn with her partner. For a moment, she glanced in his direction, their eyes meeting across the room. The warmth in her expression, the unspoken connection that seemed to spark between them, made Darcy's pulse quicken. But just as swiftly as it came, the moment was broken when she turned back to her partner, laughing at some remark he made.

Darcy's focus shifted back to Wickham and Mary. Wickham's posture had grown more animated, his hands gesturing subtly as he leaned closer to her. Mary, for her part, seemed utterly rapt, her lips parting slightly as though about to respond. Darcy's unease deepened, a knot forming in his stomach. Whatever Wickham was saying to Mary, it could not be for any good purpose.

His eyes flicked once more to Elizabeth, as if to reassure himself. She had retired from the dance floor and now stood near the refreshment table, her smile bright as she exchanged a few words with a passing acquaintance. She appeared utterly untroubled, oblivious to the peculiar drama unfolding nearby. He thought about going to her—perhaps even asking for a second set—but Caroline Bingley was now joining her, and that... well, that was not something he wished to meddle in just now.

Darcy exhaled slowly, his frustration mounting. Why could nothing about this evening remain simple?

Before he could consider the matter further, a voice broke through his thoughts.

"Ah, Mr. Darcy!" came the unmistakable, obsequious tone of Mr. Collins. Darcy turned reluctantly to find the clergyman bustling toward him, his face a mix of self-importance and barely contained agitation. "I hope I am not intruding upon your reflections, sir, but I felt it my duty to address a matter of great concern."

Darcy raised a brow, his irritation barely masked. "What matter, Mr. Collins?"

Collins puffed up his chest, clearly relishing the moment. "It has come to my attention—through means I shall not disclose—that there is a certain... wager involving your good self and my cousin, Miss Elizabeth Bennet."

Darcy's expression darkened, his body stiffening. Good heavens, had Bingley opened his fool mouth? That... that could ruin everything! The hackles on his neck rose as his voice dropped to a growl. "A wager?"

"Yes, indeed! A most improper one, I might add. It seems Miss Elizabeth engaged in a bet with her friend, Miss Lucas, regarding your esteemed self. The goal, I am told, was to gain your favor—not out of genuine admiration, but as a means to reject you publicly."

Darcy's breath caught, the words striking like a blow. She could not possibly... Not Elizabeth. Not the most genuine, artless woman he had ever... "And what proof do you have of this claim, Mr. Collins?"

Collins faltered for a moment, though his pompous demeanor quickly returned. "Proof, sir? Why, I should think the word of a clergyman sufficient in such matters! My source is... unimpeachable."

Darcy's eyes narrowed. He scanned the room and immediately found Mary Bennet, standing near the refreshment table with her hands clasped tightly together, her gaze fixed firmly on them. Her pale complexion and anxious expression betrayed her involvement. Darcy's mind reeled. Mary Bennet was Wickham's unlikely choice of confidante earlier—had she been manipulated into this?

"Your source," Darcy said coldly, "appears to be Miss Mary Bennet."

Collins stammered, his discomfort momentary before he rallied. "Miss Mary is a deeply principled young lady, who I am sure would wish to prevent... Well! while I shall not confirm or deny her involvement, I can assure you that my concern lies solely in preventing harm to the Bennet family's reputation. Lady Catherine would be most displeased were I to allow such impropriety to continue unchecked."

Darcy's fury simmered beneath his calm exterior. "And what precisely have you done to address this... impropriety?"

Collins puffed himself up even further, clearly pleased with his own actions. "I would take it upon myself, sir, to speak to Miss Elizabeth most firmly on the matter, as soon as I may. Though, I must say, when I have taken measures to reprove her on other matters she has been—alas—less receptive than I might have hoped. I believe she shall require further guidance in understanding the consequences of her actions, but rest assured, I intend to make my position clear. I thought it would be wisest to first approach you—"

Darcy's fists clenched at his sides. "And you believe Lady Catherine would approve of such meddling?"

Collins beamed. "I am confident she would, Mr. Darcy. It is my duty as a clergyman to address matters of morality, particularly where my family is concerned."

Darcy exhaled slowly, his anger sharp and focused. He glanced once more toward Mary, whose guilt-ridden expression left little doubt as to her role in this debacle. But beneath his anger lay something far more painful: doubt.

Could it be true? Could Elizabeth have wagered on his favor as some sort of game? The thought was almost unbearable.

"Mr. Collins," he said, his voice cold and clipped, "I will thank you not to involve yourself in matters beyond your comprehension. Your interference in this situation has caused more harm than good."

Collins blinked, his expression faltering. "But I only sought to—"

"That will be all," Darcy said firmly, cutting him off. Without waiting for a reply, he turned on his heel and walked away, his mind a storm of conflicting emotions.

Twenty-One

THE HUM OF THE ballroom felt stifling as Elizabeth stepped onto the dance floor's edge, her movements brisk and sharp. Her thoughts churned with Caroline Bingley's revelation, each repetition of the word *wager* igniting fresh waves of fury. Her chest tightened with every glance toward Darcy, the man who had dared to make her the subject of such a ridiculous game.

Civility. Politeness. Duty.

She clenched her jaw as those words rattled in her head, taunting her. How dare he? How *dare* Mr. Darcy, with all his self-important airs and guarded mannerisms, reduce their interactions to some shallow obligation born of a wager? Every moment she had shared with him tonight—every lingering look, every hint of warmth—felt tainted now, as if she had been foolish to ever believe it genuine.

Elizabeth's gaze swept the room until she found him. Darcy stood near the far wall, his posture stiff, his expression carved from stone as he listened to Mr. Collins. The clergyman was gesturing wildly, his voice carrying faintly over the din of the room. Though Elizabeth could not make out the words, she saw the flicker of irritation in Darcy's eyes, the subtle tightening of his jaw.

Good, she thought, her anger bubbling higher. *Let him be irritated. Let him feel even a fraction of what I feel now.*

She took a step toward him, her resolve hardening. But before she could close the distance, another figure intercepted her path.

"Miss Elizabeth," said an older acquaintance, a matronly woman with an overbearing fondness for gossip. "What a lovely evening this has turned out to be, has it not? I hear Mr. Darcy was quite attentive to you at supper. Surely, there must be some truth to the rumors?"

Elizabeth barely heard the words. Her gaze remained fixed on Darcy, her pulse pounding in her ears. She muttered a curt, "If you will excuse me," and brushed past the woman without a second thought. The other guests in her path fared no better; Elizabeth moved through them with singular determination, her every thought consumed by the need to confront him.

Her anger flared brighter as she neared, noticing that Darcy barely acknowledged Mr. Collins's endless prattle. The clergyman, oblivious to any lack of interest, continued speaking with exaggerated animation, puffing out his chest as though he were sharing some great wisdom.

Elizabeth stopped a few paces away, her hands trembling at her sides. She should not do this. Not here, not now. Confronting Darcy in the middle of the ballroom, under the eyes of half the county, would only add fuel to the gossip that already swirled around her. But the words burned in her throat, desperate for release.

Darcy glanced up then, as if sensing her presence. Their eyes met, and the tension between them crackled like a lightning strike. Elizabeth's breath caught, her anger momentarily faltering under the weight of his gaze. There was something there—something raw and unguarded that left her stomach twisting in ways she did not want to name.

"Miss Bennet," Darcy said, his voice low but unmistakable, cutting through Mr. Collins's endless chatter like a blade.

Collins turned, startled by the interruption. "Ah, Cousin Elizabeth! How fortunate that you are here. I was just—"

But Elizabeth barely heard him. Her focus was entirely on Darcy, the simmering anger surging back to the surface as she squared her shoulders.

"Mr. Darcy," she said, her tone sharper than she intended. "I wonder if I might have a word."

Darcy's jaw clenched like a rock, but he nodded. "I have nothing to say."

Oh, so he was going to take that tactic, was he? She lifted her chin. "Well, I am afraid *I* do."

Collins looked between them, his mouth opening to protest, but Darcy silenced him with a glance that could have frozen the Thames. "Excuse us, Mr. Collins."

The clergyman sputtered indignantly but stepped back, leaving them standing together in the shadow of the great chandelier. The hum of the ballroom seemed louder now, the distant sounds of laughter and music a sharp contrast to the charged silence between them.

Elizabeth spoke first, her voice low but trembling with barely contained emotion. "I have just been made aware, Mr. Darcy, of a certain... wager you made with Mr. Bingley."

Darcy stiffened, his expression hardening. "Miss Bennet, I—"

"No," Elizabeth cut him off, her eyes blazing. "You will allow me to finish. I would like to know, sir, whether your decision to dance with me tonight, to sit with me at supper, was made out of genuine regard or merely to satisfy the terms of some trivial bet."

Her words struck him like a physical blow. Darcy's jaw tightened, the muscles in his face visibly working as he fought to keep his composure. "Miss Bennet," he said carefully, his voice low and trembling with restrained fury, "you presume much."

"I presume?" Elizabeth's tone was sharp, cutting through the din of the ballroom. She stepped closer, her voice lowering but losing none of its edge. "What else am I to think, Mr. Darcy? To discover that every kindness, every gesture, was simply your way of fulfilling a wager? A game?"

Darcy's face darkened, his frustration spilling over. "And what of your own wager, Miss Bennet?" he shot back, his tone sharp enough to draw blood. "Should I assume that your attentions this evening were born of genuine regard? Or were you merely playing a role, seeking my favor as part of your own farce?"

Elizabeth's breath caught, her fury briefly faltering. "Playing a role?" she repeated, her voice trembling with disbelief as her face flushed with unwelcome conviction. "What are you talking about?"

"Do not insult my intelligence," Darcy said coldly. "I was informed quite thoroughly—by your 'esteemed' cousin, no less—of the terms you agreed upon with Miss Lucas. The goal, as I understand it, was to win my favor, only to reject it with some grand display of triumph. Tell me, Miss Bennet, was that your intent all along?"

Elizabeth's cheeks burned, her shame mingling with fresh waves of anger. "And you believed him?" she demanded, her voice rising. "You believed Mr. Collins, of all people?"

"I had no reason not to," Darcy snapped. "He seemed quite eager to play the moral arbiter of the evening."

"Because, of course, you would take the word of a pompous fool over considering, for one moment, that there might be more to the story!" Elizabeth's fists clenched at her sides, her entire body trembling with emotion. "You, who pride yourself on your discernment, would rather cling to your wounded pride than allow for the possibility that you might be wrong!"

Darcy's eyes narrowed, his gaze burning into hers. "And what of your discernment, Miss Bennet? What of the assumptions you have made about me? You stand here, casting aspersions, accusing me of falseness, when you yourself—"

"Stop," Elizabeth said sharply, cutting him off. "You do not get to turn this on me."

"Do I not?" Darcy's voice was lower now, but no less cutting. "I have spent the past weeks believing—foolishly, it seems—that we had begun to understand one another. That your teasing, your wit, was a mark of friendship, not derision. And tonight—tonight, I allowed myself to hope for more. But now I see the truth. All of it was a pretense. You never intended to see me at all."

Elizabeth's chest heaved, her anger so fierce it felt like it might consume her entirely. "And what about you?" she demanded, her voice shaking. "You speak of being misunderstood, but you have the audacity to make a wager—about me, about my family—and pretend that you are above reproach?"

Darcy's silence was deafening, his jaw tightening as he met her gaze. The weight of their words, their accusations, hung heavy between them, drawing the attention of more than a few nearby guests. Elizabeth could feel the stares, the whispers, but she no longer cared. Let them look. Let them see the wreckage of whatever connection she had thought might exist between herself and this man.

"I see," Darcy said finally, his voice cold and clipped. "There is nothing more to say."

"On that, Mr. Darcy," Elizabeth said bitterly, "we are in perfect agreement."

Darcy inclined his head, his expression an unreadable mask. "Good evening, Miss Bennet."

With that, he turned sharply on his heel and strode from the room, his departure swift and decisive. Elizabeth watched him go, her breath coming in uneven bursts as the reality of what had just transpired settled over her. The room felt unbearably loud now, the hum of whispers and the weight of judgment pressing down on her from every corner.

HE DID NOT KNOW where he was going—only that he needed to escape the suffocating press of people, the prying eyes that seemed to follow his every move. His chest was tight, his breath shallow, and every step felt like a fight to maintain his composure.

Elizabeth.

The name seared through him, as though even thinking it might burn away whatever fragile control he had left. For weeks—months—he had allowed himself to be drawn into her orbit. Against his better judgment, he had softened, let down the walls he had built so carefully, and dared to believe that she might see him as more than the cold, unfeeling man she had first met.

And tonight—tonight had felt like everything he had ever wanted. Her laughter, her wit, the way she had looked at him during their supper set—it had all felt real. Genuine. He had let himself believe that her warmth, her charm, had been meant for him. That she had seen him, truly seen him, as he was.

And it had all been a lie.

Darcy's hands curled into fists at his sides as he pushed open a side door, stepping into an empty corridor. The quiet was a welcome reprieve from the noise of the ballroom, but it did nothing to quell the storm raging within him. He leaned heavily against the wall, his head falling back as he let out a slow, measured breath. His heart pounded in his chest, the betrayal cutting deeper than he cared to admit.

How could I have been so blind?

He had seen her as genuine, unlike so many others who sought his favor for their own ends. But now, knowing the truth of her wager with Miss Lucas, every moment he had shared with her felt like a mockery. The teasing glances, the playful banter—it had all been a game, designed to draw him in, to trap him, so she could revel in rejecting him.

And yet, even as anger churned in his gut, another emotion gnawed at the edges of his thoughts. Hurt. He had been falling in love with her, helplessly and irrevocably, and the realization that she had never been sincere left him reeling. He had been a fool—a lovesick fool, blind to the manipulation behind her every smile.

No. His jaw tightened, his fists clenching harder. This was not manipulation, not in the way of the scheming debutantes who sought his wealth or status. It was something else—something more complex and, in its way, more cutting. She had played her role so well, so convincingly, that he had seen in her everything he had ever wanted: honesty, intelligence, kindness.

He shoved away from the wall, pacing the length of the corridor as his thoughts spiraled. "She never intended to hurt me," he muttered to himself, the words bitter on his tongue. "She only wanted... what? To prove a point? To win some ridiculous bet at my expense?"

The thought made his stomach churn. He stopped mid-stride, pressing his hands to his temples. He could not bear the idea of her laughter—light, musical—being shared with Miss Lucas over the success of her scheme. Did she mock him in private? Had she shared with Charlotte every detail of how easily he had fallen for her charm?

A door creaked open further down the corridor, and Darcy tensed, expecting a servant or perhaps another guest. Instead, Mr. Bingley appeared, his expression confused and concerned.

"Darcy?" Bingley approached cautiously, his affable nature tempered by unease. "You vanished from the ballroom. I was worried."

Darcy straightened, forcing his features into something resembling calm. "I needed air."

Bingley frowned, his brow furrowing. "Is something wrong?"

Darcy hesitated. He wanted to tell Bingley everything—to vent his anger, his heartbreak—but the words caught in his throat. He had already suffered enough humiliation tonight. To admit the depths of his feelings for Elizabeth, only to reveal how thoroughly he had been deceived, was a vulnerability he could not bear to share. Not now.

"Nothing that cannot be mended," he said tersely, his voice flat. "Have my valet sent for. I mean to pack for Lincolnshire."

"Now?" Bingley looked genuinely surprised. "Darcy, it's the middle of the ball! What could possibly—?"

"I said I needed air," Darcy snapped, harsher than he intended. "And I find I need more of it than this place can offer."

Bingley's expression darkened, but he stepped back, his tone careful. "If you must. But Darcy—"

"Good night, Bingley." Darcy brushed past him, the finality in his tone leaving no room for argument.

As he made his way toward the exit, the noise of the ballroom grew fainter with each step. The night air hit him like a shock, cold and biting against his heated skin. He paused just outside, staring up at the sky, the stars scattered across the darkness like fragments of something broken.

He clenched his jaw, shoving his hands into his pockets. He had let himself fall for her, and now he would pay the price. But he would not let her see the extent of his pain. She would never know how deeply she had cut him.

Tomorrow, he would leave for Lincolnshire. And after that, London. Distance was the only cure for this madness, and he would take it without hesitation.

Elizabeth Bennet may haunt me now, he thought bitterly, *but I will not allow her to destroy me.*

ELIZABETH HAD BARELY SLEPT. The events of the previous evening played on a tor-
turous loop in her mind, each memory a fresh wound. Darcy's furious expression, his
biting accusations—she could still feel the weight of his words, the sharp edge of his
disappointment. And now, with morning light streaming through her window, she was
no closer to finding peace.

As she descended the stairs, voices from the sitting room carried through the house,
sharp and agitated. Elizabeth froze midway, recognizing Mr. Collins's tones rising above
the others.

"...an absolute scandal, Mrs. Bennet! I was merely doing my duty as a clergyman and a
relative, and now I find myself accused of impropriety! Impropriety, madam!"

Elizabeth's stomach twisted as she reached the doorway. Mr. Collins stood near the
fireplace, his face flushed, gesturing wildly as he spoke. Her mother sat on the settee,
clutching her handkerchief as if it were the only thing keeping her upright. Mary hovered
near the corner, her expression taut with guilt.

"What is going on here?" Elizabeth asked sharply, stepping into the room.

Mr. Collins turned toward her, his chest puffing out indignantly. "Ah, Cousin Elizabeth, how kind of you to join us. Perhaps you might explain to your family how my innocent attempt to preserve the Bennet name has resulted in such unwarranted hostility."

Elizabeth stiffened, her hands curling into fists. "Preserve the Bennet name? By spreading gossip about me and Mr. Darcy in the middle of a ball?"

"Spreading gossip?" Mr. Collins gasped, his hand flying to his chest. "I did no such
thing! I merely acted upon the information given to me by a trusted source—"

"Mary," Elizabeth said flatly, her gaze snapping to her sister. Mary flinched, looking
down at her hands, which were folded tightly in her lap.

"I... I only told Mr. Collins what I thought he ought to know," Mary stammered, her
voice barely above a whisper. "It seemed improper... your wager with Charlotte... and Mr.
Darcy... He's not a good man, Lizzy."

Elizabeth's anger surged, her composure slipping. "What evidence have you?"

"Well..." Mary's hands twisted her handkerchief. "Mr. Wickham, he said..."

"Mr. Wickham is the man you hold up as trustworthy! On what grounds?"

"He..." Mary cleared her throat. "Apparently, Mr. Darcy deceived Mr. Wickham in his inheritance. Some long-standing arrangement in his father's will..."

"Now, Cousin," Collins interrupted. "Pray, let us not denigrate an upright man so! The nephew of Lady Catherine and my good friend Mr. Darcy would never stoop so low as to undermine his father's wishes. Why, I could write to Lady Catherine this minute for a character—she means for him to marry her daughter, of all people!"

Elizabeth gesticulated toward the man. "See? Even this fool can see through that lie. Mary, do you have any idea what you've done? What damage you caused by sharing something so personal—something so foolish—with him?"

"Now, see here!" Collins exclaimed, his face reddening further. "It was my moral obligation to intervene! Lady Catherine herself would applaud my efforts to protect a gentleman of Mr. Darcy's standing from such... from such manipulation!"

Elizabeth laughed bitterly. "Manipulation? Mr. Collins, you have no idea what you're talking about. You humiliated me—and Mr. Darcy—publicly, and for what? Your own self-importance?"

"That is quite enough!" Mrs. Bennet interjected, waving her handkerchief dramatically. "Elizabeth, how could you bring this shame upon our family? To think, wagering on a man's affections! And Mr. Darcy, no less!"

Elizabeth's breath caught, the accusation cutting deeper than she expected. Before she could defend herself, another voice interrupted.

"Lizzy?"

Elizabeth turned to see Charlotte standing in the doorway. A wave of relief and dread washed over her simultaneously.

"Charlotte," Elizabeth said, her voice faltering.

"May we speak privately?" Charlotte asked, her tone calm but firm.

Elizabeth hesitated, glancing at the others. Collins looked ready to object, but Charlotte silenced him with a look that left no room for argument. Without waiting for an answer, Elizabeth nodded and followed her friend into the hallway.

THE HALLWAY WAS QUIETER, the muffled sounds of the sitting room fading behind them. Charlotte faced Elizabeth, her arms crossed and her expression carefully neutral.

"So.. It seems the wager has taken a turn we did not anticipate."

Elizabeth winced. "Charlotte, I never meant for any of this to happen. I—"

"Didn't you?" Charlotte interrupted, her gaze sharp. "You set out to prove a point, Lizzy. To show me that you could make a man like Mr. Darcy fall for you. And you succeeded, didn't you?"

Elizabeth's chest tightened. "I did not mean to hurt him."

"Of course you did" Charlotte said, her tone softening slightly. "But you didn't think about what might happen if you changed your mind. Or if you got hurt, too."

"This was all your stupid idea! I never should have let you talk me into this."

"Oh, come, Lizzy, it was all harmless fun at first."

Elizabeth looked away, shame creeping into her voice. "It wasn't supposed to be like this. I never imagined... I did not think I would... care."

"And now?" Charlotte asked, tilting her head.

Elizabeth hesitated, her voice barely above a whisper. "And now I've ruined everything."

Charlotte sighed, her posture relaxing. "You haven't ruined everything, Lizzy. But you have to decide what you want. If you care about Mr. Darcy—truly care—then you need to stop hiding behind your pride."

Elizabeth laughed bitterly, shaking her head. "It's too late for that, Charlotte. He hates me now."

"Maybe," Charlotte said with a faint, knowing smile. "Or maybe he's just as angry with himself as he is with you."

Elizabeth frowned, her thoughts a chaotic storm. She wanted to believe Charlotte was right, that Darcy's anger wasn't entirely aimed at her. But the memory of his face—cold, distant, betrayed—loomed like a specter, and the hope Charlotte offered felt impossibly far away.

"Charlotte," Elizabeth said at last, her voice trembling, "I don't know how to fix this. I don't even know if it can be fixed."

Charlotte's expression softened, but her tone remained steady. "You have to decide whether it's worth trying."

Elizabeth shook her head, turning away slightly. "It doesn't matter. It's too late. He—" Her voice faltered. "He thinks I've been playing him this whole time. And after what Collins said—" She broke off, her fists clenching at her sides. "I wouldn't blame him if he hated me."

Charlotte studied her closely, her arms crossed. "And do you?"

Elizabeth blinked, confused. "Do I what?"

"Hate him."

Elizabeth's breath caught, and for a moment, she couldn't speak. Hate? The word seemed absurd now, even after everything. Whatever frustrations she had once felt toward Darcy, whatever pride or prejudice had clouded her view, those emotions had long since given way to something far more complex—and far more painful.

"No," she said finally, her voice quiet but certain. "I do not hate him."

Charlotte raised an eyebrow. "Then why are you so determined to let this end badly? If you care about him, Lizzy—"

Elizabeth whirled around, her frustration boiling over. "Because I've already ruined it! Don't you see that? There's no coming back from this. He thinks I've been mocking him, playing with his feelings, when all I've done is—" She stopped herself, biting her lip as tears threatened to spill.

"All you've done is what?" Charlotte pressed gently.

Elizabeth looked away, her throat tightening. "Made a fool of myself," she whispered. "And now I've lost him. The wager doesn't even matter anymore."

Charlotte's gaze turned sharp at the mention of the wager. "Doesn't it?"

Elizabeth let out a bitter laugh. "You want to talk about the wager now? Very well. I did not win, Charlotte. I didn't even come close."

"You danced with him. You shared the supper set, and then... well, you sort of 'rejected' him, did you not?" Charlotte countered. "I'd say that was enough to fulfill the terms."

Elizabeth turned back to her, her eyes blazing. "He left the ball early, furious with me! Not because I was able to turn the tables but because *he* turned them on *me!* Does that sound like a victory to you?"

Charlotte hesitated, her composure flickering. "Perhaps not. But Lizzy, you—"

"No." Elizabeth's voice cracked as she cut her off. "I did not win, Charlotte. Not the way we first agreed. And even if I had... what would it mean? What would it be worth, knowing that I've hurt him?"

Charlotte sighed, her shoulders sagging slightly. "So you're conceding, then?"

Elizabeth nodded, swallowing hard. "Yes. You were right. This was a mistake—a foolish, thoughtless mistake. I'll have something for you tomorrow."

Charlotte frowned, her brow furrowing. "Lizzy, this isn't about me collecting on a wager."

"It's about what's fair," Elizabeth said bitterly. "And fair or not, I've lost. You win, Charlotte. Take your prize."

Her friend's face softened again, but she didn't respond immediately. Instead, she placed a hand on Elizabeth's arm, forcing her to meet her gaze. "Lizzy," she said quietly, "if you really care about him, then this isn't over. It doesn't have to be."

Elizabeth laughed hollowly, shaking her head. "It is over, Charlotte. You didn't see the way he looked at me. He hates me now."

"And if he does?" Charlotte's voice was calm but firm. "If this really is the end, what then? Are you going to spend the rest of your life convincing yourself it doesn't matter? That you never cared?"

Elizabeth's breath hitched, her composure cracking further. "I don't know," she admitted, her voice trembling. "I don't know how to fix this, and I don't know if I can."

Charlotte stepped back, her expression thoughtful. "You may not know now. But you'll figure it out. And if I'm wrong about all of this—if it truly is over—then I'll concede as well. The wager can remain unfinished."

Elizabeth blinked, startled by her friend's sudden offer. "You'd do that?"

"I'd do that," Charlotte said with a faint smile. "But only if you're sure. Because if you find a way to mend this, Lizzy—if you and Mr. Darcy reconcile—then I think we'll both know who really won."

Elizabeth didn't respond. She couldn't. Her mind was too full, her heart too heavy. All she could do was nod weakly, watching as Charlotte gave her arm a final squeeze and turned to leave.

TWENTY-TWO

THE STEADY RHYTHM OF the horses' hooves against the road did little to soothe Darcy's tumultuous thoughts. The countryside blurred past the carriage windows, a patchwork of muted winter tones that should have offered solace in their familiar simplicity. Instead, they only deepened the ache in his chest.

He had left Netherfield early, much to Bingley's dismay. His friend had tried to coax an explanation out of him, but Darcy had offered none, retreating behind a wall of civility that even Bingley's good humor could not breach. There was nothing to say that would make sense of the chaos in his mind, no words to explain the sharp, unrelenting pain that settled beneath his ribs.

Elizabeth.

Her name was a wound, each repetition cutting deeper. He had trusted her—more than that, he had admired her. She was unlike anyone he had ever known, her wit and sharp tongue a welcome contrast to the artifice and affectation he had grown so weary of in society. For two months, she had teased and baited him, drawing him into conversations that felt alive in a way he had scarcely allowed himself to imagine. And slowly, against every instinct, he had let himself care.

And now, it had all unraveled.

Darcy's hands tightened into fists in his lap as Collins's words echoed in his mind. The wager. The humiliating notion that Elizabeth Bennet had courted his favor not out of genuine regard but as part of some frivolous game. A contest. A jest at his expense.

He exhaled sharply, the sound harsh in the silence of the carriage. How could he have been so blind? He had allowed himself to believe that she was different—that she was honest, genuine, unaffected by the petty schemes of society. He had believed her laughter, her warmth, her wit were meant for him. And all the while, she had been laughing at him.

His jaw tightened as fresh anger surged. He had let her into his confidence, shared parts of himself he had kept hidden even from those closest to him. He had spoken to her of

Georgiana, of his sister's struggles and vulnerabilities. And Elizabeth—Elizabeth, with her perceptive eyes and sharp tongue—had seemed to understand. Had it all been an act? A carefully crafted performance to make him fall for her, only so she could prove a point?

Darcy leaned his head back against the carriage seat, closing his eyes briefly. The memory of her face, alight with laughter during their supper set, burned in his mind. That moment had felt real. But now, doubt seeped into every memory, tainting even the smallest gestures. Had she meant any of it? Or had she simply been playing her part in this cruel wager?

A sudden pang of guilt twisted in his chest. He had hurt her, too. His own wager, though meant in jest, had been no less thoughtless. Bingley's lighthearted challenge had led him to act with the same callousness he now accused her of.

Darcy shook his head, the thoughts warring within him. Whatever her faults, Elizabeth had not deserved the coldness he had shown her in their final conversation. He had lashed out, his words as cutting as the betrayal he had felt. But beneath his anger lay something far more dangerous: longing. Even now, the memory of her voice, her smile, her presence lingered, a cruel reminder of what he had thought he might find with her.

As the carriage jolted slightly over a rough patch of road, Darcy opened his eyes, the countryside coming back into focus. Lincolnshire was still hours away, and beyond it, London waited. The thought of retreating to Pemberley, of immersing himself in the duties and routines that had once provided solace, felt hollow now. He could not imagine finding peace while the specter of Elizabeth Bennet haunted his every thought.

The carriage slowed briefly as the driver navigated a bend in the road. Darcy glanced out the window, his gaze settling on the distant horizon. The sky was overcast, the pale gray clouds heavy with the promise of snow. It matched his mood perfectly: bleak, unsettled, and cold.

He had thought Elizabeth Bennet was the one person who might see him as he truly was, who might look past the cold reserve and pride to find the man beneath. But he had been wrong. She had seen him, yes—but only as a challenge, a target, a game to be won. And now, that illusion lay shattered, leaving him with nothing but regret.

Darcy leaned back once more, the weight of his thoughts pressing heavily on him. Lincolnshire awaited, along with Georgiana. His sister would be glad of his company, he was sure, and her wellbeing was the one certainty he could cling to now. But even as he resolved to focus on her, to push Elizabeth from his mind, a single truth remained:

He had loved her. And the loss of that love, however undeserved, was a wound that would not easily heal.

"YOU LOOK PALE, LIZZY," Jane said, crossing the room to sit beside her. "I thought you might like some company."

Elizabeth shook her head faintly, her lips pressing into a tight line. "Thank you, Jane. I am not certain I am fit for company today."

Jane tilted her head, studying Elizabeth with quiet concern. "I heard some news this morning," she said softly. "Mr. Bingley mentioned that Mr. Darcy left Netherfield early—very early."

Elizabeth's head snapped up, her heart sinking at once. "He left?" she repeated, her voice sharper than she intended.

Jane nodded, her expression pained. "Yes. Mr. Bingley seemed surprised, but Mr. Darcy said he had pressing business in Lincolnshire. Something to do with collecting his sister?"

Elizabeth's stomach twisted. Yes, his sister… Lincolnshire, then London. He had told her as much during supper, before everything had unraveled. Hearing it confirmed now, knowing that he was already gone, left her feeling hollow.

"I see," Elizabeth said after a long pause, her voice subdued. She looked down at the stationery before her, her fingers tightening slightly around its edge. "So he is gone."

Jane reached out to place a hand over Elizabeth's, her touch warm and steady. "Lizzy, I know this must be difficult. But if you truly wish to make amends, perhaps it is not impossible."

Elizabeth laughed softly, though the sound lacked humor. "And how, Jane, do you suggest I do that? Shall I wait for him to return to London and then stalk him there like some forlorn heroine from a dreadful novel? That would surely end well."

"I only meant," Jane said gently, "that we could visit our aunt and uncle in Cheapside. You have been saying for months how much you miss them. London is vast, yes, but it is not entirely out of the realm of possibility that—"

"That I might stumble across him in the street? Or knock on his door unannounced?" Elizabeth interrupted, shaking her head. "No, Jane. I have made enough of a fool of myself already. To chase him to London would be the height of folly."

Jane's expression softened further. "Perhaps it would not be folly if it came from the heart."

Elizabeth met her sister's gaze, her throat tightening. For a moment, the temptation of Jane's words flickered within her. She imagined herself in London, somehow finding a way to cross paths with Darcy, to explain herself, to repair the damage she had done. But even as the thought formed, it crumbled under the weight of reality.

"No," she said quietly. "I have hurt him too deeply. Even if I could find him, I doubt he would want to see me."

Jane sighed, her hand still resting on Elizabeth's. "You care for him, do you not?"

Elizabeth's lips parted, but no words came. Instead, she looked away, her chest aching with the weight of feelings she had only begun to understand.

Rising abruptly, she moved toward the bookshelf that stood against the far wall. Her fingers brushed over the spines of her Shakespeare volumes, their worn edges familiar and comforting. She paused, pulling one from the shelf—a battered copy of Much Ado About Nothing—and held it for a moment, her thumb running along its cover.

"I suppose," she said lightly, though her voice wavered, "if I cannot make amends with Mr. Darcy, I might as well settle my accounts with Charlotte."

Jane looked puzzled. "Charlotte?"

Elizabeth forced a small smile, though it did not reach her eyes. "The wager. I lost, Jane. And Charlotte deserves her due."

"You are being too harsh on yourself," Jane said softly, rising to stand beside her. "Charlotte would not hold you to such a thing."

"Perhaps not," Elizabeth said, tucking the volume into a growing stack of books on the desk. "But I hold myself to it." Her fingers hesitated over the next book before she added softly, "It is silly, but I find myself wondering what Mr. Darcy thinks of Shakespeare. But Charlotte certainly does not care for him."

The admission stung, sharper than she expected. She pulled another volume from the shelf, her movements brisk as if to shake off the thought. "It is fitting, really," she said after a moment, her voice tinged with bitterness. "Shakespeare understood tragedy all too well."

Jane touched Elizabeth's arm gently, her eyes filled with quiet understanding. "Lizzy, you are not as hopeless as you think. You still have time to set this right."

Elizabeth shook her head, swallowing against the lump in her throat. "Perhaps. But I fear that time is slipping away, Jane. And when it is gone, I will have no one to blame but myself."

THE CARRIAGE WHEELS CREAKED softly over the gravel drive as Darcy leaned back in his seat, casting a glance toward his sister. Georgiana sat across from him, her posture relaxed for the first time in weeks. The faintest smile played on her lips as she gazed out the window at the retreating view of the Pomeroys' grand estate.

"I cannot tell you how glad I am to be leaving," she said, her voice light but sincere. "Mrs. Pomeroy means well, but she insists on speaking of nothing but London society, as though it were the only thing in the world that mattered."

Darcy's lips curved into a faint smile. "She does enjoy her gossip."

"Enjoy it? She thrives on it," Georgiana replied, rolling her eyes. "And Miss Pomeroy—she is perfectly polite, but I do not think she has ever read a book that was not about fashion or manners. I felt like an interloper every time I so much as opened the piano."

Darcy chuckled softly. "I believe Elizabeth Bennet would say the same."

Georgiana's head tilted curiously, her attention snapping to him. "Miss Bennet? You wrote about her in your last letter. What is she like?"

Darcy stiffened slightly, caught off guard by the question. How had her name slipped past his lips so readily? He hesitated, the image of Elizabeth's sharp wit and sparkling eyes flashing unbidden in his mind. "She is..." He faltered, searching for the right words. "She is... unconventional."

Georgiana's brow lifted. "Unconventional? That is not very descriptive."

Darcy's gaze flicked to the window, his jaw tightening. "She is clever, independent, and unafraid to speak her mind."

Georgiana smiled. "She sounds fascinating. Do you think I shall have the chance to meet her?"

The question struck him like a blow. Darcy's grip on his knee tightened as he forced himself to maintain an even tone. "That is unlikely," he said curtly, avoiding her gaze. "Circumstances... have changed."

Georgiana frowned, leaning forward slightly. "Circumstances? Fitzwilliam, what happened?"

"Nothing that need concern you," Darcy replied, his voice firmer now. He turned his attention back to her, softening slightly at the confusion in her expression. "Georgiana, let us leave the topic."

His sister looked as though she might press further but relented, leaning back in her seat with a sigh. For a moment, silence stretched between them, broken only by the steady rhythm of the carriage wheels.

"You seem restless," Georgiana said after a pause, her tone quieter now. "Is it because of Miss Bennet?"

Darcy's chest tightened, but he forced himself to remain calm. "I have much on my mind, Georgiana. That is all."

She studied him for a moment, her brow furrowed, but eventually nodded. "Where will we go next? Are we returning to London?"

Darcy hesitated, the thought of London filling him with unease. The idea of its bustling streets and glittering parlors, with their endless chatter and probing questions, felt unbearable. "I am considering turning north," he said at last. "To Pemberley."

Georgiana's face fell, her earlier brightness dimming. "But Richard is in London for Christmas," she said, her voice almost pleading. "I was hoping to see him before his leave ends."

Darcy's resolve wavered at the mention of their cousin. Colonel Fitzwilliam's warmth and humor were a balm for Georgiana, and she had always adored their time together. Darcy sighed, leaning his head back against the seat. "Very well. We will return to London."

Georgiana's relief was immediate, her smile returning. "Thank you, Fitzwilliam. I know you do not care for London, but it will mean so much to see him."

He nodded, though the weight of his thoughts pressed heavily on him. Georgiana turned her attention back to the window, her spirits noticeably lighter, but Darcy's mind was a tangle of contradictions. Elizabeth's advice had been sound—sending Georgiana to the Pomeroys had indeed been a mistake, and the guilt of his stubbornness stung bitterly now.

And yet, the very thought of Elizabeth brought fresh pain. How had he allowed himself to be so thoroughly deceived? Her laughter, her teasing, her charm—it had felt so real, so genuine. And now, knowing it had all been part of a wager, left him hollow. His jaw tightened as he stared out at the passing landscape, willing the memories to fade.

Georgiana spoke again, her voice soft. "Do you think Miss Bennet would have liked me?"

Darcy closed his eyes briefly, his chest tightening further. "I cannot say."

Georgiana frowned. "Why not? You seemed to think so highly of her before."

Darcy's gaze snapped back to her, his tone sharper than he intended. "Because it is a question that does not matter, Georgiana."

She blinked at his uncharacteristic brusqueness, her mouth opening slightly in surprise. Darcy immediately regretted his tone, exhaling heavily. "Forgive me. It has been a long journey, and I am tired."

THE PONY CART RATTLED along the uneven lane, its wheels crunching against the frost-touched earth. Elizabeth kept her hands tight on the reins, her jaw set in grim determination as Lucas Lodge came into view. The neatly kept house stood as serene and unbothered as ever, utterly unaware of the turmoil its occupant had caused.

In the back of the cart, carefully packed and wrapped in a blanket to guard against the cold, sat her precious Shakespeare volumes. A pang shot through Elizabeth's chest as she thought of them—her books, lovingly collected over years of careful saving. Each one held memories: evenings spent reading by the fire, passages recited aloud to Jane, and the occasional argument with her father over which play contained Shakespeare's finest wit.

And now, she was giving them up.

Charlotte met her at the door, her face lighting with a mix of amusement and—Elizabeth suspected—sympathy. "Lizzy," she greeted warmly, stepping aside to allow Elizabeth inside. "To what do I owe this honor? A friendly visit, or are you here to settle our little wager?"

Elizabeth pressed her lips into a thin line, refusing to rise to the bait. "I have come to fulfill my end of the bargain," she said briskly, brushing past Charlotte to retrieve the books from the cart. "It is no honor at all."

"Oh, but it is!" Charlotte called after her, her voice laced with mock reverence. "The great Elizabeth Bennet, bestowing her sacred Shakespeare collection upon an unworthy friend. Truly, it is a day for the history books."

Elizabeth returned moments later, her arms full of the wrapped volumes. She set them on the nearest table with a care that bordered on reverence, her hands lingering on the topmost book before she stepped back. "There," she said, her tone clipped. "I trust you are satisfied."

Charlotte tilted her head, surveying the stack with exaggerated thoughtfulness. "Hmm. Yes, I think they will do nicely. I have even been considering where they might look best on my shelf."

The jab hit its mark, and Elizabeth's frown deepened. "You do not even care for Shakespeare."

"That is precisely why they are so effective," Charlotte replied with mock solemnity, crossing her arms. "Think of them, Lizzy—sitting proudly on my shelf, a testament to your folly and my triumph. Hamlet may even find a new purpose as a teacup saucer."

Elizabeth's mouth fell open, indignation bubbling up. "Charlotte Lucas, if you so much as balance a single cup on one of these books, I will—"

"Oh, relax," Charlotte interrupted, waving a dismissive hand. "I would never disrespect them so openly. Subtly, perhaps, but not openly."

Elizabeth couldn't help the reluctant laugh that escaped her, though it was tinged with bitterness. "You are impossible."

"And you," Charlotte countered, "are far too attached to these dusty old things."

"They are not 'dusty old things,'" Elizabeth retorted, her tone sharp. "They are works of genius."

Charlotte smirked. "Genius, is it? The same genius who fills his plays with bawdy jokes and overlong soliloquies?"

"Bawdy jokes that reveal the deepest truths of human nature," Elizabeth shot back. "And soliloquies that—"

"—that you will now have to live without," Charlotte finished smugly. "Do not look so aggrieved, Lizzy. It was just a wager, after all."

Elizabeth's smile faded, her shoulders sagging slightly. "It was more than just a wager, Charlotte. For both of us."

The sincerity in her tone seemed to disarm Charlotte, whose expression softened. She stepped closer, her voice gentler now. "Lizzy, you do not have to do this. Truly, I do not care about the books. I only teased because—well, because I hate to see you so unhappy."

Elizabeth shook her head, forcing a wry smile. "You won, Charlotte. Fair and square. It is only right that you take them."

Charlotte hesitated, then placed a hand on Elizabeth's arm. "You are a terrible liar, you know. But if this is what you need to do..." She trailed off, glancing at the books. "Just know that they will have a good home. And perhaps," she added with a small, teasing grin, "I might even read one of them. *Much Ado About Nothing*, perhaps. That title seems particularly fitting."

Elizabeth rolled her eyes but couldn't suppress the small smile tugging at her lips. "You are insufferable."

"And yet, you still bring me gifts," Charlotte quipped, her grin widening. "Come, let us have tea. You can mourn your books properly before you go."

Elizabeth allowed herself to be led into the sitting room, her heart heavier than she cared to admit. The books were gone, but the weight of what she had lost lingered, far deeper than a few volumes of Shakespeare could explain.

TWENTY-THREE

THE FIRE CRACKLED SOFTLY in Darcy's study, its warmth doing little to ease the chill that had settled in his chest. The hour was late, and the streets of London were quiet, save for the occasional sound of wheels against cobblestones outside. Darcy sat in his chair, staring into the flames, a glass of brandy untouched in his hand.

He did not even hear the door open until his cousin's familiar voice broke the silence.

"Well, this is a sight," Colonel Richard Fitzwilliam drawled, stepping into the room with an easy confidence. "I had wondered if I'd find you buried under some mountain of paperwork or brooding into the night, and here you are—doing both, I see."

Darcy's shoulders stiffened. "Richard," he said flatly, not bothering to rise. "I was not expecting you."

"That much is obvious." Richard closed the door behind him and crossed the room, his sharp eyes taking in Darcy's uncharacteristically disheveled appearance. "You look terrible, cousin. No, truly. I've seen soldiers after a week-long march look better than you."

"Thank you for your concern," Darcy replied dryly, setting his glass down on the desk with more force than necessary. "To what do I owe the pleasure?"

Richard dropped into the chair opposite him, resting one ankle over his knee. "Georgiana sent me."

That caught Darcy's attention. His gaze snapped to his cousin, his frown deepening. "Georgiana?"

Richard nodded, his expression turning serious. "She's worried about you. She said you've been... unwell these last two weeks. Distracted. More irritable than usual—which, frankly, is saying something."

Darcy exhaled sharply, leaning back in his chair. "Georgiana should mind her own concerns."

"She is your sister. If you've forgotten, let me remind you: her concerns include you. She mentioned a Miss Bennet from Hertfordshire."

Darcy's jaw tightened, and he looked away, the flicker of the firelight dancing in his eyes. "She should not have mentioned that."

"Ah, but she did," Richard said, leaning forward slightly. "And now I'm here, because whatever is going on, it's clearly eating you alive. So, talk. Who is this Miss Bennet, and why does she have you looking like you've just lost a battle?"

Darcy was silent for a long moment, the tension in the room thick enough to cut. Finally, he sighed, his shoulders sagging slightly. "Elizabeth Bennet," he said quietly, the name like a confession. "She is... unlike anyone I have ever met."

Richard's brow lifted. "Go on."

Darcy hesitated, then rose abruptly, moving to the window. He stared out into the dark street below, his hands clasped behind his back. "She is clever, sharp-witted, independent... and utterly infuriating. For weeks, she teased me, challenged me—drew me into conversations I never expected to enjoy. And somewhere along the way... I fell for her."

Richard studied him, his expression unreadable. "And what happened?"

Darcy turned back to him, his face shadowed with bitterness. "I discovered that she had made a wager with her friend—a game to see if she could gain my favor. A farce."

Richard frowned, leaning back in his chair. "A wager? That doesn't sound like the kind of woman you'd fall for."

"I thought the same," Darcy admitted, his voice quieter now. "But it was true. Collins—her cousin—made it painfully clear. And yet..."

"And yet?" Richard prompted.

Darcy's gaze dropped to the floor, his jaw tightening. "There were moments, Richard. Moments when she was so tender, so unguarded, that I cannot believe it was all false. I cannot reconcile the woman I knew with the idea of her playing such a cruel game."

Richard tapped his fingers against the arm of his chair thoughtfully. "And have you considered the possibility that there's more to the story?"

Darcy's head snapped up, his expression sharp. "What do you mean?"

"I mean," Richard said, "that people aren't always what they seem at first glance. You of all people should know that. Maybe this wager wasn't what you think it was. Or maybe she started with one intention and ended with another. Either way, you'll never know unless you ask her."

Darcy shook his head, turning back to the window, his silhouette framed by the faint glow of the streetlamps outside. "I cannot go back. Not after everything that was said. She despises me now."

Richard snorted, leaning back in his chair with an incredulous smile. "I doubt that. You're many things, Darcy, but despised? No. At least, not by her."

Darcy let out a humorless laugh, his hands clenching into fists at his sides. "You did not hear her, Richard. You did not see the fire in her eyes when she confronted me. She called me out for my supposed civility, for my falsehoods, and—" He cut himself off, his voice breaking slightly.

Richard frowned, tilting his head. "She called you out for... civility? What does that even mean?"

Darcy's shoulders stiffened, and for a moment, he said nothing. Then, with aching reluctance, he turned back to his cousin, his expression shadowed with self-reproach. "Because I was not entirely innocent, either."

Richard raised an eyebrow, sitting up straighter. "Go on."

Darcy's gaze dropped to the floor, his voice low and tight. "It was Bingley. He made a wager—harmless, he said. A jest. He believed I was incapable of civility, especially toward the Bennet family, given my... initial impressions."

"Initial impressions," Richard repeated, a grin tugging at his lips. "Let me guess. She did something irreverent and you insulted her? I only guess because it would not be the first time—"

Darcy shot him a sharp look, but Richard only laughed. "Carry on, cousin. This is getting good."

"Bingley challenged me to prove him wrong. To demonstrate that I could be polite without creating unnecessary entanglements. And I—" He paused, exhaling heavily. "I accepted. It seemed harmless at the time, nothing more than a matter of pride."

Richard's grin widened. "So, let me get this straight. You, Mr. High-and-Mighty Darcy, accepted a wager to be polite, and now you're furious that Miss Bennet might have had her own wager? That's... rich."

Darcy scowled, his jaw tightening. "It's not the same."

"Oh, isn't it?" Richard leaned forward, resting his elbows on his knees. "You gambled with her reputation, Darcy. Whether you meant to or not, you made her the subject of some ridiculous game. And now you're angry that she did the same to you?"

Darcy flinched at the words, his guilt twisting deeper. "I did not mean for it to go this far."

"No one ever does," Richard said dryly. "But here's the thing—you're both idiots."

Darcy's head snapped up, his expression darkening. "Excuse me?"

"You're both idiots," Richard repeated, unabashed. "You're angry with her for making a wager, but you made one, too. And the way you talk about her, Darcy—if half of what you've said is true, then she's probably just as miserable as you are right now."

Darcy's lips parted, but no words came. He turned back to the window, his chest tightening as Richard's words struck uncomfortably close to the truth. Could Elizabeth be as conflicted as he was? Could there be more to her actions than the cold calculation he had imagined?

Richard rose, crossing the room to clap a hand on Darcy's shoulder. "Look, I'm not saying you should forgive and forget instantly. But maybe—just maybe—you should stop wallowing long enough to find out the truth."

Darcy shook his head slightly. "And what if the truth only confirms what I already fear?"

"Then you'll know," Richard said simply. "And you'll stop driving yourself mad with questions. But if you let this go—if you let her go—then you'll spend the rest of your life wondering if you made the worst mistake of all."

Darcy swallowed hard, his throat tightening around the weight of his emotions. He wanted to dismiss Richard's words, to retreat into the safety of his own anger and pride. But deep down, he knew his cousin was right.

Richard stepped back, his tone softening slightly. "You've never been one to shy away from a challenge. Don't start now—not when it's something that clearly matters this much."

Darcy nodded faintly, though he couldn't bring himself to speak. His mind was a whirlwind of conflicting thoughts and feelings, each one pulling him in a different direction.

Richard sighed, his voice tinged with amusement as he moved toward the door. "And for the record, I'd wager on Miss Bennet over you any day."

"You do not even know her."

"I do not need to. The fact that she has you this wrung-out speaks enough."

Darcy shot him a withering look, but Richard only grinned as he slipped out of the room, leaving Darcy alone with his thoughts.

He sank back into his chair, his gaze fixed on the dying embers of the fire. The memory of Elizabeth's voice, her laughter, her fiery spirit, filled his mind once more, refusing to be silenced.

Perhaps Richard was right. Perhaps he owed it to himself—and to her—to find out the truth, no matter how painful it might be.

THE WINTER SUNLIGHT FILTERED weakly through the windows of Longbourn, casting pale beams across the sitting room. Elizabeth sat in her usual chair, her hands idle in her lap, her thoughts as barren as the spot on the bookshelf where her Shakespeare volumes had once proudly stood. The emptiness there seemed to mock her, a silent reminder of everything she had lost—not just her beloved books, but the hope that had flickered briefly in her heart.

From the next room, the low hum of conversation drifted through the walls. Mr. Bingley's familiar voice carried warmth and good humor, and Jane's soft replies were no doubt full of her usual gentleness. Elizabeth knew her mother hovered nearby, likely wringing her hands and urging Jane to secure her future before the moment slipped away.

Elizabeth should have felt happy for Jane. And she did—truly. But it was a hollow sort of happiness, dulled by the ache in her chest that refused to fade. Two weeks had passed since the Netherfield ball, two weeks since her disastrous confrontation with Darcy, and still, her heart felt as though it had been trampled underfoot.

Collins had left Longbourn the day after the ball, his pride bruised and his offers of marriage rejected by every eligible lady in Meryton. Even Mrs. Bennet, who had once championed him so fiercely, now declared him "an insufferable oaf" and spoke of him only to complain. Elizabeth wished she could feel relief at his departure, but even that small victory was overshadowed by the weight of everything else.

Mary sat quietly in the far corner of the room, a book open in her lap, though her eyes barely skimmed the pages. Elizabeth glanced at her sister, her expression softening. Mary had barely spoken to her since the ball, her guilt and discomfort evident in every awkward silence. Elizabeth had assured her more than once that she was forgiven, but Mary's shame seemed impossible to shake.

As if sensing her gaze, Mary looked up hesitantly. "Lizzy?"

Elizabeth smiled faintly, trying to put her sister at ease. "Yes, Mary?"

Mary hesitated, her fingers tightening on the edge of the book. "I—I wanted to say again how sorry I am. I never meant to... I didn't think—"

"I know, Mary," Elizabeth said gently, cutting her off before she could spiral further. "I forgave you weeks ago."

Mary's eyes filled with tears, and she looked down at her lap, her voice barely above a whisper. "But you lost so much because of me."

Elizabeth's throat tightened, and she glanced once more at the empty space on the shelf. "I did not lose as much as you think," she said, though the lie tasted bitter.

Mary seemed unconvinced but said nothing more. Elizabeth rose abruptly, unable to bear the tension. Crossing the room, she paused by the window, staring out at the frost-covered garden. The cold, stark landscape felt like a reflection of her own heart—silent, empty, and unyielding.

I cannot stay here.

The thought came suddenly, sharp and clear, and for the first time in weeks, Elizabeth felt a spark of something other than despair. She turned away from the window, her steps purposeful as she crossed to the small writing desk by the wall. Sitting down, she reached for a sheet of paper and dipped her pen into the ink.

"Lizzy?" Mary's voice was hesitant. "What are you doing?"

Elizabeth didn't look up. "I am writing to Aunt Gardiner."

Mary frowned. "Aunt Gardiner?"

"Yes. I am going to ask if I may visit her in London."

Mary's brow furrowed. "London? But why—"

"Because I cannot stay here, Mary," Elizabeth said, her voice breaking slightly. She set the pen down, pressing her fingers to her temples as she tried to steady herself. "Every day, I feel as though I am suffocating. I need to get away. To think. To..." She trailed off, her eyes closing briefly. "To find out if there is still hope."

Mary was silent for a moment, then ventured timidly, "Hope for what?"

Elizabeth opened her eyes, her gaze distant. "Hope that I might not have ruined everything."

The words hung heavily in the air, and Mary had no reply. Elizabeth picked up the pen again, her hand moving steadily across the paper as she addressed her aunt. She did not know how she would cross paths with Darcy again—if it was even possible—but London at least offered a chance, however slim. Here at Longbourn, there was nothing but regret and the knowledge that she had let him slip away.

When she finished, Elizabeth folded the letter carefully and set it aside to be sent. For the first time in weeks, the weight in her chest lifted slightly. It was not much, but it was a start.

THE SNOW FELL IN thick, swirling flakes, blanketing the road ahead and muffling the steady clatter of the carriage wheels. Darcy sat stiffly in his seat, his eyes fixed on the frosted glass of the window as the landscape passed by in shades of white and gray. Despite the warmth of the carriage, he felt cold, a chill that came from within and had plagued him for weeks.

He was nearing Meryton now, the town that had become synonymous with frustration and heartache. Darcy's grip on his gloves tightened as he thought of Elizabeth Bennet, her fierce eyes and sharp tongue, her laughter that had once felt like sunlight piercing his carefully constructed walls. She had haunted him every day since their parting, her image an unwelcome but relentless companion.

And yet, here he was, traveling the same snowy roads he had sworn never to tread again. Logic had abandoned him entirely, leaving only the raw, unrelenting need to see her—to speak to her, even if it meant risking further humiliation. He could not rest until he knew the truth, no matter how painful it might be.

The carriage jolted slightly, drawing his attention back to the road. Darcy leaned forward, his gaze narrowing as he saw another carriage approaching from the opposite direction. It was an unremarkable vehicle, small and plainly outfitted, but something about it caught his eye. He squinted, his breath catching as the carriage drew closer.

Then he saw her.

Elizabeth.

His heart lurched, disbelief crashing over him like a wave. He blinked, certain for a moment that he was imagining her—that the snow, the strain of the journey, and his own fevered thoughts had conjured her apparition. But no. It was Elizabeth.

She leaned slightly out of the carriage window, her dark hair escaping in soft, wind-tossed tendrils, dusted with snow. Her cheeks were flushed from the cold, her eyes wide and unguarded, fixed on him with a look that mirrored his own: shock mingled with something raw and vulnerable.

"Stop the carriage!"

The driver obeyed immediately, pulling the horses to an abrupt halt. Across the way, Elizabeth's carriage slowed as well, coming to a jerking stop just yards from his own. For a moment, the road was silent save for the snorts of the horses and the faint rustle of snowflakes falling all around them.

Darcy threw the door open, the cold air biting at his face as he stepped down into the snow. Elizabeth emerged from her carriage almost in tandem, her movements hurried and unsteady as she stepped into the snow. Her cloak swirled around her, the dark fabric in sharp contrast to the stark white of their surroundings. For a moment, she stood frozen, her expression a mixture of astonishment and disbelief.

Her lips parted slightly, as though she were about to speak, but no words came. She simply stared at him, and Darcy was struck—painfully, powerfully—by the sight of her. She looked so achingly familiar, yet seeing her here, so unexpectedly, was like seeing her for the first time.

He stopped a few paces from her, his chest tight, his pulse thundering in his ears. He could not tell whether the cold or her presence was stealing the air from his lungs. "Miss Bennet," he said finally, his voice low and rough with the effort to contain his emotions. "What are you doing here?"

Elizabeth blinked, as if startled by the question. Then, with a faint shake of her head, she replied, "I could ask you the same, Mr. Darcy."

The sound of her voice—familiar yet distant, as though it belonged to a dream—sent a pang through him. He struggled to find the right words, his thoughts a tangled mess. "I—" He hesitated, exhaling sharply, his breath visible in the cold. "I was traveling to Longbourn."

"To Longbourn?" Elizabeth echoed, her brow furrowing. She took a half-step forward, her eyes scanning his face. "Why?"

"To see you," he admitted, his voice trembling slightly despite his best efforts to steady it.

Her lips parted in surprise, her gaze locking with his. For a long, heart-stopping moment, neither of them spoke. The snow continued to fall between them, the world beyond the road seeming to fade into nothingness.

"You were coming to see me?" she asked at last, her voice soft and disbelieving.

"Yes," Darcy said, taking a step closer. " I could not—" He faltered, swallowing hard, his gaze never leaving hers. "I could not stay away."

Elizabeth's breath hitched, her hands clutching the edges of her cloak as if to ground herself. "And I," she said after a pause, her voice shaking slightly, "was on my way to London. To see you."

Her words struck him like a physical blow. "You... you were?"

She nodded, her expression both tender and hesitant. "I—I have no idea what I thought I was going to do. Show up on your doorstep, perhaps, though I know not where that even is. I just... I could not stay at Longbourn, not knowing if..." She broke off, glancing down briefly before meeting his gaze again, her eyes shining with emotion. "If there was still a chance."

Darcy felt as though the ground beneath him had shifted. His chest tightened, his thoughts racing as he searched her face for any sign of deceit. But there was none. Only sincerity, raw and unguarded, in every word and every look.

"A chance," he murmured, the word tasting foreign on his tongue.

Elizabeth took another step closer, closing the gap between them. "Do you still hate me, Mr. Darcy?" she asked, her tone a mix of earnestness and fragile hope.

"Hate you?" Darcy repeated, his voice thick with emotion. "Elizabeth, I—" He stopped, closing his eyes briefly, gathering himself. When he opened them again, his gaze was steady, though his voice trembled. "Elizabeth, I have never hated you. If anything, I have spent these past weeks hating myself for letting you think I could."

Her breath hitched, her eyes widening slightly. "But the wager—"

"The wager was foolish," Darcy interrupted, his tone fierce. "But it was never about you. Not truly. And even if it began as a jest, it did not take long for me to see you for who you are. For everything you are."

Elizabeth's cheeks flushed, her expression softening even as her lips trembled. "And yet, I—" She faltered, swallowing hard. "I hurt you. I played a part in all of this, and I regret it more than I can say."

Darcy shook his head, his voice gentler now. "You hurt me, yes. But you also showed me a part of myself I had forgotten existed. You made me laugh, made me think, made me—" He stopped, his breath catching. "Made me care."

Elizabeth's eyes shone with unshed tears, and she laughed softly, shakily. "And here I thought I was the only one who cared."

For the first time in what felt like years, Darcy smiled—a small, genuine smile that softened the lines of his face. "You were not."

The distance between them disappeared as they stepped closer, snow swirling around them like a veil. The road was quiet, the world still, save for the unspoken understanding that passed between them.

"Elizabeth," he said quietly, his voice trembling slightly, "I—"

"Do not say it," she interrupted with a soft laugh, her smile breaking through her tears. "Not here, in the middle of the road, in the snow. Let us go somewhere warmer."

Darcy laughed—a real, unguarded laugh that felt like a release of everything he had been holding back. "As you wish."

He helped her back into her carriage, their hands lingering as they parted. Then, with a nod to their drivers, the carriages turned toward Longbourn, the snowy road stretching ahead like a blank page, ready to be filled.

TWENTY-FOUR

DARCY HANDED HER OUT of the carriage back at Longbourn, the cold air brushing her cheeks as his hand lingered on hers. Snowflakes clung to their cloaks as they approached the door, their steps almost hesitant. Elizabeth's heart fluttered wildly—not from the cold, but from the sheer improbability of the last hour. She glanced up at Darcy, his expression set with determination, but she could see the faintest flicker of nerves in his eyes.

For the first time in weeks, she felt hope bloom fully in her chest. They were walking into Longbourn together—not as adversaries, not as strangers, but as something new, something unspoken but thrilling.

The front door opened before they could knock, and the sound of Mrs. Bennet's shrill cries filled the air. "Oh, Mr. Bingley, what is this? Jane, my darling, what is—?"

Elizabeth froze as they stepped into the drawing room. There, in the center of the room, was Mr. Bingley, down on one knee before a wide-eyed Jane, his face a perfect picture of earnest devotion. Jane's hand covered her mouth, her cheeks flushed pink, her eyes shimmering with happy tears.

"Oh!" Elizabeth exclaimed, startled into a laugh as she halted in the doorway. Darcy stiffened beside her, his brow lifting in a mixture of surprise and amusement.

Bingley turned his head, startled, but instead of rising, his grin widened. "Darcy!" he exclaimed, beaming. "You've arrived just in time! I was about to—"

"You will finish later," Darcy interrupted. "Besides, it looks to me as if your business is already concluded. Miss Bennet, forgive the intrusion, but I must insist on having the room."

Bingley blinked, his brow furrowing. "The room? But I—"

"Now," Darcy said firmly, fixing Bingley with a pointed look.

Elizabeth burst into laughter, hiding her smile behind her hand as Jane's cheeks deepened in color. "Fitzwilliam Darcy!" she exclaimed, mockingly aghast. "Do you always commandeer rooms at the height of romantic moments?"

Darcy turned to her, his expression both solemn and faintly smug. "I assure you, Miss Elizabeth, this is a matter of great importance."

Bingley, ever obliging despite his confusion, rose to his feet and offered Jane a reassuring smile. "I'll only be a moment, my dear. I... I suppose I shall... speak with your father?"

"Yes, do that," Darcy urged. "And her mother, too, if you please. Off with you now."

Bingley's face reddened still further, and he gave Jane's hand a squeeze before allowing Darcy to shepherd him—and Mrs. Bennet, who had been hovering near the doorway—out of the room.

Once the door clicked shut, the drawing room fell silent. Elizabeth turned to Darcy, her eyes sparkling with laughter. "I hope you do not expect me to forget the sheer audacity of that display."

"I will gladly bear the censure," Darcy replied, stepping closer. His eyes softened, his voice dropping to a low murmur. "Elizabeth, I have waited too long already."

Her breath caught as he reached for her hands, his warmth steady and grounding. "And you think now is the time?"

"I do," Darcy said, his voice steady but his eyes warm with emotion. He stepped closer, his hands enclosing hers with a reverence that made Elizabeth's breath catch. "Elizabeth Bennet, you are the very center of my thoughts—my better judgment, my every hope for happiness. I am hopelessly and completely in love with you. Will you allow me the privilege of calling you my wife?"

Elizabeth's lips parted, a soft gasp escaping her before she could compose herself. For a moment, she simply stared at him, her heart thundering as his words wrapped around her like a warm embrace. Then, the teasing glint in her eyes returned. "Privilege, Mr. Darcy? Are you certain you can endure the honor?"

A slow, wry smile tugged at his lips, and he dipped his head slightly. "I would endure far worse, Elizabeth, if it meant securing your affection."

Her laughter bubbled up, light and full of life, and she shook her head at him, her tears threatening to spill. "Well, then," she said, her voice trembling as her smile widened. "If you are so determined to endure me, I suppose I cannot refuse."

Darcy's smile softened, his thumb brushing lightly over the back of her hand. "You cannot imagine what it means to hear you say that."

"Then allow me to make it clearer," Elizabeth replied, her voice steadier now, though her tears shimmered brightly in her eyes. She looked directly into his gaze, her words firm and true. "Yes, Fitzwilliam. I will marry you."

The relief that washed over his face was almost comical in its intensity, and Elizabeth laughed again, her heart so full it felt as though it might burst. Darcy's hands tightened slightly around hers as his expression shifted to something deeper, more vulnerable.

"You cannot know how long I have waited to hear those words," he murmured, his voice thick with emotion.

Elizabeth tilted her head, a teasing smile playing on her lips. "And yet you nearly fumbled the proposal with all that talk of enduring me."

Darcy chuckled softly, his head bowing briefly as he shook it in amused defeat. "You will never let me forget that, will you?"

"Not as long as I live," she replied, her grin widening.

"Then I shall endure it gladly," he said, his tone lighter now, though his gaze remained steady and filled with adoration.

Elizabeth stepped closer, her voice dropping to a tender murmur. "You need not endure anything, Fitzwilliam. Loving you is no hardship for me. It never has been."

Darcy's breath caught, his composure faltering just slightly, and then he closed the remaining distance between them. His hands moved to frame her face with gentle care, his eyes searching hers for one last moment before he leaned down and kissed her.

It was a kiss that held everything—every misunderstanding, every moment of longing, every unspoken word that had built between them. And as Elizabeth kissed him back, she felt the weight of the past weeks lift entirely, leaving only joy in its place.

When they finally broke apart, her face was radiant, and his expression was softer than she had ever seen it. He gathered her in his arms, holding her tightly as if to assure himself she was truly there.

"I cannot believe it," he murmured into her hair, his voice thick with emotion. "You—here, with me."

Elizabeth tilted her head back to look up at him, her eyes sparkling. "Well, you did rather commandeer the drawing room."

Darcy laughed, his head bowing slightly in acknowledgment. But then his expression turned thoughtful, his brow furrowing slightly. "Tell me," he began, his tone tinged with curiosity, "did you ever win your wager?"

Elizabeth's eyes widened in surprise, and then she burst into laughter, shaking her head. "This is hardly the time to ask such things!"

He arched a brow, his expression mockingly grave. "On the contrary, Elizabeth. It is the perfect time. If I recall correctly, the terms were that you had to break my heart. And as you did not succeed, I must conclude that you lost."

Her laughter deepened, her cheeks flushing. "I forfeited, if you must know."

His gaze sharpened with interest. "And what, pray tell, did you forfeit?"

She hesitated, her smile softening as she glanced away. "My Shakespeare collection."

Darcy stared at her, his brow furrowing in astonishment. "You are telling me that you—Elizabeth Bennet, who despises sentimental poetry—love bombastic, bawdy plays so much that losing them was a wrench?"

Elizabeth laughed, her cheeks flushing again. "They are more than that to me! But yes, I suppose it was a wrench."

Darcy's lips twitched with amusement, his eyes twinkling as he teased, "Your taste is appalling."

She poked his chest lightly, her grin mischievous. "Never fear, Mr. Darcy. I will corrupt your taste in due time, so you will not take offense to mine."

He laughed again, the sound rich and unrestrained, and she could not help but join him, the two of them standing in the center of the drawing room, surrounded by joy and warmth. Whatever awaited them, Elizabeth knew one thing for certain:

This was the start of everything.

DARCY DESCENDED THE STAIRCASE at Netherfield with a purposeful stride, Georgiana's letter clutched in his hand. The content of her words had lifted his spirits more than he cared to admit. She had written with uncharacteristic enthusiasm, detailing how she was already imagining Elizabeth as her sister-in-law, and her joy practically leaped off the page. It was a warmth he carried with him now, even as the cool winter air seeped through the hall.

As he approached the door, Darcy spotted Caroline Bingley, stationed strategically near the foot of the stairs. She turned at the sound of his boots and beamed, her smile as bright as it was insincere. He sighed inwardly but maintained a polite, if distant, expression.

"Mr. Darcy!" Caroline greeted, her voice lilting. "You are up and about early today. How very industrious of you."

"Miss Bingley," Darcy said with a faint nod, not breaking his stride. "I have business to attend to."

Caroline stepped into his path, undeterred by his brusque tone. "Oh, but you have been so diligent already, what with all the traveling back and forth to Longbourn. Tell me, are you quite settled on the matter? Or will this courtship remain an... experiment?"

Darcy's jaw tightened, though he kept his composure. "It is hardly an experiment."

"Of course not," Caroline said quickly, her tone shifting to one of affected contrition. "You know I only jest. After all, wagers can be so dreadfully misleading, can't they?"

Darcy stopped then, fixing her with a cool gaze. "What are you implying, Miss Bingley?"

"Oh, nothing at all," she said with a flutter of her hand. "Only that I do wonder about that little bet with Charles. You know, the one about proving you could be civil without falling into... entanglements." She gave him a pointed look, her smile sharpening. "And yet, here you are, thoroughly entangled. Are you certain it is too late for you to cry off?"

"Quite too late for that, I am afraid."

"Oh, but I would not say so! Charles could be easily persuaded—"

Darcy's expression remained impassive, but his words were dry. "Your brother's wager was hardly binding, Miss Bingley. He is free to draw his own conclusions."

"Indeed, he is. And I am free to lament his stubbornness. Honestly, Mr. Darcy, if Charles had simply agreed to sell that dreadful mill, you would have both profited handsomely, and none of this would have—"

Darcy held up a hand, silencing her. "Charles's business decisions are precisely that—his business. If he wishes to ruin himself with sentimentality, that is his prerogative."

Caroline blinked, momentarily stunned by his bluntness. But she quickly recovered, her smile returning with a forced brightness. "Oh, I am sure you mean that kindly."

"I mean it truthfully," Darcy said evenly. "And now, Miss Bingley, if you will excuse me, I have somewhere to be."

He stepped around her, leaving her gaping after him, and strode toward the door. The crisp air outside was a welcome relief as he made his way to the waiting carriage.

Climbing inside, he allowed himself a moment to glance again at Georgiana's letter, her neat handwriting a testament to her growing confidence.

> *I cannot wait to meet Miss Elizabeth properly*, she had written. *You must bring her to London soon, Fitzwilliam, and then Pemberley. I think she will love it—and I suspect she will not be shy in telling you what improvements it needs!*

Darcy chuckled softly to himself, folding the letter and tucking it into his coat. Georgiana's insight, though playful, was strikingly accurate. Elizabeth had already managed to shake the foundations of his carefully ordered life, and he found himself looking forward to the ways she would continue to do so.

"Longbourn," he instructed the driver, settling back against the seat as the carriage rolled forward. Whatever nonsense Caroline Bingley wished to spin, it was nothing compared to the clarity of purpose that now filled him. He had Elizabeth, and with her, he had everything.

DARCY STEPPED OUT OF the carriage at Longbourn, the familiar house bathed in the golden light of a winter afternoon. The snow had stopped, leaving the world hushed and pristine, and the faint scent of woodsmoke hung in the air. His heart quickened at the thought of seeing Elizabeth again, though he did his best to temper his eagerness.

The door opened before he reached it, and there she was, standing on the threshold with her cheeks flushed and her eyes bright. Elizabeth smiled, that particular smile of hers that sent a jolt straight through him.

"You are becoming rather predictable, Mr. Darcy," she teased lightly as he approached. "Arriving here with alarming frequency."

"And yet, you keep letting me in," he replied, a faint smile tugging at his lips.

"I suppose we shall have to reconsider our hospitality," she quipped, stepping aside to allow him entry. "Though I suspect you would not take offense."

"Not in the slightest," Darcy said, his tone warm as he shrugged off his coat. "I am quite determined to be undeterred."

As they moved toward the sitting room, laughter spilled out from within, and Darcy caught the distinct sound of Elizabeth's younger sisters' voices. When they stepped inside, Kitty and Lydia were perched together on the settee, clearly in the midst of a spirited discussion. Mary sat nearby with a book in hand, though she appeared more interested in the conversation than the pages.

"He's here!" Kitty exclaimed, nudging Lydia and giggling.

Lydia leaned forward, her eyes alight with mischief. "That took longer than I thought. I win."

"You do not," Kitty protested. "The wager was five minutes, and it's barely been four!"

Elizabeth arched a brow, her arms crossing as she regarded her sisters. "What are you two conspiring about now?"

"Nothing," Kitty said quickly, though the smirk she shared with Lydia gave her away.

Lydia, less inclined to subtlety, grinned wickedly. "We were just discussing how long Mr. Darcy's next kiss will last."

Elizabeth's cheeks turned a delightful shade of pink, and Darcy coughed, his composure slipping for a moment. "A wager, is it?" he asked, his voice calm but edged with amusement. "And what were the terms?"

"Oh, nothing too scandalous," Lydia said, waving a hand. "Just a bit of fun."

"More like a test of endurance," Kitty added with a giggle, earning a sharp look from Elizabeth.

"You two have far too much time on your hands," Elizabeth said, though her tone was more exasperated than stern. She turned back to Darcy, her expression softening. "I apologize for my sisters. They seem to have no concept of propriety."

Darcy stepped closer, his voice low enough that only she could hear. "I find myself rather curious about their wager."

Elizabeth's lips twitched, and she tilted her head, her eyes sparkling. "And what would you say if I told you they were wagering on your fortitude?"

His gaze held hers, his voice dropping to a murmur. "I would say I intend to exceed expectations."

Elizabeth laughed, the sound warm and unguarded, and it took every ounce of Darcy's restraint not to pull her into his arms right then and there. Instead, he offered his arm, his tone playful but his eyes full of meaning. "Shall we?"

She placed her hand on his arm, her touch light but steady. "If we must."

As they exited the room, Lydia called after them, "We'll be counting!"

Elizabeth shook her head, muttering something under her breath that made Darcy chuckle. They stopped in the quieter corridor, and Darcy turned to face her fully, his expression softening.

"Elizabeth," he said quietly, brushing a strand of hair from her face, "if I may be so bold..."

"You are always bold, Mr. Darcy," she replied, her voice teasing but her eyes warm.

"Then I shall live up to the reputation," he murmured, leaning down to capture her lips in a kiss—gentle at first, then deepening as she responded with equal fervor.

When they finally parted, her cheeks were flushed, her eyes sparkling with laughter. "I think you've just ruined their wager," she said breathlessly.

"Good," he replied, a rare grin curving his lips. "They should never doubt my resolve."

Epilogue

ELIZABETH ADJUSTED HER BONNET as the pony cart trundled along the snowy road toward Meryton, her gloved hands steady on the reins. Beside her, Darcy sat as stiffly as ever, his posture impeccable even in the relative discomfort of the cart. His expression was a study in composed indifference, though Elizabeth could detect the faintest flicker of curiosity in his eyes.

"You are remarkably silent today, Mr. Darcy," she said, her tone light. "Have I already exhausted your tolerance for my company?"

"Not at all," he replied, a faint smile tugging at the corners of his mouth. "Though I confess I am curious as to why you were so insistent on this trip to town."

Elizabeth hesitated, biting her lip to keep from smiling. "It is nothing of great importance," she said casually.

Darcy's brow arched. "Elizabeth, when you insist upon something 'unimportant,' I am inclined to believe the opposite."

She laughed, unable to resist his dry tone. "Very well, if you must know, I have... a small wager to settle."

Darcy turned to her fully, his expression equal parts incredulous and exasperated. "Another wager?"

"Indeed," she said breezily. "With my aunt Philips. She is positively convinced that you are less than six feet tall, while I maintain that you two inches over."

Darcy blinked, clearly unprepared for such nonsense. "You are dragging me to Meryton to measure me?"

Elizabeth grinned. "Not at all. *I* know how tall you are. I simply thought my aunt might like to see the proof with her own eyes."

Darcy stared at her for a moment, his jaw tightening as he fought to suppress a smile. "You are impossible."

"I have been told so before," she replied cheerfully. "And before you protest, I should inform you that the stakes are quite high."

"Pray, enlighten me," he said, his voice dry but edged with curiosity.

"My aunt has wagered her finest tea set," Elizabeth said with mock solemnity. "And as I am quite in need of a new one, I could hardly decline."

Darcy groaned softly, leaning back in the seat as if the weight of the world had just been placed upon him. "Elizabeth, if a tea set is all you desire, I will gladly buy you one. There is no need for these... absurd wagers."

Elizabeth sighed dramatically, her eyes sparkling with mischief. "You are quite missing the point, Mr. Darcy. It is not about the tea set. It is about the principle of the matter."

Darcy turned his head to regard her, his expression a mixture of disbelief and reluctant amusement. "And what principle might that be?"

"That I never win," she said with mock solemnity. "Not a single wager in all my life—unless you count the time I bested Mr. Wickham over Sir William's long-windedness, but as he never paid up, I do not think that one counts. But *this* one, I was certain of. After all, I have stood beside you often enough to know."

Darcy shook his head, his lips twitching with suppressed laughter. "Elizabeth, I will not humor this foolishness."

Elizabeth glanced at him, her eyes narrowing slightly. "Very well," she said with a mock sigh. "If you are so determined to deny me the tea set, I shall have to content myself with my second wager of the day."

"Second wager?" he repeated, his brow furrowing.

"Yes," she said lightly, her tone almost careless. "With the bookseller. I wagered that a certain volume of essays my father ordered would arrive today."

Darcy pinched the bridge of his nose, though his shoulders shook faintly with suppressed laughter. "And did it?"

Elizabeth sighed again, this time more dramatically. "That is what I mean to find out, but according to my Aunt Philips, who called at Longbourn this morning, no parcels were delivered to the bookseller this morning by the post. So, it probably did not."

Darcy chuckled, shaking his head. "You have a remarkable talent for losing wagers, Elizabeth."

"It is a gift," she said with a wry smile. "And one I appear destined to keep."

As the pony cart came to a halt outside the Meryton shops, Darcy climbed down first, his boots crunching against the snow. He turned to offer her his hand, his gaze still alight with amusement. "Elizabeth," he said, his tone half-teasing, "I refuse to be complicit in your wagering schemes."

She took his hand, her lips curving into a playful smile. "Then wait here, Mr. Darcy. I shall face my defeats alone."

Darcy crossed his arms, leaning against the cart with an air of feigned sternness. "Very well. But do not expect me to rescue you from the consequences of your folly."

Elizabeth laughed as she turned toward the bookshop. Over her shoulder, she called, "Perhaps you should wager on how long it will take me to settle this one, Mr. Darcy. Then you might understand my plight."

Darcy's laughter followed her inside, a warm sound that lingered even as the door closed behind her. Elizabeth couldn't help but smile as she approached the counter, her heart light despite the inevitability of her latest loss. For with Darcy, even losing seemed like winning.

Darcy stood outside the bookshop, the brisk December air carrying the scent of roasted chestnuts and freshly cut pine. Around him, the town buzzed with activity—merchants calling their wares, children darting between stalls, and townsfolk exchanging holiday greetings. Darcy's attention, however, was fixed on a singular figure: George Wickham.

The man's usual charm had vanished, replaced by a thin veneer of composure that was fraying at the edges. Wickham stood opposite a stern-faced woman dressed in fine but practical attire. Her stance was commanding, her chin tilted high as she glared at Wickham. Darcy couldn't help but feel a grim satisfaction at the sight.

"What is happening there?" Elizabeth's voice interrupted his thoughts. She stepped to his side, her hand slipping lightly into the crook of his arm.

"It appears," Darcy said, "that Mr. Wickham's penchant for wagers has finally caught up with him."

Elizabeth arched a brow, her gaze shifting back to the scene. "What has he done now?"

Darcy's lips curved into a faint smile. "If I heard correctly, he made a rather large wager with Mrs. Abernathy—the widow of a naval captain—on a game of cards last week at a tea gathering. Unfortunately for him, she is not only a skilled player but also a woman of considerable influence in town."

As they watched, Mrs. Abernathy gestured sharply toward a document in her hand. Wickham's face paled further as she spoke, her voice carrying just enough for Darcy and Elizabeth to catch fragments of the conversation.

"...out of my sight by sundown, or I'll see to it that your reputation—or what little remains of it—is shredded entirely! I shall go to Colonel Forster myself!"

Elizabeth stifled a laugh behind her gloved hand. "I must say, I never expected Mr. Wickham to meet his match in a card game."

"Nor in a woman unwilling to be charmed by his usual tactics," Darcy added, his tone edged with satisfaction.

Wickham's shoulders slumped, his attempts at placating Mrs. Abernathy clearly failing. Finally, he turned on his heel, his expression a mixture of anger and humiliation as he stalked away. The crowd, sensing the drama had concluded, dispersed with murmurs of interest and the occasional smirk.

Elizabeth tilted her head toward Darcy, her eyes sparkling with mischief. "So, Mr. Darcy, would you consider this the final triumph over Wickham?"

Darcy's lips twitched. "It is certainly a satisfying one. Though I suspect he will resurface somewhere else, as he always does."

"I would think, after all you have told me about his wrongs against you, you would not see him go so lightly."

Darcy lifted his shoulders. "He has made his bed. I doubt it is a comfortable one, but mine... mine *certainly* will be," he finished with a suggestive grin.

She laughed. "You think that now, sir, but I mean to keep you guessing regularly."

Darcy turned toward her, his expression softening. "And what of your wagers, Future Mrs. Darcy?"

"I thought we agreed not to speak of them."

"On the contrary," he said, a teasing glint in his eyes. "I distinctly remember you promising to corrupt my taste in literature."

She grinned, her cheeks flushing faintly in the cold. "Ah, yes. That is a wager I fully intend to win."

"Do you?" Darcy's voice lowered, his gaze holding hers. "And what, pray, will be my forfeit?"

Elizabeth pretended to consider, her smile widening. "Your solemn vow to read *Twelfth Night* without complaining."

Darcy chuckled, shaking his head. "A steep price, but one I am willing to pay."

They began walking again, her hand linked under his arm. The sounds of the market faded into the background as Darcy looked down at Elizabeth, his heart full. The road to this moment had been anything but smooth—fraught with misunderstandings, wagers, and wounded pride—but standing here with her, he knew it had all been worth it.

"And you, Elizabeth," he said, his tone light but his gaze warm, "have you any wagers left to settle?"

Elizabeth's smile turned soft, her eyes shining as she looked up at him. "None that matter, Mr. Darcy. None at all."

As they walked hand in hand through the snowy streets of Meryton, Darcy could not help but feel that, at last, all the wagers that had once seemed so important had led to the only victory that truly mattered: a future shared with a woman worth betting his life on.

CATCH MORE SWOONY DARCY and Elizabeth romance in *Raising the Stakes!*

FROM ALIX

THANK YOU FOR INDULGING with me and spending a little time with Darcy and Elizabeth.

I hope you've had a delightful escape to Netherfield! I'd love it if you would share this family with your friends so they can experience a love to last for the ages. As with all my books, I have enabled lending to make it easier to share. If you leave a review for *All Bets are Off* on Amazon, Goodreads, Book Bub or your own blog, I would love to read it! Email me the link at **Author@AlixJames.com.**

Would you like to read more of Darcy and Elizabeth's romance? I have a fun Darcy and Elizabeth Memoir for you to try next! Dive into Raising the Stakes and laugh along with our favorite couple as they find the love they were destined for!

And if you're hungry for more, including a free ebook of satisfying short tales, stay up to date on upcoming releases and sales by joining my newsletter: https://dashboard.mailerlite.com/forms/249660/73866370936211000/share

Raising the Stakes

Chapter One

"Get your hands off me!" Broadshaw shoved his opponent hard enough to send the smaller man stumbling back. The other man, dressed in the fine but mud-streaked coat of Miles Stanton's steward, recovered quickly, his face twisted with rage.

"You will regret this, Broadshaw!" the steward barked, lunging forward. "You think you can raise a hand to a servant of Miles Stanton and walk away? I will see you hauled before the magistrate before the sun sets."

Broadshaw surged forward again, his fists raised, but another farmer stepped between them, his arms outstretched as though to hold them both back. "Stop it, Broadshaw," he said, his voice low and urgent. "Think of your family."

Broadshaw ignored him. "You come onto my land and accuse my son of poaching? My boy was out with the sheep on grazing land we have used for generations! You think I will let you put up fences where they do not belong and let you take what is not yours?"

The steward adjusted his coat and pointed a finger at Broadshaw. "Your son was where he had no right to be, Broadshaw. That land belongs to Miles Stanton now, and if the boy sets foot there again, it will not be the sheep we are hauling off to market."

Broadshaw's face darkened, his fists trembling at his sides. "Do not think you can scare us into giving up our rights, Stanton's man. You put your fences where the law does not allow, and then you have the gall to come here and call us thieves?"

Darcy swung down from his horse, the reins slipping from his hands as he strode toward the commotion. His presence drew the eyes of several onlookers, but no one moved to intervene. Stanton's steward squared his shoulders and jabbed a finger toward Broadshaw.

"This man struck me, Mr. Darcy," the steward said, his voice ringing with indignation. "You saw it. I demand he be taken before the magistrate. Sir Frederick will not stand for this lawlessness."

Darcy stepped into the circle, his gaze fixed on the steward. The man's bravado faltered under Darcy's stare, though his mouth pressed into a defiant line.

"Broadshaw, step back," Darcy said, his voice steady. Broadshaw hesitated, his fists still clenched, but then took one slow step away. His eyes, blazing with fury, remained locked on the steward.

Darcy turned to the steward. "You will leave. Now."

The steward blinked. "Leave? This man assaulted—"

"I said leave." Darcy's tone was calm, but there was steel beneath it. He took a deliberate step closer, forcing the smaller man to crane his neck to meet his eyes. "You are on my land, delivering threats to one of my tenants, and I will not have it. If you wish to report this incident, you may do so through the proper channels. But understand this: if you press charges against Broadshaw, I will personally ensure that every aspect of Stanton's dealings in this county is brought under scrutiny."

The steward's face paled. He opened his mouth to retort, but no sound came out. Finally, he gathered himself enough to speak. "Stanton will hear of this."

"I am counting on it."

The steward's lips thinned, and he glanced around at the gathered crowd, as if realizing for the first time that he was outnumbered. He straightened his coat, muttered something unintelligible under his breath, and strode toward his horse, his boots sinking into the muddy path. Within moments, he was mounted and riding away.

Darcy turned back to the farmers. Broadshaw stood rigid, his jaw clenched, his chest heaving with restrained fury. The crowd remained silent, their eyes darting between Darcy and Broadshaw as though waiting for one of them to erupt.

"You have jeopardized your position. Had Stanton's man pressed charges, there would have been little I could do to stop the magistrate from ordering your arrest."

Broadshaw let out a bitter laugh. "And what does my position matter when Stanton is taking it all anyway? They fence our grazing fields and send their men to intimidate us when we protest. Do you think the law will save us, Mr. Darcy?"

"I think violence will destroy you," Darcy said. "And if you persist in attacking Stanton's men, you will lose the small ground you still have."

Broadshaw shook his head, his fists unclenching at last. "The law is not on our side. If it were, none of this would have happened."

Another man, younger and leaner, stepped forward from the crowd. "They talk in the villages," he said, his voice sharp and clear. "They talk about France and how it started. If Stanton pushes us too far, what choice will we have?"

Darcy felt the weight of those words settle over the group. The murmurs that followed carried an edge that sent a chill down his spine.

"You think rebellion will solve this?" Darcy asked, his gaze sweeping the crowd. "Look to France, and you will see only ruin. Families torn apart, cities burned, blood spilled for generations."

"And what would you have us do?" Broadshaw demanded. "Stand here until we are starved out? Do nothing while they take everything from us?"

Darcy exhaled slowly. "I will speak with Stanton's steward. I will see what can be done."

"You think he will listen? His men have been at our farms, marking fences like we are cattle for slaughter. They say the land is his now, that the grazing fields are closed. They even dragged my boy off when he tried to herd our sheep across the old paths."

Darcy looked at the man he had shoved, Davies, who now stood silent, rubbing at the sleeve of his coat as though it pained him. Broadshaw's words hung in the air, and several others murmured agreement. The muttered discontent spread through the small crowd like kindling taking flame.

"You believe I am the one with influence over Stanton? That I can dictate his decisions, when the law—"

"The law is nothing but a cudgel for men like him!" Broadshaw interrupted, stepping forward. "Do you think we are fools, sir? Do you think we do not see what is happening? They tell us it is all for progress. But progress leaves us empty-handed while their coffers grow fat."

A murmur of approval rippled through the group. One of the younger men standing near the back stepped forward, his face taut with a mixture of defiance and desperation.

"And what are we supposed to do, then? Bow and scrape? Watch our families starve? You tell us violence is not the answer, Mr. Darcy. Tell us, what is?"

Darcy looked at him. The young man was perhaps nineteen, his frame still awkward with youth, but his gaze burning with something dangerous. Darcy thought of the mobs in France, of the fires that swept through the cities and left only ash in their wake.

"Violence will only bring soldiers to your doors," Darcy said. "And soldiers answer with blood."

"That is what they want you to say," Broadshaw shot back. "That is what they want us all to believe, so we will roll over like sheep and accept it."

Darcy turned his gaze to Broadshaw. The man's shoulders were set in defiance, but his hands trembled where they hung by his sides. There was no strategy in his rebellion, only despair.

"You believe I am the one holding you down? That because I stand here with an estate and the duty to steward the land, I am the same as Stanton? Let me assure you, I am not."

"And what difference does that make?" Broadshaw's voice cracked as he stepped closer. "You are comfortable at Pemberley. You have your land, your family, your fine house. We have nothing but promises, and promises do not feed our children."

The younger man spat on the ground. "France happened because of men like Stanton, because of men who turned their backs on the people. If the gentry will not listen, sir, we will find ways to make them listen."

Darcy felt the air shift, the gathered men nodding, the agreement unspoken but clear. He thought of Georgiana, of the people at Pemberley who trusted him, who expected him to ensure their safety and prosperity. He could see the faces of those who had fled to the towns, abandoning generations of work because there was nothing left for them.

"I will speak with the magistrate, Sir Frederick," Darcy repeated. "I will make it clear that these grievances must be addressed."

"You will speak," Broadshaw repeated. "And what then? More talk? More promises? It will not be enough, Mr. Darcy. Mark my words. It will not be enough."

Darcy did not flinch. He kept his eyes steady on Broadshaw's until the man broke away with a muttered curse. The younger man lingered for a moment longer, his stare hard and unrelenting. Then he, too, turned and walked away.

As the men dispersed, Darcy stood in the center of the clearing, unmoving. A single thought burned through his mind. It was not the defiance in their words or the bitterness in their faces that disturbed him most. It was the undeniable truth behind them.

He could not stop this from coming. Not by standing still.

Darcy returned to his horse and mounted without a word. His steward approached, his expression anxious, but Darcy raised a hand to silence him. He would think on this later. He would decide what must be done.

For now, the only certainty was that he would not sleep that night.

Darcy stepped into the library, the air thick with the remnants of a dying fire. His cousin, Colonel Richard Fitzwilliam was already leaning against the mantle, arms crossed, wearing his "colonel" expression. His uniform was as neat as ever, but his boots were caked with dust, as though he had come straight from the road without pause. Darcy closed the door with more force than necessary.

"You sent no word of coming," Darcy said, walking to the decanter on the sideboard. He poured a glass, ignoring Richard's raised eyebrow. "I thought you were still in London."

"Would you have responded if I had?"

Darcy swirled the liquid in his glass. "What is it this time, Fitzwilliam? More tales of revolution from your travels? More speeches about the duty of the privileged class to preserve the order of society?"

Richard pushed off the mantle and walked to the table, where a stack of correspondence lay untouched. "I have no speeches for you today, Darcy. Only facts."

"That sounds ominous."

"Does it? That is what I was hoping for. I had word from Sir Frederick that there was some little 'misunderstanding' between one of your tenants and Miles Stanton's steward."

"There was. Sir Frederick was kind enough to promise to speak with Stanton himself. I hope that shall be the end of it."

"You know better than that, Darcy. Six months... eight incidents. Stanton's men are throwing their weight around."

Darcy did not respond. He took a measured sip of his drink and gestured for Richard to continue.

"Miles Stanton," Richard said, "has held his seat for two decades by playing both sides—just enough to appease the gentry, just enough to quiet the rabble. But things are changing. You saw it yourself this week, did you not? The farmers are no longer whispering about their grievances; they are shouting them."

Darcy set the glass down with a deliberate clink. "And what would you have me do about it?"

Richard's gaze sharpened. "Stanton is not invincible. He used to be—five years ago, his position was unassailable. Even your father could say or do nothing against him, but he has become complacent. His allies are dwindling, and there are men—young men—who would see him replaced. Men who look to you, Darcy."

"I am not a politician."

"No, you are not. Bloody miserable politician you would make, if you ask me."

Darcy grunted. "At least we are in agreement about that."

"But you are a man with influence, with connections, and with the respect of those who matter. These younger landowners, they do not have the weight to stand against Stanton alone. But with you? With my father behind you?" He stepped closer, his tone lowering. "You could unseat him."

Darcy turned away, staring at the unlit candelabra by the window. "And why would I want to? To leave Pemberley, to embroil myself in petty debates and alliances? The cost of this—of leaving what I know, what I value—would be far too high."

"And the cost of doing nothing? Have you considered that? I heard all about what happened, Darcy. A man's son was threatened—a boy who, by all accounts, was doing nothing wrong. That was not discontent. That was desperation. And enough desperation leads to fire, to blood, to chaos. Stanton's greed has made him blind to the storm he has sown. If someone does not step forward, that storm will come here, to Derbyshire, and could even spread."

Darcy turned sharply, his expression taut with frustration. "You are asking me to abandon my life for a world of schemes and manipulation. To stand against Stanton, I would need more than influence. I would need allies, support, and—"

"You have them," Richard interrupted. "You have Lord Matlock, who can rally the old guard. You have the respect of men who are tired of Stanton's games. You have your tenants, who trust you more than they trust their own neighbors."

"And I have my father's legacy to uphold," Darcy snapped. "He did not send me to Eton and Cambridge so I could become a puppet for political maneuvering."

"No one is asking you to be a puppet. They are asking you to be a leader."

The silence between them was thick, broken only by the crackle of the fire as Richard stepped back toward the mantle. Darcy remained by the window, his hands gripping the back of a chair, his gaze unfocused.

"Speak to my father," Richard urged. "Hear what he has to say. If you still believe this is not your fight, then I will say no more."

Darcy's jaw tightened. "You will not say no more. You will continue to hound me, as you always do."

Richard smiled faintly. "Probably. But you can hardly blame me for that."

Darcy released his grip on the chair and straightened. "Very well. I will speak to your father. But I make no promises."

"That is all I ask."

Darcy crossed the room and rang the bell for the butler. When the man came to the door, he gave his order. "Prepare a carriage for tomorrow morning. I will be traveling to London."

Chapter Two

THE GRAND ENTRY HALL of Lord Matlock's London townhouse was a riot of light and sound, the kind of spectacle that swallowed people whole. Chandeliers glinted like stars overhead, their crystals catching every flicker of the candles beneath them. The hum of voices, laughter, and the faint strains of a string quartet floated through the air, and Elizabeth could feel the swell of the music already pulling at her feet.

She adjusted the lace at her sleeve for the third time in as many minutes and glanced sideways at her aunt. Mrs. Gardiner looked equally uneasy, though she disguised it better, her posture straight, her chin lifted. Her uncle, in contrast, seemed to fit the scene with ease, exchanging pleasantries with a gentleman by the doorway as if they were old friends.

The invitation had arrived only two days before, as much a shock as a delight. Mr. Gardiner's recent success brokering a complex trade agreement across the Channel had brought him to the attention of Lord Matlock himself, an acknowledgment so unexpected that Elizabeth had nearly dropped the letter when her aunt handed it to her. The Earl's gesture—inviting them to this gathering of London's elite—seemed both a reward for Mr. Gardiner's hard work and a challenge to their place in society.

Elizabeth had overheard her aunt say as much to her uncle that morning: "It is not only an honor; it is a test. We must give them no cause to think us unworthy of the company."

That thought had stayed with Elizabeth, its sharpness piercing her like the stiff new stays she had reluctantly tightened to perfection earlier that evening.

Elizabeth smoothed her skirts and tried to ignore the tiny tremor in her hands. She had never been so determined to disappear into the background of a room, but the sheer opulence around her made it feel impossible.

"Do not fidget so, Lizzy," Mrs. Gardiner murmured, leaning closer. Her tone was firm, but her eyes betrayed her own nerves. "You are drawing attention."

Elizabeth swallowed. "I am trying to look inconspicuous," she whispered back. "I fear I am failing spectacularly."

Her aunt gave a wry smile, but before she could reply, a liveried servant approached them, inclining his head with crisp precision. "Lord Matlock requests the pleasure of your company in the main drawing room," he said. "If you would follow me."

Elizabeth's pulse quickened as they were led through a gilded archway and into a space that seemed even grander than the one before. The drawing room was enormous, its high ceilings adorned with intricate plasterwork and frescoes of pastoral scenes. A sea of elegantly dressed men and women mingled beneath them, their movements fluid and practiced, as if they had rehearsed this very tableau for years.

Her uncle gestured for her to follow, and she clung to his side like a lifeline as they navigated the crowd. The sheer number of unfamiliar faces was dizzying, but a few names reached her ears as her uncle whispered them under his breath.

"Lord Cowper... the Duke of Somerset... ah, and there is the Earl of Matlock himself."

Elizabeth's eyes darted toward the tall, silver-haired man standing near the far wall. His presence was commanding, his stance relaxed but watchful, as though he were both host and sentinel. He was deep in conversation with another gentleman, who carried an air of importance despite his unassuming appearance.

"That," her uncle continued, his voice lowering, "is Monsieur Lapointe, the French minister."

Elizabeth's stomach flipped. She had heard whispers about the Frenchman during the carriage ride over—hushed remarks about secret negotiations, delicate matters of diplomacy, and a web of intrigue that seemed far removed from her quiet life in Hertfordshire. Seeing him now, she was struck by how ordinary he seemed, with his thinning hair and plain black coat. And yet, the way others kept a careful distance spoke volumes.

Her uncle drew closer to Lord Matlock, bowing slightly as he introduced himself. Elizabeth and her aunt curtsied in turn, murmuring polite acknowledgments as the Earl greeted them with practiced charm. His sharp blue eyes flicked briefly to Elizabeth, and she felt an odd sense that he was weighing her somehow, measuring something unseen.

"The Gardiners, of course," he said smoothly. "I trust you are enjoying the evening."

"Very much, my lord," Mr. Gardiner replied. "It is an honor to be included in such an august gathering."

"Indeed," Matlock said, his tone neutral. His gaze shifted to Elizabeth again, lingering a fraction too long. She resisted the urge to fidget.

Elizabeth felt the weight of his scrutiny and the unwelcome prickle of heat rising to her cheeks. She knew what he saw: a young woman plainly dressed compared to the glittering fashions around her, her gown simple and modest but decently tailored, with no attempt at the daring necklines or vivid silks worn by the ladies of the ton. Her dark curls were neatly arranged, though without the intricate twists and jeweled pins that adorned the other women in the room. She had taken care to carry herself with dignity, aware that one wrong step—or word—could undo not just her own reputation but that of her aunt and uncle as well.

And yet, her eyes always gave her away. Elizabeth knew they were too bright, too alive with curiosity as they darted around the room. She could not help herself. Every face, every gesture, every detail was a puzzle waiting to be unraveled, and though she knew better than to stare, her gaze lingered just long enough to make her feel out of place. She clasped her gloved hands tightly in front of her, willing herself to appear as composed as her aunt, and offered Lord Matlock a small, polite smile.

Before she could overanalyze Lord Matlock's lingering gaze, a figure approached from the far side of the room. The newcomer—a tall gentleman with an air of importance and the slightly hunched posture of one accustomed to discretion—leaned in to murmur something to the Earl. Elizabeth caught the low murmur of words.

"Mr. Darcy has arrived."

The Earl's hand paused mid-gesture, his eyes narrowing slightly as though he doubted what he had just heard. "Darcy?" he repeated, his voice still quiet but edged with clear surprise.

The other man gave a single nod. "He is in the hall, my lord."

"Indeed! Show him to my study. Tell him I will join him directly." Matlock straightened, his focus shifting back to the Gardiners and Elizabeth. "I must ask you to excuse me," he said, his tone impeccably polite despite the abruptness of the interruption. His gaze softened as it fell on Mrs. Gardiner. "Please, make yourselves at home and enjoy the evening. My staff will see to it that your every comfort is met. It was a pleasure to meet you, madam, and you as well, Miss Bennet."

Without waiting for further acknowledgment, the Earl strode toward the doorway, his long strides purposeful, the murmuring crowd parting instinctively before him.

Elizabeth glanced at her uncle, whose brow furrowed slightly in thought. Mrs. Gardiner shifted closer to Elizabeth, her fingers brushing Elizabeth's gloved arm. "Did you hear that?"

"I did. Who is Mr. Darcy that his arrival should disturb the earl?"

"His nephew, I believe. I grew up nearly in the shadow of the Darcy estate, Pemberley, and I recall hearing much good of his father. I wonder if the son is anything like him."

"It must not be so, given the look on the earl's face just now."

"Perhaps! Oh, Lizzy, let us step away from this crush. I feel everyone's eyes on me, and I fear I may do or say something terribly embarrassing. My dear?" she asked, turning to her husband. "Might we go to the refreshment tables?"

Elizabeth let out a quiet breath, her shoulders easing as the Gardiners stepped away. She glanced around, unsure whether to follow her aunt and uncle or remain where she was. Her fingers twisted the edge of her glove, a nervous habit she had tried to break, but her attention had now begun to drift. Perhaps she could look about on her own. After all, when would she ever have another opportunity to make herself welcome in the home of an earl?

Another glance at her aunt and uncle—they were by the refreshment table now, deep in conversation with a merchant about trade routes. While she respected her uncle's business acumen, she would never make sense of half the terms being discussed. Her curiosity about the room had grown into a ticklish nuisance, and surely no one would notice if she wandered a little closer to the gathering near the far wall.

The press of bodies grew tighter as she moved deeper into the drawing room, the hum of conversation punctuated by the occasional burst of laughter. She tried to stay out of the way, hugging the edge of the crowd, but she misjudged the flow of the group. Suddenly, she found herself in the midst of a small cluster of gentlemen, their faces stern and their voices low.

It took her a moment to realize who they were. One of the men, standing slightly apart from the rest, wore an unadorned black coat that seemed almost plain against the grandeur of the room. His features were sharp, his eyes quick and calculating, and though he was not tall, there was an air of authority about him that marked him immediately. Monsieur Lapointe. The French minister.

Elizabeth's breath caught. She froze, her mind racing as she realized she had wandered straight into the company of not just the minister but several of his attendants. Their accents, their reserved manner, even the way they carried themselves—it was clear that these men were not mingling like the other guests. She should leave immediately, but her feet refused to move. The room around her seemed to tilt as the conversations nearest to her began to falter, and unfamiliar gazes nearly stung her exposed shoulders.

Monsieur Lapointe turned to her. His expression remained calm, but his brow lifted slightly in curiosity. He spoke, his voice low and fluid, the cadence unmistakably French.

Elizabeth blinked. She understood enough to know he was addressing her, but the words slipped past her grasp like water through her fingers. He must have mistaken her for someone else—a member of his host's staff, perhaps, or an invited guest of higher station. Her mouth opened, but no sound came out.

"I—pardon, Monsieur," she stammered in English, her cheeks burning. The minister tilted his head, a faint smile playing at the corner of his lips, but before he could respond, another voice murmured nearby.

"Is that her?" someone whispered. The words were not meant for her, but she heard them all the same. A sharp glance from one of the minister's companions swept over her, and she felt her heart thrum painfully in her chest. The scrutiny, the judgment—it was unbearable.

Elizabeth took a step back, nearly colliding with a servant carrying a tray of folded notes. Her pulse quickened as she looked around for a way out, but she saw the table where the notes were being deposited, and her curiosity prickled once again. One of the minister's men had just placed a small folded slip onto the tray, the motion subtle but deliberate.

Elizabeth tried to ignore it. The note could be anything—a harmless message or arrangement for the evening. But then why the furtive glance? The servant deposited the notes at a side table, then disappeared into the crowd.

Her stomach churned as she realized how deeply compromised she must already look, standing among these men, the French minister himself having addressed her. She had to make it seem as though she had purpose—some explanation for why she had been there at all.

She glanced toward the side table. If the note were important, surely it was better to deliver it directly to Lord Matlock. Her gaze flicked around the room, but her aunt and uncle were nowhere in sight. Her pulse pounded as she stepped toward the table. One small action. One quick correction. That was all.

Her gloved hand brushed the edge of the note just as a sharp voice cut through the air behind her.

"Young lady, you are standing in the path of the servants."

Elizabeth startled, her foot catching the edge of a chair. She collided with the very servant returning to collect the tray, the tray tipping as several papers fluttered to the ground. A mortified apology tumbled from her lips as she crouched to gather them, her movements hurried and clumsy. Her hand closed instinctively around the nearest note, the folded edge pressing into her palm.

"I am so sorry," she stammered, rising to her feet. The servant gave her a tight-lipped nod and moved on, balancing the tray once more as though nothing had happened.

Elizabeth hesitated. The note felt oddly heavy in her hand, though it was only paper. She glanced at it, her curiosity piqued by the dark, flowing script visible through the fold. It was not hers to read, and yet she could not seem to stop herself.

Her gaze darted around the room. No one was watching. Carefully, she unfolded it.

The words leapt off the page, sharp and undeniable:

The prisoner exchange will proceed as agreed. Ensure the envoy is delayed. Our man will handle the rest.

Elizabeth stared at the note, her pulse pounding in her ears. Prisoner exchange? Envoy? The language was cryptic, but the implications were clear. This was no innocent message.

Her mind raced. Who had written it? Who was it meant for? And why had it ended up in her hands?

"Miss Bennet."

Elizabeth's head snapped up, and her blood froze. Standing before her was one of the British dignitaries, his expression unreadable but his gaze sharp as a blade.

"What, precisely, do you think you are doing?"

When a clever country miss, a reluctant politician, and a meddling earl fake a romance to win votes and save reputations, sparks fly—and hearts may just catch fire.

ELIZABETH BENNET NEVER MEANT to cause an international incident. But when her sharp tongue and innocent curiosity lead to a spectacular misunderstanding with a foreign dignitary, she finds herself at the mercy of the formidable Earl of Matlock. To clear her name—and save her family from ruin—Elizabeth must agree to a preposterous scheme: a fake engagement to his brooding nephew, **Mr. Fitzwilliam Darcy**.

Darcy has no interest in standing for Parliament—or marrying, for that matter. But with political tensions rising and his uncle pressuring him to secure his seat in the House of Commons, Darcy reluctantly agrees to the charade. Elizabeth's wit and charm make her an ideal partner to win over voters. There's just one problem: her ability to set his world spinning with a single mischievous smile.

As Elizabeth and Darcy navigate society balls, political rallies, and the chaos of campaign life, their carefully staged affection starts to feel dangerously real. Can they keep their hearts out of the equation, or will this fake engagement turn into the most unexpected love match of all?

Raising the Stakes is a sparkling Regency rom-com full of sharp banter, tender moments, and a romance worth voting for.

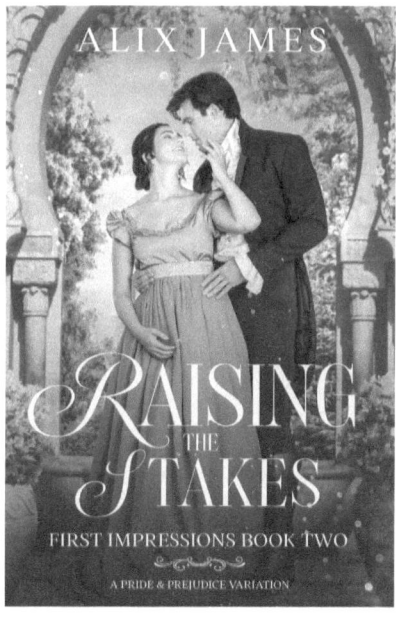

ABOUT ALIX JAMES

Short and satisfying romance for busy readers.

Alix James is an alternate pen name for best-selling Regency author Nicole Clarkston.

Always on the go as a wife, mom, and small business owner, she rarely has time to read a whole novel. She loves coffee with the sunrise and being outdoors. When she does get free time, she likes to read, camp, dream up romantic adventures, and tries to avoid housework.

Each Alix James story is a clean Regency Variation of Darcy and Elizabeth's romance.

Visit her website and sign up for her newsletter at AlixJames.com

Also By Alix James

The First Impressions Collection:

All Bets Are Off

Raising the Stakes

The Measure of a Man Collection:

The Measure of Love

The Measure of Trust

The Measure of Honor

The Measure of a Man Box Set (Coming December 2024)

The Mr. Darcy Collection:

Mr. Darcy Steals a Kiss

Mr. Darcy and the Governess

Mr. Darcy and the Girl Next Door

Mr. Darcy: Swoonworthy Collection

———————

The Heart to Heart Collection

These Dreams
Nefarious
Tempted

Darcy and Elizabeth: Heart to Heart Box Set

———————

The Sweet Escapes Collection

The Rogue's Widow
The Courtship of Edward Gardiner
London Holiday
Rumours and Recklessness

Darcy and Elizabeth: Sweet Escapes Box Set

———————

The Sweet Sentiments Collection:

When the Sun Sleeps

Queen of Winter
A Fine Mind

Elizabeth Bennet: Sweet Sentiments Box Set

––––––––––––––

The Frolic and Romance Collection:

A Proper Introduction
A Good Memory is Unpardonable
Along for the Ride

Elizabeth Bennet: Frolic & Romance Box Set

––––––––––––––

The Short and Sassy Collection:

Unintended
Spirited Away
Indisposed
Love and Other Machines

Elizabeth Bennet: Short and Sassy Compilation

––––––––––––––

Christmas With Darcy and Elizabeth

How to Get Caught Under the Mistletoe: A Lady's Guide
The Scotsman's Ghost: Or How to Wreck a Yule Party
Mr, Darcy's Christmas Kiss

North and South Variations

Nowhere but North
Northern Rain
No Such Thing as Luck

John and Margaret: Coming Home Collection

Anthologies

Rational Creatures
Falling for Mr Thornton

Spanish Translations

Rumores e Imprudencias
Vacaciones en Londres
Nefasto
Un Compromiso Accidental
Reina del Invierno
Una Mente Noble

Cuando el Sol se Duerm

A lo largo del Camino

Reina del Invierno

Una Mente Noble

El señor Darcy se roba un beso

Cómo quedar atrapado debajo del muérdago

Italian Translations

Una Vacanza a Londra

www.ingramcontent.com/pod-product-compliance
Lightning Source LLC
Chambersburg PA
CBHW020550180626
46810CB00007B/2448